The Island
Legacy

With love from Cornwall,

Roth x

RUTH SABERTON

Cornwall Edition

The Island Legacy
by Ruth Saberton
Cornwall Edition

Published by Millington

A catalogue card for this book is available from the British Library.

Editor: Jane Griffiths

Cover illustration © Jane Dixon-Smith

ISBN: 978 0 9955901 4 4

Printed and bound in Great Britian by
TJ International, Padstow, Cornwall

DEDICATION

To all the people in beautiful Cornwall who have so patiently put up with me exploring their homes, from the smallest and quirkiest cottage to magnificent castles, who have answered my questions – however strange they must seem – and who have helped so generously with all my research for this novel.

Prologue

The old man was dying.

No one had told him so; they didn't need to. He saw it in their faces, heard it in the hushed whispers spoken when they thought he was asleep, and felt it in the dragging weariness of his soul. His time was coming; it wouldn't be long now. Did they really think he wouldn't know?

The girl was crying by his bedside, her hand holding his tightly as though this grip alone could keep him tethered. Sometimes she blew her nose and sometimes she dabbed her eyes with her sleeve. He wanted to tell her not to weep, that he was at peace with it all and how much he appreciated everything she'd done, but the words could no longer form on his lips and all he could do was sigh. She wasn't a girl any longer, of course, but a woman in her forties. He wondered whether she'd be able to stay here once he'd gone. He hoped so. Would she be in trouble for what she'd done? Had he asked too much? Stretched her loyalty too far?

Maybe. But what other choice had there been? When the dream had come again, the water closing over his head followed by the fruitless diving, he'd known what he had to do. He should have done it from the moment he first started to have doubts, but time had seemed elastic back then: there had always been a reason to wait and see, a thousand arguments why there ought to have been another way. It was only when he'd overheard a conversation never intended for his ears that the old man had realised how quickly time's sands were trickling through his weak grasp. If the girl hadn't been willing to help him and there hadn't still been friends he could trust, the future for his home would have been as bleak as the Cornish winters.

There were answers for her unspoken questions too. These were in the music and at her fingertips. Would she find them? He'd never know, but he'd left hints and breadcrumb trails to lead her to them. He wanted to set straight the mistakes of the past. In time, perhaps, she'd discover the pages of his diary that he'd torn out and hidden; until then, the music of his heart was silenced, awaiting the turn of a key. The clues were in the games they'd once played to while away the long winters. Would she remember? He had to trust so.

The days were slipping into one another now, merging into a shuffle of footsteps, low-voiced conversations, and warm sunshine on his face when the curtains were open or velvet blackness when night fell. Sometimes he dozed, and occasionally he slept so deeply that he thought his time had already come, but mostly he lay back against the pillows and watched the world beyond his window. As the clouds tumbled by and the waves danced their endless ballet across the mouth of the bay, the music played through his memory, as clear and as fresh as though he'd written it yesterday rather than half a lifetime ago.

His music. His life's work. His true legacy. Would she understand what he'd tried to tell her? Would she know that he hadn't forgotten but instead had left her the most precious gift of all? The old man hoped his faith in her hadn't been misplaced. If it had, it wouldn't be the first time he'd been wrong to trust a woman, but at least it would be the last. There was no greater disappointment, no sharper pain than that of betrayal.

Outside the view was the same as ever. The old man had seen it almost every day of his life and it was as familiar to him as his own face in the looking glass – maybe even more so. Unlike his own reflection, St Pirran never changed. Even when his eyes became too heavy to open, he knew the town would still be perched on the steep hillside, each whitewashed building clinging on as the land fell away to the glittering sea below. In between the cottages and houses was greenery: gardens and hedges and gaudy flowerbeds laced up with steep narrow lanes threading through the town like ribbons on a patchwork corset. Lichen-speckled rooftops and crumbling stone walls freckled both sides of the River Pirran, which opened out onto the horseshoe beach. The beach was empty now, on an early spring day, but come high season it would be peppered with windbreaks and picnicking visitors.

How he wished it was summer. Then he would have heard the cries of excited children, carried up to his window on a warm breeze, their laughter ringing with the joy of long sandy days, ice creams and sunshine. Those were the sounds of life and possibilities, sounds he had transposed to his musical scores and knew he'd never hear them again. Today all that broke the silence was the mournful calling of gulls and the breaking of waves onto the sharp rocks. The world beyond the castle walls had a music all of its own; it played its own symphony.

The crashing surf and the harshness of his breathing seemed to become one, a rasping sigh like the tide as it rose up the beach then fell back in the endless rhythm the town and its inhabitants lived by. It was the same cadence that saw the fishing boats rise and fall, or that enticed the wading birds into the shallows. It was a perpetual, teasing dance that hid and revealed the causeway – a silver sparkling path leading to St Pirran's Island.

St Pirran's Island. His home. His place. His penance.

The old man's eyelids were leaden but he could open them just enough to see that the tide was in – a mile of blue water stretching between the island and the town. The surface looked deceptively smooth, yet underneath it lurked currents and serpent-toothed rocks waiting to snare the unwary and the careless. How many times had he and his brothers sailed their dinghy across the bay to the town? Or later on sprinted across in speedboats, loud and self-assured and so blissfully unaware of what was yet to come? Even all this time on it made his tired heart lurch to think about the catastrophe that had been awaiting them. In every nightmare since, he'd tried to warn them all but the words had shrivelled on his tongue. In his dreams, as in real life, he could only watch. There they were on the quayside: Addy, red-haired and reckless, and Maudsley so serious – yet both so full of the confidence and certainty that only comes with youth. Beth was always there too, in a wide-brimmed hat and with her long limbs honey-gold from endless Cornish summer days, sitting on the prow and watching them with those knowing feline eyes. When that cool green-eyed gaze had flickered to him he'd felt her power; it was only on his deathbed that the old man finally understood that none of them had ever had any real choice.

The fate of three was sealed from the moment Armand brought Beth home to Pirran Castle.

The old man closed his eyes again. He could see those long-lost faces just as vividly as he'd seen the white-tipped waves racing across St Pirran's Bay. Sometimes he thought he glimpsed all three in the shadowy corners of the bedroom, as though they were only waiting for the right moment to step forward and take his hands. If he listened hard enough he could hear them talking – Addy's bitter tones rising and falling with the tide, Maudsley's words harsher than the salt spray hurling itself against the windows, and Beth's laughter drifting in the breeze in rippling, silvery notes.

Beneath the warmth of his quilt, the old man shivered. The time for him to join them was drawing closer with every seagull's cry and every breaking wave. It wouldn't be long now. The final movement of his life was almost played out.

Yet time seemed to pause. Hang heavy. Hold its breath. Maybe he slept a little, he could no longer tell, but when he opened his eyes again the sun was already sinking into the sea. The sky was streaked with orange and red and peach, and across the bay lights were coming on in cottage windows, their reflections trembling in the river and the harbour. Soon the inky night would seep in and St Pirran's Island would be cut off; the small castle perched atop it would once again be a lost kingdom floating in the dark sea.

This was the old man's domain, but not for much longer. He knew that his grasp on the place was loosening. It was time to let it go. The thought of release was becoming more welcome with the turn of every tide. Yet, weary as he was, his mind was as sharp ever. The old man knew that for some it was now a matter of waiting and watching and rubbing their greedy hands together.

Well, let them wait and watch and plot. It was time to make amends.

The one thing he could do had been done. The ink had only been dry for a matter of days but no matter; the documents were legally signed and witnessed and sealed. The answers had been placed where only the true heir would ever look. How he'd struggled to organise it all! It had been such an effort to drag himself through the castle: every footstep had felt like a thousand miles and each part of the plan had required every drop of his rapidly draining energy. Still, nobody would be able to contest his state of mind and nor could anyone undo what he'd set in motion. The old man would have laughed if he'd had the strength. There would be surprises and anger and struggles, just as there had always been at the castle – but these were no longer his concern. He'd made his choices. His time was almost finished.

Were those choices the right ones? Could they compensate for the sins of the past? The old man couldn't tell, but perhaps his quivering signature had been an atonement of sorts. The rest the youngsters would have to decide for themselves; his island family would need to close ranks in order to survive. As for the future of the island, the nesting birds, the colony of seals, the crumbling castle with the nodding dog roses, the roofless chapel still heavy with the prayers of ages – all these were out of his hands.

The sun was sliding into the water now without any resistance, as though saying ease was all, there was no need to fight. The day was letting go and as the light began to bleed from the sky the old man felt something in himself release too.

It was time. He wouldn't see the turn of this tide.

Was the island's legacy safe? He could only hope so. His time as its guardian had drawn to a close.

Holding out his hands to those who'd set out before him, the old man slipped into the gathering shadows and the music of his long life gently faded away.

Chapter 1

May time in Cornwall always arrived with a sense of anticipation. After long winter months of quiet lanes, empty cottages and deserted beaches the area burst back into life just like the hedgerows that were exploding with bluebells, wild garlic and foaming cow parsley. A similar explosion took place over the Tamar Bridge as vehicles poured into the county, stuffed from dashboard to boot with suitcases, food and squabbling children, and with surfboards strapped precariously to roof racks like colourful Mohicans. Narrow lanes, untraversed for weeks, soon became the scene of much stress as city folks in huge cars tried to squeeze past one another without hitting banks or ending up in ditches. Meanwhile the locals resigned themselves to the usual inconvenience of reversing or taking alternative routes in order to get anywhere at all.

In the pretty seaside town of St Pirran the holiday cottages had been cleaned from top to bottom and their shutters thrown wide open in anticipation of the bank holiday influx. The owner of the local deli had been flat out making up picnic baskets crammed with goat-cheese tartlets, olives and artisan breads – no bog-standard pasties and saffron buns for St Pirran's clientele. The manager of the town's clothes store was busying herself redesigning the window display to showcase the usual peak-season items: fishing smocks and sailing slacks in pastel-hued fabrics that no self-respecting local would dream of wearing when working on a boat, and spotty hessian bags with price tags that made many townspeople see dots dance before their eyes.

In the art gallery the splashy seaside-themed paintings had been adjusted to their most saleable positions and a selection of chunky silver jewellery was now backlit in the window. The bookshop, meanwhile, was featuring the latest tome by a celebrity second-homer. The gift shop's proprietor had wheeled out spinning displays of postcards and had piled buckets and spades in a prime position for attracting beachgoers. Traffic crawled along the main street as new arrivals tried their best to spot their holiday cottages; as usual, they seemed oblivious to the narrowing of the road and the fact that only the river's edge lay beyond. Every season somebody managed to get their car tightly wedged, and The Castle pub always ran a sweepstake on when this would be. Each year it happened earlier than the last. It seemed that the cars were becoming bigger and the drivers were getting dafter – either that, or the wet winter had made St Pirran shrink.

As well as running sweepstakes for the locals, the harbourside pub was preparing to up its culinary game: it had recently abandoned its limited selection of basket meals, in favour of a Rick Stein inspired menu. The new fare was beautifully advertised on a chalkboard covered in italic writing. Not to be beaten, St Pirran's chip shop was promoting In Cod We Trust's very own gourmet chips, made from Cornish potatoes. The town's tea rooms were selling home-made scones and locally sourced jam – and even the ice cream at the beach kiosk was organic and from a nearby dairy.

Cornwall was on the up, foodies were in heaven and organic was the buzzword. If some of the older townsfolk missed their steak pasties and muttered darkly that they were far from impressed by the Stilton and venison variations, then they did so quietly because the tills would soon be ringing. At least, everyone hoped that was going to be the case. Three wet summers in a row, cheap deals to Spain and having the future of Pirran Castle hanging in the balance had made the locals nervous. Living in a picturesque fishing town was blissful in the summer but wages were low, house prices were high and the winters were dark and long. This season needed to be a good one and those in the town who depended on tourism would be working gruelling hours from now until October. This was the reality of life in Cornwall.

The quayside had been spruced up in anticipation of the influx too. Trawls were tucked into net bins, yellow fish boxes had been stacked into tottering piles, and ropes were coiled neatly alongside the fishing boats that bobbed on the tide and strained impatiently at their moorings. Even the seagulls looked cleaner than usual, their feathers Persil-white and their beady eyes bright as they perched on the rooftops to scope out another season's easy pickings.

Cornwall in the holiday season was big business and St Pirran was raring to begin. The weather was on the town's side today as well, the grey skies and endless rain of the past few weeks having cleared away to reveal a day that was mild and full of promise. The tang of salt filled the air and lemon-sharp sunshine drizzled over the valley, turning the remaining sliver of beach to glistening gold and making the sea sparkle as brightly as any gift-shop window. The breeze had died away and the sea was calm now, shimmering in the sunlight; St Pirran's Island and its tumbledown castle floated in the hazy bay like something from a fairy tale. With the tide in at the moment, small boats were already doing a roaring trade taking visitors on trips around the bay.

Merryn Hellier knew from experience that when the sun shone in Cornwall you made hay fast – or at the very least did the St Pirran equivalent, which was to take day trippers on boat rides. Although it was only late morning he'd already taken Guardian Angel out on two packed trips and was now setting off on his third. As he stood at the wheel with the wind blowing through his thick blond curls and the sunshine coaxing a cinnamon dusting of freckles across his nose, Merryn reflected that there was a lot to be said for this way of life. Sparkling open water lay ahead and lace-doily wake trailed behind as his boat danced across the waves. He rolled up his sleeves and braced his strong legs against the swell that he knew always broiled beneath this part of the channel. The currents below the deceptively calm-looking surface were deadly to the unwary; sometimes they surprised even those who were familiar with these waters, a fact to which the town's graveyard bore testament.

Merryn knew every inch of this coastline. Having grown up in St Pirran he'd spent most of his childhood messing about in boats and exploring the cliffs. There wasn't a creek or a hidden cove he hadn't discovered or a wreck he hadn't snorkelled. As a boy, his every spare moment had been spent on the water in the small boat he'd saved for from his pocket money. Later on, he'd worked as crew on the trawlers, loving the dawn starts and the sense of possibilities as the big fishing boats rolled out to sea. Harsh quotas and a dwindling fleet had changed that lately, but there was still a living to be made on the sea if you knew where to go and were smart. Merryn smiled to himself as he opened up the throttle and let his boat surge forward like an eager horse. He might not have A levels or book learning, but he'd quickly realised that in the summer months it made far more sense to fish for a very different kind of haul. Tourists were certainly easier to catch. They lined up on the quay clutching ice creams and trendy hessian bags from the overpriced gift shops and practically fought to be helped down the slippery green steps into the tripping boats. Then all Merryn had to do was sit them down, take them out for half an hour and collect the money. And he even got to suntan at the same time and enjoy all the pretty girls who, in their bikini tops and shorts, liked to giggle and flirt with the skipper. What wasn't to like about this job? Everyone was a winner!

His boat was now past the narrow channel that divided the island from the mainland – and even though he'd made this journey thousands of times, Merryn heaved a sigh of relief. Now that the water beneath Guardian Angel's hull was deep and blue, he could enjoy the run to the back of the island. He knew there would be seals there to delight his passengers and hopefully earn him some good tips. Sometimes, if he was really lucky, Merryn might spot a basking shark or a dolphin, which was certain to boost the day's takings. Not that it was all about money. Far from it. Merryn wasn't mercenary. If he had been, he would have snapped up one of the wealthy holidaymakers who were always coming on to men like him. Abandoned to their second homes for the summer by their city-boy husbands, they had nothing else to do but prowl the town on the lookout for some excitement to relieve the monotony. There were plenty of these women about; Merryn knew enough friends who were more than happy to humour them and enjoy the fast boats, expensive gifts and no-strings fun they offered. All the same, this lifestyle didn't appeal to him. He wasn't a saint by any means – women were attracted to Merryn, and he liked them too and had indulged on more than one occasion – but being a kept man wasn't for him. As long as he had enough money to pay his diesel bill, keep the boat ticking over and cover his own expenses then Merryn was happy. He was his own man and owed nothing to anyone, which was exactly how he liked it.

It was freedom, Merryn decided as he slowed the boat, pure and simple. Maybe eking out a living by fishing and tripping and working in the castle grounds wouldn't be for everyone, but it worked for him. Even his caravan on the far side of the island was basic by most people's standards but it suited him perfectly. It was a simple life and a good one.

Merryn hoped it was going to stay this way but lately there had been far too many changes. There was a sense of uncertainty hanging in the air nowadays, like the early-morning mist that hung over the River Pirran. Life was moving in the same rhythm it always had, but Merryn had listened to the rumours in The Castle and overheard several conversations that had unnerved him. Just as he always instinctively knew when the wind would swing from the south-west to the north-east, some sixth sense was telling him that something important was poised and waiting, that unseen events were ready to unfurl.

Merryn laughed out loud. God, listen to him! He sounded just like his nan. He'd be looking in the tea leaves in a minute or scrying in the shiny screen of his plotter. Rose Hellier loved all that nonsense and fancied herself as something of a psychic; with her wrinkled walnut skin and thick white hair she looked the part of a wise old soothsayer. For years townsfolk had come knocking at her door for a reading or a lucky charm. She'd certainly always had second sight when it came to knowing what her grandson was up to. Merryn had been brought up by Rose when his mother had walked out, the colourful harbourside lights of St Pirran having been no competition for the bright lights of London. Merryn adored Rose and would do anything for her – if only she'd let him.

"I'm not dead yet, boy!" was her usual protest when Merryn attempted to carry her shopping up the steep steps to her cottage – and woe betide him if he ever presumed to chop her logs. Fiercely independent, Rose would rather drop dead than admit defeat, and Merryn guessed that was where he got it from. Girlfriends often berated him for never allowing them to get close. Merryn knew that they were probably right, but if you let someone in then it was only a matter of time before they let you down. Hadn't his mother proved that? His father had never got over her leaving. Will Hellier had soon stopped going to sea; his boat had fallen into disrepair and after that he'd spent the majority of his time propping up the bar in The Castle. It hadn't been much of a surprise when cirrhosis had claimed him six years later.

So if that was what love and dependence on somebody did for you, then no thanks. It was the open sea and freedom every time for Merryn. But even though no woman had ever been able to tie him down, the sea and St Pirran had a far greater hold on Merryn's heart. God, he loved this place. Like a stroppy mistress the weather could turn in an instant, her storms whipping up the waves and spurring white horses to the shore, or her silent sea mists coiling themselves along the coastline and rubbing out the world. Merryn adored the place just as much then as he did on glorious days like this. Perhaps he was a simple soul who lacked ambition? Merryn wasn't sure and didn't much care what the answer might be. He only knew that this slice of Cornwall – with its slow-flowing rivers, shallow secret creeks and rocky smugglers' coves – was enough for him.

Maybe he should be driving himself hard to buy one of the big houses up on the cliff top. With their huge windows and commanding views, they were practically shrieking just how much their owners were worth. Property developers had snapped those prime sites up years ago when their former owners, ageing and tired of struggling along the cliff path to reach them, had been only too happy to swap breath-taking vistas for a pile of cash and a new-build bungalow elsewhere in town. Nobody born and bred in St Pirran stood a chance of buying a house with a view now, unless they won the lottery or happened to have a world-class talent for football. Most of the year these cliff top houses stood empty, which Merryn thought a wicked waste. It was a real case of spending money for the sake of it, and he shook his head in bemusement. Take the furthest house along the cliff, for example. This one had only recently been renovated. Rumour had it that the new owner, the Max Reynard of Reynard Developments, had gutted the place totally in favour of open-plan, glass-and-chrome loft-style living. There was even an infinity pool and a hot tub and, if Polly Pipkin in the newsagents was to be believed, there'd been all-night parties and twenty types of decadence. Lots of locals did believe her too. If the new owner was wealthy enough to buy somewhere like that, he could certainly afford to live like Hugh Hefner.

Merryn laughed at this. He might live in a tatty old caravan in an overgrown meadow on the far side of the island but his views were equal to (if not better than) those from Max Reynard's newly developed house. And who needed an infinity pool when only steps away was the bluest and most perfect natural rock pool, where you could swim alone and uninterrupted day or night? And all for the princely sum of keeping the causeway clear and doing his best to maintain the castle's grounds. The owner of the island, Armand Penwellyn, had promised Merryn that as long as he did this there would be a place for him there. He hadn't cared about Merryn's wild teenage reputation or that he'd been kicked out of school. The old man had given him a chance and a home, and for that he would always be grateful. Rose had worked on the island donkey's years ago and Merryn guessed that removing her grandson from any possible trouble on the mainland was Armand's way of thanking her. It had worked. Merryn had lived here for almost six years now and he couldn't imagine waking up anywhere else.

Sudden fear fluttered in the pit of Merryn's stomach because Armand was dead, gone three weeks already, and who knew what would happen next? Armand's niece, Lucy, was red-eyed and silent; her younger brother, Jamie, had yet to skulk back; and even Annie Luckett, the local historian and Armand's oldest friend, appeared to be in the dark. The local solicitor, David Brown, presumably knew what the deal was, but he couldn't say anything even if he wanted to. The island was special and to think that its future was hanging in the balance made Merryn uneasy. Armand was scarcely cold and already the developers were circling. Merryn had spotted Max Reynard walking on the beach this morning, sketchpad in hand and eyes fixed on the island. Merryn would have wagered the few possessions he had that those cream pages didn't contain artwork but neatly labelled plans and notes for some swanky development. He could only hope that the old man, who in life had been as sharp as the rocks surrounding his island, had been equally canny in planning for his death.

The island was fast approaching now and, as he slowed the boat, Merryn reflected that even though he saw this view every day he never tired of it. There was something about the way the island rose out of the sea, the granite cliffs towering above and the walls of the castle even higher still, that filled him with awe. It didn't matter that the castle was crumbling or that the once formal gardens were overgrown and filled with nodding wild flowers: the enchantment of its ancient stones and secrets was still there. Every time he reached this point on the trip, chatter on the boat died away as the day trippers gazed up wide-eyed, pointing at the nesting seabirds and snapping away with their phones and cameras. It was pure Enid Blyton, of course: a small island with a castle set just off the coast and easily reachable by boat or causeway. The place reminded all who saw it of childhood dreams of picnics and smugglers. Even Merryn, who lived on the island and knew it for exactly what it was in the hard winter or during a howling gale, never failed to have goose bumps dusting his brown arms when he stared up at it. Maybe he was just being fanciful, but he was convinced there was Cornish magic here. St Pirran's Island was a special place. That was why it had to be protected, why Jamie Penwellyn mustn't be allowed—

"What's the history of this island?"

The question interrupted Merryn's thoughts and, ripping himself away from his worries, he knocked the boat into neutral and turned his attention back to the visitors. His concerns about the future of the island would have to wait because it was time for the spiel, the words he knew off by heart yet never tired of telling.

"OK, folks. This is St Pirran's Island, or Pirran Island as we call it here. It's a small island just a mile off the coast. Pirran's an area of outstanding natural beauty and home to all kinds of seabirds. If we're lucky today, we may even see some seals because there's a colony at the back of the island."

There was a ripple of excitement at this idea and Merryn crossed his fingers that the seals wouldn't have vanished. They'd been basking in the sunshine earlier but it wasn't unknown for them to have enough of being gawked at. A bit like celebrities being chased by the paps, they often took themselves off for some peace and quiet – the lighthouse three miles further south being their usual port of call.

"There's a legend that Jesus visited the island with Joseph of Arimathea," Merryn continued, smiling at the gasps this story always brought. He was pretty certain this was all nonsense, but the tourists loved it and those who made the journey across always headed straight to the ruins of the twelfth-century chapel – a visit that was swiftly followed by a trip to the castle's tea room. Lucy Penwellyn made the most amazing cakes, thought Merryn, remembering now that he had a big slab of her coffee and walnut sponge in his lunchbox to enjoy once his passengers had disembarked.

"Did Jesus really visit?" asked a pretty blonde tourist.

"Absolutely," said Merryn. After all, who was he to say? There was no doubt that the ruined chapel had a special peace. He winked at her. "We certainly like to think so, anyway. How many Cornish seaside towns can claim that Jesus took his holidays there? The Son of God certainly beats a celebrity chef, don't you think?"

There was the usual laughter at this, and with thoughts of cake and tea in mind, Merryn pressed on. "The castle you can see is known as Pirran Castle. Parts of the building date back to Norman times and maybe even before that. The story goes that the castle was built to defend the town and over the years has been added to. Parts of it are ruined, like the walls we're looking at now, but there are sections that are still inhabited today. If you visit on a Tuesday or a Thursday, you'll be able to have a tour. There's a lovely tea room too. It's definitely worth a trip. I have some leaflets which you can take when we get back."

There, that was his cake paid for, thought Merryn. If he sent a few more visitors over, that would be a couple of quid extra in Lucy Penwellyn's pot – and God knew, she could do with the money. The last time he'd seen her she'd been wondering whether nettle soup was a goer and, as overgrown with weeds as the island was, he didn't think she'd been joking.

"People still live in the castle?" asked a little girl, her eyes wide. "Is there a princess?"

Merryn smiled at her, his blue eyes crinkling at the thought of Lucy Penwellyn as a princess. Hardly. With her work-roughened hands, those overalls she wore and that wispy blonde hair of hers, she was more like a worn-out Cinderella, still waiting for her prince but so busy tending to a succession of elderly relatives and the demands of a listed building that she was unlikely to ever find the time to seek him out. And as for glass slippers – well, Lucy was far more likely to be found in wellies as she walked her dog, Biscuit, along the causeway or worked on the vegetable patch.

"There have always been people living in the castle," he told the little girl, "although I'm afraid there isn't a princess. The Penwellyn family live there at the moment."

At the moment. Who knew how much longer they'd be staying? Merryn felt a prickle of unease along his spine. He took a deep breath and did his best to ignore it.

"In the twentieth century the island was bought by the naturalist Edmund Penwellyn as a home for his family and a place to write his books. You'll come across them in the town as well as prints of the drawings he did. He lived there with his wife and three sons. One of those sons was Armand Penwellyn, the composer."

"I've heard of him!" gasped a lady in a spotty raincoat. "He's famous, isn't he?"

Merryn swallowed. God, it was hard to talk about Armand in the past tense when he still expected to see the old boy walking along the pier or sitting in his tower window frowning out over the water. Since his death there'd been a strange stillness about the place, as though the island was holding its breath. Realising that his audience was waiting for a response, Merryn collected himself and returned to his well-worn speech.

"That's right. Armand Penwellyn wrote the Island Suite and Seashore Melodies, which I'm sure you've come across at some point."

There was the usual nodding at this.

"Now, I'm not musical," Merryn continued, "but they tell me that had Armand continued to compose he'd be as famous now as Vaughan Williams or Benjamin Britten or even," he turned to grin at a couple of teenagers, "One Direction!"

As always everyone laughed at this.

"So why did he stop writing music?" asked Spotty Raincoat.

Merryn shrugged. "I have no idea. All I can tell you is that he never published another piece of music after that. People said he'd written a great symphony but that he never published it. If he did write that and if it did exist, then it's certainly never seen the light of day. It's a secret that he took to his grave."

"So he's dead now?" said a wide-eyed little boy. "Is his ghost in that castle?"

If it was then poor Lucy would certainly know all about it, Merryn reflected. Demanding and temperamental in life, with the mood swings and short fuse of the truly creative, Armand had bawled her out for years and wasn't the kind to let death stop him. Merryn only wished the old man would haunt bloody Jamie Penwellyn and scare the idiot away. Now that would be something.

"No ghosts," was all he said.

"So is the castle empty now?" asked another tourist.

Merryn shook his head. "The last of the brothers died recently but his niece still lives there with some staff." He wondered if staff was the right term to describe the three of them: himself; Fred Tamblyn, the ancient gardener; and Fern, a fairly recent addition who worked in the tea room and did a bit of cleaning from time to time. If Merryn was honest, the phrase Armand Penwellyn's charity cases probably described them all far better. Where else would they all fit in?

"So is it hers now?"

"I wish she'd sell it to me!"

"It would make a great hotel!"

The trippers were chatting again now, excitedly discussing the castle and their dreams about living there.

Their words washed over Merryn. He couldn't answer any of their questions because he really didn't know the answers to them; no one had told him anything. Meanwhile, the townsfolk could only gossip and speculate. Until they knew for sure what was going on, all kinds of stories were being bandied around. A rock star was buying the island. Jamie Penwellyn was selling it to an oligarch. A developer was going to turn it into a luxury hotel. Merryn had heard every rumour and each one turned him cold.

Knocking the engine into gear and heading off in search of seals, he could only hope that whatever the old man had chosen to do with the island would keep it safe. Anything else would be unbearable.

Chapter 2

The roads were narrow in Cornwall, narrow and alarmingly steep as they wiggled round hills or plunged into wooded valleys. As she steered her hire car around a sharp bend, only to be overtaken by an enormous four-by-four, Nessa Penwellyn held her breath and pulled in as near to the high hedge as she possibly could. God, she really hoped the car wasn't scratched. The last thing she needed right now was another massive bill. The flight to the UK had almost cleared out what small funds there had been in her bank account, and taking unpaid leave meant that there was no hope of anything coming in to replace it from any direction – the solicitor had made that very clear.

With her heart hammering against her ribs, Ness waited for the black Range Rover to pass. Its driver had his foot to the floor, and when he drew alongside her the look he gave her was nearly enough to make Ness turn around and head straight back to Heathrow. There wasn't even a nod of acknowledgement from him. So much for people in the countryside being relaxed and friendly! That supercharged monster of a vehicle wouldn't have been out of place in downtown Miami, and judging by the murderous expression on the driver's face she was probably just as likely to be shot here.

This was her home? Ness couldn't have felt more alien if she'd landed on Mars. From the minute her plane had touched down at Heathrow she'd felt lost and out of place. She might have an ancient Cornish name, but that didn't mean she belonged here.

She was just as much a foreigner in her own country as she was in the United States or the Caribbean, or anywhere else for that matter.

Ness supposed this was what came of having a nomad for a father. Addy had never been able to settle anywhere for long. He'd been a restless soul, always on the lookout for the next adventure, the next wonderful place to be, the next crock of gold at the end of the rainbow. Fun and feckless, there'd been something in him that just couldn't rest. Ness had lost count of all the houses they'd lived in over the years, and she'd stopped hoping that one day he would stay long enough in one place for her to make friends. She'd quickly learned that there was no point trying to fit in or get to know anyone; instead, she became an expert at packing up her room in a matter of minutes. She was even more of an expert in comforting the women whose hearts her father inevitably broke.

People only let you down, Addy would explain as they drove to a new town or sometimes even a new country. It was better to keep moving and keep yourself safe than to have to depend on anyone. Preferable by far to keep yourself independent. Ness, perched shotgun beside him, had nodded – but she hadn't really understood. Even as a child these moonlight flits had looked to her less like bold strikes for independence and more as though her father was running away. Now that she was older Ness was absolutely certain that running away was exactly what Addy had been doing. Why he'd needed to do this she'd never asked; she'd merely accepted that it was as much a part of him as his flame-red hair and fun-loving nature.

The irony was, Ness now realised, whatever it was her father had been attempting to escape had always come with him. He could run as fast as he liked, break as many hearts as he wanted, quit jobs, take her out of school, swap continents, race motorbikes at breakneck speed, but none of it ever worked. Even whiskey hadn't succeeded, although towards the end it had certainly helped him slide into oblivion. He'd still shouted out in his sleep every night. Countless times Ness had rushed into her father's bedroom to find him clawing thin air as tears streamed down his cheeks. What the dreams were about she never did discover, but the constant running, drinking and risk-taking didn't chase it away. Whatever it was that had haunted Addy Penwellyn had pursued him until the second he'd drawn his final breath.

Ness needed to know what that had been. Maybe now she'd have the chance to find out.

The big car passed by, hurtling along the lane and with its brake lights flashing angrily as it took the next bend. Ness braced herself for the sound of screeching and wasn't surprised when seconds later there was a furious blast on the horn. Perhaps crazy driving was a Cornish thing and this was where her father's love of speed had come from. If so, then Addy had done well to have lasted as long as he did before his motorbike claimed him.

The traffic here was certainly heavier than she was used to, but then Ness had been living on a small Caribbean island where everyone was as laid-back as a deck chair. The cars there dawdled along at much the same pace as the meandering iguanas, and dodging fallen coconuts was about as dangerous as the daily commute got. Everyone waved and called hello. Nobody ever glowered like Range Rover man, that was for sure. Thinking about St Antonia, her home for the past year, made Ness feel even more lost. Already she missed the gold-medallion sun, the bright blue sky and the hot pinks and acid greens of the vegetation. Here it felt as though somebody had muted the colours and not fed enough coins into the meter to get the heater running.

This was May, wasn't it? The sun might be out but she was freezing. Thank goodness the hire car had heated seats. Shorts and vest tops and glittery sandals might work in the Caribbean, but for spring in Cornwall she was distinctly underdressed. As soon as she reached St Pirran she'd raid what was left of her funds and buy some warm clothes, Ness decided. She supposed she should have done this when she was at Heathrow, but all she'd wanted to do was head west. Clothes shopping had been the last thing on her mind, and with her thoughts racing faster than the traffic on the M5, Ness had headed straight to Cornwall. Jet lag, nerves and unsuitable outfits didn't matter. She'd needed to reach St Pirran and find out exactly what was going on. She hadn't been able to think about anything else for days.

Exhaling shakily, Ness uncurled her fingers from the steering wheel. Pins and needles buzzed through her hands. Finally, the adrenalin of her long journey was passing and the reality of what she was doing began to dawn. Travelling to St Pirran was no longer just a fun idea to discuss in the bar or the result of a fairy-tale style bequest; it was something actually happening to her, and happening right now. Something she alone had put in motion. No wonder she was filled with trepidation.

Once she arrived in St Pirran there would be no going back. The solicitor had made it clear that she had responsibilities and big decisions to make and, although he hadn't said as much, Ness suspected she'd meet opposition and resentment too. Maybe coming here was a mistake? She'd been living abroad for most of her life and these narrow lanes winding through green tunnels of trees felt strange. The rolling fields of buttery-coloured wheat and corduroy plough, the ancient churches snoozing in the shade of yews, and the villages of whitewashed cottages were undeniably English, dreamily familiar from TV shows yet foreign too.

Yet again Ness experienced that unpleasant sensation, as if her stomach was freefalling to her sandals: the old fear that she was insubstantial and didn't belong anywhere or to anything. Usually when she felt like this she reached for her snorkel, losing herself in the world beneath the waves and soothed by the vastness of the ocean where everything was inconsequential in comparison to the endless depths and the teeming life. Steadying her breathing as though preparing for a dive, Ness reminded herself that being here was an adventure, maybe the biggest she would ever have. It was certainly one she'd never expected.

Or dreamed of. How could she? Things like this didn't happen to girls like her.

Ten days ago, Ness had been preparing for another normal day – or as normal a day as was possible when you worked as a waitress in a dive hotel. The boats always left early; as soon as the stars faded and soft pink light blushed the sand, the stillness was broken by the clanking of nitrox cylinders and the cries of excited voices. As usual the cicadas' call, as much the backing track to Ness's nights as the whirr of air conditioning, had been replaced by the thrum of engines and the thud of dive gear being hurled onto decks. Although her blinds had still been down, Ness had been awake by then: the stripes of light on the walls, coupled with the singsong Caribbean tones below, were telling her it was time to head outside.

She'd lain on her back watching the ceiling fan whir in never-ceasing circles. The thin cotton sheet was sticking to her and she'd kicked it off impatiently, abandoning all hope of drifting back into sleep. It might only have been early but already the temperature had reached the eighties; by noon it would climb even higher. If she hurried she could join the divers for the morning. Once she was in that turquoise world all would be cool and silent – the perfect place to be on a rare day off.

Ness had checked Addy's chunky watch, which even three years on she couldn't bear to take off, and seen that it was gone half seven – high time she was out of bed and pulling on her bikini and shorts. Already her friends would be stowing the gear and running through their safety checks. Pretty soon they'd be taking the roll call of the morning's divers before setting sail across the shallows to the deep blue beyond the reef. Heaven!

Ness loved the water and had been drawn to the ocean all her life. Maybe it was why she'd never settled but drifted from one job to another? Moving from chambermaiding in hotels to mixing drinks in beach bars to waiting tables. It might sound exotic but the hours were long and the money wasn't so great. The only compensation was the diving and the sunshine. Life with Addy hadn't been conducive to a great education, or at least not in the traditional sense. She was well read and well travelled, and practical too. For now working here was enough but Ness didn't want to wait tables forever.

The trouble was Ness didn't know quite what it was she did want. She'd always had a sense that there was something she was just missing, an answer tantalisingly out of reach, and if she could only grasp it everything would make sense. Maybe that was her father's true legacy? She was always going to be rootless?

These had been Ness's thoughts as she'd pinned up her long red curls and made her way to the lockers where the wetsuits were kept. Then the arrival of an unexpected visitor bearing a letter had changed her plans for that morning and maybe for the rest of her life...

Sitting in her hire car now, with the handbrake jammed on and her heart hammering, Ness wondered what would have happened if she'd been five minutes earlier or had opted to have a lie-in? Would the bemused solicitor, prawn pink and sweating even at that early hour, have given up looking for her and handed the envelope to one of the girls at reception, where it would have lain buried under magazines and totally forgotten while they played on their smartphones and chatted about weekend plans? He'd already tried six resorts that week and looked as though he was ready to drop. If Ness had already gone diving, he probably would have flown back that same afternoon and told his firm how he'd done his very best to trace the sole heir to Pirran Castle but that she was nowhere to be found. Who knew what might have happened then? Either way, it wouldn't have been her problem.

Maybe ignorance was bliss.

Ness's heart thudded even harder. The sole heir. Her! Nessa Penwellyn! It sounded incredible, ridiculous even, but she'd seen the documents and spoken to the solicitor and it was true: her elderly uncle really had chosen to leave her his castle in Cornwall.

She had felt like Cinderella.

"It sounds far grander than it is," the solicitor had warned Ness. "I should tell you that the building itself is in very bad repair.

Put simply, it's a money pit. Once the death duties have been paid the estate will be in no small degree of debt."

Addy had lived his entire life in no small degree of debt, so this came as no surprise to Ness. Why should his brother be any different?

"But why leave it to me? I've never heard of this uncle and my father never mentioned the family home. I didn't even know he had two brothers. We've lived abroad my whole life!"

"I believe there was an estrangement," the solicitor said, pulling a hankie from his top pocket and blotting sweat from his shiny face.

You don't say, Ness thought. Biting back impatience, she asked, "What happened?"

The solicitor's mopping paused. "I'm afraid I have no idea, but I should imagine it was a very long time ago. And even if I did know, I wouldn't be at liberty to say. Our client's family circumstances were his private business. You'd have to ask your cousins, Jamie and Lucy Penwellyn."

If these two members of her newly discovered family were as tight-lipped as her father had been, Ness could imagine it would be easier to prise secrets out of clamshells. Head still spinning, she tried a different tack.

"OK then. You've just told me I've got cousins, so why wouldn't he have left it all to them? Especially if one's a guy? The male always inherits, right? Isn't that how it goes?"

It certainly did on Downton Abbey anyway. Addy's last girlfriend had been obsessed with that show. Lord, thought Ness, starting to feel hysterical giggles bubbling up. Gloria would pop if she knew her tattooed biker beau had grown up in a real-life castle. She'd loved his English accent.

The solicitor had shrugged. "Pirran Castle isn't entailed and there's no title, so your uncle could leave it to whomever he chose. Having no children himself it was entirely his choice – and his choice was you. What you decide to do with the bequest is up to you."

And that, it seemed, was the end of the matter. Regardless of whether she liked or wanted it, Nessa Penwellyn, previously of no fixed abode and with no close relatives or roots, now possessed the family home – and had also acquired a couple of long-lost cousins.

Did she want a castle? Did she want to meet her cousins? Could she perhaps turn it all down and just stay here? Surely she'd be crazy not to at least go and have a look though. Inheritance aside, she might find out something that would help her understand Addy. St Pirran was the key to unlocking his secret, Ness just knew it. She only wished that the thought of it didn't make her feel so nervous.

"If you don't go to Cornwall to check it out and shag Ross Poldark senseless," her friend Mel had said that evening, when after a Google search and several cocktails Ness was starting to waver, "I'll never talk to you again."

"I don't know," Ness had said slowly. The night had fallen, the air was soft, and inky waves were lapping against the dive boats. It was perfect here. Why leave paradise for a place her father had spent a lifetime trying to escape? She could turn this bequest down if she chose to. The solicitor had admitted this was a possibility.

"What don't you know?"

"Whether I want anything to do with it. It's weird, Mel. I don't even know this uncle."

Mel had shrugged her tanned shoulders. "So what?"

"So it doesn't make sense. He and my dad hadn't spoken in years. Why choose me rather than my cousins?"

"Maybe he didn't like your cousins? Or perhaps he wanted to piss them off? Who cares why! The point is that you own a bloody castle with suits of armour and battlements and everything! Stop stressing about it and just enjoy!"

Ness had laughed. Mel's enthusiasm was wonderful but probably a bit misplaced.

"From what the solicitor said I think the place is a bit of a wreck," she'd commented. The solicitor had certainly implied that there was a huge amount of work required and no money in the pot to pay for any of it. Ness bit her lip. The phrase poisoned chalice sprang to mind.

Mel's brown eyes were big circles of disbelief. "So what? It's yours! God, I have no idea why you look so bloody miserable. I'd have caught the first plane out of here."

"I can't just take off," Ness had protested. She'd poked the melting remains of her cocktail with a straw and frowned. "There's too much to do here and I've got my job to think about."

"Jeez, girlfriend! You've just been told you've inherited a stately home. Go and check it out! There are zillions of girls who'll wait tables in the sunshine." Then her eyes narrowed thoughtfully. "Please tell me you're not still hoping Stephen will sort his shit out. You're not hanging on for him, are you?"

Stephen Ambrose was Ness's ex. Fun, good-looking and (courtesy of his venture-capitalist father) wealthy too, he'd swept her off her feet when she'd first arrived on St Antonia, showering her with gifts and romantic trips to idyllic beaches. Unfortunately, a love of gambling and a weakness for pretty faces were also high on his list of personal qualities. Ness knew she'd wasted far too much time and energy, not to mention too many tears, on him. She hadn't needed the psychoanalytical skills of Freud to figure out why she'd been attracted to Stephen and which way their relationship was headed. Ending things with him had been one of the best decisions she'd ever made, although her ex was finding it hard to see it that way. He definitely wasn't used to hearing the word no and from a lowly waitress too! Leaving him behind would be a definite bonus.

"That's well and truly over. No more spoiled playboys for me," she'd said firmly.

"Or only very rich ones with big willies and even bigger yachts," Mel had grinned.

But Ness had shaken her head. "No way. I'm through with shallow idiots. Never again."

"So there's nothing keeping you here then, is there? Go and check that castle out. If you don't like it then sell the place, buy a hotel out here and I'll work for you instead," Mel had said happily. "Sorted!"

Ness had smiled at this. Her friend's enthusiasm was infectious and for the first time since she'd learned about her legacy she'd felt excitement fizzing deep in the pit of her stomach. Maybe this was the missing piece of her puzzle.

"Sorted," she'd agreed, and they'd clinked glasses. It had sounded like a plan, especially after a few drinks.

So, one plane ticket and a long drive later here Ness was, at the foot of a hill and on the brink of the unknown – and definitely on the brink of turning around and driving away. This all felt too big and too weird.

Ness had missed Addy every day since his accident. Yes, he'd been infuriating, irresponsible and totally feckless, but he would have known exactly what to do now. Parked in a lane he would surely have known, only a mile from the place where he and his brothers had grown up, Ness missed her father more than ever. She had so many questions she needed to ask, but Addy would never be able to answer them now. She'd never been brave enough to enquire about his past or demand to know more about her mother. Discussions about Beth had always been off limits and Ness had never known why. She'd been beautiful. She'd played the violin. She'd drowned when Ness was a baby. That was it. End of story. Addy had lived in the moment and been determined to stay there, right until the second the motorcycle tyres had veered off the tarmac; he'd always skirted questions, like a skater zigzagging across the surface of a frozen pond. And now it was too late. Ness would never have the chance to glean answers or know more about her family unless she screwed up her courage and faced this odd legacy head-on.

She wound the window down and inhaled the salty air. The lane was empty now and rose steeply ahead. Before she could change her mind, Ness released the handbrake with a determined clunk, put her foot down and let the car surge forward into the unknown. Within moments she had crested the hill, and suddenly the world fell away with dizzying speed. The sea below was a glittering kaleidoscope of blues and greens and turquoises, spread out at the foot of a town filled with higgledy-piggledy houses almost paddling in the shallows. Floating in the blue, like something from a fairy tale, was an island tethered to the shore by a winding sandy ribbon. On top of the island a ruined castle slumbered in the sunshine, keeping watch over the bay with the quiet dignity of ages.

The journey, her worries and even her jet lag were instantly forgotten as Nessa Penwellyn fell head over heels in love with her inheritance.

Chapter 3

Thank goodness the tide was starting to go out and she could soon walk across the causeway, thought Lucy Penwellyn as she scurried down Fore Street with her wicker basket in one hand and Biscuit's lead clutched in the other. It had been sweet of Merryn to give her a ride to shore earlier on, but she'd been drinking tea and chatting with Annie Luckett for far too long and now she was dreadfully behind.

Lucy glanced at her watch, relieved to see that it was only just coming up for noon. Jamie wasn't due to arrive until mid-afternoon, which meant she should have plenty of time to rustle something up for supper as well as being able to air his room and stumble around in what was left of the cellar to see if there was anything he would deem good enough. Her brother had exacting tastes and would rather drink seawater than the cheap white Lucy bought now and again as a treat. Yes, she would be able to do all of this and be back before he turned up, thank heavens.

If Jamie arrived at the castle before Lucy, today of all days, there'd be all kinds of awkward explanations. He'd never believe that she'd nipped into town solely to pick up milk and the papers. He'd stare at her suspiciously and make barbed comments until Lucy found herself confessing to anything he wanted just to break the mood. Then Jamie would berate her and Lucy would feel so guilty she'd do whatever she could to make up for supposedly upsetting him. It was the circle of guilt.

"We're family," was his usual lament, blue eyes wide and hurt. "You're supposed to be on my side! We're Penwellyns. We're meant to stick together!"

Usually they did stick together – or at least, Lucy had always done her best in the circumstances. When they were younger, Jamie had been sent to public school and Lucy had stayed at home to look after their widower father, who'd become increasingly ill. When Maudsley had taken a turn for the worse some years later, she'd hoped her brother might be a little more supportive, but by then Jamie was far too busy being something important in the City. (Lucy never really understood quite what it was he did; it seemed to involve playing with vast amounts of imaginary money, as far as she could see.) By the time their father passed away she'd been lucky if Jamie visited once a month.

It was too hard for him, he'd said. He couldn't handle seeing their father deteriorate. Lucy often felt she couldn't handle it either, but unfortunately she hadn't been given a choice. When she'd asked Jamie for some help with their father's care, tentatively suggesting she would like to go back to work, her brother had scoffed. In his opinion, baking cakes in a local café was hardly a proper job and she was far more use where she was. Lucy had supposed he was right. Baking wasn't a high-flying city career. Nevertheless, she'd loved her job and had shed many quiet tears on the day she'd handed in her notice, knowing she'd miss chatting to the customers and bantering with the other staff. She'd also miss the wonderful alchemy of combining ingredients into a bowl, then transferring them into tins for the oven and watching them become buns, cakes, scones or loaves of bread, the crusts thick and golden. Maybe like Jamie said it wasn't much of a talent, but it had meant a lot to Lucy.

She'd felt desperately lonely watching her father slip away. Lonely and terrified. If it hadn't been for friends like Annie Luckett and, latterly, Uncle Armand, Lucy wasn't sure she would have made it through such a bleak time. It had pained her to see Maudsley, once such a sharp-witted intellectual, become a demanding yet tremulous ghost of his former self. Annie would sit with him and chat to him, not seeming to mind that he belligerently asked her the same questions over and over again, and responding with a patience and good humour that Lucy could only aspire to.

"Years of being a teacher, my love," was Annie's explanation when, awed and a little intimidated, Lucy had asked what the secret was. "You don't teach for as long as I did without getting used to repeating yourself on a daily basis. It must be second nature now."

Lucy had felt guilty whenever she'd left her father for a few hours, but without those afternoons of freedom to walk Biscuit on the beach or simply to sit in the café in St Pirran and chat to her friends she wouldn't have clung on to her last few shreds of sanity. And without Uncle Armand she would have been totally lost. Even though he hadn't spoken to his brother for decades, Uncle Armand had been adamant that once Maudsley's funeral was over Lucy should come and set up a tea shop of her own in the castle. If it hadn't been for him she'd have been homeless too, since Jamie had needed to sell the family home as soon as possible to raise funds for his latest investment. He was supposed to have given Lucy half of the profits but said the recession had wiped them out. This was, he'd pointed out, the risk you took when you played the markets. Lucy couldn't recall ever telling Jamie she wanted to play the markets, or indeed him mentioning it either, but then she'd been in a very dark place and most events of that time were nothing but a blur.

She sighed. Almost forty-two, unemployed and homeless. She would have been in huge trouble if it hadn't been for her uncle. Grumpy and determined and difficult he might have been, but if it hadn't been for him her future would have been very bleak indeed.

Uncle Armand. Larger than life with his bright eyes, lined face and shock of white hair, he had terrified and delighted Lucy in turn. The castle had become her own private kingdom, and when she hadn't been baking for the tea room or cleaning (which was easier said than done when half the place was falling down and the other half was smothered in black mould), Lucy had loved nothing more than to pluck a book from the library shelf, blow off the dust and read aloud to him by the fire. Afterwards, she would listen to his tales, about the smugglers and wreckers who'd once made the place theirs. Sometimes she'd played the violin or the piano for him. At first she'd been embarrassed by her stumbling attempts, but gradually she'd been encouraged by his stillness and the notes had become less hesitant. When he'd asked her to play his own compositions she'd thrilled with pride. They solved crosswords and the complicated music puzzles Armand loved, and slowly Lucy had stepped out from the shadows and back into the sunlight. Her uncle had helped her through her grief and given her a home; Lucy knew she'd be grateful to him for the rest of her life. Nursing Armand through his short illness had been an honour and a privilege and not, as Jamie had put it, "yet more arse-wiping".

If she died with half as much dignity as Armand she'd be proud, Lucy thought, recalling how he'd held her hand in his and stared out of the window, each second that passed taking him to a place where she knew she could no longer reach him. With his eyes fixed on the ceaseless waves and his breath becoming ever shallower, her uncle had never once complained or made any demands. Maybe he felt he'd already asked more than enough of her by asking her to—

Although she was in the middle of Fore Street, Lucy stopped in her tracks and swallowed hard as a fresh knot of panic tightened in her throat. She wouldn't think about that. Not now. Tourists flowed around her as she stood still and tried to fight the rising terror. What was it that Fern had said she should do? Chant something, wasn't it? But what? Not that om sound that the castle's latest waif and stray liked to make when she was sitting cross-legged in the herb garden, that was for sure! Dr Russex would be running out of the surgery and sectioning her if she did that. The town's GP had been worried about Lucy for months and was always gently suggesting some counselling or a mild antidepressant. Lucy resisted all his offers; she didn't need any of that. She just needed the next few weeks to be over with and for Jamie to have no idea she'd been instrumental in what he was bound to consider the ultimate betrayal.

"Calmness in and stress out, wasn't it?" Lucy asked Biscuit. The little spaniel wagged his plumy tail in agreement, as though saying that this was indeed the right mantra. If Biscuit concurred then that was good enough for Lucy. She took a few deep breaths of salty air, relieved to feel her heartbeat slow to its usual rate. I must tell Fern when she gets home, Lucy thought. She'll be pleased to know I've listened to her about something, even if I draw the line at nose piercings and tattoos! Being in her early forties, Lucy considered herself far too old for such things – even if age was, as Fern insisted, just a number. When Lucy looked in the mirror and saw her pale face, dark-ringed eyes and limp mousy hair, she felt every one of her forty-something years – and a few more besides. Her reflection gazed back, a sad middle-aged spinster no matter what Fern told her to the contrary.

Unlike Lucy, the free-spirited Fern with her long pink plaits and rainbow sweaters couldn't be more than eighteen and had arrived only a year ago. A dark blue smudge on her cheekbone and a series of angry scars on her arms had spoken volumes and Armand, who was nowhere near as irascible as he liked to make out, had instantly given her a room and put her to work in the garden. Being as green-fingered as her name might suggest, Fern had soon produced the most glorious vegetables and had also proved to be a dab hand in the tea room. She was a pink-haired sunbeam and Lucy could no more imagine Pirran Island without her than she could imagine it without Fred the gardener (who slept more than he gardened and cost them a fortune in broken ride-on mowers) or lovely Merryn, who camped at Grace Note Bay on the far side of the island and did all the heavy work around the place in return for his pitch. What a strange little family they'd been: the grumpy old landowner, his dowdy niece, an ancient Cornish gardener, a fairy child and the town heart-throb. The island had been home to all of them.

What would happen now was anyone's guess, although admittedly Lucy had a greater insight than most into the island's possible future. Her part in the proceedings was making her more nervous with every mile that brought her brother closer. If Jamie assumed that she was up to something by being in the village on this Very Important Day, then he wouldn't be so far off the mark – and if he discovered what Lucy had really been up to these last few months, he would flip.

Her mouth dried at the very thought. She hoped Annie Luckett could resist the urge to gloat, or at the very least could manage not to mention Lucy's role in it all. Uncle Armand had taken the secret to the grave and David Brown, the affable family solicitor, certainly wouldn't be breathing a word of it – so at least there she was safe. Lucy wasn't scared of her brother but...

OK. There was no point in denying it. She was scared of her brother. She was terrified of Jamie and his rages. Most people were. Fern probably had a mantra for standing up for yourself, but Lucy knew it was far too late now to break the habits of a lifetime. She ought to have stood up to Jamie years ago, before their patterns of behaviour had become so ingrained – rather like the years of dirt on the castle's kitchen table. Life might have been very different if she'd told her demanding sibling when they were children that he couldn't have her toys, or if she'd refused to take the blame for his various misdemeanours. The trouble was, Lucy's younger brother was the kind of person you couldn't easily say no to. From the moment his eyelids had opened he'd literally been the blue-eyed boy, and nothing much in the following years had changed this. Her mother had been besotted with the new baby, during a time when Maudsley had been suffering one of his many bouts of depression, and soon the word spoilt hadn't come close to describing Jamie.

I was besotted too, Lucy reminded herself – because sometimes, when Jamie was in one of his moods, it was easy to forget this.

She was equally to blame for indulging him. The problem was, a tantrum in a six-year-old translated to a nasty temper in an adult. Vesuvius erupting had nothing on Jamie Penwellyn losing his cool. Peaceful and easy-going by nature, Lucy was petrified of conflict; the adults in her life had provided more than enough of that. Consequently she'd spent most of her life attempting to keep her brother calm. This task was proving harder and harder as time went on. It was a full-time job: some might even say that taking care of Jamie had been her life's work. In view of all this, what she'd done recently had been very much against her usual instincts – and she lived in terror of Jamie ever finding out.

Sometimes you had to do what was right. Maybe that should be her mantra?

Heartened by this idea, Lucy continued down Fore Street towards the causeway. In another twenty minutes the waves would have danced away to reveal the glistening cobbles that led to home. Although she'd made the journey hundreds of times, Lucy still felt the excitement of seeing the secrets of the seabed laid bare, the deep pools and weed-strewn rocks that were home to all kinds of shy creatures and flickering fish. As a child she'd stared out at the island from her bedroom window, unable to believe that she had a mysterious composer uncle who lived there all alone, and imagined that she saw mermaids darting through the rolling waves and lolling on the distant shore. It was fanciful but even all these years on Lucy still shaded her eyes against the glare and looked out for them. Admittedly the only semi-naked girls to appear on the island nowadays were the ones lucky enough to spend a night in Merryn Hellier's caravan.

Lucy felt a twist of longing and shook her head. How ridiculous was she? A middle-aged woman with a crush. With his salt-stiffened blond curls, crinkly-eyed smile and bronzed body, twenty-something Merryn Hellier was as out of her reach as the moon. If he noticed her at all then it was definitely for her baking rather than her body. Lucy couldn't think of anyone who'd be interested in that.

Moving through the town on foot was certainly easier than driving during the tourist season, and as she traced the familiar route home Lucy took time to look around her and enjoy the beauty of St Pirran. There was The Castle Inn at the end of the road, where it overlooked its namesake. Outside the pub, a jaunty sign rocked gently in the breeze and the smell of stale beer floated onto the street. Lucy had spent some fun nights there as a teenager, listening to dodgy bands, ordering basket meals and sipping Malibu and pineapple (which had seemed the height of sophistication then). She hadn't been into the pub for years now. Judging by the immaculate sage paint on the woodwork, and by the window boxes filled with blooms rather than the dried earth and cigarette ends she remembered, fried food and cocktails were as far in the past as her hopes of romance.

Closer to the quay and the causeway were the gift shops, art galleries and designer clothes outlets filled with flowery fabrics and espadrilles. Slowing her pace, Lucy dawdled by Frock Box, admiring a pretty fifties-style prom dress in red cotton embroidered with white spots. It had been teamed with a pair of strappy shoes and a floaty white scarf, and the mannequin was also clutching a gorgeous matching purse. For a split second Lucy imagined how it might feel to wear that outfit, to maybe even push a pair of Victoria Beckham style sunglasses onto her head and toss a mane of glossy blonde curls. How would it feel to be the kind of woman who could wear such a dress and draw admiring looks wherever she went? Catching a glimpse of her reflection, Lucy winced; that dowdy woman in shapeless jeans and a faded fisherman's smock would never know. She was better off putting such daft ideas firmly away. Women like her weren't made for romance or glamour – and even if Lucy Penwellyn had been, her time was well and truly past.

"You should buy it," said a cheerful voice.

Jolted from her thoughts, Lucy looked up, straight into twinkling brown eyes. While she'd been daydreaming, a man had paused beside her and had also been admiring the dress.

"I don't think so," she said, with a nervous laugh. "It's hardly the sort of thing I'd wear."

The man frowned. "Why not?"

Why not? Where did she start? Because she was too old? Too frumpy? Would look ridiculous? Had nowhere to wear it?

"It's just your colour," he added.

Was he laughing at her? She wasn't sure. He had a friendly face and didn't look the type to mock anyone.

"I know these things," the man continued conversationally. "I'm an artist."

With its scoured light and breath-taking views, St Pirran was a magnet for arty types. Usually they liked to drift around in paint-stained smocks, holding pencils up at the horizon and squinting thoughtfully. They didn't tend to wear dusty combats with knee pads, though – and they were seldom seen holding hard hats. This smiley man with his thick blond hair and outdoorsy tan looked nothing like an artist.

"Technically I'm a stonemason," he told Lucy, seeing her surprised expression, "but that's pretty artistic in my book and I've been known to sketch in my spare time, so I think I'm qualified."

"Right," said Lucy. Her face felt hot and she was oddly flustered by this peculiar conversation. "That's great. Fantastic."

"I think so," said the man cheerfully, "and it pays the bills and means I've been able to move to Cornwall. My boy loves St Pirran and it's much better here for kids than London is, don't you think?"

Lucy nodded. This was something she did feel qualified to talk about. She was just about to tell him that growing up in St Pirran was wonderful, when they were interrupted by a blasting horn as a white van drew up alongside them.

"Hey, Adam! You can't stand here all day chatting up the locals!" the driver called as the window hissed down. "Some of us have work to do!"

Lucy's new friend rolled his eyes. "That's my summons. Better go. I meant what I said though. You really should buy that dress."

Then he hopped into the van, leaving Lucy bemused. As the driver pulled away, with another cheery blast on the horn, she saw the familiar red fox logo and swirling scarlet script of Reynard Developments. Ah. Now it all made sense. Another of Max Reynard's builder teams, shipped in from London to turn around a development in record time. She felt oddly disappointed.

"Time to go home," Lucy said to Biscuit.

Further down the hill, past the new deli (which had once been a very basic grocers where Lucy had faithfully bought her father's favourite shrimp paste for years), was the expensive wine merchants boasting London prices so that the likes of Jamie could show off. Beyond that was the chandlery and the small fish market where the St Pirran fleet landed their catch. At the far end of the quay was the church, facing patiently out to sea as though waiting for Jesus to return. If He did, He'd be disappointed because Reynard Developments had bought that beautiful building eighteen months ago and was converting it into luxury apartments. For a figure that took Lucy's breath away and sent the hopes of locals nose-diving, Londoners could buy themselves a slice of heaven on earth with views to die for and even a private parking space, something that was like gold dust here. Both of Lucy's parents' funerals had taken place in that church, and she'd been to more weddings and christenings and midnight Masses there than she could even remember. To think that all this history had been smothered by oak floors, designer kitchens and Farrow and Ball paint turned Lucy cold – but Jamie, who was thick as thieves lately with Max Reynard, called it progress.

Annie Luckett called it a crime and her opinion wasn't unique. There were tensions in St Pirran as locals found themselves priced out of a town that had been home to their families for generations. Fishermen struggling to make a living or townsfolk doing seasonal work for minimum wage in the pubs and cafés couldn't afford to pay London prices for the privilege of living in their home town. Gradually they found themselves relocated to the top of St Pirran in new-build accommodation. In the winter the cottages and houses where generations of their families had once lived were empty as second-homers went skiing or in search of sunnier climes. It was only Armand's tenacity and stubborn refusal to sell up and move to the mainland that had saved Pirran Castle from a similar fate. Towards the end, hardly a week had gone by without a letter arriving from a developer or some other would-be purchaser.

"Kindling," Armand would say, screwing these letters up and lobbing them into a basket – but once he'd left the room Lucy would smooth each one out and read it, her forehead crinkling like the paper. The vultures were circling. What would happen when her uncle wasn't there any longer? What would happen when her brother inherited the place?

As her feet slithered down the steps to the causeway Lucy wondered if it was a coincidence that Max Reynard and Jamie seemed so pally lately. She didn't think so and, as it turned out, neither had Armand thought so. Thank God the old man had always been ten steps ahead of his nephew.

If he hadn't been, seeing Jamie's black Range Rover lumbering over the causeway would probably have made Lucy feel even worse than it already did.

She gritted her teeth and picked up her pace. It was time to face her brother.

Chapter 4

Fern watched the black Range Rover cross the causeway as she sat on the jetty and dabbled her toes into the cool water below. She'd rolled up her flowing gypsy skirt, tucking it into the waistband, and the wood was warm and crumbly beneath the bare brown skin of her thighs. This was one of her favourite spots on St Pirran.

She'd actually be hard-pushed to pick just one favourite spot, Fern thought, because there were so many to choose from. Sometimes it might be the highest point on the old ramparts; the masonry was loose there, but if you made the climb there was nothing better than being as high as the gulls and buzzards. On other days Fern loved to sit in the stillness of the ruined chapel to let the peace of ages quieten the chatter of her mind. Then there was the walled garden, where in the summer she'd tended the vegetables and cut swathes of nodding sweet peas from the canes, burying her face in the blooms and feeling almost drunk with their scent. Or there was Merryn's secluded bay, with its deep rock pools and slice of silvery sand. How could anybody choose just one place when every corner you turned on this magical island revealed somewhere more beautiful than the last?

Not that Jamie Penwellyn appreciated any of this. Fern knew he wouldn't see the beauty of this place unless it could be measured in pounds. Money was everything to men like him and they were so much the poorer for it. Armand hadn't even been dead an hour and his nephew had been on the phone to the family's solicitor, demanding that the will should be found and read immediately. Poor Lucy had been in pieces but her brother had remained dry-eyed. In fact, he'd looked as though he'd won the lottery rather than lost his uncle. It hadn't even been supper time before he'd been closeted in his office, talking to Max Reynard and making plans. He'd been so sure everything was in the bag, even more revoltingly arrogant than usual if such a thing was possible, bossing his tearful sister about, nosing through all Armand's private papers and striding through the passageways as though he already owned the place.

Served him right when he got a big shock, Fern thought with satisfaction. Perhaps she shouldn't have been listening behind closed doors, but in fairness his howl of rage could probably have been heard in the town anyway. He'd stormed out of the library (sending Fern and her duster flying) and minutes later had been in his car tearing over the causeway – and that had been the last they'd seen of him. Until now.

As the big car drew closer, Fern's pretty face creased into a scowl. She always tried hard to live in harmony and balance with the universe and send out good vibes to everyone, but there was something about Jamie Penwellyn that set her teeth on edge.

Right now her skin prickled with anticipation of the storms ahead. The island was usually such a peaceful spot and Fern loved it with all her heart. It was a healing place and serenity wrapped itself around her like a hug as she fell asleep every night, lulled by the waves and the whisper of the wind through the grass. She cherished the hours she spent working in the garden with Fred, her hands buried in the rich red soil. Sometimes she would pause to contemplate the miraculous potential of a seed held between her fingers, before she planted it deep and sent it blessings for the months ahead. She enjoyed helping Lucy in the tea room too, and chatting to the visitors as they tucked into her cakes and pasties. She even loved cleaning the place, although it always felt like a losing battle: the grime was centuries old and there was hardly enough money to heat the water, never mind buy silver polish or beeswax. Come to that, there was barely enough money to pay her – not that Fern was worried about being paid. She'd have worked for free if necessary, because Pirran Island was her home now. The Penwellyns and the island had saved her and Fern would do anything for them. Anything.

"Maybe draw the line at listening to private conversations, though? You'll crack your chi!" Merryn had teased when Fern had attempted to tell him what she'd overheard. Merryn had put his hands over his ears and refused to listen, which meant she'd had nobody to confide in apart from Fred the gardener or the seagulls. Fred didn't count because he was as deaf as the proverbial post and hadn't heard a word she'd said anyway, and the seagulls had been too busy nesting to care what Fern thought. Consequently, she'd been stewing for weeks and was fit to pop.

Merryn could be as self-righteous as he liked, Fern decided. If listening at doors was what it took to be two jumps ahead of Jamie Penwellyn and Max Reynard, then a few cracks in her chi were a small price to pay.

But luckily for Fern, and for the island, the old man had been even further ahead...

Shielding her eyes against the sun's glare, Fern watched the Range Rover advance across the cobbles. She shivered. With every inch the tyres crept closer, the atmosphere seemed to swell slightly more with tension. The breeze seemed to hold its breath, the waves broke with just a little less certainty and even the gulls muted their shrieking. Everyone and everything was on edge whenever Jamie arrived. If you believed in soul energy, which Fern did with all her heart, then Lucy's brother possessed more than his fair share of the negative variety.

A small figure was poised at the furthest end of the causeway and Fern could just make out the wicker basket tucked over one arm and the dancing spaniel at the person's feet. From these clues she realised it was Lucy – a fact confirmed by the way the person was almost running across the slippery path in her haste. Lucy always raced about when Jamie was in residence. It broke Fern's heart to see how nervous she became in her brother's presence; Lucy's usually sunny disposition and easy laugh vanished completely in the onslaught of his critical comments and sly put-downs.

Arse, thought Fern. Jamie Penwellyn deserved everything that was coming to him. As far as she was concerned, whoever it was that the old man had decided to leave the castle to couldn't be worse than him. Jamie might have been shocked to discover that some mysterious female cousin had inherited the lot, but Fern hadn't been at all surprised. Armand had had the measure of his nephew. Fern would have wagered all she owned (a daisy headband and some tarot cards being about the sum of it) that he'd also known that if he'd left his estate to the far more deserving Lucy it would only have been a matter of time before Jamie bullied it out of her hands. Armand had had no choice.

Fern shuddered. She hated bullies. It was one of the reasons she was here.

She scrambled to her feet, her skirt still tucked up into her waistband, and sprinted from the jetty to clamber up the steep bank, where parts of the wall had long since fallen down. Her bare feet easily finding footholds in the worn stones, she heaved herself up to the halfway point where it was possible to press her spine against the granite and watch proceedings through a veil of ivy. Merryn would probably disapprove of this and accuse her of spying, but as far as Fern was concerned this was a case of know your enemy.

The four-by-four, having made the crossing, now swung to the left, turning under what remained of the gatehouse arch and crunching across weed-smothered cobbles until it drew up alongside the entrance. Nobody actually used the original entry to the castle. Lucy said she couldn't ever recall seeing the door open, and a previous investigation had shown that the hinges had long since seized up. Nevertheless, even if it wasn't functional it was pretty. It was woven through with ivy, and in the summer it had been heavy with nodding dog roses. Nest-making swifts had darted in and out of the gaps above, like arrows fired by long-ago archers. On days when the island was open to tourists they loved to take pictures of the castle entrance, and it featured on many local calendars and postcards. To park across and obscure it was just typical of Jamie. Never mind that his uncle had faithfully parked his Morris Minor around the back or that Lucy's ancient 2CV was relegated to the old coach house; Jamie Penwellyn was going to park right outside the front door of his castle.

Except that it wasn't his castle, was it? Pirran Island belonged to somebody else now, somebody who would be arriving very soon. Fern could hardly wait. That even from beyond the grave Armand could put his nephew in his place was very satisfying. She just hoped that the mysterious Nessa Penwellyn was up to the task of keeping him there.

From her vantage point Fern saw Jamie swing his stocky frame out of the car. He looked out of place for Cornwall in his city suit, shiny shoes and designer sunglasses. People in St Pirran didn't tend to bother with expensive tailoring; they were too busy battling with the elements and paying the bills. Admittedly some out-of-towners liked their vintage flowery fabrics, shabby chic macs and pretty shoes, but that kind of look was hardly practical for day-to-day life here. Everyone else dressed like Lucy in jeans and boots, ready to face a gale or a downpour. Fern knew she stuck out in her sequinned skirts, biker boots and flowing scarves, but even she had a raincoat and some wellies tucked away.

Jamie was leaning against the car with his phone clamped against his ear, deep in conversation.

"It's absolutely fine, Max. There's nothing to do now but wait," he was saying, his voice just holding back its usual note of impatience. While the person on the other end of the line was speaking, Jamie pushed his glasses onto the top of his neatly cut hair and squinted critically up at the walls. Spotting Fern, who gave him a jaunty wave, he scowled.

Fern wouldn't lose any sleep over it. She knew Jamie thought she was a "scavenger", a "freeloader", a "street rat" – and those were some of the nicer things she'd overheard him say about her

– so she didn't expect him to be thrilled to see her. Unfortunately for him, his uncle's will stated that her future on the island was entirely at the discretion of his beneficiary. So as much as Jamie might love to be able to kick her off, he was stuck with her – just as he was stuck with Merryn and Fred. Well, for now anyway. Who knew? This Nessa Penwellyn could be even worse than him. Unlikely, Fern thought, but since they shared some of the same genes it was a possibility.

"Arriving tomorrow, apparently," Jamie said, turning his back on Fern and pulling a sleek Louis Vuitton holdall from the front seat. "Some cousin, or so I'm told. Yes, I know I promised – but look, there's no need to be concerned, Max. The deal's still on. We just need to go about it slightly differently. Fine. Tomorrow."

Having ended the call, he pushed the phone into his jacket pocket, swung the bag onto his shoulder and flipped the remote control to lock the car with a sharp horn blast that sent the nearby seagulls soaring and screeching.

Fern raised her eyes to heaven. What a knob! Who did he think was going to steal his car here? Her? The castle cat? Or maybe old Fred might fancy a joyride before quiz night in The Castle?

Jamie was plotting something and with Max Reynard too. It was hardly a surprise; the developer had been eyeing up the castle for months, and if rumour was to be believed he'd made Armand several eye-watering offers in the past. Of course, he'd be looking to add the island to his portfolio.

Making her way down from the wall, Fern concluded that Nessa Penwellyn couldn't arrive soon enough.

Chapter 5

Max Reynard ended the call and leaned back in his chair. Narrowing his eyes against the sun's glare, he stared thoughtfully out across the bay and watched the little tripping boats slicing white lines through the shimmering water as they raced to reach St Pirran before the tide caught them out.

You had to act swiftly to stay ahead in business too, Max reckoned. He prided himself on his ability to spot an opportunity and cut a deal before anyone else had even thought of it, the ink barely dry on the contracts before he was moving forward to the next challenge. From turning dilapidated Georgian seafronts into smart flats, to snapping up mouldering stately piles and converting them into luxury apartments, to completing niche developments like St Pirran's Church, Max Reynard had an uncanny ability to see potential and exploit it. Like his namesake, the fox, once he had something in his sights he pursued it and pounced on it. In his thirties and with a multimillion-pound property development business to his name, Max was now in a position to acquire a magnificent addition to the Reynard portfolio. St Pirran's Island would be his best catch yet.

Or so he'd thought. Suddenly things were looking rather different and Max didn't like this turn of events one bit. He hadn't made all those plans or put things in motion this far – or even lent that little weasel Jamie Penwellyn all that money – only to be cheated of his prize at the eleventh hour.

Max's dark brows drew together. Above him the gulls were circling, as keen to scavenge leftovers as he had been to pick up the remains of his greedy school friend's inheritance. The problem was that Jamie had been a little too hasty in assuming that his uncle would bequeath the estate to him. It was understandable that Jamie had dismissed his sister's chances of inheriting it. Max had met Lucy Penwellyn on several occasions and could see why Armand wouldn't have left the place to her: she'd have given the lot away to her waifs and strays by teatime. But to leave Pirran Island to a completely unknown entity? Jamie certainly hadn't seen that coming.

Part of Max (the part that wasn't infuriated by the delay in proceedings) was secretly pleased that the old man had seen through his nephew. All Jamie's visits and toadying to his uncle had been fruitless – and bearing in mind how he'd loathed every minute he'd had to spend with his elderly relative, it served him right.

Max took a sip of his drink and gazed across at the island again. The tide was out now, leaving the wet sand glistening in the early afternoon sunshine. The beach was freckled with holidaymakers, all determined to make the most of the weather. Beyond it, the causeway was visible now above the waves and people were making the mile-long walk across to visit what was left of the chapel, gawp at the ruins and eat scones in that shabby excuse for a tea room. That would all stop once he owned the place. The clientele who could afford the exclusive apartments Reynard Developments would be offering wouldn't want their privacy compromised. There would be some legal wrangling, of course; that was inevitable when you purchased an old property. But Max's lawyers never had any difficulties getting around these things – it was why he paid them so much money. Money, Max had learned very early on, greased a lot of wheels and almost always persuaded people to share your point of view.

He'd no reason to think this unknown Penwellyn cousin would be any different. Jamie hadn't said much about her, mainly because when Max had seen him last Jamie had been too apoplectic to string so much as a sentence together. What little Max had managed to glean had come not from his old school chum but from his contact at the solicitor's office in St Pirran. After dinner and a few drinks in The Castle, Cally the PA – with her ample curves, soft mouth and brain like an Aero – had been only too happy to tell him all she knew. It certainly took the phrase "pumping someone for information" to a whole new level, Max reflected now, although in fairness Cally hadn't needed much encouragement. Women never did, in his experience.

They were there for the picking, like ripe fruit, and if he'd wanted to gorge then it would have been exceedingly easy to do so. This town was full of bored wives and pretty girls in shorts and bikinis. They were always thrilled to cruise around the lanes in his convertible Aston, and they tumbled so easily into his bed too. If he wanted he could have enjoyed a different date every night of the week. Nobody would have blamed him and there wasn't one man in St Pirran who didn't secretly envy him. After all, he was rich, good-looking and single. Max Reynard had it all.

Self-indulgence wasn't Max's style though. Yes, he enjoyed more than his fair share of no-strings encounters, but he was choosy and more than aware that it wasn't just his lean muscular body, stormy grey eyes, sharp cheekbones or handsome face they were attracted to. The houses, cars and luxurious lifestyle were equally, if not even more, alluring. Would those same women find him quite as appealing if he was still living in a council house and working on-site with his father? And if the designer clothes were exchanged for overalls? Or if he still had his old wooden boat rather than the shiny Sunseeker yacht moored in St Pirran's marina?

Max's lip curled. Somehow he didn't think so. He was tired of pretty, empty heads and gold-diggers who were so obvious that they might as well be approaching him with sifting pans and pickaxes. He liked sex and he enjoyed the chase, but anything else soon bored him. As far as Max was concerned there was no greater turn-on than a business deal and a challenge.

Which was what it looked as though he was about to get now.

"Another drink, Mr Reynard? Or maybe some lunch? We've got mussels on today and a lovely monkfish special." A waitress was hovering at Max's elbow, balancing a tray in one hand and proffering a laminated menu with the other. Her heavy false eyelashes were fluttering so much that she was in danger of doing her lids an injury, Max thought.

"Mineral water, thanks angel," he replied, treating her to a slow and white-toothed smile. He was amused to see her blush in response. She was pretty enough, in a plump and freckled way, and she had a Cornish accent that reminded him of a character from Poldark. She couldn't have been more than twenty though, which made him feel bloody ancient. He might be kicking his heels while Jamie Penwellyn sorted out his shit, but a guy had to draw the line somewhere. All the same, Max was no use at sitting still: he was much happier when he was flat out with a deal or even helping to carry out some of the renovations. There was a lot to be said for actually getting your hands dirty. Max might be the boss but that didn't mean he couldn't point a wall or lay bricks with the best of them. His father had seen to that.

"Nothing stronger?" Flutter, flutter went the eyelashes. Max almost felt his hair blow in the breeze.

He shook his head. "I don't drink. Mineral water's fine."

Not drinking was a choice that lots of people found hard to understand. They either assumed he was a recovering alcoholic (he wasn't) or thought he was a control freak (possibly), and they usually tried their hardest to persuade him that just one wouldn't hurt. Max found it tiresome. He'd enjoyed drinking in the past but he liked having a clear head and clear judgement even more – and when he'd unexpectedly found himself in charge of Reynard Developments these qualities had been invaluable. You didn't drag a company out of imminent receivership and into enormous profit by spending your time drinking.

A concept Jamie Penwellyn hadn't grasped...

As the waitress fetched his drink, her peachy little ass sashaying across the terrace, Max reflected that if Malcom Reynard could have seen him now, drinking designer water and lolling around in the afternoon sun on the deck of a boutique hotel, he'd have had a fit. His father had been working class to his marrow and a firm believer that real men got on with real jobs. He wouldn't have been impressed with the smart suits and flash cars, being the kind of person who preferred to roll up his sleeves and get on with the job in hand. Reynard Developments had been his pride and joy; Max just wished he'd lived to see what it had become. In Max's hands the business had certainly prospered. It had grown from a small building company in South London to one of the UK's premier developers boasting an impressive portfolio. Max hoped that wherever Mal was now he was proud and not spinning in his grave, clutching his copy of the Socialist Worker and ranting over his son's capitalist ways. He'd never know now, of course, but Max suspected that his workaholic personality would be a psychiatrist's wet dream. If studying hard and winning a scholarship to public school hadn't been enough to make his father proud, it was hard to imagine what would have pleased Malcom Reynard. Sometimes Max had even had the impression that his father was embarrassed about his son's public school education, which was a peculiar inverted snobbery.

The waitress returned with his drink and, sensing his introspective mood, didn't pause to flirt – which Max was thankful for. Reaching into his holdall, he drew out a battered sketchpad and the pouch that contained his charcoals. Then, with his eyes narrowed, he began to sketch the castle. It was a view Max never tired of; already the pad was nearly filled with drawings of it from all perspectives. He loved to sketch, although it was something of an indulgence these days. More often than not his artistic leanings were channelled towards plans for buildings and renovations. Working with architectural plans had taught him technicality, but drawing from the heart gave him peace.

The castle bloomed on the cartridge paper, rising from the white background just as it rose from the sea; it transformed the space with its magic and possibilities. As he sketched Max was filled with determination. He had to have the island. He had to. There was no doubt in his mind that it was meant to be his. Jamie Penwellyn had gloated about his inheritance all the way through school, never missing the chance to look down his nose at scholarship boys. After all, what did brains matter when you would one day be bequeathed your own castle? Working-class oiks like Max were to be sneered at.

Or rather, they had been back then. Twenty years on Jamie had sung a very different song when he'd arrived at Reynard's London offices deep in debt and with an interesting proposition. Max had enjoyed watching his old schoolmate sweat as he'd sat at his big leather-topped desk listening to Jamie choke out what it was he wanted. Jamie's puffy face and pallor spoke volumes about the life of excess that had led him to this point, and Max despised him for squandering all of his opportunities. Never mind the proverbial silver spoon; Jamie Penwellyn had been born with the entire cutlery set wedged in his mouth. Although Jamie's parents had passed on, leaving him an investment portfolio as well as their pretty Georgian manor house, he'd even managed to let these assets slip through his pudgy fingers.

He was utterly pathetic, Max thought scornfully. Still, it never hurt to hear what people had to say – and in his experience the more desperate they were the more useful they could be.

"Max, old man, I need a bit of a favour," Jamie had said, once they'd exchanged pleasantries. He'd run a finger around his shirt collar and flicked a pink tongue over his lips while Max had remained silent. It was a favourite tactic of Max's, to let the other party do all the talking and dig themselves in as deep as they wished while he waited to see exactly which move to make. Business was a game of chess to Max – and he'd had a feeling that this one could literally end with him taking the castle. He'd been looking forward to checkmating his old tormentor.

Max had narrowed his eyes. "I'm not sure I follow."

Jamie had shifted on his seat as Max regarded him with a cool grey gaze. "The thing is, I'm in a bit of a spot."

"A spot? What kind of spot?"

Jamie had cleared his throat. "Some of my investments haven't performed quite as expected and I've had to liquidate quite a few assets to keep things afloat. I even had to sell the house and Ma and Pa's things. Lucy was very upset but what's a man to do?"

So he'd flogged the family silver then, thought Max, and now there was nothing left. No surprises there. In the past, whenever Jamie Penwellyn had managed to get his hands on any funds the money had soon gone down his neck or up his nose – so why would he be any different now? He even looked the same: weak-chinned and sandy-haired and with the petulant expression Max recalled only too well from school. Thank God Max had been strong and sporty and more than a match for Jamie and his cronies.

"I'm sorry to hear that," Max had said evenly. "They've been tough times recently. We're pulling through now though. Globally the markets are doing well; they definitely seem to be in recovery."

"They are, they are." Jamie was nodding like the Churchill dog.

If I told him the earth was flat right now he'd agree, Max had thought, and in spite of himself his interest was piqued. Desperate people sometimes made offers that were unexpected. Unexpected and lucrative.

"Something that's definitely on the up is Cornwall. Everyone wants a piece of the place," Jamie had declared, as though this would be a surprise to Max. Perhaps Jamie was unaware that Reynard Developments had already bought several plum spots in that county already. "Which is where we might be able to help one another out – scratch each other's backs, if you like?"

Max had steepled his fingers under his chin. Although he hadn't allowed his face to show any emotion, a knot of excitement had tightened in his belly.

"Really? In what respect?"

"My uncle owns an island off the coast of St Pirran, with a castle on it? You visited once when you came to stay with us that time in the school holidays? Remember?"

Of course Max remembered. It was hard not to, since Jamie had spent most of their schooldays boasting that he was to inherit the lot. When Max had visited that one weekend, the beauty of the place had taken his breath away. It was certainly nothing like Croydon. In the years since, Cornwall had remained in Max's mind as somewhere that seemed enchanted. Of course, it was doubly enchanted now, thanks to the influx of celebrity chefs that had sent house prices skyrocketing. So far as Max could tell, property values looked set to continue on an upwards trajectory for some time yet, and there was money to be made by investing now. His company had recently purchased several buildings in St Pirran, one of which Max had renovated as a holiday home. He loved water sports and hiking the rugged cliff path, and he worked bloody hard too, so he reckoned it was the least he deserved.

"So I was wondering whether you'd be interested in a potential project?" Jamie was asking, his braying tones breaking into Max's thoughts. "You put up some collateral now as surety and when I inherit I give Reynard Developments first refusal on the place and a guaranteed price."

Max hadn't even twitched an eyelash. "What on earth makes you think Reynard Developments would be interested in a ruin?"

"A run-down castle, not a ruin. It's still inhabited. My uncle and a bunch of hangers-on live there," Jamie had corrected him swiftly.

What a charming way to talk about his sister, Max had thought. Having spent some time in St Pirran lately, he knew that Lucy Penwellyn was run ragged caring for her sick uncle as well as managing the tea room, maintaining the castle and manning the visitor centre on the island when the need arose. A team of dedicated local volunteers helped her, but the bulk of the work and responsibility fell to Lucy. On the few occasions when Max had seen her, scuttling along the High Street with a shopping basket in one hand and a spaniel's lead in the other, she'd looked ready to drop.

"There must be hundreds of people who'd kill for a luxury apartment in a castle on a private Cornish island. You could develop it and make a fortune," Jamie had pressed, leaning forward. His blue eyes were bright with zeal. "If you pay me a sum upfront as a guarantee, I'll make sure that when I inherit you can buy the island and the castle at an agreed sum. We can get it all drawn up and legal if you'd rather."

Max would certainly rather. He could throw the castle further than he trusted Jamie Penwellyn. "Saying we were interested, which I'm not necessarily saying, why would you want to do that?"

"It's simple: I need the funds. Bloody embarrassing but true. Besides, the old place costs thousands a week just to maintain. It's a millstone to me and I'd be glad to see the back of it."

A millstone he didn't even own yet, Max had thought wryly.

"And you're certain you're inheriting?"

"Nobody else to leave it to. Lucy's bloody useless, Uncle Adric buggered off years ago and died in the States, and the only other relative is some bint living God only knows where. So I'm the only male heir. Don't worry about Uncle Armand leaving it to a cats' home or something either. The old man wouldn't do that. He's been banging on about family lately – a bit bloody ironic really, since he didn't talk to his brothers for years and only saw Lucy and me in passing when we were kids. He won't let the place go out of the family."

Max was amused at the irony here. "But you would?"

"For the right sum. Let's face it, the place is a liability unless somebody with a tonne of cash buys it." Jamie had held out his hand across the desk. "For the right sum I'll sell it to you. I'd want a share of the profits and a small apartment too, but you'll more than double your money. I promise."

He didn't need to promise; Max's sharp mind was already doing the maths and his artist's imagination was picturing the castle fully restored and offering sumptuous apartments with breath-taking views. Jamie was wrong. Max wouldn't double his money: he'd quadruple it. How could he not reach out and shake his ex-classmate's hand?

So, deeply in debt to Max now, Jamie had promised that the island and castle would be sold to Reynards just as soon as the old man snuffed it and the legalities were in place.

Max's pencil scored a groove in the paper as he recalled their agreement. Jamie had been so certain that he was the heir, and Max hadn't hesitated to strike a deal. Developing the castle was going to make him wealthier than he'd ever imagined – already he had buyers lined up for apartments in the luxury renovation. But it was about more than that to Max. Owning Pirran Island would be proof that he'd made it in life. From council house to castle – it would be a big V-sign to Jamie Penwellyn and his kind.

Was this some sort of class revenge? Max wasn't sure. Would his father be cheering him on or horrified that he'd embraced capitalism so wholeheartedly? All he knew was that the castle was going to be his and that nobody was going to get in his way, least of all some random Penwellyn relative. He'd poured too much time and money into this project to let it go now. Whoever she was, she had better step aside.

"All I know is that she's definitely a niece," Cally the PA had said, placing her hand on Max's leg and moving one of her red-tipped fingers slowly up his thigh.

"I thought Lucy was the only niece?" he'd asked, linking his fingers with hers in an attempt to halt that teasing digit.

"Not according to David. There were three brothers and for some reason they all fell out. The youngest brother lived abroad for years, and I don't think I've ever seen him here. It's his daughter Armand's left everything to."

Her hand had slipped out of his and crept higher up his leg – which to all intents and purposes had ended the conversation and led to something far more interesting. A little bit of extra digging later on had revealed that the estate was in huge debt, the heir to it all was some kind of dropout, and the massive death duties would wipe out anything left in the pot. There was no way some flower child could possibly afford the upkeep on the place. Max had felt much better knowing this. It was only a matter of time before she sold to him, and in the meantime he'd have some fun making Jamie Penwellyn squirm as he paid back his loan.

Who said revenge wasn't sweet?

So, all he needed to do was sit back and enjoy his stay in St Pirran. Then, once this niece realised that her inheritance was actually a bottomless money pit, he'd make her an offer she couldn't refuse. It might even work out in his favour, Max reflected. He'd offer her a couple of million less than Jamie had been demanding and she'd be bound to accept because it would seem like a lottery win to her. Then he'd own the castle without having to give Jamie the apartment and settlement that had been part of their original agreement. It was a win-win situation.

Max smiled. This unknown niece inheriting was turning out to be the best thing that could have happened.

And for now? Well, he'd just enjoy some much-deserved rest here in Cornwall. That wouldn't be such a hardship, not when there was blue water and sunshine – not to mention pretty girls like the cute redhead over there who was checking him out. With her lush curves, golden tan and flame-red hair she was exactly Max's type. Catching her eye and raising a questioning eyebrow, he was rewarded by a rose-petal blush. Yes, Cornwall in the summer. What wasn't to like?

Gathering his bag and his sketchpad, Max decided it was time to find a sunny spot where he could spend the afternoon drawing up some more plans for what would soon become Reynard Developments' greatest venture.

Chapter 6

It was far too early to turn up at the castle, Ness had decided as she'd guided the hire car through St Pirran's warren of narrow streets. Nobody was expecting her until tomorrow – when, accompanied by David Brown, the family's solicitor, she was due to meet her newly discovered cousins and hear her uncle's will being read. Until then she was on free time and perfectly at liberty to wander around the town and explore like any other tourist. There were certainly enough of them here today, licking melting ice creams and stepping out in front of her bonnet as though being on holiday afforded them some kind of magical protection from being squashed flat. It was with relief that she'd finally headed into the car park of the Island View Hotel.

She'd do her best to avoid driving through the town in future, Ness had thought as she'd pulled into a space and killed the engine. At least she could leave the hire car to be collected. She wouldn't have any further need of it, having booked into the hotel for two nights. In theory perhaps she could have stayed at the castle instead: it was technically hers (even if Ness was finding it even harder to grasp this concept now that she'd actually seen the castle). Nevertheless, it had seemed unwise to presume that she'd be welcome. There were people who already lived there, and to just turn up would be insensitive. She had no idea how things were going to unfold, and while she got the lie of the land it seemed best to stay in neutral territory.

And what neutral territory it was too. Perched on the headland overlooking the bay, the hotel had an unrivalled view over the water and boasted a large terrace that wrapped itself around the building. As she climbed a steep flight of steps towards the reception area, Ness saw that the terrace was filled with people seated under huge calico umbrellas. Those nearest her were sipping white wine and tucking into towering buckets of mussels. One man was busy making a charcoal drawing of the scene in front of him, his fingers flying over the creamy paper of his sketchpad as he narrowed his eyes and regarded the horizon. Ness, pausing to get her breath back after climbing the steps, couldn't help but notice him. He was one of those men who drew the eye instantly. It wasn't just because of his physique (lean, yet broad-shouldered); there was something about his intensity as he gazed across the bay, assessing the scene. His dark hair fell over his forehead every now and again, and he pushed it away with an impatient hand as though furious with anything that might get in the way of his sketching. He must be an artist, Ness thought with a pang. Addy had behaved exactly like this. When her father had been painting, which admittedly had happened less and less as the years had gone by, he'd locked himself into whatever room served as a studio and refused to emerge until the piece was finished. This man's all-consuming concentration was very familiar – and when he glanced up and caught her staring, Ness pretended to be busy adjusting the handle of her case. He was extremely attractive, with those piercing grey eyes and sharp cheekbones; he must get women gawping at him all the time. Perhaps he'd assume she was doing the same. When he raised a quizzical eyebrow she felt her cheeks start to glow. He really did think she was checking him out! How embarrassing! For a second Ness considered walking over and explaining that she'd only been staring because he reminded her of her father, but how rude and odd would that sound? When she finally felt brave enough to look up again he'd returned his attention to his sketching. Relieved, Ness was able to reach the reception desk without making an idiot of herself.

Inside, the hotel was a treasure trove of quirky designs and funky furnishings. As she checked in Ness admired a pair of zebra-print sofas, the big splashy paintings on the white walls, and the glass lobby showcasing the shifting seascape beyond. Every time she saw the island rising from the bright blue, Ness's stomach churned. How was it possible that this belonged to her? And that Addy had grown up in such a magical place yet barely mentioned it, just as he'd hardly ever mentioned her mother? All the information she had about Beth had been gleaned from chance remarks but Ness felt sure her father's reluctance to talk about either her mother or his home were linked. Was coming to St Pirran and accepting this inheritance the key to unlocking the mysteries of Adric Penwellyn? The tingling feeling that swept over her each time she looked across to the castle certainly seemed to suggest as much.

The receptionist, a woman in her fifties with a round face and warm smile, checked Ness in. Her eyes widened when she saw the Penwellyn surname.

"Welcome to St Pirran, Miss Penwellyn. I didn't realise you would be American!"

Ness laughed. "I guess I sound it but I promise you I'm British. I've just lived abroad for a very long time, that's all. I can show you my passport if it helps?"

The receptionist looked flustered. "Oh no, no! That won't be necessary. It's so wonderful to meet you. Let me upgrade you to the Castle Suite." Her fingers flew over the keyboard. "It's our nicest room and it has a wonderful view."

Thinking of her bank balance, Ness was alarmed. "That's really kind of you but—"

"The upgrade's on the house," the receptionist interrupted. "My goodness, it's the least we can do to welcome you to St Pirran, Miss Penwellyn. Anyway, if I didn't my sister Annie would skin me alive." She held out her hand and beamed at Ness. "I'm Val Brown, Annie Luckett's sister."

Ness was jet-lagged, but even if she hadn't been it wouldn't have made much difference. She had no idea who Annie Luckett might be or why she'd want a total stranger to have an upgraded room.

"Don't look so surprised; we're all related here," Val added, handing Ness a big set of heavy brass keys held together with nautical-looking rope. "I'm your solicitor's aunty too, and the vicar's cousin."

"Right," said Ness. Her head was starting to thud. The long drive and lack of sleep were beginning to take their toll, never mind the thousand and one questions she needed answering. Val Brown's information overload was more than she could handle right now.

"Listen to me prattling on! You'll be wanting to get to your room and freshen up, won't you?" Val said, turning sideways and easing her ample frame out from behind the desk. "It's just that everyone's so excited to have you here."

As Val led her through a maze of corridors, all white and covered in colourful artwork, she chatted away nineteen to the dozen. Ness did her best to listen carefully, but the words crashed against her like the waves on the island's rocky shore and made little sense.

"It was such a shame your uncle stopped composing," Val was saying as Ness followed her large backside up a flight of stairs. "I think he'd have been one of the greatest composers of the past century if he'd carried on, don't you?"

"Mmm," said Ness, wondering when would be a good time to let Val know that until recently she hadn't even been aware that she had an uncle, let alone a reclusive one who lived in a castle and was a gifted composer. The first she'd heard about Armand Penwellyn had been when she and Mel had done a quick Wikipedia search. Although she'd never even met her uncle and didn't have a musical bone in her body, Ness was saddened to think of him ending his days with his talents going to waste.

"We've all been really worried that Armand would have left everything to Jamie, and then who knows what would have happened? Anything, probably!" Val continued once she'd gained enough puff to talk again after climbing the stairs. "There'd be a theme park or a strip club on the island before we knew it if that one had his way. That was why Annie was so determined to trace you. Well, her and Lucy, of course – although that's supposed to be a secret! Oops! Me and my big mouth! Could you forget I mentioned that? I'll be in huge trouble and Jamie would probably murder Lucy!"

Ness thought she would have no problem keeping anything Val had said a secret, since she was hardly registering a word. Her temples were starting to beat more aggressively now, and battalions of black dots were mustering in the corners of her vision. She needed to lie down before she fell down.

"Here it is, our very best suite," Val announced. "I'll leave you to freshen up and I'll have one of the lads carry your bag up. If you want dinner, best book now. I recommend the monkfish. It's fresh off the boats this morning."

"It sounds wonderful," Ness said, even though the thought of food made her feel queasy. All she needed was some rest.

"Just call down to reception if you do want a reservation," Val said. "It's holiday season, see, and we'll be very busy tonight. If you don't book, you could miss out."

And with this warning, she lumbered away down the corridor, leaving Ness nonplussed. The torrent of names and facts had been overwhelming and she was glad to step into the sanctuary of her room at last.

Goodness. Val hadn't exaggerated about the view. The suite was in the highest part of the hotel and the bay stretched out before Ness like a living picture. The beach was covered with colourful towels and windbreaks; from here it reminded Ness of a sponge cake sprinkled with hundreds and thousands. Beyond it, boats zipped across the deep water, towards the castle that basked in the sunshine. Her castle.

Shaking her head, and wincing as her brain seemed to swivel inside her skull, Ness pulled the curtains closed. Much as shutting out the view and the sunshine seemed criminal, the instant pools of darkness were a relief. She was too tired to think about it all for a second longer, too tired even to explore the suite and check out the luxurious bathroom. Instead, Ness kicked off her sandals and fell back onto the bed.

The softness of the mattress and the cool caress of the cotton pillows were like a balm to her aching head. Ness's heavy eyes closed and even the endless calling of seagulls and the crashing of the surf faded away. Within moments she was fast asleep.

Ness woke with a jolt, her heart hammering as she tried to work out where she was. It was dark and chilly now; the curtains at the window drifted in the breeze and the air was sharp with the tang of salt and seaweed. The familiar clicking sound of the ceiling fan, the thrum of the air-conditioning units and the chirping of the cicadas had been replaced by the sighing of waves and the gentle tinkle of cutlery from the terrace below where the evening's diners were enjoying the monkfish Val had proudly recommended.

Cornwall! Of course. She was in the hotel overlooking the bay. Here she was, poised on the brink of something exciting and scary and wonderful all at once. Ness sat up and rubbed her eyes. Goodness, she must have slept for over five hours, judging from the fact that the daylight had seeped away.

Her headache was gone, replaced by a raging thirst. Ness swung her legs over the edge of the bed and padded into the bathroom, where she gulped down two glassfuls of water. Then she went to the sitting area and curled up on the big sofa positioned in the bay window. Tucking her legs under her, she looked out over dark water to the few lights that came from the castle. Whoever was living there, they were certainly being prudent with their electric, Ness thought – in contrast to the town, which was lit up like Oxford Street at Christmas. Recalling the solicitor's warning about money pits, she frowned. David Brown was right: it was one thing to feel excited and romanticise this unexpected inheritance, but in reality being the custodian of a castle might be a very different proposition.

"All I can do is wait until tomorrow," she said out loud. Maybe the full reading of the will would reveal some useful extras that David Brown had overlooked? Like a nice trust fund that could pay for the place, maybe? Or a stray Picasso nobody had identified? Wasn't that what usually happened in movies? Then she could sell the Picasso and everything would be fine.

She laughed. She'd obviously been watching too many Richard Curtis films; she might as well be expecting Hugh Grant to turn up and play the romantic hero too. Hugh, with his upper-class charm and cut-glass accent, would certainly fit the part of castle owner much more neatly than a tangle-haired, suntanned diver with an accent that was a mishmash of all the places in which her father had raised her over the years. What on earth had her uncle been thinking? She didn't belong here.

Time to explore and stop navel-gazing, Ness told herself firmly. Closer investigation of the suite revealed that her bag had been delivered, so she had a quick shower and got dressed, her brow crinkling when she saw just how few clothes she had. White jeans, a green vest top and glittery sandals were all very well for balmy Caribbean nights, but in the cool May air of a Cornish seaside town she was going to freeze. Clothes shopping had to go to the top of the list, Ness decided as she made her way down to the hotel bar in search of a snack. At the very least she needed a pair of boots, some socks and a hoody – because she doubted very much that the castle came with central heating.

Following the noise of chatter and clinking cutlery, Ness found herself passing through a set of French doors and back out onto the terrace, which was now heaving with drinkers and diners. Val had certainly been right about the restaurant's popularity. Now that it was night-time, the place was lit by hurricane lanterns on every table and hundreds of white fairy lights that trembled in the breeze. The sky was speckled with stars and the moon smiled down from above the castle. The whole scene was magical. There was only one problem: unlike the Caribbean, where everyone headed for the shade or a fan, the fight was on here to find a seat near one of the patio heaters pumping warmth into the chilly Cornish night. The place was so busy that she couldn't see a vacant table anywhere. With goose bumps on her arms, Ness was just about to head inside again when a man stepped into her path.

"Would you like a seat? There's a spare one here if you don't mind sharing?"

Ness looked up and found herself gazing into a pair of dark grey eyes starred with fine lines. They were astonishing eyes, their pewter-grey irises ringed with black as though traced around with a fine liner, and as they held hers Ness was lost for words. She might be on a dimly lit terrace, but even in the shadows and with his dark hair falling over his swarthy face she could see that he was handsome, albeit not in a way she'd ever encountered before today. Although he was smiling there was an air of ruthless masculinity about him. He was tall, long-limbed and muscular, the shoulders beneath his white shirt broad and powerful. As she stared into those piercing grey eyes, Ness realised he was the man she'd seen sketching earlier on. He was pretty hard to miss.

"I saw you earlier. You're an artist, aren't you?" she blurted. She could have torn her tongue out. Now he really would think she'd been checking him out.

The man laughed. He had a nice laugh, deep and gravelly. It made the fine hairs on Ness's arms stir.

"I'd hardly call myself an artist but I do like to sketch from time to time – badly, I might add! Look, it's only going to get busier here, so honestly, if you want a seat you really should grab one now. They'll be fighting for them in fifteen minutes."

"Fighting?"

He nodded his dark head and the grey eyes glittered. "You'd better believe it. Fighting for seats in restaurants and pubs is something the locals here take very seriously in the season. It could get ugly; don't say you weren't warned. It's also a very long way to the nearest hospital. If I were you I'd grab a chair and fast."

Ness felt her mouth curve into a smile. "I'm not sure I'm ready to engage in chair wars. Not without some serious training anyway."

"Very wise of you," the stranger agreed. He pulled out a seat and, still smiling, Ness slipped into it. Instantly the warmth of the patio heater curled around her bare shoulders like a wrap and she sighed with pleasure. St Pirran was certainly pretty but it was about fifteen degrees cooler than the climate she was used to.

"I'm about to order some supper. You're very welcome to join me, if you like?" the man added. "The food's not bad here."

"I hear the monkfish is good," Ness recalled.

"Ah, Val's been trying to sell you the catch of the day has she? Never misses a trick, that one. Her son owns a trawler and it's amazing how much fish this hotel needs."

"This is a complicated place. Everyone seems to be related to everyone else," Ness observed.

The man grinned. "That's St Pirran for you. Luckily, I'm an incomer so you can't offend me. I'm Max, by the way."

He held out his hand. It was strong and large, the fingers tapering and sensitive. Artist's hands, thought Ness – and, unbidden, an image of her father sketching came to mind. The sudden lump in her throat took her by surprise. Addy had been gone for over three years now and the stabbing grief of the early days had gently receded. Being here, in the place where he'd grown up, must be making everything sharper again. He'd have seen these views every day of his childhood and would have known all the people in the town. This had been his home.

Pushing these thoughts aside, she took Max's outstretched hand. The jolt she felt as his skin brushed hers made her eyes widen – and the glitter in his said he'd felt it too.

"I'm Ness."

"Nice to meet you, Ness," said Max. He shook her hand, holding it in his for just a fraction longer than was necessary. "May I buy you a drink? To welcome you to St Pirran?"

The look in those dark eyes suggested that he'd like to do far more to welcome Ness than buy a drink, and her pulse skittered. She could take his hand, lead him back through the restaurant, up the stairs and to her suite if she wanted, she found herself thinking.

What? Ness never thought like this. No-strings flings were her father's style, not hers – but for a split second she was tempted, before common sense took over. This was a small town; the last thing she needed was gossip.

"I'd love a glass of wine," she answered. "But I should warn you I'll probably pass out. I've had a long-haul flight and a busy drive today, so my body clock's shot to pieces."

Max's gaze flickered across her bare shoulders and he raised a dark eyebrow. "That tan certainly isn't from Cornwall. California? Or maybe Florida?"

"The Caribbean, St Antonia?" Ness said. It was a small island and not many people had heard of it, but her new acquaintance was nodding.

"It's a diving Mecca, isn't it? I went there years ago. Gorgeous place."

"I work in a dive hotel there and, yes, it's lovely but in a very different way to this." Ness looked out towards the island, a dark mass now in the inky water, and for the hundredth time found herself marvelling that this was hers. It was crazy. She was a nobody. A waitress. A drifter's daughter. How could this possibly be true? Surely David Brown had made a mistake?

"Cornwall's special," Max was agreeing, "and the water's as good as anywhere in the Caribbean, if a bit colder. There's a spot off the back of the island where there's an old wreck that's become a natural reef. You should dive it sometime while you're here."

"I think I'm way too soft to dive in the UK," Ness admitted. It was hard to imagine plunging into icy cold water after the bath-warm Caribbean Sea.

Max laughed. "Nonsense! All you'll need's a good wetsuit. If you're about for a few days, check out the dive sites around here. Honestly, you won't regret it. It's a special place."

"You sound like you know it well. Is this home for you?"

He shook his head. "No, but I have got a holiday place and I spend as much time here as I can. My builders are finishing some work, so I'm staying out as long as I can tonight to preserve my eardrums! I love it here though. I came here on holiday and when I was a kid I was obsessed with Armand Penwellyn's music. I tried to play his Island Suite on the violin and drove my poor parents mad."

"They didn't like the music?" Ness had only recently downloaded Armand's works and was gradually working her way through them. The notes were strident and at times discordant, not always easy on the ear, yet now she saw the landscape that had inspired his work she totally understood why. This was an unyielding place.

He grinned. "They liked the music very much – just not the way I was butchering it! I'm a hopeless musician. Far better for everyone that I appreciate his work rather than attempt to play it."

Ness teetered on the brink of telling him that Armand Penwellyn was her uncle, but before she found the right words Max was busy catching the attention of a waiter and ordering drinks. The moment having been lost, their conversation turned instead to the town and tourist attractions. Before long Ness was sipping ice-cold Pinot while Max poured mineral water into a tumbler.

"I don't drink," he explained, when he caught her looking. "No real reason why, except I'm just too busy to have hangovers and I prefer to keep my judgement clear. Probably makes me a real bundle of fun to hang out with."

Ness thought of Addy, who could never say no to a beer. Or a short. Or a whiskey. Or anything alcoholic. "Not at all. It probably makes you far more fun. I'd say it takes more control not to drink."

Max swirled his water thoughtfully. "You mean I'm a control freak?"

"No! No I didn't mean—"

"I'm teasing you." He reached across the table and laid his hand on hers. Leaving it there, he traced the inside of her wrist with his forefinger.

Ness felt her knees turn to water. Maybe it was jet lag, maybe it was exhaustion, she wasn't sure – but if those factors weren't to blame then she would have said she'd never felt such a powerful attraction before. Her skin was tingling.

"Anyway, I am a control freak. Ask anyone who knows me," he said with a grin that lit his eyes and made a dimple dance in his cheek, as unexpected in that stern countenance as sunshine peeping out of storm clouds. "But enough of me. Tell me about you. What brings you to St Pirran from the sunny Caribbean?"

Max moved his hand from her wrist and instantly Ness missed his touch. It had been too long since Stephen, that was all, she told herself firmly. That and the large glass of wine hitting her empty stomach.

"It's just family stuff," she said, since I've inherited the castle you were sketching would have sounded like the worst kind of boasting, especially to someone who presumably made his living from his sketches. Everyone knew how poor artists were; Addy had never had two pennies to rub together. She thought about offering to pay for the drink but something about Max suggested that he wouldn't be best pleased. "It's a long story but the short version is that there are a few things I need to take care of here."

Max looked as though he was going to ask more questions, but at this point the waiter arrived with their food and another glass of wine for Ness. As they ate the monkfish, which was as good as Val had promised, they chatted easily. When Ness looked around she was amazed to find that the terrace had cleared and the moon had risen even higher. She checked her watch. It was almost ten, UK time. Her body clock was indeed all over the place, just as she'd told Max. In spite of herself, she yawned.

"I'm keeping you up," he said. "You've had a long day."

Tomorrow was going to be even longer, thought Ness with a little stab of nerves, and she nodded. She reached into her bag for her purse – and then her heart sank because she didn't have any English money. David Brown was supposed to be sorting that out. At least, she hoped he was – or Pirran Castle was in big trouble.

"This is really embarrassing but I don't have the right currency on me," Ness confessed.

"Looks like you'll be washing up then," deadpanned Max. Then his lips curled upwards. "Don't look so worried. This evening's on me. Call it a welcome to St Pirran."

"I couldn't let you do that," Ness protested. "Besides, I do have a debit card. It's just that I've gone and left it up in my room with my passport. It'll only take a moment to fetch it though."

"No need for that," said Max. "I insist on getting this. I waylaid you, after all. I've got my card behind the bar and I'm sure they can take care of it. But in return, before you turn into a pumpkin I want to show you what I think is the best view in the place. If you're happy to get your feet wet, that is?"

This was turning into a very strange evening, Ness thought as Max took her hand in his and led her across the terrace and down a flight of steps onto the beach. Then again, life in general had been peculiar lately, so why not walk on the beach with a handsome stranger?

Ness kicked her shoes off and stood with the cold sand between her toes, staring across the bay to the island. Max was right: this was an amazing view. From here, with the water only inches from her feet, the island looked as though it was floating on the edge of the world. The moon was spilling liquid silver across the dark sea, and the lone light in the castle threw a trembling reflection over the waves. Tomorrow she would cross that water and see the castle for herself. She shivered.

"Cold?" Max asked. He slid his jacket off and draped it around her shoulders. The heat from his body warmed her skin and Ness shivered again, but not because of the chilly night. Maybe it was the wine or the moonlight or just because she was on holiday, away from her usual life, but she rose onto her sandy tiptoes and traced the sharp line of his jaw with her forefinger before brushing her mouth against his.

Max was motionless for a moment. Then he took Ness's face in his hands and kissed her back; a slow, teasing, tempting kiss. His lips strayed to her cheeks, her neck, her eyelids, covering her in delicious and tantalising caresses that melted her inside and made her long for more. At last he returned to her lips, with a kiss that spoke of passion held in check and the promise of delights to come. In the light of the moon and with the sigh of the waves as a soundtrack, Ness was kissing a total stranger and she never wanted it to stop.

Cornwall was full of magic, that was for sure.

"Mr Reynard! There's a call for you!"

The shout from the edge of the terrace was like a pistol shot. Max drew his mouth away from Ness's and they stood for a moment, staring at one another, their breathing ragged. He looked so surprised that Ness wanted to giggle.

"That wine must have been stronger than we thought!" she said.

"I had water," Max reminded her. "Control freak, remember?" He reached forward and brushed a curl away from her cheek. "I'm totally sober."

"Mr Reynard? I'm sorry but they say you have to take this call! It's from New York."

He sighed. "I turn my phone off and what happens? They call bloody reception."

Ness stepped away; her heart was hammering against her ribcage. She hadn't kissed someone for months, since Stephen in fact, but kissing her ex had been nothing like this. Kissing Stephen had been nice, a damning word if ever there was one, but kissing Max had been something else entirely. She didn't think she'd ever wanted someone so much.

Maybe this was delayed shock?

"Mr Reynard?" A figure loomed out of the shadows and Val's face floated above them from the terrace. "I'm sorry to interrupt but it's the New York office and they say that – oh! Miss Penwellyn! I had no idea you were here. I do apologise."

Ness had only been in St Pirran for a few hours but already she had a good idea of how the place worked. She suspected Val was now bursting to tell all and sundry that she'd caught the new mistress of Pirran Castle snogging the local artist on the beach. Mind you, he must be a successful artist if he was receiving calls from New York.

"What did she call you?" Max was staring down at Ness. Shadows danced across his face and filled his eyes.

"My name?"

"She called you Penwellyn?" Max's dark eyes held hers and Ness had the sensation that they were boring into her soul. For some reason the answer was crucial.

"That's my name. I'm Nessa Penwellyn."

"You're Nessa Penwellyn? Jamie's long-lost cousin?"

She nodded.

Max raked a hand through his dark hair. His mouth, so soft and so right, hardened. Although he'd only taken one step back from her he was suddenly thousands of miles away, the closeness of moments earlier vanishing like the surf into the sand.

"I need to take that call," he said curtly. "You should get some sleep. Goodnight, Ness."

And with this he was gone, taking back his jacket and leaving Ness alone and staring after him, her head whirling and her lips burning as though his kiss had been a branding iron.

Exactly who was Max Reynard? And why had her name shocked him so deeply?

Chapter 7

Jamie was in a foul mood, even worse than usual – which was really saying something, thought Lucy as she made her way out of the castle's kitchen and across the courtyard. She was heading for the tea room with a tray of scones, partly because she was stocking up the cake cabinet in anticipation of a busy day ahead and partly because this was the one place she knew her brother wouldn't venture. There was only so much glowering and sniping a girl could take and Lucy had reached capacity. Her head thumped from all the door slamming and the slightest thing she said was likely to send him off on another rant.

Nessa Penwellyn might have inherited the castle and thus the bulk of Uncle Armand's wealth, but Lucy was very glad indeed not to be in her shoes. Jamie had been shut in the library all morning and, unless he'd suddenly developed a passion for reading classic literature, he was busy plotting something. When she'd stuck her head in to ask if he wanted breakfast, he'd looked up from an involved phone call to bellow at her to get out. Lucy hadn't needed asking twice.

"Sorry about that, Max. A man can't get a minute's peace in this lunatic asylum,"

she'd heard him say as she'd beat a hasty retreat.

The sooner the full will reading was over the better, Lucy decided as she backed into the tea-room door and shoved it open with her rear end. Then everyone would know where they stood, including her. Jamie might be miffed that he was losing out on what he'd assumed was his inheritance, but she could be losing her home – and so could Merryn and Fern, who were currently sitting at the table by the window, drinking tea and sharing a bacon buttie.

"Here, let me take those." Merryn was on his feet instantly, receiving the heavy tray from Lucy and depositing it on the counter. "Mmm. They smell wonderful."

Lucy's heart lifted as it always did when somebody appreciated her cooking.

"Take a couple for your lunch," she said, blushing when he smiled at her with those sleepy turned-down eyes. "There's some jam and cream in the fridge too."

"Don't you bloody dare! You eat far too much of our profits as it is," said Fern as Merryn reached out, about to grab a couple. "It's going to be boiling today and I bet we'll be inundated."

The castle's tea room was converted from what had once been the stables, and with tables set on the grassy slope beyond the remains of the outer keep it had stunning views over the bay. Although it was only early, the sun already had the kind of warmth that promised a beautiful day to come. Lucy knew that as soon as the hotels had finished dishing up breakfast there would be a steady stream of visitors. Fern was right: by half ten they would be packed. Lucy sent up a silent prayer of thanks for this. Her uncle's full will and testament might not have been disclosed yet, but she'd seen enough of the castle's expenditure to know that every scone helped.

"I can always bake another batch," she began, but her pink-haired helper was already jumping up from her seat and blocking Merryn's path.

"You'll have to get past me first!"

Fern was five feet tall and probably weighed about seven stone, whereas Merryn was a tanned six feet of sinew and muscle. In a heartbeat he'd picked Fern up under one arm and swiped a scone with his free hand while she twisted and pummelled him with her fists. For a pacifist Fern certainly fought hard. Feeling ancient, Lucy shook her head; it was like supervising a pair of five-year-olds. They adored each other though and she often thought there was more just beneath the surface – if they would just take the time to look.

"Put the scone down!" Fern shrieked, her giggles punctuating the words. "You're going to get so fat your boat will sink and none of the emmets will fancy you anymore!"

As if that would ever happen, thought Lucy fondly. With his blond hair bleached almost white and his limbs already the colour of warm honey, Merryn was undeniably attractive. Even dressed in a faded blue fisherman's smock and tatty coral board shorts, he looked like the adverts for Ralph Lauren she saw when flicking through glossy magazines she couldn't afford.

"Did somebody say something?" asked Merryn, swinging Fern around several times then winking at Lucy while his dizzy prisoner kicked him with her bare feet.

"I'll bake some more, Fern." Lucy tied her apron and tried to avoid flailing limbs by ducking behind the counter. "It won't take long and I promise we won't run out."

"You've got enough on today with the will stuff and Nessa arriving, without doing extra baking," Fern gasped out between shrieks of mirth.

Instantly Merryn's laughing face grew serious. Setting Fern down, he regarded his pilfered scone regretfully.

"I totally forgot. I'm really sorry, Lucy. You've got a massive day today and the last thing you need is me dicking around. Is there anything I can do to help? Apart from not scoffing the cakes, obviously."

The truth was that nothing made Lucy happier than to feed Merryn and listen to his cheerful banter. In the dark days since Armand had died and her future had been left dependent on the whim of an unknown cousin, the time spent in the tea room with him and Fern and the small but devoted group of volunteers from the town had been all that had kept her from hiding in her tower bedroom with the duvet pulled over her head. She'd realised how bad things were when she'd even been thrilled to see Fred the gardener, an old man so grumpy he made bears with sore heads seem good-humoured.

Oh dear. Maybe Dr Russex was right after all and she did need a little help?

"Don't you dare think about putting it back!" cried Fern as Merryn dithered, scone held aloft and rather gingerly.

"Eat it for lunch," Lucy said firmly. "It's one scone; I think we'll cope."

While Merryn wrapped his prize in a paper napkin and Fern took the chairs down from the tables, Lucy glanced around the tea room and felt the thrill of pride that came with knowing she'd created something special. It wasn't the smartest venue but with its cobbled floors, ancient beams and scrubbed trestle tables and benches it was unique and true to the building's original purpose. The walls were lime washed white, and at the far end the original stalls had been cleverly transformed into seating booths thanks to Merryn's handiwork and some help from her friends in the town. Their love of history and the castle was in every joint and nail and brushstroke. Armand had given her free rein with the project and, although he'd never said much about it, Lucy knew he'd been impressed. The modest income stream it had produced had made her feel that in some small way she'd been repaying him. The roof was rotten and needed replacing before the winter but she was putting it off, partly because of the cost and partly because who knew what her mysterious cousin might choose to do with it?

A lump rose in her throat. Would Nessa Penwellyn allow the tea room to continue or would she want to shut it and turn the visitors away – or even sell the place to a vulture like Max Reynard? Suddenly the smell of scones made Lucy's stomach churn. To distract herself she flicked on the coffee machine and retrieved the chocolate brownies from the fridge. Usually she'd have one with a cup of tea as a little treat to herself, but today Lucy felt so panicked she couldn't face a thing. She'd be able to fit into that red spotty dress in no time if this went on for too long.

Quite unbidden, at the thought of the spotty dress the associated image of twinkling brown eyes and a cheerful smile flickered through her memory – and Lucy found that she felt slightly better. If a total stranger could be kind then surely a relative, however distant, would be sympathetic?

"Time for me to go and catch some tourists before the tide turns," Merryn declared once he'd finished setting up the tables outside. Already his nose was turning pink and freckles were peeping out from underneath.

"The seals are basking on the rocks at Grace Note Bay this morning. I saw them when I was saluting the sun," Fern told him, glancing up from the chalkboard where she was busily writing up the day's menu in swirly pastel writing.

"Thanks for the heads-up," Merryn said. "Any specials I should tell the punters about?"

"I'm making sweet potato and parsnip soup and there's going to be a mackerel pâté made by Annie," Fern replied, turning the board around.

"I'll make sure I mention it," he promised. "I'll do my very best to send as many this way as I can so you sell the lot."

"It shouldn't be too hard. Annie's mackerel pâté's to die for," Lucy said.

Honestly, she didn't know how she'd survive without her stalwart team of volunteers. Apart from making food for the tea room, they got involved with the fundraising and helped out with the twice-weekly guided tours of what bits of the castle were good enough to show off. All in all, they were an absolute godsend. And talking of godsends, here was Annie Luckett now, bowling into the tea room with a giant wicker basket over her arm and dressed for action in her stripy apron. As always her weathered face was beaming, and just the sight of her was enough to make Lucy feel better. From running the St Pirran Guide pack to beekeeping to retained firefighting, Annie Luckett was one of those people for whom organising and taking charge was in the DNA. Maybe it was something to do with all her years in the classroom, but when Annie Luckett told people to do things there was very little questioning. Even Jamie hadn't the guts, or maybe more accurately the stupidity, to try that.

"Who's taking my name in vain?" Annie demanded, placing her basket on the counter with a thud and pulling off her headscarf to release her springy grey curls.

"We were just talking about your mackerel pâté," Merryn explained. "You're today's special."

Annie gave him an arch look. "I'm every day's special, aren't I? Still, there's enough in here to feed an army." She patted the basket. "Tom's boat had a good catch yesterday. You should have a word with him. He's looking for crew."

Merryn shook his head. "No thanks. I'm more than happy doing my own thing."

Annie looked as though she was going to argue. She'd taught Merryn at the local high school, Lucy recalled, and often said privately that his being expelled was a complete balls-up.

"He was bright as a button, that one," was her usual take on it, "and totally let down by all the adults in the equation, as per bloody usual. He shouldn't be wasting his time tripping on a boat. He could do anything."

Lucy fully agreed. It was abundantly clear how clever Merryn was, especially when it came to all things mechanical. He'd single-handedly kept her old Citroën going for the past year and all the fisherman called on him when their trawlers had problems. On the other hand, there weren't many people who appeared as contented with their lot in life as he was, and from a purely selfish point of view she would miss him dreadfully if he ever did decide to leave. Or, as she was starting to fear, if this Nessa Penwellyn wanted her inheritance all to herself.

Luckily Merryn's charm was enough to pre-empt a lengthy lecture from Annie.

"As much as I'd love to stick around and sample your latest batch, I need to catch the tide." He picked up his battered rucksack, pulled it onto one shoulder and gave Lucy an encouraging smile. "Good luck with everything today. I'll be thinking of you."

"Thanks," said Lucy. Her cheeks felt a little warm at the idea of Merryn thinking about her, however platonically, which made a nice change from the cold lump of dread in her stomach. "I'm sure it's all going to be fine."

Annie, already unpacking ingredients and lining them up on the counter in rigid rows like pupils in the classroom, snorted. "I'm afraid I'm not so convinced, not after what I've just been told."

"What does that mean?" asked Merryn, pausing in the doorway. "What have you heard?"

"Is it about the castle?" Lucy asked. Her hands were trembling, so she tucked them into her apron pocket. This was not the time to go to pieces.

Annie nodded. "It is indirectly, I suppose. I'm not sure if it means anything, but I bumped into our Val this morning when I went down to the quay to buy the mackerel from Tom. Val works at the hotel, remember?"

Lucy did remember. Working as the hotel receptionist meant Val Brown was party to some very interesting information and was none too discreet about who she shared it with either. If Lucy ever had a secret love affair (which was highly unlikely), the last place she'd go to conduct it would be the Island View Hotel.

"Tom said he'd give me a ride over on the boat, so Val came too because there was something she thought we should know," Annie continued, clearly enjoying having their full attention. She paused for dramatic effect and Lucy found she was holding her breath. After all, not much went on in St Pirran that Annie Luckett didn't know about. Apart from having taught most people here under the age of fifty, she was related to several of the key families in the town, including the local solicitor. All this, added to the top-secret fact that the old school teacher had been instrumental in helping Lucy trace the whereabouts of Nessa Penwellyn, made the possibilities for her knowing about any impending disasters endless.

"Go on then, what did you hear?" demanded Fern.

Annie leant heavily on the counter and regarded them all with bright boot-button eyes. "I don't like to spread gossip but on this occasion I'll make an exception because knowledge is power, after all. Val told me that yesterday she checked Nessa Penwellyn into the hotel – and upgraded her too because she mistook her for an American."

"She's American?" Lucy was confused. She'd thought Nessa had been born in Cornwall.

"No, she's British but she certainly has an American accent, which is what threw Val – although to be fair that doesn't take a great deal," said Annie tartly.

Fern's eyes were wide. "Oh my God! What does she look like?"

"Does her appearance bear any relevance to this issue?" Annie asked.

"If she's hot it might," grinned Merryn. "That was a joke, Annie!" he added quickly when the older woman shot him her best teacher look.

"Well, you might not be laughing in a minute," Annie said darkly. "Still, to answer your question, Fern, Val said she's very pretty with long red hair and green eyes."

Lucy gasped. Her uncle Armand had possessed a thick mane of red hair when he was a boy, and his brothers too. The portraits in the castle's Small Hall showed all three as young men with bright red hair. This gene had bypassed her and Jamie, but to learn that it lived on in this unknown cousin thrilled her. There was a link! Heritage! Surely Nessa would feel it?

"So pretty, in fact, that within a few hours of arriving at the hotel she was seen having dinner on the terrace with a man," Annie continued, disapproval written clearly across her hawk like face.

Fern rolled her eyes. "What a crime. Shall we tar and feather her now? Or maybe burn her alive, the slapper?"

Annie ignored this remark, just as she must have ignored countless silly comments in her classroom. "There's nothing wrong with that, of course, and neither is there anything wrong with her walking along the beach with a man. She's an adult. The problem is that it wasn't just any man she was with and, from what Val says, they're clearly very close. Val thinks he'd arranged to meet her there, since there's absolutely no other reason for him to be at the hotel, not when he's got a holiday home and owns half the town."

Fern and Merryn were looking confused but Lucy experienced a horrible moment of clarity. Oh God. She really hoped she was wrong.

"It was Max Reynard, wasn't it?" she whispered, and Annie inclined her head gravely.

"I'm afraid so," she said. "I very much fear we've invited a viper right into our bosom and it appears she hasn't wasted any time hatching plans with the enemy. We'd better all be on our guard with Nessa Penwellyn. She is not to be trusted."

Chapter 8

When she woke up, Ness's mouth was dry and her head was pounding. The evening before seemed like a strange dream. Had she really kissed a total stranger on the beach?

It must have been the jet lag and all that wine on an empty stomach, Ness decided as she showered and pulled on last night's rather crumpled white jeans, the bottoms of which were dusted with sand – proof that the moonlight and a change of time zone hadn't caused her to hallucinate. So it had happened, and what a kiss it had been too. Ness felt a blush cover her cheeks as she recalled how his mouth had strayed from her lips to her neck and down to her collarbone while her stomach had collapsed in on itself with longing. If Val hadn't interrupted them when she did, who knew what might have happened next? Would they have broken apart and said goodnight so that she could get the early night she needed, or would she have taken his hand, led him up the twisty stairs and invited him into her suite?

Her heart fluttered beneath her ribs because deep down she knew the answer to that question, even if she didn't want to admit it. Besides, she felt rather stupid now. Max couldn't have raced away from her any faster. What was that all about?

Then she groaned because it was obvious: he was married and the whole business about "the New York office" having called was nothing but an elaborate charade, a code he'd dreamed up with the hotel staff. Of course it was. Why would anyone in New York be urgently needing to talk to an artist? Ness was willing to bet her entire and very new inheritance that Max Reynard was a player. He probably hung out at the hotel all the time on the prowl for silly single women with empty stomachs and even emptier heads, because this was exactly what men like him did – she'd seen enough of such behaviour in the Caribbean. It had been Stephen's *modus operandi* too.

"Honestly, Nessa Penwellyn," she said out loud. "Don't you ever learn?"

Well, from now on she'd be on her guard, Ness told herself as she tugged a brush through her wild curls and bullied them into a messy topknot. She'd make sure she gave Max Reynard a wide berth in future no matter how bone-meltingly sexy he was. Handsome artists were bad news – she'd mopped up enough of Addy's girlfriends' tears to know that much.

And talking of Addy, Ness had far more important things to worry about than the mysterious Max Reynard. Today was the day she was going to cross the causeway and see her father's former home. She'd also be meeting the family. Would they be pleased to see her or would they be seething with resentment that a stranger had turned up to claim the family home?

She'd know soon enough, Ness thought as she checked her watch, because David Brown was picking her up as soon as the tide was far enough out for the causeway to clear. Unknown and potentially unhappy relatives aside, she'd be stepping into a world that had been her father's, and her mother's too.

Ness shivered. Addy had barely spoken about her mother and Ness had never pressed him, partly because she'd been too small to remember Beth or miss her, and partly because she could always see how hard he found it to talk about the past. All she knew was that her mother had drowned and Addy had taken their daughter, little more than a baby, away from Cornwall to start again. Sometimes Ness had caught him looking at the faded few pictures he'd kept, and as she'd grown older he'd said she looked like her mother, but the conversations had rarely gone any further than that. She had no idea how Beth Penwellyn had come to drown or why Addy would cut off all contact with his family, but she was determined to find out. As far as she was concerned, the chance to uncover the truth about her past was the most important thing she'd inherited. Coming here was already raising so many questions about Addy, and Ness hoped the answers wouldn't prove too hard to hear.

Wearing a long-sleeved blue tee shirt with the Caribbean hotel's Dive into Paradise! emblazoned right across her chest, Ness made her way to the dining room. She noticed that the tee shirt seemed to be attracting some faintly disapproving looks from the guests of this rather more genteel Cornish hotel. Finding an empty seat in the restaurant window, she stared across the bay at the island. Whereabouts had the icy water swallowed Beth? By those rocks maybe? Or had she been swimming in a hidden bay and fallen foul of a current? Ness had no idea. Today the sea was oily smooth and it was hard to imagine that it could ever be anything but gentle, but Ness knew that the ocean had a habit of taking people by surprise.

Somebody in St Pirran would be bound to know what had really happened; this was a small town and people in small towns had long memories. Maybe her cousins would be able to help?

The thought of today's events was so daunting. Ness ordered a lunch she knew she had no appetite for, and picked up her phone. She was hoping for a friendly message from Mel, but there was nothing except a short text from David Brown saying that he would meet her by the causeway at half twelve. Until then there was nothing to do but sip coffee and try her best to eat the obligatory Sunday lunch. It was going to be a long afternoon and probably best faced on a full stomach, Ness decided, but it was hard to eat when it felt as though you were waiting for the dentist.

Ness pushed her food around the plate and watched the tide ebb. Cobble by cobble the causeway was exposed, gleaming in the sunshine and fringed by acid-green weed. Jagged rocks, invisible before, rose from the shallow water – some of them retaining bright rock pools that mirrored the blue sky. Within a matter of minutes people were crossing, the first few wading to begin with while the sea teased the path with a few last waves before it finally parted to allow access for a steady stream of holidaymakers. The way was clear and there was no point delaying the inevitable; the time had finally come for her to meet David and go across. This was it. She took a deep breath, then stood up and made her way outside.

"Good afternoon!" David was waiting in a dark blue Freelander and reached across to open the passenger door. "Are you ready for this?"

"As ready as I'll ever be," said Ness, hopping in. "Will I make it through in one piece, do you think, or will somebody toss me from the battlements?"

"It's a difficult situation for everyone but I'll do my best to make it as painless as possible," David replied. He let up the clutch and the car crept forward onto the causeway. Although the vehicle was well sprung, every cobble made it jolt. Ness noticed that the solicitor's hands were clutching the wheel so tightly that his knuckles glowed chalky white through the flesh. A frown traced a line between his brows as though he was worried about something.

She was being silly, Ness told herself sharply. Of course David was tense. He wasn't chilling out on a Caribbean beach anymore, drinking cocktails and mulling over the possibilities of this odd bequest, but on home turf and faced with the reality. No doubt the other Penwellyns weren't quite as happy about the state of affairs as she'd been, and her flippant remarks probably weren't helping.

"They're expecting you," he continued as the car crept forward and Ness's nervousness intensified. "We'll get the introduction and the formalities done first and then Lucy will show you around. After that it's over to you."

Ness nodded. Now that she was almost at the island it was becoming clear just what a huge deal her uncle's bequest was. The place was simply breath-taking, but the closer they got the more she began to realise what a state it was in. The causeway was cracked in some places, which gave it a rather pockmarked appearance and forced David to steer around the gaps as best he could. Once they were on the island, the causeway petered into a path which initially bore to the right and hugged the quayside for a few hundred metres, before curving left and climbing a grassy slope that was peppered with picnic tables.

"That's the island's tea room," David said, following her gaze to a wooden building tacked onto a thick wall. "It's in the old stables and very popular. Lucy runs it with some local help."

Ness was craning her neck and trying to take it all in. Below her, the grass rolled away down to the small quay and the rocks, while above her grey stone walls towered into the blue. The castle felt organic, as though it had sprung to life from the island of its own accord, as much a part of the landscape as the rugged cliffs and calling gulls.

"This is the Pilgrim's Gate," David said as they drove through a gateway in what must once have been an impressive castle wall. "There used to be a chapel just to the right here, but it was torn down in the Reformation and never rebuilt. The family are buried in the churchyard on the mainland now."

His words hardly registered; Ness was too distracted by the scenery around her. They were crossing a big courtyard and heading to the foot of a tower that looked as though it had come straight out of a Disney film. Grasses swayed in the breeze and ivy's fingers clawed the stonework. Set in the middle of the tower's base was an enormous wooden door, complete with gigantic black hinges and oversized locks. Weeds choked the cobbles here, daisies clustered in swathes at the top of overgrown banks and there were sizeable holes in the walls, as though giant stone-eating moths had been having a picnic. Across the courtyard were ruined towers, linked by precarious walls and crumbling structures that still had echoes of past magnificence. Through the chinks in these walls were glimpses of the sea, blue and bold in the sharp light. All around, seabirds and swifts darted in and out of nooks and crannies.

"It's beautiful," Ness whispered, but her heart sank because although this was true it was also dilapidated. Ness had struggled enough to afford to rent a one-bedroomed apartment in St Antonia. How much would a place like this cost to maintain? All of a sudden the solicitor's warnings about death duties and empty bank accounts felt very ominous indeed. This place couldn't have been touched for years and Ness wouldn't have been surprised to find Sleeping Beauty inside catching a few zeds.

"That's the ruined area, in case you hadn't guessed. The family live in another part of the castle, which is more intact," David explained.

Ness was glad to hear it. For a moment she'd imagined her cousins camping out in tents within the ruins, Famous Five style.

"Did my uncle never want to sell? It can't have been easy getting old here, and I bet there are lots of people who'd love to buy it," she mused as David drove past the castle door and through a large gap in another wall, before pulling up in an inner courtyard.

He looked at her askance. "Of course there are but Armand loved this place. He would never sell it to a developer. That's up to you now, however, if that's what you've decided. There are several companies who would be most interested."

"I wasn't saying I want to sell," Ness said, stung by how quickly he'd jumped to this conclusion. She hadn't seen the castle yet or explored the island, but already her pulse had quickened in much the way it had when Max Reynard's hard mouth had captured hers on the beach last night. This place could take a serious hold on her heart.

But it wasn't just her heart involved, of course, and this knowledge troubled Ness. "What about Lucy Penwellyn? Shouldn't the inheritance have gone to her? It doesn't seem right I inherit all this when she looked after our uncle and this is her home."

"Well," David said, "that was Armand's decision. Believe me, if he'd wanted Lucy to inherit his estate then he would have made sure that was what happened. He wanted Pirran Island and the castle to be left to you."

"But it doesn't make sense. He didn't even know me!"

"Lots of things Armand chose to do didn't make sense. That was the kind of man he was, but he certainly wasn't one to make decisions lightly. If he chose you then he did so for a good reason. Why not accept your good luck and see what happens?"

"That's what my friend keeps telling me," Ness admitted. She could almost hear Mel yelling in her ear to just take the bloody island and shut up!

"From waitress to heiress! It's like Cinderella!" Mel had said. "Can't you just be happy? It's a fairy tale come true."

Ness sighed. She was happy and excited too but she was also uneasy because this wasn't really her fairy tale, was it? It should have been Lucy's. She was the real Cinderella in this story.

"What if I decided to give the island to Lucy? Could I do that?"

David flicked her a glance. "Is that what you want to do?"

Ness shrugged. "It seems fairer."

"I appreciate that, Nessa, and I know this must all feel very strange," David replied. "But the point is that, strange or not, it's what Armand wanted. If you don't wish to be the beneficiary of his will then I suppose technically we could make alternative arrangements. If everyone was in agreement then perhaps Lucy could have the island. On the other hand, both Jamie and Lucy might feel that Jamie ought to receive it, being the eldest male relative living. That was how Armand came to have the island, after all. I daresay we could organise things so that Jamie would own it instead, but I can tell you with absolute certainty that would be the antithesis of what your uncle wanted."

"But why? Why not Jamie?" Ness asked.

But David wasn't prepared to answer this.

"You'll meet him soon enough," was all he said.

Ness didn't press him and the solicitor killed the engine. Moments later he was opening the passenger door for her.

Ness stared upwards, her eyes widening when she noticed battlements and crenulations. She owned battlements? And were those actually cannons that she could see? If she wasn't already black and blue from the drive over, Ness would have pinched herself. Surely any minute now she'd wake up in her narrow bed, the sheet sticking to her, and with the air con roaring away? With her head spinning as much from the surreal nature of everything as looking upwards, she grabbed her bag and followed David Brown across this smaller courtyard.

"The kitchen's over to our right; what remains of the Great Hall is on the left, and then there's the winter parlour," he was saying. "The rest of the rooms beyond that are in the tower where the family live, although sometimes they open the music room up too. At Christmas there's always a wonderful tree in the hall and a carol concert featuring Mr Penwellyn's Cornish Winter from his Island Suite."

"You sound like a tour guide," Ness remarked.

"That's because I am. Twice a month I volunteer my services and show the visitors round." He stopped so abruptly that Ness almost slammed into him, and he spun around to face her. "Don't be fooled by the grandeur of what you're seeing. This place is run and tended by volunteers from the town who give their time and energy to looking after it, as well as a few folks who live here and work for a pittance."

She nodded. The size and beauty of the castle were breath-taking but there was no hiding the fact that nature was doing her best to capture by stealth what sieges and gunfire had failed to fully destroy.

"And don't underestimate the strength of feeling that exists about this place, either. It's very much a part of St Pirran and its local history. You've inherited a huge responsibility, and what you choose to do with it is going to have significance above and beyond the Penwellyn family."

That sounded like a warning if she'd ever heard one, Ness thought. What on earth did David think she was going to do with the place? Sell it to Disney? Build a nightclub? Bulldoze the lot and build a carbuncle?

She was just about to ask him when a liver-and-white spaniel shot out of a doorway and hurtled towards them, jumping up at David and barking joyously before hurling itself at Ness.

"Biscuit! Get down, boy!" David lunged for the spaniel's collar but missed. Seconds later Ness found herself on the ground with a pink tongue licking her and silky ears brushing her face.

"Biscuit! Biscuit! You naughty dog!" A woman scuttled down the worn steps, her wispy blonde hair falling into her face as she ran, and tugged the spaniel away. "I'm so sorry. Are you all right? He hasn't got you dirty has he? Oh, Biscuit! You bad boy!"

"I'm fine," Ness assured her as she got to her feet and brushed dried grass and mud from her white jeans. With hindsight it was a bad idea to have worn them; white clothing always seemed to invite muddy-pawed dogs or some other kind of trouble.

"He never usually does that. He must really like you. Perhaps he knows you're family?" Biscuit's owner said, biting her lip in distress and regarding Ness with worried forget-me-not blue eyes. Keeping two fingers of her left hand curled tightly into the dog's collar, the woman held out her right one. "I'm Lucy Penwellyn – and you must be Nessa. Welcome to Pirran Island."

Ness took the hand and shook it. The fingers were rough and the nails had been nibbled almost to the quick, but the grip was firm and Lucy's smile was warm. Since Addy's death Ness had been on her own; until this second she'd had no idea just how adrift and lonely this had made her feel. There was an enormous lump in her throat. This woman was her cousin and they were related. They were family.

She had a family.

"Please, call me Ness," she said.

Lucy smiled again. "It's wonderful to see you, Ness. Everyone's waiting in the library." She turned to David. "I thought that would be the best place?"

"Everyone?" David said as they climbed the steps to the arched door. Lucy raked a hand through her hair. Judging by the way it was standing on end at the back, she'd been doing this quite a bit already.

"I mean Jamie," Lucy said. "Oh dear. He feels like more than one person at times."

David didn't reply but nodded. Interesting, thought Ness. Her welcome from Jamie wouldn't be quite as warm as Lucy's and certainly wouldn't be anywhere near as enthusiastic as Biscuit's. Then again, Jamie Penwellyn would have assumed he was inheriting everything and was probably seething now that he'd been proved wrong.

She raised her chin. Well, let him seethe. For some reason their uncle had chosen her over him and, no matter how intimidated this place made her feel or how nervous she was right now, Ness was determined not to let Armand down. She already had the strange impression that David no longer trusted her, and judging by the way Lucy was gnawing her thumbnail she was on edge too. The sooner the full will was read and everyone knew exactly what they were dealing with, the better.

Ness hesitated beneath the arched doorway as the others stepped inside. The entrance pooled with shadows and for a moment the only sounds were Biscuit's claws clicking on the flagstones and the calling of the seagulls high above. This was it. Once she stepped over the threshold she was inside the castle and setting foot in Addy's childhood home. Mysteries and secrets and angry cousins lay ahead. Was she ready for them? Ready for the undercurrents and unsaid words swirling like the sea beyond the rocks? The answer was probably not, but it didn't look as though she had any choice in the matter; like it or not, this place was now her home and her responsibility.

Taking a deep breath, Ness stepped into her castle.

Chapter 9

The castle was cool and still; only the steady ticking of a longcase clock and the sounds of paws on stone broke the silence. It felt to Ness as though the place was holding its breath. Dust motes and dog hair twirled in the beam of sunlight filtering down from a high slit window, and the walls bulged as though the weight of the old muskets and staffs on display here were too much for the ancient stones to bear.

"This is the Small Hall. The Great Hall's in ruins now," Lucy told Nessa. "It's really nice here in the winter when the fire's lit, but otherwise we don't tend to use it much. Mostly we just pass through."

Small Hall? Ness could have fitted most of the dive hotel in this cavernous space. She looked around her in interest. The hall contained a large refectory table with benches either side, as well as a sofa. A coat of arms was emblazoned above a huge fireplace that was easily six feet tall and topped by a blackened beam, and three oak doors led off from the far end into narrow tunnel-like passageways going who knew where.

Dusty, mournful-eyed hunting trophies regarded her from on high and a faded tapestry hung on the far wall, but what struck Ness were the four large portraits that dominated the wall directly opposite her.

Her hand flew to her mouth. There was no mistaking that bold style; she would have recognised those confident, vivid brushstrokes anywhere.

"My father painted these!"

"There's quite a lot of your father's work here. Uncle Armand kept it all but I know these portraits were especially important to him," Lucy said.

"That's Dad!" Ness stared up at the first portrait in amazement. It was Addy all right, but younger and without the deep lines that had crisscrossed his face in later life. Those gas-flame blue eyes and that mane of deep red hair were all his, as was that characteristic lack of self-consciousness as he stood with one hand in the pocket of his jeans and the other resting loosely on the windowsill. The shock of being confronted with him so soon on her arrival was overwhelming – so much so that Ness had to breathe deeply to try to calm her racing pulse. History, both her own and that of the castle, was all around her. This self-portrait was from a time before grief and fear and loss had changed him forever, and Ness was both thrilled and saddened to catch a glimpse of the young man he'd once been.

The next two portraits were of her uncles, Maudsley and Armand himself – both caught forever in time as young men, preserved for posterity like dragonflies in amber. As she looked at the paintings Ness had the unnerving experience of seeing her own features reflected back at her across the years. The slightly too long nose and the high brow were theirs too, as was the determined chin, but the heart-shaped face and wide green eyes belonged to the subject of the fourth painting: Beth Penwellyn, her mother.

Unlike the three brothers, who had been depicted in casual clothes and inside the castle, Beth was outdoors and yet formally dressed. She was wearing a crimson ball gown that exposed her golden shoulders, around which fell her glossy curls of long brown hair. With her back to the painter, and looking over one shoulder beyond him, she was standing on the rocks with the waves breaking behind her. Her attention was held firmly by something, or someone, in the distance. A violin hung loosely from her left hand and a bow dangled from the right.

"That's my mother." Ness was overwhelmed. Any mental images she had of Beth had been gleaned from Addy's few faded snapshots. They'd shown a pretty young woman with laughing green eyes, but none of these snaps had captured Beth's pure sensuality the way this portrait did. Every brushstroke and swirl of paint brimmed with desire and, oddly, danger.

Ness shook her head. Danger? What a strange thing to think.

"I'm sorry," she said, realising that David and Lucy were waiting for her. "It's a bit of a shock. Dad's only been gone three years and as for my mother—" The word caught in her throat and for a moment she struggled to continue. "I've never seen a proper picture of my mother before. Not like this one, anyway. Addy never really spoke about her."

Lucy laid a hand on her arm. "I'm sorry, Ness. It didn't occur to me this might be upsetting for you."

Ness shook her head. "Please don't apologise. It's not upsetting exactly, maybe just a little strange."

How did she feel, Ness wondered? Punched in the solar plexus. Winded. That described it. As soon as she'd looked at the picture her skin had prickled. Was it a coincidence that Beth was framed by the same ocean that had claimed her life? And why would her uncle have kept the portraits when he'd been estranged from both his younger brothers? Something here was as discordant as the notes in her uncle's compositions.

"There's a lot of family history here," David said gently. "It's going to take some getting used to. Maybe we should get the official business out of the way? Then you and Lucy can talk."

Lucy nodded. "I can tell you what I know, although I should warn you that it's easier to pull limpets off the rocks than it was to get Uncle Armand to talk about the past. He had that in common with your father, at least."

There were family secrets here more convoluted and confusing than the twisting passageways that Lucy was now leading them through, Ness thought, still feeling shaken. As she followed her cousin's denim-clad backside, she had the unsettling sensation that she was being led into a deep labyrinth. If she lost sight of Lucy, she didn't think she could find her way out again: the corridors zigzagged erratically and the flights of tight curving steps wound ever closer into the centre of the place. The only light came from arrow-slit windows or skylights high above, through which she glimpsed slices of blue. Otherwise all was dark and oak-beamed and claustrophobic. What a place for her uncle to shut himself away. It was a fortress of the mind just as much as it was a physical fortress.

After what seemed like an endless climb, they reached a small room with latticed windows filled with the bright blue of the sea. Below was a dizzying drop to emerald-green gardens and a jigsaw of overgrown walled terraces, with the town lying beyond the golden apron of sandy beach. A steady crocodile of people wound to and from the causeway. Having taken a moment to absorb this view, Ness looked around her at the rest of the room. Two battered sofas flanked a stone fireplace and there were several well-stocked bookcases crammed with a mixture of classic fiction and romances.

Seeing Ness looking at this selection of novels, Lucy blushed. "All mine, I'm afraid. They're my guilty pleasure. This is the solar, the room I use the most."

"It's a lovely space," Ness said. After the darkness of the enclosed passageways the solar felt like the architectural equivalent of heaving a sigh of relief. "And anyway, there's nothing wrong with reading for pleasure. Jilly Cooper and Jackie Collins have got me through some tough times."

Lucy looked pleased. "Oh! I do love a good Jilly. I think I've still got Riders tucked away somewhere. I have such a soft spot for Rupert Campbell-Black."

"And what a lovely place to read about him," Ness remarked. Wow. Talk about Rapunzel's tower, with Lucy as a rather faded princess. Had a handsome prince rocked up to rescue her at any point? Judging by how nervous she was every time somebody mentioned Jamie, Ness didn't think so. Poor Lucy was totally in thrall to her brother.

Well, now Ness was in charge that could change for a start. Girl power hadn't ended when the Spice Girls broke up!

"After the medieval wing it's nice to have some daylight, isn't it? I always think whoever added this part on in the seventeenth century did a good job," Lucy was saying, interrupting Ness's daydreams of platform shoes and Union Jack dresses. Giving herself a mental shake, Ness dragged her concentration back to what her cousin was telling her.

"So it's not all Norman?" she asked, hoping her question made sense. She'd been doing her best to read up on the place, but her British history was vague to say the least. She'd had little education in such things, whereas she could recite the McDonald's menu like a parrot – another thing to thank her father for.

"Not all of it. Some parts were added to later on, or the older parts adapted. I'll give you a proper tour of the place later," Lucy promised. "I know it must feel like a warren but, honestly, it isn't that bad. You'll soon get the hang of it. If you keep it, of course."

Ness was about to ask Lucy how she felt about all this when a door flew open and a scowling young man burst into the solar.

"For Christ's sake, Lucy. Give her the bloody history lecture later on, can't you? I've been waiting for hours and, unlike you, I've got real business that needs attending to."

This had to be Lucy's brother Jamie. What a charmer, thought Ness. Although he had the same colouring and blue eyes as his sister, there any similarities ended. Whereas Lucy's blue eyes were lined and a little faded, exhaustion and sadness having taken their toll on the pretty lively girl she must have been, her brother's were as hard and chilly as sea-washed glass. His sandy hair was receding and his chin seemed to have acquired excess flab; in general his facial features had an odd blurriness to them, as though they were composed of pencil lines that somebody had tried to erase. His was a petulant and bloated look that was all too familiar to Ness from her long experience of a certain kind of expat: self-indulgent and self-important people who gorged at brunches, drank too many cocktails and spent far too much time in the hotel bars congratulating themselves for merely existing while barking orders at the locals.

Instantly she was on her guard.

"Nessa, this is your cousin, James Penwellyn." Ever the professional, David was making polite introductions – although he was no doubt bracing himself for what was already promising to be a difficult hour or two.

"Pleased to meet you," Ness said, holding out her hand.

Her cousin took it reluctantly, just about managing to brush her fingers with his own pudgy ones before stepping away as though he'd come into contact with something nasty. An inheritance-stealing virus maybe? thought Ness, fighting the urge to giggle.

"Likewise, I'm sure," Jamie replied with maximum insincerity. "Shall we go into the library?"

Turning on his heel, Jamie stalked into the next room, while David gallantly held the door so that Ness and Lucy could follow.

The library was a circular room, with one large leaded window that was in a recess filled with scarlet cushions and framed with matching velvet curtains. The walls were lined with row upon row of books with faded spines and pages edged in gold; all of them were a little dusty and unloved, but to Ness they seemed to be crying out to be held and read. The wooden floor must have glowed with beeswax once, but was now dull and scuffed where it was visible at the perimeter; the rest was covered with threadbare carpet. A standard lamp threw buttery light into what would otherwise have been the darkest part of the room, where there was a huge armchair that looked perfect for curling up and reading in. The centre of the library was occupied by a large mahogany table with four chairs pulled up around it – one of these being at the head, where Jamie immediately seated himself.

"Sorry," Lucy whispered to Ness. "He's a bit upset."

Ness shrugged. She wasn't worried. Let Jamie throw his weight around for now if it made him feel better.

Once everyone was seated at the table, David Brown opened his briefcase and drew out a sheaf of thick parchment. He was about to speak, but was interrupted.

"Before we start, just open the door and make sure that little rat, Fern, isn't skulking outside," Jamie ordered his sister. "You know what a little snooper she is."

Two red spots burned on Lucy's cheeks. "Jamie, that's not very kind. Fern's busy in the tea shop – and, anyway, she doesn't snoop."

"For God's sake, do I have to do everything myself?" her brother exploded, standing up so fast that his chair toppled over as he strode across the room and wrenched the door open. Presumably the passageway outside had been empty; Jamie slammed the door shut again and stormed back to his seat. "Makes a bloody change, that's all I can say. She probably ran off."

"Fern lives here," Lucy whispered to Ness. "It'll all make sense soon, I promise."

Ness doubted that anything about this strange family was going to make sense any time soon. Everything still felt unreal. Her fingers stole to her lips. Why was it that the memory of Max Reynard's kiss felt more solid than this ancient castle, and a thousand times more real than the legalese David was reading aloud?

"I, Armand Penwellyn, eldest son of Edmund Penwellyn and resident of Pirran Castle in Cornwall, do hereby revoke all my former wills, codicils and testamentary dispositions made by me. I declare this to be my last will and testament."

There was a sniff from Lucy, at which Jamie rolled his eyes.

"Do you think we could cut all this guff and just get to the bit that we're all actually interested in?" he said.

"I'm afraid not. It's an important legal document, and I'm sure the others would like to hear it," David replied stiffly.

Jamie gave a theatrical sigh. "Oh very well; let's just get it over with then, so that it can be contested. The old man was clearly losing his marbles leaving this place to a Yank."

Ness bit back the retort that flew to her lips. She could see that Jamie was upset.

David cleared his throat. "I maintain good mental health and possess a sound mind¬. This will is made by me of my own independent will and free volition."

Jamie snorted. "I hardly think so. This is where it all stops, and right now. The old boy had lost it. Who says he was in sound mind? You, Lucy?"

Lucy shrank into herself. "Not just me."

"I was joking!" Jamie screeched. He rounded on Lucy, a fat worm of a vein pulsing in his neck. "You knew about this?"

Poor Lucy looked close to tears.

"You knew what the old man was planning? You knew all along that the old bastard was intending to cut me out?" His voice dripped menace.

Lucy shrank further into her seat. "He asked me to help him so I called David. I couldn't say no, Jamie. He was our uncle."

"And I'm your bloody brother! What about me? Didn't you stop to think how I might feel while you were plotting with him?"

"Lucy was only doing as your uncle requested," David interjected. "As was Annie Luckett—"

"That old dyke? What the hell has this got to do with her?" Jamie's pale eyes bulged.

"Miss Luckett witnessed the will and helped to trace Nessa Penwellyn, all in accordance with your uncle's wishes," the solicitor said calmly. "Dr Russex, who witnessed the will as well, will be happy to confirm that Mr Penwellyn was in sound mind. It says so in the will too, if you'll allow me to continue?" He shuffled the papers. "Now, may I?"

Jamie spread his hands helplessly, too angry to speak. Although she'd never met her uncle, Ness wanted to high-five Armand for checkmating his nephew so neatly. Within seconds of meeting Jamie Penwellyn, she'd known exactly why Armand had decided to bypass him and leave the castle to someone else instead. Jamie was a bully. It was as simple as that. But to leave Lucy out seemed unfair at best and malicious at worst. She'd clearly loved him and Pirran Island was her home.

Ness felt a twist of guilt. She didn't have anything like Lucy's claim on the place, so why her?

David read on, confirming that Armand was childless and that Ness was to inherit his castle and most of its contents, as well as the island, the marine rights and whatever money was left after any debts and expenses had been taken care of.

"I must warn you," David said, pausing from his reading and regarding Ness solemnly over the top of his glasses, "that this won't be a large amount. This estate takes an enormous amount of money to run. The castle alone costs over five thousand a month to maintain, and the amount remaining will soon run out."

She gulped. "I understand."

Jamie turned to Ness, his chilly eyes scanning her and clearly finding what he saw lacking. "Nobody here would blame you if you chose to walk away from it. It's not as though you've been raised to handle this kind of thing. You're an American anyway, so all this is very alien to you. I'm sure we could come to some understanding that would be to your advantage. You'll never have to wait tables again, if that's what you're worried about?"

The nerve of him! Trying to buy her off during the will reading. Unbe-bloody-lievable.

"That's a kind offer, but I'll take my time and work something out, thanks all the same," she said. "And by the way, don't be fooled by my accent. I'm not an American. I'm as English as you are."

"You're an idiot then. The estate will be in receivership by Christmas," Jamie snapped.

"I'm sure Miss Penwellyn has lots of thoughts about this, but now is not the time or the place for such a discussion." David gave Jamie a stern look. "If I may, I'd like to move on to the bequests allotted to yourself and Lucy."

"Uncle Armand left me something?" Lucy looked up and her eyes were bright. "Really?"

David nodded and returned to his will reading. "To my nephew, James Penwellyn, I leave whichever one of the following he chooses: either my entire share portfolio, or alternatively the rights to my compositions and the royalties pertaining to these. To my niece, Lucy Penwellyn, I leave whichever of these two possibilities her brother does not choose."

"And you said he was of sound mind?" Jamie scoffed.

"Do you have a preference?" the solicitor asked.

"Isn't it obvious? The shares, of course. They'll bring in a good income." He shot Ness a triumphant smile. "You could have done with those to keep this bloody place afloat."

"So I can have the music?" Lucy looked thrilled. "It's mine? That's amazing!"

"You're mad, sis," said Jamie. "Everyone knows the music's bloody worthless now the world's forgotten the silly old fart. You'd be best lighting a fire with it."

"That's not true! Uncle Armand was a genius!" Lucy cried.

"A genius who hasn't written a note for decades!" sneered her brother. "Do you think anyone outside of here even remembers who he was?"

David held up his hand in warning. "I will note and detail your choices but there's more. Mr Penwellyn also leaves personal effects – and again the decision is yours, Jamie. The Steinway piano in the music room or the small upright that's in Armand's bedroom; which you keep is up to you."

Jamie laughed. "And you're telling me that the old man wasn't gaga? The grand, of course. What on earth would I want that shabby old thing he kept in his bedroom for? It's only fit for firewood."

"He so loved that piano. I used to play it to him towards the end," Lucy said softly. A tear rolled down her cheek and splashed onto the table.

"Well, it's all yours now, sis." Jamie leaned back in his seat and grinned. "Not such a bad day's work for me as I'd feared. Ness gets the money pit and I get the money. Maybe we can do a deal?"

It was on the tip of Ness's tongue to say that she'd rather eat vomit than do a deal with him, but somehow she managed to keep quiet. None of this made any sense to Ness. Poor Lucy, the only person here genuinely grieving for their uncle, had been totally overlooked. All Lucy had were the rights to some unfashionable music and a tatty piano. It seemed dreadfully unfair.

"Before we finish, there are a few minor details to attend to," David said. "Ness, Mr Penwellyn has requested, although it can't be legally enforced if you aren't in agreement, that Merryn Hellier, Fred Tamblyn and Fern Morris be allowed to reside on the island for as long as it remains in your possession."

Fern. That was the name that Jamie had spat out earlier, Ness recalled. Suddenly overcome with the childish urge to annoy him as much as possible, she nodded. "Absolutely. I'll be delighted."

"And also that for as long as the island remains in your possession, Miss Lucy Penwellyn be allowed to reside here and run the tea room."

Ness smiled at Lucy. "I'm a hopeless cook. I even burn water. Please stay."

"What about me?" interrupted Jamie. "Do I have a right to stay?"

"There's nothing mentioned here," David said, looking up and raising his eyebrows. "I can only assume he correctly guessed what items from his estate you'd choose and felt you'd be sufficiently taken care of."

"And that's it? He's thrown me out of my home?" Jamie was white with rage.

"Uncle Armand hardly threw you out of your home, Jamie: you live in London," his sister said gently.

But Jamie wasn't listening. Instead he'd leapt to his feet and, jabbing a finger across the table at Ness, was screeching about birth right and heritage and usurpers and hundreds of other things that she couldn't really hear because his furious words were so incoherent. Biscuit, cowering under the table, whined.

"This isn't over," Jamie promised, still jabbing that finger and glaring at Ness. "Believe me. It isn't. This is only just beginning. I'll contest this pathetic excuse for a will and I'll have you out on your ear, you bitch. So watch your back. This isn't over. Far from it!"

He stormed from the library, slamming the door so hard behind him that the table shook. Looking down at her hands, Ness realised she was shaking too. To be the target of such venom was very disconcerting.

Lucy exhaled slowly. "I think that went pretty well. At least Jamie didn't lose it."

Ness stared at her. "You're kidding me? That wasn't him losing it?"

"Lord no," said Lucy, pulling a face. "That wasn't even close. Trust me, when Jamie's really angry you don't want to be around. He'll be furious right now but that's nothing to how he'll be later. It's just as well he's not staying."

Why was a scene from Macbeth running through her mind all of a sudden? Ness wondered. Blood-dripping daggers and castles and dark deeds of greed and ambition? She felt a twinge of nerves. Life had been simple in the Caribbean. Would Mel have encouraged her to come here if she'd known that her best friend was walking straight into a drama of Shakespearean proportions?

Forget Mel, Ness thought grimly. Would I have come?

Probably not, but it was too late now. She was here and there was nothing else for it: she had better find out where the portcullis was, buy a few crocodiles for the moat and order several vats of boiling oil, because she was at war with Jamie Penwellyn. He'd drawn the battle lines and made it clear how things were going to be from now on.

To her surprise, Ness realised that she was up for a fight. She might be new here but there was no way he was getting his hands on Pirran Castle. Not if she could help it. Armand had chosen her for a reason and, whatever that reason was, Ness wasn't going to let him down.

The battle to save this place was on.

Chapter 10

No matter how many times she gave a tour, Lucy never grew tired of showing the island and the castle to visitors. Sometimes seeing the place through their wide eyes was just what she needed to fall in love with it all over again. What did steep steps, narrow passageways or awkward tides matter when you had an ever-changing panorama of waves and diving seabirds? Recently the strain of nursing and then losing her uncle had clouded Lucy's vision, as had her fears about losing her home. She'd been trudging from one day to another with her head down and all the steadfast determination of a plough horse. Now, as she showed Ness around, Lucy felt as though she was taking a deep breath, filling her lungs with fresh salty air and starting anew.

It was beautiful here. Really beautiful. And how lucky was she to have been able to spend even a couple of years in such a place? I mustn't complain, whatever happens, Lucy told herself firmly as she led Ness up the sharply rising path to the island's highest point. How many people could say they had been blessed to live somewhere like this? Whatever happened next, whatever Ness decided to do with her unexpected legacy, Lucy could never regret the time she had passed on Pirran Island.

"This is steep!" Ness called, sounding short of breath. "St Antonia's totally flat! I'm out of practice with hills!"

"Nearly there now," Lucy promised. Her boots scrambled up the last incline, scree and dry earth falling behind her as she dug in to propel herself to the summit. Goodness, she ought to come up here more often; the view truly was amazing. She'd forgotten just how much more of a vantage point you got from here. The town looked like a model village and the houses along the cliff top were strung out like beads on a necklace. There was a lot of activity at the furthest one – Max Reynard's, of course. No doubt he was sitting in his very expensive sitting room and staring out at the castle, lurking like a spider in his luxurious web and waiting to move in for the kill.

Lucy frowned. From what Annie had said earlier, Ness and Max were already as thick as thieves. She might be making all the right sounds and appearing to be blown away by the island, but who knew what was really going on inside that pretty red head? For all Lucy knew, her long-lost cousin could already be working out what to spend her new-found millions on. Maybe a ranch? Or a condo? Didn't Americans like those? But then again, Ness wasn't an American at all. Oh! It was all so confusing.

"Oh my God, that was some climb." Ness was bending down with her hands on her knees and gulping in air. The breeze whipped long curls of red hair across her face and the exertion had brought out the roses in her cheeks. With those wide-spaced green eyes and her delicate heart-shaped face she really was quite stunning – no wonder Max Reynard was interested. The looks in the Penwellyn family had clearly flowed across to Addy's side of the gene pool, Lucy thought ruefully, although she also saw in Ness a marked resemblance to the portrait of Beth that hung in the hall. It was strange to see a face so similar to the one Lucy had passed every day for the past few years, and to witness it coming to life right in front of her rather than captured in oils. Not for the first time, Lucy found herself wondering exactly what had happened between the Penwellyn brothers and whether Beth Penwellyn had played a greater part in their falling out than anyone professed to know.

"What?" said Ness, plucking Lucy out of her reverie. "You're staring at me."

"Oh! Sorry!" Lucy was mortified and her face flamed. "I was just thinking how much you look like the portrait in the hall."

"Do I?" Ness looked surprised. "I know I've got Dad's red hair – everyone's always said that – but I never knew my mum. Do you really think I look like her?"

"Absolutely," Lucy said.

Her cousin's brows drew together as she stared out across the water. "Dad and I were a team, and I was often told I looked like him. Nobody knew my mother though, so I guess they couldn't comment. Addy hardly mentioned her."

Uncertain quite what to say to this, Lucy could only nod. "Uncle Armand never spoke about her either but I know he treasured that portrait. Not a day passed when he didn't look at it. Even when he was really weak towards the end he liked to walk through the hall. It was like he had a silent conversation with the images in that room."

As she said this, Lucy's arms prickled. What exactly had her uncle been saying? She supposed she'd never know now that he was gone, and anyone in the town who might have been able to shed some light on the matter was still guarding those old secrets. All the same, some sixth sense told her that Ness's legacy was part of the puzzle.

"It's actually quite weird to come face to face with her. She's never been a part of my life and suddenly here I am in the place where she lived and died." Ness bit her lip. "I wonder why our uncle kept her portrait?"

Lucy couldn't answer. "I've no idea, I'm afraid. He was a very private man."

Ness laughed bleakly. "Yeah, so was my dad. It must have been a family trait. I don't even know what really happened to my mum, only that she drowned when I was a baby."

They both stared out across the bay. What should she say to this, Lucy wondered? She'd always known her parents, and had taken care of them until the end. Even now if she chose to she could go and visit them in the stillness of the town churchyard.

(Max had yet to get his hands on that. Hopefully exhuming graves to gain a nice slice of real estate would be a step too far even for him.) But to not know about her family? She couldn't begin to imagine how that would feel.

"I don't know very much about it either," she admitted, wondering now why she'd never thought to ask more. "All I do know is that the brothers fell out and were never reconciled. Annie from the tea shop might have some idea; she's a bit of a local historian. Or maybe Merryn's gran? I think she worked at the castle for a while."

Ness sighed. "What will it achieve, digging the past up now? Things are already weird enough."

She looked so bleak that Lucy's heart went out to her. This situation wasn't easy for any of them. "Maybe it will help explain why our uncle made the choices he did?"

"After meeting your brother earlier I don't need to find out about my mother to understand that," Ness said. "I don't want to be rude, Lucy, but is he always like this?"

Lucy sat down on a tussock, wrapping her arms around her knees and exhaling wearily. Above her the gulls called and whirled, just as wildly as her feelings and loyalties. As Ness joined her, they watched the tide begin to turn and creep slowly back towards the same causeway that Jamie's big four-by-four had hurtled along only a little while ago.

As always, thoughts of her younger brother filled Lucy with conflict. On the one hand she could understand why Jamie was so upset, and she felt she was betraying him by being so glad that he hadn't inherited. On the other hand, if his response to the grand piano was anything to judge by then her brother would have sold the island to Max Reynard before the tyres of his Range Rover had even reached the town.

"He's upset," was all she could say. "He hadn't imagined you would inherit."

"Well, that makes two of us," answered Ness. "I can't say it makes much sense to me, except that I don't imagine your brother loves the place. But I can see how much the island means to you. Everyone I've met so far has sung your praises and I know they wish you'd inherited rather than a total stranger. Merryn and Fern look as though they'd like to stab me."

It was on the tip of Lucy's tongue to explain why, but she managed to stop herself just in time. If Ness was planning something with Max, then it would be better to bide her time. Quite what she was biding her time to do Lucy had no idea, but Fern or Annie were bound to come up with something; they usually did.

"The thing is," Ness continued, shading her eyes and looking out to sea, "you nursed Armand and you live here. So why not leave the place to you?"

Lucy laughed. "I think we both know the answer to that one. I've never been much use at saying 'no' to Jamie. Uncle Armand knew that, and he also knew that Jamie's always desperate for money. Maybe he thought that by leaving the place to somebody who wasn't emotionally involved with it, the right choices would be made?"

"Hmm," replied Ness. She looked unconvinced and Lucy didn't blame her. Even to her it sounded a bit of a long shot as far as explanations went. "None of this seems fair on you. Jamie got to choose what he wanted while you had the leftovers and I get the island. None of it makes sense. If our uncle knew Jamie well enough not to leave him the island, then surely he must have known that Jamie would pick the shares and the expensive grand piano?"

"That's Uncle Armand for you," said Lucy mildly. Nothing in her uncle's will had surprised her in the least. She could see him now, arms folded and bushy eyebrows meeting in a scowl as he refused to do what she was asking, be it eat less salt or call the doctor. "He was a law unto himself. Anyway, I'm thrilled to have the music and that old piano. They actually meant something to him." She glanced at her watch. "We'd better get a move on if you want to walk across to the mainland. The tide will be over the causeway in half an hour."

"You really don't mind me moving in?" asked Ness.

She was looking so worried that Lucy's kind heart went out for her. This must be an awful lot to take in. She seemed a nice girl, and her admiration of all that Lucy had shown her so far appeared to be genuine. It was hard to believe she was embroiled with Max Reynard. Still, no doubt her true colours would soon be revealed – and what would happen next was anyone's guess. Lucy knew that her own future was as rocky as the island shore; some royalties for unfashionable music would hardly be enough to live on if and when Ness sold the place. She made a mental note to call the agency that had represented Armand, as soon as she had a moment spare. Perhaps they could find a way of boosting his portfolio a little? There had been a flurry of interest a few years ago when the BBC had made a documentary, but since then all had been quiet. That his work had stopped at the very peak of his career both drew and repelled the music industry. Now and again somebody raised the matter of the missing symphony, but if it still existed – or indeed had ever existed – her uncle hadn't been willing to say so.

And now he'd taken that secret, along with all the others, to his grave.

"I can stay in the hotel for a little longer if it helps," Ness continued when Lucy didn't reply.

"Don't be silly. This is your home now." Dragging her thoughts away from her financial troubles, Lucy smiled warmly at her cousin. "Of course you should move in. That way you'll have more idea about what to do."

"What to do?"

"Whether you sell or not." Lucy rose to her feet, brushing dried grass from her jeans. "Nobody would blame you if you did. This place is a huge burden, especially without the income to run it."

"I'm not going to sell!" Ness's eyes were green circles of outrage. "No way! This island's special and I'm going to do everything I can to keep it. Of course I am. Isn't that why our uncle left it to me instead of Jamie?"

"You heard David. There's no money for the upkeep," Lucy warned, but Ness just shrugged.

"Then we'll have to find some, won't we? Don't look so worried, Lucy. I know I'm new to it all but it's amazing here and it's where my father came from. That means so much and there's no way I'm letting that go. We'll find a way to make this place pay."

Heartened by this and by the "we", although a little sceptical still, Lucy followed Ness back down from the cliff top, pointing out Grace Note Bay, the Devil's Teeth rocks and Merryn's caravan. Then they walked across the causeway, with Biscuit joining them for a Sunday afternoon run. Lucy smiled when she saw Ness's surprise at how fast the water was approaching the cobbled path.

"But there were acres of beach just now!" Ness remarked in amazement.

"The tide comes in very fast," Lucy explained. "Here's a top islander tip for you: when you see the water bubbling against the rocks each side of the causeway, that means you've only got about five minutes to make the crossing on foot – and if the water's looking scummy, usually on a northerly wind, not even that. You'll have to wade at best and get swept away at worst. My advice would be don't risk it. Wait for a boat."

Ness seemed to take this in and they parted by the hotel. Feeling a little more optimistic, Lucy decided to take Biscuit for a long run across the beach before catching Merryn's boat back. She'd have a word with Merryn too, to ask him to go gently with the new arrival. She'd see if she could persuade Fern to follow suit. Until they knew for certain that Ness really was plotting with Max, Ness deserved the benefit of the doubt. Besides, as her uncle's will stated, they were all only able to stay living here for as long as Ness wanted them. Unlike Jamie, who now had a fair income to enjoy, Lucy only had her savings and cake-making skills to live off. Her options were frighteningly limited. For now, and until she had managed to figure out what was really going on, they would need to play nicely. Antagonising Ness wouldn't be a smart move.

For once the May weather had held fair, and as she made her way along the tideline – with Biscuit racing in and out of the surf with his tongue lolling and ears flapping wildly – Lucy raised her face to the sunshine and enjoyed the warmth on her skin. Families were picnicking on the beach, ice cream sellers were doing a roaring trade on the quayside, and on the far harbour steps where people were queuing for the boats she spotted Fern busily painting henna tattoos onto sunburned limbs. Was there no end to that girl's talents? She was far too clever to bury herself away on the island. Sometimes she gave away just how well educated she was by mentioning books she'd read or plays she'd seen, yet when anyone tried to ask her more Fern clammed up as tightly as the barnacles on the rocky shore. Yet more secrets on the island.

Lucy sighed. Was it really too much to ask for a simple life? That was all Lucy wanted. Perhaps Jamie was right and she was just middle-aged and dull.

The tide was coming in, so Lucy decided not to walk to the furthest part of the beach but instead to head up the steps by the quay and then back through the town. That way she could pick up a coffee before making her way to the boats and catching a ride home with Merryn. By the look of it people were already starting to queue for trips, which hopefully meant that Annie and her helpers would have a busy time in the tea room. Without the income from her uncle's estate Lucy was only too aware that finances were precarious at best and a total disaster at worst. She'd glimpsed the figures earlier on and although she was no Stephen Hawking, Lucy knew a black hole when she saw one. Unless Ness was either stinking rich (unlikely) or had a killer fundraising plan up her sleeve (even more unlikely judging by the look of utter terror in her eyes when David had mentioned how much it cost to run the place), the island was in big trouble.

Lucy retraced her footsteps across the wet sand. She was so deep in thought that at first she hardly noticed the knot of children gathered at the foot of the slimy beach steps. When the tide came in this was the perfect spot for crabbing or jumping into the chilly water. As soon as the tide retreated it was a favourite place for the local youngsters to practise parkour and hone their climbing skills; rarely a summer passed without a broken bone or two. In spite of all adult attempts to stop these activities it was a local rite of passage to climb to the top of the wall when the tide was out; most townsfolk had done so at some point, and Lucy still had the pins in her arm from when she'd been dared to make the ascent. As clumsy then as she was now, she'd tumbled to the compacted sand with a wallop and a nasty-sounding crack. That had been the summer Max Reynard had come to stay with them, Lucy recalled. Max had been the one who'd run to fetch help while Jamie had laughed. Strange to think that such a kind little boy had grown into such a hard-hearted man. If that was what having money did for you then she was happy to be poor.

As she grew closer to the wall, Lucy saw that although half a lifetime might have passed since she'd fallen onto the beach that day, some things never changed. A gaggle of local children stood at the foot of the steps, while a good fifteen feet above them a small boy clung to the quay wall. Even from several metres away, Lucy could see he was gripping so tightly that his knuckles shone white through his skin as he tried his hardest not to fall and his feet scrabbled for a foothold.

"I can't go any higher," Lucy heard him call. There was a wobble in his voice.

"Go on, you pussy! Right to the top!" yelled a boy from below.

"He's scared!" jeered a freckly lad.

"You're such a girl!" called another, and all the rest started laughing.

Lucy's temper began to simmer. She couldn't bear bullies, which she knew was ironic seeing as she spent most of her time being bossed about by one. Maybe that was why? She knew exactly how that little boy felt – she even had the scar on her pinned arm to prove it.

The pale-faced climber stretched his hand out to try to grasp a hold, but his fingers slipped and for a few heart-stopping seconds he slithered down the wall before clawing a grip. The children below laughed and jeered. It was like a scene from a Cornish version of Lord of the Flies.

"You're crap!" cried the freckly one, whom Lucy recognised as one of Val's many grandchildren. Danny, she thought he was called – although there was such a tribe of them it was hard to remember them all. And wasn't that Polly Pipkin's daughter? If she looked closely she was bound to know the others too; St Pirran was a small town and it was impossible to get away with anything here.

As Nessa Penwellyn would soon discover.

The boy scrabbled for a surer foothold and slithered further down the wall, only managing to cling on through luck rather than skill. Lucy's heart catapulted into her mouth. If he fell onto the sand from this height, which judging from his precarious grip was very likely, there was going to be a nasty injury. Before she could think twice, she strode towards the group of children.

"Danny Polmartin! What on earth do you think you're doing? You know how dangerous this is! I'd have thought better of you at your age. Just you wait until I see your mother!"

Instantly six pairs of eyes were on Lucy; the seventh pair was still trained on the wall as the climber focused every ounce of his concentration on not falling. Lucy didn't recognise him. He must be a new arrival to St Pirran. That would explain why he was having to try so hard to prove himself.

"We're just having some fun, Miss Lucy," muttered Danny mutinously.

"Don't give me that! I know exactly what you're up to and it certainly isn't fun!" Lucy was seething. "I'll be having words with your parents, young man." She glanced around at the others, all of whom were now suddenly very keen to be elsewhere. "In fact, I'll be talking to all of your parents, so you'd better get home and speak to them first, don't you think? And count yourselves lucky I haven't called the Harbour Master... yet."

The children didn't want to stick around for a telling-off from the biggest and shoutiest fisherman in the town; seconds later they were gone, running up the steps and back into the busy streets. Only the young climber remained exactly where he was – glued with terror to the rough stones.

"We need to get you down," Lucy called up, trying her best to sound calm. Drat, he was higher than she could reach to lift him. She'd need to guide his feet stone by stone until she could catch him.

"I'm stuck and I'm going to fall," he gasped.

"No you won't," Lucy told him firmly. "Just listen to me and do what I tell you and it'll be fine. I promise. I've climbed this wall myself and I know exactly what to do. It's easy really; you'll see."

"Really?"

Lucy crossed her fingers. "I promise." It'd probably be best not to mention that she'd broken her radius during this exercise, she thought wryly.

Fortunately her bluff worked. The boy's blond head was nodding now, and as she told him where to put each foot he seemed to trust her enough to do exactly as she suggested. Lucy held her breath as he made the treacherous descent, inch by terrifying inch, until at last he was at a height where she was able to reach him.

"I'm going to hold onto you now while you do the last bit," she said, putting her hands up and grabbing his waist. "If you fall now you'll have a soft landing because I'm underneath."

There was a sharp intake of breath. "I don't want to squash you."

Lucy laughed. "You won't squash me. Besides, I'm so fat I need flattening, so you'd be doing me a favour anyway. Come on, last bit now. You're nearly there."

There was a scrabble, a slither and then a tangle of arms and legs as he tumbled the last few feet. Somehow Lucy managed to catch him and not fall over, which was probably the most agile feat of her life, and then he was back on the sand without any broken bones – his or hers. Big brown eyes gazed up at her from a face so white that the freckles stood out like a rash. The poor little chap must have been terrified.

"Well done," Lucy said warmly. "That was really brave."

But the little boy was shaking his head. "No it wasn't. I didn't make it to the top because I was too scared. They're right: I'm just a wuss and now they'll never let me join in. I won't have any friends."

He looked close to tears. Lucy knew that nothing she said would make him feel better. Kids were so cruel to each other and, come to think of it, so were adults. Why couldn't everyone just be kind?

"Is that why you were trying to climb the wall? So they'd be your friends?" she asked.

He nodded miserably. "They said if I did it then I could hang out with them and I'd have people to sit with at school. They don't like me because I'm from London. They think I'm a wuss."

Lucy snorted. "I think you're very brave moving here from somewhere else and starting all over in a new place. I don't imagine that many of those children have done that."

"But I can't climb the rocks or dive off the quay or drive a boat," he said sadly.

"No, but I bet you can catch a tube train or cross a busy road – and you've probably been to the Natural History Museum," Lucy countered. "Anyway, in my experience people who make you do things to become their friend really aren't worth the effort." She held out her hand. "I'm Lucy, by the way."

They shook hands and she noticed that his nails were nibbled right to the quick. The poor kid really was having a rough time.

"I'm Josh," he said, and then added with a frown, "You said you were fat to land on but you're not fat at all!"

Lucy laughed. "That's very kind of you, Josh. I think I maybe just eat a few too many ice creams in the summer. That's one nice thing about Cornwall – lots of ice cream."

"I like Cornwall," said Josh. "I just don't think I like the other kids very much."

At this point Biscuit, who'd been chasing seagulls by the water's edge, came bounding over, thrilled to see Josh because boys of his age generally enjoyed endless games of fetch. Biscuit jumped up at Josh before Lucy had a chance to tell the lively springer spaniel to get down. For a moment she felt anxious about this (after all, Josh's day had been hard enough without Biscuit knocking him flying), but the little boy seemed delighted and laughed.

"He's brilliant! Is he yours?"

"That's Biscuit and yes he's mine, but I can tell he really likes you," said Lucy. "There's one friend made, even if he is a bit slobbery and sandy."

Josh was busy patting Biscuit, who stared up at him adoringly.

"I'd love a dog. Dad said we could get one when we moved here but we haven't got one yet."

"Dogs are hard work. They need a lot of walking," Lucy warned.

Josh shrugged one shoulder. "I can do that. Then I'd have a friend with me all the time. I don't have any friends here. Nobody likes me."

Lucy didn't want to patronise him by offering platitudes. "That must be pretty lonely," she remarked instead.

"Yeah, it is. Dad said we were coming here for a new start but he's working all the time on the church now."

Ah, so his father was working for Max Reynard. That figured. Who else would expect his employees to work on a Sunday and be prepared to pay them the weekend rates? No wonder Josh was at a loose end; from what Lucy knew of Max he'd be making sure he got value for money.

"What did you like to do when you were in London? There must have been things you enjoyed there?" Lucy asked as they climbed the steps up from the beach and made their way along the quay towards the town.

"It was different then because my mum was still... hadn't..."

His voice tailed off, the unsaid words telling Lucy all she needed to know. Poor little boy. Meeting him was certainly putting her own woes into perspective.

"I liked to play the violin," Josh told her, looking thoughtful. "I play the piano too but we don't have room for one here so I haven't done that for ages. Mum played duets with me sometimes. She was really good but she said I was even better."

"You're musical. That's great," said Lucy.

Josh looked unconvinced. "The kids here think liking music makes me weird. When I have my violin lessons at school they all laugh at me."

"Don't listen to them. Being musical is brilliant," Lucy replied staunchly. "I bet they like Kanye West and all the girls are mad about One Direction, aren't they? Those guys are musicians and I can't imagine anyone thinks they're weird."

At least she thought Kanye and One Direction were musicians; Lucy wasn't quite sure, being more of a Take That fan herself. Still, her words seemed to do the trick and Josh looked slightly more cheerful.

They were nearing the ice cream kiosk and Lucy decided to buy them both a cornet to help overcome the earlier trauma. As they queued, she told Josh about her Uncle Armand and how he'd been a famous composer.

"He's not as popular as he used to be but he's still pretty well known. Google him when you get home and you'll soon see. He wrote most of his music over there." She pointed across to the island.

Josh's eyes widened. "In Max's castle?"

Max's castle? So that was the rumour going around among the workers, was it? Interesting, thought Lucy.

"It certainly isn't Max's castle," she said firmly. "It belongs to my family and it's our home. There's a wonderful music room there with a lovely grand piano. My uncle loved to play that when he was younger. You must ask your father if you can come and visit one day and play it."

Josh's eyes lit up like the lights on the seafront. "Cool! Yes, please! Can I come now?"

Lucy laughed. "I think you ought to ask your father first."

"He won't mind; he's really busy. Anyway, I can text him – and his friend lives over there in a caravan. He can give me a lift home or bring Dad."

"You mean Merryn?" Lucy asked, handing him an ice cream. Another nod.

"Merryn's got a really cool boat and all the girls at school fancy him," Josh said through a mouthful of mint choc chip.

Not just the girls at school, thought Lucy. Oh dear. She really needed to get over her crush – and soon, before it got embarrassing. She'd be fancying Justin Bieber next.

"You could text him now then, and tell him you'll be with Lucy Penwellyn and Merryn Hellier," she suggested. "Everyone knows me here so he won't need to worry."

"And I can see Biscuit." Josh was busy texting with one hand and feeding the spaniel some of his wafer with the other, a feat of great dexterity. No wonder he was good at playing the piano, Lucy thought.

Before she'd even managed to finish her ice cream, Josh's mobile pinged and he punched the air.

"Yes! Dad says he knows who you are and that's fine as long as I come back with Merryn by half six," he announced, all earlier woes forgotten. "Let's go now!"

"I didn't realise I was so famous," said Lucy. She ate the rest of her ice cream and then brushed the crumbs from her hands.

"OK, let's go. I'm already looking forward to hearing what you can do," she told Josh.

Needing no encouragement at all, Josh and Biscuit bounded ahead of her. It was hard to tell who was more excited. Lucy felt her own spirits lift. She hadn't touched the piano or her violin since Armand had died; the music room now echoed with memories rather than the rich notes of the Steinway. Why not make the most of the beautiful grand piano before Jamie sold his inheritance?

Yes, decided Lucy as she followed Josh across the beach, an hour or two of music was exactly what she needed to clear her tangled thoughts.

Everything else would just have to wait

Chapter 11

You couldn't really moan about working on a Sunday afternoon when you were being paid handsomely, the sun was pouring golden warmth down from a blue sky and one of the best views in Cornwall was spread out before you, Adam Miller decided. The mallet in his right hand might be heavy and he was having to take extreme care to prevent the chisel from slipping on the ancient stone, but working on this beautiful old church against the backdrop of St Pirran's Bay made up for any difficulties. The texture of the granite beneath his fingers and the way the masonry was coming back to life after years of neglect were hugely satisfying too. So the project was complex and the hours were long, but that was what he'd signed up for and Adam wasn't complaining. This certainly beat life on-site in London. The move here had been a good one.

Beneath his tools, the same basic ones his medieval forebears would have been familiar with, a gurning gargoyle was slowly emerging in sharper detail. Centuries of gales and prevailing westerly winds had weathered the stone and blurred the mischievous features, but with Adam's skilled touch the years were peeling away.

Stepping back from his bench Adam laid his tools down for a moment and, flexing his aching fingers, pushed his dusty blond fringe out of his eyes. Note to self: he must get his hair cut – and properly this time too, rather than hacking it off with the kitchen scissors. Elly had always cut it for him before and, as with most of the jobs his wife had done so well, Adam's attempts were a very poor second. There was also something intimate about hair cutting, and to have another woman brushing the hair from his neck and snipping around his ears felt like a betrayal, almost an infidelity.

"I know, I'm being bloody ridiculous," Adam said to the gargoyle – and then laughed out loud. He was talking to a piece of stone now? That said it all. Never mind being ridiculous; he was going mad. It had always been a matter of time. If the grief hadn't crazed him then the stress of trying to complete Max's latest project on time was certainly driving him insane. They were already running three weeks behind schedule and Max, being Max, was starting to put on the pressure.

Adam picked up his tools and resumed his task, chipping away with a precision that belied the crude instruments. The speed of this operation was painfully slow, but that was the way it had to be. One slip of the chisel, one false move and that would be it: game over, with the artefact ruined beyond repair. Much as it irked his friend, Adam knew from long experience as a master mason that you couldn't rush these things. Like grief, working stone had its own timescale. Sometimes you felt as though you were getting nowhere. Other days it felt as though life was starting to become a little easier. And then there were those days when no matter what you tried, even making a start felt pointless.

Adam blew more dust away and continued his work. He knew that his perseverance would eventually reveal something fantastic. Granted, it might never be quite the same as it had once been, but it would certainly be close – and it would be just as beautiful in its own way. Likewise, if he kept chipping away at this new life he was carving out for himself and Josh here in St Pirran, then surely something good would come from it?

He had to hope so and to hold onto this thought in any case. It had been over two years now and although Adam knew he would never, ever get over losing Elly, there was a sense of getting used to the loss. That raw, unbearable grief had eventually ebbed like the tide from the causeway and the ache had become a dullness rather than a searing pain. Nevertheless, Adam knew that he and Josh would never be the same again. They were changed forever, like the stone beneath his chisel.

He paused again and squinted at the ugly face leering up at him. It was the product of almost a week's work, and he felt a tingle of pride as he contemplated this piece of restoration. Let Max moan. Fast wouldn't be good and if Max didn't want the best then he wouldn't have hired Adam Miller. If Reynard Developments had wanted nothing more than a quick fix job then they could have had their pick of anyone, but master stonemasons were few and far between. Adam Miller had years of experience. He'd worked his apprenticeship the old-fashioned way, starting as a sixteen-year-old in Malcom Reynard's building yard before moving on to work with the National Trust and English Heritage, growing his reputation as an expert in his field and as one of a handful of master masons who could be trusted with the most delicate projects. He'd had his pick of the best jobs, and a very comfortable life in London too, and his old friend had had to make it worth his while to move all the way to Cornwall.

Adam brushed off some more dust with his forefinger, then picked up his tools again. Working like this was almost meditative, and sometimes hours could pass in what felt like moments. He was lucky to have been given the chance to make this move. So many people were caught up in the rat race, scurrying around to make a living and becoming slaves to huge mortgages that they could just about pay. Most of his friends back in London were trying to spin so many plates that just watching them had made him feel giddy. Adam had worked hard, but his expertise had commanded the best fees and he'd been able to take the jobs that really appealed to him. He'd travelled all over Europe and worked on some incredible buildings, from cathedrals to palaces. Adam adored his job, and when Elly had still been alive the travelling hadn't been an issue at all – but once she'd died everything had shifted. Suddenly Josh had needed him in every way. Quite apart from the grief, Adam's life had become a complex game of juggling child minders, jobs and pitying neighbours.

None of this had been much help for Josh, of course. As brilliant as Adam's friends and neighbours had been, making stews and doing the shopping and collecting Josh from school, they weren't Elly. His son had grown more withdrawn by the day and it had broken Adam's heart all over again to see the formerly outgoing and sociable little boy sink deeper into himself. Josh's music had stopped too, although in truth the closed piano lid and the dust falling on top of it had hardly featured in Adam's consciousness at the time. Just the sight of an old lipstick in the glove box or a cardigan hanging on the back of the door had been enough to break him; he'd barely been aware of anything except his wife's absence. The house, the street and the daily routines had all reminded him of Elly. Although he might have looked as though he was functioning, inside Adam had been falling to pieces.

It hadn't been unexpected, not when Elly had found the third lump. They'd both known then that all the treatments were only to buy time. Towards the end she'd been so exhausted that putting her through them had felt like the worst kind of cruelty. When the doctors had told them that there was nothing more they could do except keep her comfortable, Adam had thought he was prepared. He'd seen counsellors, knew what Elly wanted done and had made sure that Josh understood too. This was death by numbers: something expected, planned for and that he was almost at peace with – or so he'd thought. The reality was that when she'd finally slipped away from him, the shock and the anger had been overwhelming.

Some days they still were...

Losing Elly had turned Adam's world inside out. Nothing looked the same anymore. Nothing seemed to work. A bit like a tune played slightly off-key, parts of his life had seemed hauntingly familiar and yet not quite as they ought to be. He'd felt constantly on edge. But he had to carry on for Josh – and for Elly too, because she'd fought so hard and been so courageous. He couldn't respond to that by being weak. Life without her was lonely at times and difficult and empty, but at least he still had a life. Adam knew he owed it to his wife to keep going.

"Time heals everything," was what people had kept telling him, and they'd been right – to some extent. The trouble was that everywhere he'd gone, Adam had kept seeing Elly. She'd be in the kitchen making one of her pasta concoctions that always involved using every pan and utensil they possessed, or she'd be in their tiny courtyard garden coaxing blooms from the smallest patch of earth. And somehow she was always sitting at the piano with her slender fingers flying over the keys, filling the small house with fluttering notes. She was everywhere and nowhere all at once. Although the sharp sting of his grief had lessened somewhat, Adam had known that if he was ever to come into a real time of healing, something big had to happen – for him and for Josh.

The problem was that he simply hadn't had the energy to figure out what that "something" ought to be. Trying to carry Josh through and remain strong for him whilst coping with the demands of his job had been wearing him out; most evenings it had been as much as Adam could do to make it from the sofa to bed, never mind decide what the hell to do next.

The change had come when he'd least expected it. One Tuesday morning he'd been sitting at the kitchen table after dropping Josh at school. He'd been staring sightlessly into a cooling cup of tea, when there'd been a sharp rap of knuckles on the front door. Who now? Adam had wondered. The neighbours weren't quite as frantic about his welfare as they had been (although they were still visiting regularly enough to ensure that he had a freezer full of casseroles), and it was a bit early in the day for Jehovah's Witnesses. Deciding to ignore it, Adam had almost jumped out of his skin when there had been another sharp knock and a voice had called, "Don't ignore me, Windy! I know you're in there. Open the bloody door, for God's sake! I'm scared I'll get mugged if I stay out here much longer. Bad enough my car will end up on bricks without some little scrote stealing my wallet too!"

It was Adam's friend, Max Reynard, shouting through the letterbox. What on earth was Max doing here on a weekday when he should be busy taking over the universe while mere mortals watched The Jeremy Kyle Show?

Adam and Max had grown up together – Adam's bricklayer father working for Max's – and the two had been best friends at primary school, where they'd got into all kinds of scrapes. Even now, Adam had the silvery scar on his palm from their decision to become blood brothers. They'd pinched a Stanley knife from his dad's toolkit and there had actually been far too much blood; both boys had been taken to A & E for stitches. He still had the bump in his nose too, which he'd acquired during a bout of overenthusiastic play-fighting with Max. Although their paths had diverged years ago when Max had won a place at public school and Adam had chosen to embark on a training scheme, they'd stayed in touch and had the kind of friendship that meant it didn't matter if they only saw each other once in a blue moon. Max was Josh's godfather and for all his ridiculous wealth had always seemed just as content hanging out with Adam and Elly, eating pasta and chatting together on their Ikea sofa, as he was swanning about in The Ivy. He might seem like the stereotypical rich businessman, but Adam knew he was equally, if not more, devoted to his charity work than to making a profit. The homeless shelter Max had set up in his father's memory took up huge amounts of his time, and it might surprise the readers of the business pages to know that Max Reynard was just as likely to be found dishing up dinners or unblocking a toilet as he was chairing a board meeting.

He was the velvet fist in the iron glove all right – or, as Elly had often said, a soft heart locked inside a safe. Somebody surely would find the combination one day and set it free? Elly had thought Max was wasted on his own, because he had so much to give. Adam would tease her and call her a hopeless romantic but actually they were in perfect agreement: Max was one of the most generous people they knew. He just played his cards close to his chest, that was all.

When Elly had died, in that bleak time that now felt like a black and white blur, it had been Max who'd moved in for a week, taken charge of the funeral arrangements and made sure that Josh was looked after. He'd let Adam cry too; rather than giving him platitudes Max had simply handed him a loo roll and poured them both a drink (albeit a non-alcoholic one for Max).

Yes, there was no doubt about it: Max Reynard was the kind of friend you wanted around when the chips were down.

But at nine-thirty in the morning when Jeremy Kyle was about to start? Well, that was a different matter.

"This is Hoxton, not the Bronx," Adam had pointed out as he'd let Max in. "We're up and coming here these days, you know."

Max did know; of course he did. Reynards had completed a big warehouse development down the road only six months previously. All the same, Max liked to wind Adam up about the area as much as Adam had always enjoyed teasing Max about his posh accent and bubble-brained girlfriends. Although Max always claimed not to be with any of them for their intellect, saying the last thing he wanted was a brainy woman giving him grief, Adam knew that in reality this was exactly the kind of girl his friend needed. Elly had also said so – and his musician wife, the epitome of a clever woman, had never been wrong.

"Christ, what's gone on in here?" Max had stared around the kitchen in surprise.

"Cleaner came yesterday," Adam had replied. He'd hardly noticed how neat and tidy the place was. In the past, Elly – queen of clutter – had filled it with everything from glass painting to clarinets to piles of sheet music. Now that she was gone the place might be tidy but, just like him, the heart had gone out of it.

"That woman's worth her weight in gold. I'd better double her wages and steal her. If she's pretty I'll triple them," Max had grinned, sitting down uninvited at the table and stretching out his long legs. As he'd done so, his dark hair had fallen over his face and he'd pushed it back impatiently.

Adam had seen that gesture a thousand times; if they'd been playing poker, it would have told him all he needed to know. "Whatever you want, the answer's no," he'd said.

Max hadn't bothered to deny that he wanted something. "You'll change your mind when you hear what it is."

"My car's crap; you hate my house; my clothes are George at Asda, not Giorgio Armani; and you don't need to borrow a tenner." Adam had ticked all these off on his fingers and then frowned. "There's nothing I have that you need."

"Apart from this tea. God, I need a cuppa." Max had helped himself to Adam's mug of builder's best and was glugging it happily. Then he'd caught sight of the television. "Christ, tell me you're not seriously watching Jeremy bloody Kyle? I'm not a moment too soon."

"Not a moment too soon for what?" Adam had asked. He didn't think Max was here to borrow his Transformers collection this time (Optimus Prime had never been the same since Max had got his hands on him as a child), but you could never be too sure. His friend certainly had that old *I'm going to go after what I want and get it* gleam in his eye.

"To take you away from a life of daytime TV," Max had said, with a theatrical shudder. "You'll be watching Loose Women before you know it. We may as well just shoot you now."

"I quite like Loose Women," Adam had protested, but his friend wasn't listening. Instead Max had reached into his beautiful grey cashmere coat – which had probably been selected by some adoring woman to match the colour of his eyes – and pulled out a sheaf of papers and photographs that he'd spread across the table.

Plans. Of course. Max was on another project. In the years since Max had first started running the company, Reynards had changed beyond all recognition: it was no longer the small family building firm of their fathers' time, but instead was one of the UK's foremost developers. From warehouses to stately homes, Max was developing pretty much everything – and very successfully too, if The Sunday Times Rich List was to be believed. What now?

Intrigued in spite of himself, Adam had leaned forward to have a look.

"What do you think, Windy?" Max had asked.

Adam was still looking. The photographs showed a castle on an island; it was set in a pretty bay, across from a town full of ice-cream-coloured houses. The steep valley, clear seawater and granite rocks suggested this was in the West Country, and the beauty of the place took his breath away. Next to the glossy photographs was a series of plans, neatly drawn up by the leading firm of architects Reynards favoured.

"I think it's bloody amazing, Mangey," Adam had replied, slipping just as easily back into the old nicknames. Windy Miller and Mangey Reynard might be men in their thirties now, but deep down inside every adult male is still a schoolboy, be he a master stonemason or a multimillionaire businessman. "You've bought a castle. Crikey. I was pleased to buy this place! I take it this is your next project?"

Max had nodded. "I haven't technically bought the property yet but it's pretty much in the bag. We should be moving on it sometime in the not too distant future. I'll be sending two teams down to Cornwall to join the one already in St Pirran."

"If you haven't purchased it, isn't it a bit premature to draw up the plans and get a workforce mobilised?" Adam had asked with a frown.

This wasn't like his friend. Usually in business, and matters of the heart, Max was cautious to the point of icy coldness. The sparkle in his eyes and the excitement in his voice were both unusual. Adam realised that Max was head over heels in love with the place.

"The owner's elderly and very unwell," Max had said, smoothing the plans with his forefinger, almost as though he was caressing the castle's walls. "His nephew, an old school alumni of mine, is going to inherit and has already decided to sell. Christ! That sounds really callous. I don't wish the old boy any harm but according to my old school friend it's only a matter of time – and, as you can imagine, every developer in the country will be circling. If it's my company that buys the place at least any work on it will be done sympathetically. That's respectful to him, don't you think?"

Adam had nodded then peered closer at one of the pictures. "The place looks like it's gone to rack and ruin, fam. The walls are in a really bad way and the masonry on the arch is about to go. I take it the place is listed?"

"Grade one," Max had said, "which is where you come in."

"Me?"

His friend had fixed him with a determined stare. "This is the project of a lifetime, Ad. I'm staking everything on making this development the jewel in the company's crown. It needs the best of everything. I'm going to restore it and I need to put together a highly skilled team. I want you to come and work with me as Project Manager. We're talking at least three years' worth of work here, possibly more. Can you imagine having free rein to work on something like this? To really show what you can do and leave a legacy for generations?"

Adam could, and for the first time in ages he'd felt a flicker of excitement. Max knew him so well; this was exactly the kind of project he'd always dreamed of. It was a chance to draw upon all his skills, hone his creativity and pay homage to the work of men who were long dust. Just imagining what he could do with this place was making his pulse race.

"I'll pay you double whatever your usual rates are," Max had added. "What do you say?"

Adam had smiled. "I'd say I'm flattered and very tempted, but I think the commute would kill me."

"That's the whole point. You'd have to move there and stay for at least the next three years. It's the new start that you and Josh need." Max had glanced around the kitchen and then said gently, "Mate, I know you miss Elly and it must be bloody awful for you and Josh – I can't even imagine how awful – but isn't it time to move on?"

Adam had shaken his head. "I can't uproot Josh. This house is his stability."

"You're his stability," Max had corrected. "You'll always be that, but maybe it's time to make life a bit different now? You've done a brilliant job of carrying on just like before – but it's never going to be like before, no matter how hard you try, is it? Not in the only way that matters."

He was right, of course. Adam knew that. He and Josh were doing all right, on the surface at least, and most days they got by – but it wasn't always easy when there were memories everywhere. What if this was the opportunity he'd been needing? A chance to make a new kind of life for him and his son? One where he'd be working locally and not having to rely on an endless stream of blank-faced au pairs or put-upon neighbours? Cornwall was full of fresh air and beaches; it would be much better for Josh than being cooped up in London. It would be a new start for them and one that he was sure Elly would have been up for. She'd have been opening the laptop and booting up the webpages of RightMove before Max had even finished rolling up the plans; by dinnertime she'd have been experimenting with pasties and listening to the Island Suite as she chopped and fried and made her usual mess in the kitchen.

It made sense. He'd be able to give Josh the time he deserved. Besides, if he was honest Adam was tired of travelling across the continent, living out of suitcases and eating alone. It wasn't practical for him to do that now anyway. The idea of working on a castle appealed to him too; it was a once-in-a-lifetime project. Like Max said, it was a chance to really show what he was capable of and to leave a lasting legacy. Adam didn't live for his job, exactly, but since losing Elly he was finding that working stone brought him a level of comfort that talking to counsellors didn't offer. This project filled him with excitement – and it would be no bad thing to have secure employment for a few years, either.

Cornwall would be perfect. Adam and Elly had holidayed there many times and had loved the bright scoured light, the space and the sense of freedom. They'd rented cottages in picturesque villages, drunk cider in waterside pubs and gorged on delicious pasties, and all Adam's memories of the place were sun-drenched and happy. There was a different pace of life in that part of the country, and the people there seemed friendlier. Children played outside rather than hunching over their Xboxes, and everyone had the healthy glow that came with fresh air and outdoor living. Maybe Josh could have a dog and learn to sail as well? It could be just what they needed.

Adam hadn't rushed the decision. After all, everyone told him that stability was what Josh needed the most. On the other hand, Adam had started to feel that a change could be good for them both. It wasn't that he wanted to forget Elly or start again – she would be in his heart forever and Adam knew he'd miss her every day for the rest of his life – but maybe it was time to begin a new chapter? She would have been the first person to tell him to go for it; nothing would have saddened or angered her more than to see him still in a state of inertia nearly two years on. Elly had lived every minute to the full, even when she'd been desperately sick, and Adam knew he owed it to her to do the same.

He'd done the sums and found that Max was right: the move to St Pirran made perfect sense. He and Elly had bought their flat when prices had been comparatively low. Now that Hoxton was trendy he could sell it for a sum that would buy him and Josh the perfect family home in Cornwall.

Although it had still hurt that Elly wasn't there to help view cottages or share in the excitement, Adam and Josh had enjoyed some fun weekends away exploring St Pirran. Eventually they'd chosen the tiny converted net loft that was now their home.

The gargoyle was complete and Adam stepped back to assess his work. There wasn't much to show for all those hours of effort, but being slow and patient was the essence of his craft. The same approach had been applied to the new house, so that the tired, unloved holiday cottage he'd bought had gradually been transformed into a warm and welcoming home. Adam had stripped away the layers of paint from the walls and beams, peeled up the carpets to reveal oak floors and worked late into the night to make the wood gleam again. He particularly liked the big windows that overlooked the bay; on sunny days the light gushed through them, and on stormy ones you could curl up on the oversized leather sofa and watch the waves race in. Josh had a bedroom high in the eaves, which he loved. The house wasn't the only good thing about their new life though: they owned a boat as well, and weekends were now spent on the beach or sailing across the bay. Everything seemed to have fallen into place. Josh seemed happy too, although he was still far quieter these days than he'd been before Elly's death. At least he was out playing with some of the local kids this afternoon and making friends while Adam put in some extra time on the church conversion. So much for life in Cornwall being slower paced. He'd never worked so hard.

Adam lifted the stonework and carried it to the far side of the workshop, carefully placing it with the gargoyles he'd already restored. Only four more to go, he thought wryly. If Max thought that Pirran Castle's restoration was going to be complete within three years then he was in for a nasty shock. Adam had visited the island several times since he'd arrived in the town, and to his expert eye it was apparent that the place was in need of serious work. One part was almost too far gone to restore and would require a team of specialists to rebuild it, and the rest hadn't been touched for years. It would be a challenge, that was for sure.

As he put his tools away the text-message alert on his phone sounded.

the lady who owns the castle says I can come and play the piano now. Can I? plz?

The lady who owned the castle? Adam frowned. What lady? Armand Penwellyn had been dead a short while – but hadn't Max said that his old school friend was inheriting? Or was there truth in the pub rumours after all?

He sent a quick text back asking his son who exactly this lady was, and within seconds he received a picture message in response.

The subject of the picture clearly didn't know she was being captured for digital posterity; instead she was intent on devouring a 99, an expression of utter bliss on her face and oblivious to her blonde hair blowing into the ice cream. Adam recognised her at once. She was the woman he'd chatted to outside the dress shop – the one who'd been gazing at the spotty dress as hungrily as she was now eating her ice cream.

She's called Lucy and Merryn will give me a lift on a boat and it's a grand piano plz?

Adam's heart lifted. He couldn't remember the last time he'd heard his son sound so enthusiastic. He wasn't sure whether Josh was excited about the music or just the idea of having a ride on Guardian Angel. Josh hadn't played the piano since Elly had died. It was a shame because – as everyone who knew anything about music agreed – he was gifted. He took after his mum in that respect, whereas Adam was tone deaf. Josh and Elly had played duets together and she'd often said that her son's talents would way exceed her own. Had Josh stopped enjoying the piano because playing it was too painful without his mum? He'd certainly been adamant when they'd left London that there was no point in bringing a piano to such a tiny house. Now, as he reread the text message, Adam was heartened that Josh wanted to play again. It had to be a good sign.

Adam had heard of Lucy Penwellyn. She was well known in the town and, unlike her brother, everyone spoke most highly of her. Adam knew all about how she'd nursed her father and then her demanding elderly uncle without ever complaining. He also knew that she baked the best cakes in Cornwall. Her tea shop on the island was definitely worth a visit; he'd already enjoyed several cream teas there. Without doubt she inspired loyalty in St Pirran. Even scary Annie Luckett sang her praises, as did the shopkeepers, the fishermen and his friend Merryn Hellier, who lived on the island and had known the family forever. From all he'd heard of Lucy, Adam had been picturing a matronly soul in a pinny – and maybe even a halo too. A kind of saint crossed with a motherly figure, perhaps.

But what he hadn't been expecting was a curvaceous blonde with the bluest eyes he'd ever seen and skin as fair as the clotted cream he'd been spooning onto her scones...

Adam shook his head and then laughed at himself. Skin as fair as cream? He was sounding like one of the pink novels Elly had gobbled up! Still, sometimes only clichés really worked, didn't they? Lucy had been so surprised when he'd complimented her too, blushing sweetly and unable to look him in the face. He'd meant it though. That dress would have really suited her; she'd have looked like a 1950s film star in it, all curves and smiles. Was he being disloyal to Elly to think like this? Adam hoped not. He might be a widower but he was still able to appreciate women, surely? Nobody would ever replace his wife and he would never want them to – but he wasn't past it yet.

In any case, now he'd made the link between the dress woman and all the good things he'd heard about Lucy, Adam was more than happy for Josh to go and play the piano at the castle. Merryn, who'd become something of a friend since Adam had moved to the town, could bring him home; Josh always loved a trip in Guardian Angel. Adam would put a couple of pints behind the bar as a thank you, since Merryn always refused to accept money.

Fine! he texted back. I know who she is now. Have fun. I'll ask Merryn to pick you up at half six. xDx

He knew that his son would roll his eyes at the punctuation and kisses, but so far as Adam was concerned it was all part of his job as a dad to be embarrassing.

When the message had been sent, Adam checked his watch. For once he found himself with a free hour to spare after work. Maybe Max was around for a drink? He didn't often socialise in the town but it was high time they caught up. Besides, Adam was starting to feel a little uneasy. Having moved his entire life and his child lock, stock and barrel to St Pirran for the express purpose of working on the castle project, he wanted to make sure it was still going ahead. The town had been rife with rumours since Armand Penwellyn had died, but nobody seemed to know for certain what was happening. Adam generally kept himself to himself and didn't listen to gossip, but if anyone did know the truth then it would be Max Reynard.

As he scrolled through his contacts, Adam hoped that his best friend wasn't about to come unstuck with this project and fail for the first time in his hugely successful life. Max had seemed so convinced he'd be buying the castle that Adam had also believed it was a done deal. It was only when the stonemason had been in the town for a while that he'd learned that this business transaction wasn't quite as straightforward as he'd been led to think.

Reynards had to buy Pirran Island. Everything Adam held dear was depending on it. He was being paranoid, Adam told himself firmly. Max always won and nobody would get in the way of this development, not even somebody as sweet and as gentle as Lucy Penwellyn.

Adam pressed the call button and waited for Max to answer. It was time he found out exactly what was going on.

Chapter 12

Ness had collected her bag and checked out of the hotel, and was on her way back to the castle. Her head was still spinning. This had to be one of the strangest days of her life.

She owned a castle. How crazy was that? There was no longer any doubt about it; David Brown had completed the legalities and she'd seen for herself just what an undertaking this was going to be. Jamie was furious but at least he had the private income. How Ness was going to make the island pay now was her first problem. Sweet as Lucy was, Ness didn't think selling scones was going to do it.

What skills do I have that might be useful? Ness asked herself as she shouldered her bag and walked towards the queue for the boats – the tide having well and truly swept over the causeway now. Life with Addy had made her independent and resourceful; she'd needed these qualities in order to survive when he'd vanished on painting binges and only emerged, paint-speckled and dazed, several days later. Working at the hotel in St Antonia had honed Ness's people skills too, although these seemed to be failing quite spectacularly today. Indeed, today it appeared that Ness Penwellyn was about as popular in St Pirran as the dive-bombing gulls.

As she joined the queue of waiting tourists, Ness felt bewildered. There was a marked change in the way people were behaving towards her and she had absolutely no idea why. Take David Brown, for instance. He'd been so friendly before, but today there had been a noticeable chilliness about him. It wasn't simply that he was trying to remain reserved and professional as the family solicitor; instinct told Ness that it was more than that. He'd barely been able to look at her when she'd met him by the causeway – and as soon as the official legalities had been concluded, he'd departed with the very briefest of farewells.

Then there were the women in the tea shop who, despite Lucy's warm introduction, had hardly managed to say more than a civil hello. And the girl with the pink plaits, Fern, had looked as though she wanted to stab her with a cake fork. Perhaps Ness could have put this antipathy down to worry about the future of the island, but having met Jamie she felt they ought to be thanking their lucky stars he hadn't got his pudgy hands on the place instead. Surely they could see that if Lucy had inherited the island it would only have been a matter of minutes before her brother would have schemed and bullied his way into taking charge? Ness had only known her cousins a short while, but already it was obvious to her how the dynamic in that family worked. Ness could understand the cold reception and suspicious looks from those closest to the family, but when she'd checked out earlier, even Val Brown had been positively glacial.

Ness frowned. Last night the hotel receptionist had been so welcoming and kind. She'd even upgraded the room free of charge and taken the time to recount a potted history of the island. In contrast, today Val had struggled to even go through the formalities of checking out – and Ness had been sure that the two women in the back office were whispering about her. Unless there was something in the water making her have paranoid delusions, the whole town felt hostile. The sun might be out and the sea glittering but the atmosphere in St Pirran was decidedly frosty. Something had changed and she hadn't a clue what it was or how she could put it right.

Was it her imagination or were the skippers of the tripping boats also glowering in her direction? There was one there now, shooting Ness a black look while he readied his little blue vessel for the journey to the island. As her queue wound its way closer to the pontoon she realised that she was going to end up on his boat.

Great. If she made it back across without being forced to walk the plank then it would be a miracle. For such a handsome guy (a dead ringer for Brad Pitt in his pre-Angelina heyday, but with much blonder hair), he certainly had a face on him that could curdle milk.

She edged her way down the steps and onto the pontoon as, one by one, the holidaymakers were directed into the boats. Sure enough, by the time Ness was at the front of the queue it was Brad Pitt's turn to accept passengers. Just her luck, she was the first on. Although Brad looked as though he'd like to turn her away, the lure of a couple of pounds was fortunately strong and Ness stepped on board. He didn't hold his hand out to steady her, though. Ness was used to dive boats and more than able to hop over the gunnel and adjust her balance to the shifting water, but it was interesting to notice that this lack of manners wasn't repeated with the rest of his customers, male or female.

So it wasn't her imagination then. Fine. Maybe Lucy would be able to shed some light on all this? If not, then let them carry on until they got used to the fact that she was here and she wasn't about to run away. Ness raised her chin and fixed her gaze on her island, floating in the sea beyond. She hadn't come this far to be intimidated by a bunch of stroppy locals.

With the passengers now seated, the skipper cast off. Before long the boat was zipping across the bay towards the island. In spite of the hostility she could sense in the eyes that were now shielded behind his black sunglasses, Ness ignored the skipper and focused instead on the short journey. Her heart lifted as the craft picked up speed and danced across the waves. She loved the space and sense of freedom that came with heading out on the open water. For as long as she could remember she had been drawn to the sea. Maybe it was in her blood? After all, Addy had grown up on the water and boating must have been a huge part of his life. Not that you would ever have known this in his later years, given that he'd avoided the sea almost as if he had an aversion to it, instead preferring the Californian desert or the wilds of Montana.

The ride across the bay to the island's small and, she now noticed with alarm, crumbling quay only took five minutes – but it was long enough for Ness to enjoy the wind in her hair. It was a shame there wasn't enough money for her to buy her own boat. Did this mean she'd have to rely on the fishermen and the sullen hunk here when the tide was in? Independent to her last cell, Ness didn't like this idea at all. She'd rather swim across than be beholden to anyone.

"Here we are, everyone: St Pirran's Island," the skipper was saying, as he popped the engine into neutral and hopped out onto the worn quayside. "Home to one of the best tea shops in Cornwall and a huge variety of natural life too, from seals to puffins. Untouched for centuries, this island is a sanctuary – for wildlife and for people. Let's hope it always stays that way."

As he said this, the skipper pushed his shades up into his thick blond hair and stared straight at Ness. What on earth had she done to inspire such antipathy? Then he turned away and busied himself mooring up and helping passengers to disembark. Again, no steadying hand was offered to Ness and she made the jump across unassisted and feeling perplexed. Was this guy a good friend of Jamie's and upset on his behalf? It was an explanation of sorts but Ness wasn't buying it. She'd only met her cousin once but he didn't strike her as the kind who'd socialise with fishermen. He'd only just about managed to lower himself sufficiently to speak to the local solicitor.

The sun was still high in the sky and although it was late afternoon Ness grew hot as she trudged up the steep route to the castle. The worn path circled the lower keep and then passed through a ruined gateway, threading across a massive expanse of grass where today people were picnicking and enjoying the sunshine or seated at the café tables tucking into cream teas. It was a stunning spot, Ness decided, and maybe they could do something here? A concert? Or a play? Or glamping?

She laughed. Lord, she'd not even been on the island twenty-four hours and already she was thinking of ways to raise funds! Maybe she should settle in first and get a feel for the place before she started making plans? On the other hand, she'd seen the bleak accounts and the concerned expression on David Brown's face, and she knew that she wouldn't have the luxury of waiting to see how everything panned out. Things were probably going to get bumpy. She was bound to ruffle feathers, tread on toes and generally mix lots more metaphors, but if Pirran Island was to escape the developers then Ness would have to act soon.

Ignoring the impressive castle door that didn't open, Ness made her way around the building to another, more modest entrance. Inside, all was dark and cool; for a moment she stood motionless while her eyes adjusted. The longcase clock tick-tucked from the shadows and somewhere a melody was being played on a piano, the haunting notes drifting through the empty hallway like a sigh. Following the music, Ness found herself crossing the Small Hall, where the steady gazes of the portraits seemed to monitor her, and walking into a dark passageway that led deep into the castle. Just as before, she felt as though she was wandering into an intricate labyrinth – and yet the notes drew her deeper until she pushed open a door and stepped into a beautiful room filled with sunshine. A grand piano stood in the centre of a polished floor, like a stately galleon afloat on an oaken sea, and curved shelves lined the walls, weighed down with piles of yellowing sheet music and instruments. Seated on the piano stool, his legs not even long enough to reach the pedals, was a little blond boy whose fingers were flying over the keys. The concentration on his face was matched only by that on Lucy's as she turned the pages. Ness felt herself sink into the magic of the melody as it rose and fell like the tide, then soared and swept in perfect unison with the seabirds outside. It was only when the final notes died away that she realised she'd been holding her breath and that tears were in her eyes.

Lucy looked at Ness and smiled. It was the first smile Ness had seen for a while and the relief of seeing a friendly face was immense.

"Did you like it?"

"Like it?" Ness shook her head. "I loved it. That was beautiful. It matches this place, if that makes sense?"

Her cousin looked pleased. "I'm glad you think so. That was Spring Tide, the first movement of the Island Suite. Uncle Armand wrote it in this very room and at this piano."

"Wow." Ness was overcome by a sudden sense of legacy and her heart lurched. Was she up to the task of guarding it? There was so much more at stake here than bricks and mortar. "I think I've heard it before."

"I expect you have," Lucy agreed. "It's his best-known piece and it's been used in quite a few adverts – luckily for me, since I've inherited the rights! He was still enjoying the success of this when he began his symphony. Or so I've been told. Of course, he never finished the symphony, if it even existed."

She collected up the music and gently shut the piano lid, while the little boy swivelled on the stool and swung his feet.

"Why wasn't it finished?" Ness asked, struck that – just like her father – Armand had squandered a huge talent.

"Nobody really knows," Lucy replied sadly. "I asked him, of course, but he never told me. I don't think he ever told anyone. It's such a shame because he was poised for great things and the music world was waiting to see what came next. He's often been described as the greatest lost talent of the twentieth century."

"But if he started it then it must be somewhere," Ness said.

"If he started it. Big if, but yes I suppose so. And what a find it would have been! But I can promise you, Ness, there's nothing left behind. I cleared his rooms and it would break your heart to see how few possessions he actually had."

"My father was exactly the same." There was a lump in Ness's throat. When she'd discovered that the evidence of Addy's existence amounted to little more than a couple of rucksacks full of empty tobacco pouches, tee shirts and jeans as well as the crumpled heap of his beloved motorbike, it really had broken her heart. It wasn't a lot to show for the vibrant, infuriating, charismatic man she'd loved so much.

"Well, there you go. Must be a family thing. I can't say I own much myself," Lucy remarked. Then she pulled a wry face. "Jamie tries to make up for it though!"

Ness had only met Jamie once but she could see Lucy was right. The way his eyes had lit up when he'd inherited the Steinway said it all. Ness, who'd lived a nomadic life with Addy and had never truly had a home to call her own, found his avarice repellent.

"Until I inherited this place I didn't have a lot either," she told Lucy. "You're right. It must be a Penwellyn thing."

Saying this gave Ness a glow she'd not experienced before. This was what it was to have family then? Shared traits and history linked her to her cousins, and slowly but surely being here would uncover even more of her past. Her roots were here.

"That was brilliant!" exclaimed the little boy, still swivelling on the stool. His freckled face beamed at Lucy. "Can I come again, please?"

"You can come as much as you like, Josh," said Lucy, with a wink at Ness, "at least while we still have the piano, anyway."

"Cool!" The child slipped off the stool. "I'm going to find Merryn now. Dad said I could go back with him. He'll be at the quay."

"We'll come with you," said Lucy. "I expect he'd like to meet Ness."

"Merryn lives at Grace Note Bay," Lucy reminded her as the three of them made their way back through the castle and across the courtyard. "He's our handyman and water taxi. He's great fun and I can't imagine life without him."

By now they were walking under the gate and out past the ruined tower. The grassy slopes below the crumbling walls were dotted with picnic tables and the last few customers were still enjoying tea and cakes. The tide was high now and boats were busy in the bay or mooring up. Among them was the little blue vessel she'd come over on; stroppy Brad Pitt was sitting on the bow fiddling with a rope, while a girl with pink braids helped trippers in.

Lucy waved delightedly at Brad. "There he is! Hey! Merryn! Wait up! There's one more here!"

As Josh sprinted across the grass and towards the quay, Ness's heart plummeted. So this was the guy her uncle had wanted to stay on the island? The one who'd looked as though he wanted to throw her overboard. Just her luck.

Lucy turned to Ness. "Come and say hi. I'll introduce you."

Ness hesitated. The girl with pink braids had also glared at her earlier on, as had the elderly gardener and the old woman sitting at the stern. They'd all been in the tea room when Lucy had given her the tour, and their welcome couldn't have been colder if the freezer door had been left wide open.

"Ness? What is it?" pressed Lucy.

She took a deep breath. "This probably sounds silly, and you're bound to tell me it's all in my imagination, but I get the distinct feeling that your friend Merryn isn't very pleased I'm here. I have no idea what his problem is either, since I've never even met him before. And the girl with the pink plaits – Fern, was it? She was really off when you introduced us earlier. Are they good friends with Jamie? Is that what it is?"

Lucy laughed. "Oh Lord! Hardly!" Then, seeing that Ness was still frowning, she sighed. "Look, I'm not really sure if I should say this, and it's probably none of my business, but this is a small town and people talk, you know? In a place like this, everyone knows everyone."

Ness understood. Having lived on a tiny Caribbean island for a while, she knew exactly how gossip spread in a small community.

"So you're telling me I'm not imagining it then? I really am public enemy number one?" She raised her eyes to the blue sky. She'd only been here two minutes and already she'd upset the town? Seriously? "Go on then. What have I done? Sold the island to Disney?"

"Close," said Lucy, and now her blue eyes were narrowed. "How about Max Reynard?"

Hearing that name was like a jolt to Ness's system. She saw again those compelling grey eyes and felt the insistent pressure of his mouth on hers. That kiss had been haunting her, and remembering it now made her pulse race.

"You know Max?" Ness asked.

"Everyone knows him. The question is, how do you know him?"

Ness wasn't sure how to answer this. I met him in a bar and almost slept with him didn't sound great and, although she might be misjudging her cousin here, Lucy didn't exactly look like the type who picked men up for wild nights of sex.

In any case, her answer didn't matter because Lucy then added, "You were seen on the beach, Ness, so there's no point denying you know him. It's obvious you're more than friends."

The town spies had been out in force then. Val from the hotel probably.

"I'm not going to deny it," Ness said. "I met him in the bar, we had a drink and then we went for a walk. I'm a big girl; I can do that. And before you ask, yes I was kissing him. Did I sleep with him? No."

Lucy turned scarlet. "I wasn't going to ask that. I wondered if he was a friend."

Ness shrugged. "He was friendly, he's attractive and it was fun, but he got called away and I haven't heard from him since – and probably never will."

"You really don't know him?"

What was this? "I really don't," Ness replied. "Not that I need to justify myself to anyone."

Her cousin seemed to turn even redder, which a moment earlier Ness would have thought impossible. "I know. Sorry. It's just... just... well, we thought..."

"What?"

Lucy looked miserable. "We thought you knew him and that you were planning something together." She swallowed. "The thing is, Max Reynard isn't a holidaymaker. He's a property developer and one of the biggest in the country. He owns Reynards. You must have heard of them?"

Max was a property developer? A horrible cold feeling started to spread from her core right to the tips of her fingers and toes as a nasty suspicion took root.

Lucy pushed her hair behind her ears. "He's got a few properties in the town – second homes mostly, and all far too expensive for locals. He's been wanting to buy the island for months and I know he was talking to Jamie about it. When he was seen with you yesterday, we all thought..." Her voice tailed off. "Well, you can probably guess."

"You thought I was planning to sell the island to him," Ness answered. She could tell from Lucy's face that this was exactly what her cousin had thought. Now she understood why Merryn and Fern and just about everyone else had been so frosty.

Lucy bit her lip. "I'm so sorry if we've jumped to conclusions."

Ness could see how this must have looked. Almost as bad as it felt to realise that the gorgeous man who'd had you melting in his arms had been playing you for a fool. Max Reynard must have seen her coming, waited for her and then picked his moment. It wasn't Ness he wanted: it was the castle. How stupid she'd been. He must have been laughing because she'd made it so easy for him, hadn't she? Thank goodness Val had interrupted them, otherwise Ness knew for sure that she'd have ended up feeling even more foolish.

Max had been using her. He was nothing but a cynical manipulator and she was an idiot. That kiss had meant nothing to him.

It had meant nothing to her either, Ness reminded herself sharply. It was just a bit of moonlit fun. She would put it out of her mind now for good. It would never happen again.

But as for Max Reynard? There was no way Ness was letting him get his hands on her castle. She wasn't sure whether she had a drawbridge or whether the village shop stocked boiling oil, but as far as she was concerned she was digging in for the long haul.

Max Reynard had better watch out. This was war.

Chapter 13

Pirran Island ran on its own timescale. Minutes seeped into hours, slipping into days and flowing into weeks. The tides turned, water dimpled the wet sand, clouds raced by and each day stretched out just a little longer than the one before. As one week melted into a fortnight and then another, the castle's labyrinthine passageways became more familiar to Ness, until she no longer felt tempted to scatter a trail of crumbs behind her like Hansel and Gretel.

Just as the castle was becoming ever more familiar, so too was the island; before long Ness had explored every inch. From the charged stillness of the ruined chapel to the ferocious rocky teeth of the Devil's Mouth beyond Grace Note Bay, her new home felt less strange every day. It was comforting to think of her father growing up here. Ness liked to picture him as a small boy scrambling over the rocks to catch darting fish, or rolling down the grassy banks of the motte and chasing his brothers through the long passageways. Now she could understand the rawness of his painting; the savage skies and wild waters that seethed from every brushstroke made perfect sense.

Her mother had also lived here for a while and died here. Ness had tried to find out more about Beth Penwellyn, but the details were hazy. Even local historian Annie Luckett, who was a little less frosty now that she'd realised Ness wasn't in cahoots with Max Reynard, wasn't able to tell Ness more than she already knew. It seemed that all the people who'd lived and worked on Pirran

Island in that era were now long gone, taking the truth of that dark stormy night with them. Coming to Cornwall hadn't revealed anything new: all Ness had to work with were the same bare facts she'd arrived with. A young and beautiful violinist, Beth had originally come here to work on the Island Suite with Armand. She'd subsequently married Addy and then drowned several years later. None of these facts explained anything.

I can't leave it at that, Ness told herself for what had to be the thousandth time. How had her mother drowned? Why had Addy fled from his home? Why had the three brothers fallen out? And why, a question that troubled Ness greatly, had Armand Penwellyn really left her the bulk of his estate? If he'd wanted to protect the island from Jamie, surely he could have left it to a wildlife charity or maybe the National Trust? Something deep down inside told Ness that there was more to this. The difficulty was how to prove it now that all three brothers were gone.

"Stop being such a misery!" she told herself sternly. None of these questions were new, after all. It was just that being here was bringing everything into sharper focus.

Besides, it was hard to be melancholy when the sun was out and the world outside seemed all newly scrubbed and shiny. Lucy had helped settle Ness into one of the spare bedrooms, and Ness didn't think she'd ever slept as well as she now did in this circular chamber with its thick walls and latticed windows. Here she could watch the sun rise from one side and set from the other, while at night the stars shone more brightly in the velvet-black sky than anywhere else she could recall.

"We've not used this room for years," Lucy had told Ness apologetically when she'd helped her move in (which hadn't been the most onerous of tasks, given that Ness only possessed one rucksack). "Uncle Armand kept it shut up, which I think's a real shame because it's such a pretty room, isn't it? Before he died he suggested you might like it."

Ness had been in perfect agreement; it was a beautiful room, simple and uncluttered and yet full of peace and warmth. During the daytime it was flooded with sunshine, and its views stretched out to sea. The room contained a large four-poster bed, a tallboy and a huge carved chest. The flagstone floor was covered by a threadbare rug, its rose design faded now, and sun-bleached pink drapes hung from heavy curtain poles. Set beneath the furthest window – the one that looked across the bay and back to the town – was a big saggy armchair with fat cushions, next to a bookshelf crammed with yellow-paged paperbacks. Ness could imagine curling up in the chair and reading, or maybe to watch the shifting view.

"I've dusted and aired it," Lucy had continued, not waiting for Ness to answer, "and all the bedding's clean. The tallboy's empty for your clothes to go in, but I'm afraid I haven't had a moment to sort out the books or see what's in the chest. There must be a key for it somewhere but heaven knows what's happened to it."

Ness had laughed and placed her bag on the bed. "Everything I own is in this rucksack, so I think it'll easily fit in the tallboy. We can sort the chest out later."

"We'll have to break the lock if we can't find the key," Lucy had sighed. "I can't find it anywhere."

"That seems a shame," Ness said. The lock was beautiful: brass and ornate. "Don't rush on my account. I've not got a lot anyway."

"It might turn up. I'm still sorting through Uncle Armand's belongings. I even found his diary. He'd thought ahead and ripped most of the pages out," Lucy had said sadly.

"Was this his wife's room?" Ness had asked, glancing around. "It certainly feels feminine in here."

"Uncle Armand never married," was Lucy's reply. "I don't know much about this room, only that it's not been used for a long time. He lived here on his own for years, until I moved in to help."

Now, as she ran down the spiral stairs that led to the Small Hall, Ness thought that she really must have a hunt for that key. It hadn't taken long before she'd realised that if she carried on wearing her Caribbean wardrobe she'd freeze. Accordingly, she'd driven into Truro with Lucy to stock up on warm clothes. Although the Cornish weather had been beautiful since she'd been here, it was still chilly and the castle was far colder inside than out. If it was a choice between her tan and catching pneumonia, then Ness was resigned to swaddling herself in jumpers and jeans and swapping her glittery flip-flops for boots. She now had more clothes than the tallboy could cope with and the chest would be very handy. At the moment she was heaping her clothes on it, but they'd be much tidier inside.

"Hello, Ness!" called Josh, when she reached the foot of the steps. Sitting on one of the benches flanking the refectory table, he was working his way through a doorstep of toast and scribbling notes across a buttery-yellow manuscript.

"You're keen," Ness said, looking at her watch and seeing that it wasn't even nine. Goodness, he must have been up early and walked across the minute the tide had started creeping out.

Josh shrugged. "It's teacher training day and Dad's at work. 'Sides, I like it here. I'm doing a music puzzle. Lucy's been teaching me. They're well cool. I'm teaching her to use her iPhone. She's rubbish."

In the weeks since Ness had arrived, Josh too had become something of a fixture at the castle. Most afternoons found him in the music room playing the piano or accompanying Lucy on his violin. Weekends would see him eating cake in the tea room, sitting in the kitchen chatting to Fern or helping Merryn with the boat. His father must work dreadful hours for the evil Max, Ness thought. At this her heart hardened all the more. She hadn't seen anything of him since their kiss (not that she was thinking of that, of course), but when she did eventually bump into Max Reynard he'd better watch out. As the time had gone by her anger had been growing, not dissipating.

"Annie's made toast and scrambled eggs," Josh told Ness through a mouthful. "She said to have some before Merryn scoffs it all."

In St Antonia Ness had barely eaten breakfast and had watched her diet carefully – you had to if you spent ninety percent of your time in a bikini – but here she was eating non-stop. It didn't help that Lucy was a great cook or that Annie had a habit of turning leftovers into delicious meals. Most evenings they all sat around the table in the kitchen and tucked into whatever had been thrown together that day in the tea room.

They were an odd mix, Ness thought, but there was comfort in knowing there was always somebody around. Growing up with Addy had meant she'd never had a family, so Ness was enjoying feeling part of something now. It had taken a while before Merryn and Fern had stopped looking at her suspiciously – and Annie had certainly taken longer to thaw out – but after several weeks had gone by without Ness flogging the island to Reynards, they'd come round. Her unwitting association with Max had been exceedingly unfortunate and was yet another big blot in his rapidly filling copybook.

Although she'd told each person in turn that she had no intention of selling the island (she'd even taken the trouble to speak to old Fred, who hadn't heard a word anyway), Ness was become increasingly aware that very soon she was going to have to take some action regarding their finances. Quite what form this should take, she wasn't certain. Maybe she would call a council of war and see if the friends of the island could brainstorm some ideas together. Without the income from Armand's portfolio, things were looking bleak – and Lucy's royalties wouldn't arrive until the autumn.

Ness continued on her way to the castle's kitchen, which adjoined the Small Hall. The kitchen was generally the place where everyone congregated. It was a long room with an enormous open fireplace at the furthest end, its chimney still blackened with the soot of centuries. It also contained a very battered oak table, plus an ancient Aga that pumped out warmth. It was to the latter that Ness headed now, to warm her chilly fingers on the rail.

Merryn was seated at the table, his socked feet propped up alongside the marmalade as he cradled a mug of tea in his strong brown hands and chatted to Annie. Seeing Ness, he smiled. Now that the warmth reached those blue eyes she was reminded of the inviting waters of the Caribbean. She thought of the slow pleasure of sinking into the gin-clear sea and letting the waves wash over her sunburned limbs, and then felt her cheeks heat up. He was even more attractive now that he wasn't shooting the stare of death at her. She hadn't seen that much of him since she'd arrived, but when they did bump into one another he'd been friendly enough.

"Have I got crumbs on my face?" Merryn asked, brushing cheeks that were dusted with golden stubble. "You seem to be staring at me, Miss Penwellyn."

Embarrassed to be caught gawping like some teenager with a crush, Ness felt her flush deepen. It was a curse of being red-haired, along with a hot temper and skin that took forever to tan.

"No crumbs, but you are running late – and take your feet off the table!" Annie scolded, reaching across and tapping his legs. "What manners!"

Merryn grinned at Ness. "She still thinks I'm a naughty boy in her classroom."

"That's because you are," the older woman said tartly.

His blue eyes held Ness's. "You'd better listen to Annie. It's true. I can be incredibly badly behaved."

His meaning was unmistakable. Flustered, Ness turned her attention to filling the kettle. She felt like plunging herself under the cold tap too, because a sudden throb of heat was coursing through her every cell. There was something wild about Merryn that was very appealing. Max Reynard had been all control and brooding sexuality, whereas the bronze-skinned, golden-haired skipper was pure energy and sunshine.

"Tea, anyone?" she asked. She was aware of how British she sounded; her American friends would be laughing if they could hear her now.

"I'll have another cup and I'll take one to Lucy in the tea room," said Annie, holding out her mug. "Merryn here is going to work. There's a broken toilet to attend to and Fred needs a hand fixing the ride-on before he can start mowing."

"Oh, the glamour," Merryn said ruefully. "It seems you'll have to learn all about my bad deeds and misbehaviour another time, Ness."

"I'll look forward to that," she said, and blushed even deeper when she saw the way his lips quirked upwards and his eyes darkened with promise. Lord, but he was a rogue. She'd really have to be careful, otherwise Merryn would think she wanted to jump his bones. Which she did, in an abstract way, because he was undeniably sex on a stick. Not that it mattered whether she fantasised about him; in reality, she knew that getting involved with him would make life even more complicated than it already was, which was saying something.

Once Merryn had departed, munching toast with those strong white teeth and laughing, Ness made tea and joined Annie, who gave her an arch look.

"Careful," she said.

"I can look after myself," Ness assured her.

"It isn't you I'm worried about," Annie replied. "But none of my business anyway. Now," she continued, her voice shooting up several decibels in true teacher style when Ness looked poised to protest, "after our chat the other day I've been doing some research and it seems that there is still one person in the town who was working on the island when your parents lived here – and she might know a little more than me."

"Really?" Ness was thrilled. Anything that would help her to know more about Beth Penwellyn would be a bonus.

Annie nodded. "Merryn's grandmother, Rose. I'd forgotten all about it but she was working in the kitchen back then. Your uncle used to throw the most amazing parties. He really was something of a celebrity, you know. The Island Suite was so popular and everyone touted him as being the next Vaughan Williams. Rose is an interesting character but she's notoriously difficult to deal with. If she does know any more than I do, then she'll have kept it to herself for a long time."

"Do you think she might know more?" Ness asked.

Annie looked thoughtful. "Maybe. I'll agree with you that it all feels a little odd and unfinished. Now, it might just be the historian in me, or maybe I'm a nosy old boot, but yes, I think she might know something. Armand certainly looked after her, and of course Merryn lives here too and has done for ages. Your uncle was a strange man but he was steadfast too. Once he made his mind up about something or someone, that was it."

"Like not speaking to his brothers?" Ness could see this was the case. "Or leaving most of his estate to a niece he'd never met?" And locking up rooms, abandoning his music and leaving odd bequests? The more she thought about it, strange didn't come close to describing her uncle.

"Just so," the older woman agreed. Then she sighed. "Ness, I can't pretend that I knew what was going on in Armand's mind. Lucy was probably the closest to him out of anyone and even she's in the dark. It might be an idea to have a chat with Rose but I must warn you, she's very spiky and totally devoted to Merryn. Anyone who upsets him won't want to come across her in a hurry – and she certainly wouldn't want to help them."

The warning couldn't have been clearer. If Ness broke Merryn's heart his granny would have something to say about it and anything she did know about the past would remain a secret. It was all a bit ironic really, since from what Ness had gleaned about Merryn Hellier, he was the Don Juan of St Pirran. She was sure his heart was very safe.

Leaving Ness to ponder on all this, Annie rose and began to stack the dishwasher. Ness's temples started to throb. This was all becoming so complicated. What was it that David Brown had warned her when she first met him? That her inheritance could prove to be a poisoned chalice? Untangling secrets was the least of it. She needed to find some money as well, and fast. She'd never known an electricity bill could have so many noughts on it – and this was in the summer too. What would happen when the winter arrived didn't bear thinking about.

Before she could even get started on the horror that was the council tax, Ness's thoughts were interrupted by the sudden appearance of Josh. White-faced and wide-eyed he stood in the doorway, panting.

"You've got to come at once! Come on!"

Ness was out of her chair and at his side in a heartbeat. "Josh! What's happened? Are you all right?"

"They're here! The men! You've got to stop them!" He was speaking wildly, the words so choked that he was almost incoherent. "They say they're taking it away! Come on, Ness! Stop them."

He tugged her hand, trying to pull Ness after him. "Hurry up! They're taking the piano! You've got to stop them! They can't take your piano!"

Annie's hand flew to her chest. "Jamie must have sold it. I thought he'd gone quiet."

Jamie Penwellyn had certainly been lying low. Since storming out after the will reading he'd not been in touch with Lucy and was yet to reappear at the castle. Although Ness was relieved not to have been confronted with his antipathy, she'd known it was only a matter of time. He'd probably been holed up somewhere, plotting her downfall.

That and selling the Steinway.

"It's not my piano, Josh," she told the little boy as gently as she could. "It was left to Lucy's brother and he can do whatever he likes with it."

"But it belongs here!" Josh wailed. "The Island Suite was composed on it! He can't take it! He can't!"

He began to cry, huge gasping sobs that shook his body.

Ness turned to Annie helplessly. "I can't do anything about this, can I?"

"Of course you can't," Annie said. "Now listen, young man, you're going to have to be very brave about this. Lucy's going to find saying goodbye to that piano even harder than you, so we need to look after her, don't we?"

Josh gulped and wiped his hand across his eyes. "I 'spose."

"Good boy." Annie patted him on the shoulder. "I think Lucy needs to know what's happening so that she can say goodbye to the piano. Would you be able to go and fetch her from the tea room? It's very important you look after her now. She's going to need you."

He sniffed. "OK, Miss Luckett."

Once he was out of earshot Annie's mouth set in a bitter line. "I hope Jamie enjoys his one hundred thousand pounds, or whatever it is he's sold it for."

Ness thought that she would have enjoyed it too. A hundred thousand would go a long way towards paying the bills and making a start on some urgent repairs. Then she gave herself a sharp telling-off. After all, that piano belonged here. It was as much a part of the castle as the thick walls and arrow-slit windows. Musical history had been made in this place with that piano's ivory keys and delicate wire intestines; it belonged in the middle of the sun-filled music room where it could be played, silver streams of notes cascading into the air, rather than sitting with its lid shut and its frame covered, in some millionaire's drawing room. Jamie was wrong to sell it, and she would be making sure that whatever other items were integral to the castle's character remained here. There were other ways to find the money she needed rather than selling off the few pieces they still possessed. She'd think of something.

The music room looked odd once the piano had been removed. Swaddled in layers of protective material it looked as though it had been bound and gagged as it was wheeled away. The space the Steinway had filled now yawned raw and empty; all that remained were the scars on the wooden floor where it had once stood. Suddenly the drapes looked tatty and dusty, the rugs seemed more worn than ever, and the shelves appeared thick with grime and yellowing, as though the spell the piano had cast over the room for decades had suddenly been broken. Even the strings on the harp seemed slack, while outside the sun had slid away and turned the sea to pewter.

"I don't think I can bear to watch them try and load it into a van," Lucy said. Her voice was tight with unshed tears. "What will it do to the piano to be bumped over the causeway?"

"It came here that way," Annie pointed out briskly. "It will survive."

Lucy inclined her head and put her hand on Josh's shoulder. "I know it sounds ridiculous but it feels like I've just said goodbye to a dear friend I know I'll never see again."

Ness had a lump in her throat – and she'd only lived here for a short time and didn't have a musical bone in her body. How on earth must Lucy feel?

"Why ever did our uncle let Jamie choose?" she wondered out loud. "He must have known he'd pick that piano."

"It was stupid," Josh muttered angrily, scuffing the toe of his trainers on the floor and leaving ugly rubber snakes on the wood. "Stupid, stupid, stupid."

Lucy shook her head. "Uncle Armand was far from stupid. He must have had his reasons, even if we can't work out what they were." She took a deep breath. "Anyway, he left me a lovely piano all of my own. It's the one I used to play to him in his bedroom when he was poorly, so it too has its own special place here. I'll ask Merryn and Fred to move it into the Small Hall. Then we can all enjoy playing it."

"Not me," said Ness. "Chopsticks is my limit! But I'll enjoy listening to you guys."

"It's not the same," Josh responded bitterly.

"No," was Lucy's gentle reply, "but sometimes things change, Josh, and then they're different. It's how we handle those changes that counts. Come on, let's go and have a play on my piano. You can tell me what you think."

Ness watched them go. She was impressed by Lucy. Her cousin might appear gentle and meek but there was a quiet strength underneath – the same edge of steel that she too possessed, and which was right now hardening her heart even further against Jamie Penwellyn.

He could keep his piano and his money. He might think he'd won, and he might be lurking in the shadows gloating and waiting for her to admit defeat, but he was in for a very long wait because Ness had made up her mind. She was going to find a way to save the castle.

Chapter 14

"Stop mooning around, for heaven's sake. It's getting depressing. Go and do something fun. Hang out with Ness for a bit. She could do with a break."

Merryn, on the deck of Guardian Angel, looked up to the quayside. Shading his eyes against the sun's glare he saw a pair of slim brown legs poking out from a swirling scarlet skirt and dangling merrily over the vertiginous drop. Toes tipped with acid-green varnish swung in a lime blur, and a host of ankle bracelets jangled in perfect rhythm.

"Don't give me that look," said Fern. "You know exactly what I'm talking about."

"I'm not sure I do," Merryn said. He leaned against the wheelhouse door and enjoyed the warmth of the sun on his face – well, that and the fact that the brightness meant he couldn't see Fern's knowing expression.

She snorted. "I know you way too well, Merryn Hellier. I heard you turned Cally Davey down too. You fancy Ness, don't you?"

Merryn rolled his eyes. Having lived here all his life he really shouldn't be surprised when the local gossip machine swung into action – but this was fast even for St Pirran. Cally Davey, with her sloe-black eyes, bee-stung pout and long brown hair, was certainly tempting. Usually Merryn wouldn't have thought twice about getting together with someone like Cally, but when she'd joined him in The Castle Inn and suggested they went back to hers after last orders, his heart hadn't been in it.

"Since when did my not going home with Cally have to mean anything?"

"Err, since you had a pulse?" said Fern. With a rattle of bells and a swirl of her skirt, which she swiftly tucked up between her legs and into her waistband like a pirate costume, she descended the broken ladder and joined him on the deck.

Merryn sighed, knowing that he was about to get one of Fern's interrogations. Quite what his answers would be he wasn't sure; after all, Fern had a good point. He liked Cally well enough: she was fun to be around and they'd enjoyed a few nights out together. Yesterday evening, though, he hadn't felt tempted in the least and had gently but firmly made it clear that he would be heading back to the island – alone. Cally hadn't seemed offended and had turned her attention to one of the young fishermen instead, leaving Merryn to walk back across the causeway with only the distant waves and the moonlight for company.

"That's rather sexist, isn't it?" he remarked mildly.

Fern, on the deck and rearranging her skirt, just grinned. "Like I say, I know you. Something must be the matter with you if you turned Cally down."

"Maybe I wanted to be alone?"

Her lips quirked. "You had a Garbo moment? Yeah, right. Come on, Merry! This is me you're talking to! I've noticed how much time you've spent with Ness lately."

"We've all spent time with her, showing her around," Merryn pointed out. "Ness owns the island now, remember? We're only able to stay here on her say-so. You've shown her the garden and taken her into town. Lucy has too. Why should it be any different for me?"

"Err, because you're a bloke?" Fern said. "And she's gorgeous?"

Merryn couldn't deny either of these claims. He was most definitely a bloke and Ness was undoubtedly gorgeous too. That fiery Penwellyn hair and those big green eyes set in a heart-shaped face were quite a striking combination, even before taking into account her slim but curvaceous body. She was the sort of girl any man would look at twice and come back to for a third glance. There had been many women in Merryn's life. He loved women – enjoyed their company, their beauty and their moods – but none had ever held his attention long enough to weave her way into his heart. And that was just the way he'd liked it. The only constant woman in his life was Fern and she clearly wanted nothing more than friendship. Whenever he tentatively asked about her past she shied away and she never seemed bothered when he spent time with other girls. Now she was teasing him about Ness. Fern was complicated and she fascinated Merryn. He couldn't work her out no matter how hard he tried or how much he wanted to. She wasn't interested in him, that was clear. Why else would she try and push him and Ness together?

Fern had a point. He did like Ness. After an awkward start, when they'd all thought she was plotting with Max Reynard, the island's new owner had made a good impression on Merryn – and not just because she was attractive and tended to dress as though she was still in the Caribbean rather than Cornwall. He admired her decision to quietly and respectfully learn about the place, instead of throwing her weight around as they'd all feared she might. It would have been easy for the newcomer to have made Lucy feel uncomfortable; knowing the gentle Lucy as well as he did, Merryn had been quite worried about that. However, Ness had soon made it clear that Pirran Island was Lucy's home just as much now as it had always been, and that the same was true for all the other people who resided there. Merryn had given Ness a brief boat tour around the island and the bay, pointing out the places where the seals liked to bask and where the puffins nested, but Lucy had been present too and they'd had little time alone. Now and then Ness had caught a ride across to the town in Guardian Angel or passed him when walking along the causeway, but Merryn always sensed a hesitancy in her and blamed himself for having been so antagonistic when she'd first arrived. He'd like to make it up to her.

"I thought you didn't trust her?" he said to Fern.

She raised one skinny shoulder. "You know me. I don't trust anyone."

This was certainly true. Fern had lived here for almost a year but Merryn didn't know anything more about her now than he had done on the day he'd first met her. She was well-spoken and in their conversations revealed an education that surpassed anything he'd received from St Pirran Comp, despite Annie's best efforts. The bruises she'd arrived with had certainly told a tale, but apart from these clues Merryn didn't know much more about Fern than her name – if indeed this even was her real name. She was a pretty girl and fun to be with, and Merryn had grown very fond of her. Several times he'd thought there might be something more between them but she always fluttered out of reach, leaving him wondering whether it was all in his imagination. He always felt she was holding something back and this made it impossible to feel closer to her. Armand had probably known far more, but Fern's story was yet another secret he'd taken to the grave – along with his missing symphony, as well as the real reason he'd stopped composing and the truth about how Beth Penwellyn had died.

This reminded Merryn that he really should visit his grandmother. Annie had asked him whether he thought his grandmother might know something about Beth, and Merryn had made a mental note to sound Rose out. She spoke little about the past but she'd worked on the island at one point, so she might be able to help. One thing Merryn did know for sure was that Rose Hellier was as sharp as a gutting knife; even now he never got away with anything. She would remember everything. Whether she chose to reveal it, however, was another matter entirely. He hoped he could find something out that would help Ness. If he could give her a piece of the jigsaw that might allow her to find out more about her parents, perhaps it would go some way towards making up for his frosty welcome.

"Why don't you show Ness the saltwater pool?" Fern suggested. "There are hardly any tourists today, the tide's turning and the tea shop's quiet. She's in the garden with Fred and could probably do with rescuing. It's a gorgeous day and she should be enjoying the island. The gardening will still be there tomorrow. You could do with chilling out too."

Fred, deaf as a post, liked to carry on conversations even if he couldn't actually hear them. They were a bit one-sided and he tended to shout so loudly that your ears rang for hours afterwards. Poor Ness could certainly do with a break from that.

Merryn exhaled. The sun was growing hotter and the faint sea mist was starting to burn off. It was going to be another beautiful Cornish day – one for skiving work, visiting secluded beaches, picking sand out of picnics and throwing crusts to beady-eyed gulls, before diving into cool green water and feeling the waves take the sting out of hot limbs. A day for living in the moment.

Fern was right: everything else could wait. It was time to introduce Ness Penwellyn to one of the island's best-kept secrets.

Ness placed the last of the strawberries in her basket and straightened up. Her back was aching from all the crouching down and her eardrums were throbbing from Fred's endless hollered chat as they'd worked their way around the neat rows of plants. On the plus side, she now knew an awful lot about what was planted and when. On the negative side, any questions she'd tried to ask about her parents had literally fallen on deaf ears.

"These are Elsanta strawberries," Fred bellowed as they carried their crammed baskets towards the tea room, where Annie was waiting for them. "Best taste and longest season."

Ness, who'd already sampled far more strawberries than she should have done, nodded. They were truly delicious. In St Antonia all fruit was imported from Miami and generally tasted of nothing, so these sweet berries had been a revelation. She'd probably have the mother of all stomach aches, but it would be worth it.

Maybe they could sell organic produce to raise funds for the island? She knew she was clutching at straws here, but there had to be a way they could make the castle and island financially viable. It was either that or give in and sell to Max Reynard – and there was no way Ness was going to do that. He'd underestimated her if he thought she was going to give up without a fight. His kisses had been good but not that good.

As she left the walled garden and stepped onto the path leading down to the tea room, Merryn Hellier was coming the other way. He was wearing a white tee shirt and faded cut-off Levi's that clung to his narrow hips and showed off his strong, tanned legs. His wild gold hair was held back from his brown face by a scarlet bandana. When he saw Ness he waved.

"I've come to make you play truant for a bit," he said, joining her and instantly taking the baskets of fruit from her and the elderly gardener. "Christ! These are heavy. Fred, you're a terrible slave driver."

"Onions and leeks," agreed Fred. "Not till the autumn though."

Merryn caught Ness's eye. His lips twitched. "You seriously deserve some time out. You do know that?"

Ness nodded. "I feel as though I've been in a strange parallel universe."

"Ah yes, Planet Fred. I know it well." Merryn pushed open the door of the tea room and held it for Ness. "Special delivery, Annie!"

The older woman looked up from scrubbing the counter. "Wonderful! I'll put some in a sponge cake and use the rest for jam. Just pop them down over there, love. I'll deal with them in a bit."

Merryn placed the strawberries on a table. "Can I pinch a couple of pasties and some drinks? I'm taking Ness down to Grace Note Bay for a swim and some lunch."

He was? This was news to Ness.

While Merryn selected two golden pasties and several bottles of pink lemonade, Annie chattered merrily about Josh's piano playing ("He really is talented. He only has to hear a tune once to remember it; I swear the child's a genius!") and the big surge in holiday bookings in the town. By the time Ness and Merryn headed back outside into the sunshine, Ness's ears were ringing even more. She found that she was looking forward to the idea of a swim, her first since arriving in Cornwall, even if the water was going to be a great deal colder than the Caribbean Sea she was used to.

"Do you need to pick up any swimming gear?" Merryn asked, his freckled face crinkling into a cheeky grin as he added, "Unless you fancy skinny-dipping, of course?"

There was something in his eyes that made Ness's heart beat faster and her cheeks grow warmer. Merryn's skin was sun-kissed and his body muscular; all of a sudden Ness could picture him in the water, curls like springs and with rivulets running over the sculpted pecs and strong arms.

God. She hoped the sea was really cold or else she'd be in trouble here...

"I've got my bikini on under my shorts and vest," she said. "It's a Caribbean habit – you practically live in your bikini out there."

"I like the sound of the Caribbean," he grinned.

It would certainly suit him, Ness thought as they skirted the castle and set off to the small bay where Merryn's caravan stood sentinel over the marching waves. He was made for St Antonia and she could picture him running a dive boat or drinking mudslides in tiki bars as his skin turned the colour of smooth butterscotch. Mel would go crazy for him. All the girls would.

But was Ness prepared to go crazy for him? She wasn't sure. Why did she keep thinking of eyes as grey as a wintery sea and recalling that slow sardonic smile?

She needed help if she was still thinking of Max Reynard.

Grace Note Bay was tucked away on the far side of the island. Although Ness had walked this way several times, it had always been at high tide; until now she'd never seen the pale sliver of sand or the ridge of darker rocks rising out of it. She followed Merryn along the narrow path, which zigzagged down past the plateau where his caravan was pitched, and onto the beach. As her sandals slithered she skidded a little, and he reached out and steadied her by resting one strong hand lightly upon her waist. Once they reached the sand, though, he dropped it away and she was strangely bereft. There had been something so solid and safe about his touch. She hadn't realised just how alone she'd felt before.

Unaware of her thoughts, Merryn gestured at the sweep of sand and sky. "Here it is: Grace Note Bay. I think your uncle named the place."

"It's beautiful," said Ness. Then she frowned. "What does it mean, a grace note?"

"No idea! That's one for Lucy to answer, or maybe our new child genius? Anyway, the best is still to come."

He placed the bag of food onto a rock and kicked off his deck shoes. Minutes later the white tee shirt was tugged over his head and he was bare-chested and golden. He waited for Ness to follow suit.

She gulped, partly because his muscular body was powerful and partly because she was suddenly nervous. Telling herself off for being ridiculous – after all, back in St Antonia she lived in a bikini, and Merryn was just a friend in any case – Ness stepped out of her shorts and removed her vest top. The sun might have been warm but goose bumps dusted her skin when she saw desire flicker in those blue eyes. It felt as though she was on the edge of a precipice. The question was, did she want to topple over?

Merryn held out his hand. "Are you ready?"

"Ready? Ready for what?"

"For this!"

And then he was tearing down the beach and tugging Ness after him, laughing at her shrieks when they splashed through puddles on their way to the tide's edge. He was going to pull her in and the water was bitterly cold.

"Stop! Stop!" she gasped, but Merryn was still laughing and shaking his head.

"You're not in the Caribbean now! This is how we do things in Cornwall – although I must admit we usually have wetsuits."

They had reached a band of rocks that were sticking up from the sand like a crown. Releasing Ness's hand, Merryn climbed upwards and called for her to follow. Limpets and barnacles and green weed made the surface treacherous, but Ness had never been one to shrink back from a challenge. She gritted her teeth and launched herself after him, wincing at the roughness of the shells against her bare feet. Merryn reached down and caught her hands, pulling her up until she was standing beside him and looking down into an enormous rock pool.

"Oh!" Ness exclaimed in astonishment.

"Do you like it?"

There was something very touching about his hopeful question and Ness was struck again by just how magical the island was to so many people.

"It's amazing," she answered. It was too – and there was no way Ness would have known this pool was here unless Merryn had shown her. At high tide it would be hidden by rolling waves, and even when the waters receded it was out of the general eye line. It was yet another of Pirran Island's secrets. How many more remained to be uncovered?

"I'm so glad you like it, Ness. It's such a special place – such a special island."

"I know," she said softly. "I see that, I do, and I promise that I'll do whatever I can to keep it safe."

In answer he slipped his fingers from hers and dived into the water in one fluid arc, then struck out across the pool.

"Come on!" he called as soon as he was at the farthest side. "If you're brave enough, that is?"

Ness didn't need asking twice. The sun was high and hot, the pool deep and inviting. She leapt in, rising to the surface with a splutter.

"It's freezing!"

"Don't be so soft," Merryn teased while Ness rubbed at her arms and shivered. "The sun's been on this since the tide turned. It's positively tropical."

Ness would have disputed this if the shock of the temperature hadn't robbed her of all coherent speech.

"Anyway, you'll go numb soon," he added soothingly.

He wasn't wrong. Either her limbs had lost all sensation or she'd adjusted to the chilly English sea, but before long the shock of the temperature had worn off and the water felt pleasantly refreshing. Mel would have had a fit if she'd had to work in such conditions, Ness thought with a smile as she floated on her back and watched the clouds drift overhead.

They swam for a while, splashing one another and competing to see who could do the best dive. Eventually Ness realised that her teeth were chattering, so she pulled herself out to dry in the sunshine. The call of the gulls, the heat on her body and the fresh air made her sleepy and she drifted off with the sound of the waves. It was only when Merryn dripped water over her as he rummaged for their lunch that Ness opened her eyes.

"Hey, sleeping beauty, this is yours." Merryn held out a pasty.

Sitting up, Ness took the pasty and bit in hungrily, groaning with delight at the deliciousness of the steak and potato. The sharp air and exercise of her Cornish life were giving her such an appetite – and she didn't think anything had ever tasted as good as this pasty picnic washed down with pink lemonade.

"Tide's on the turn," Merryn remarked once they'd finished and all that was left were crumbs. "This will be underwater in an hour or so, like it doesn't even exist."

"I feel that way about lots of things here," Ness said.

"You're thinking about your parents?"

She nodded, her fingers picking at a limpet. Its shell was as unyielding as the secrets held here.

"There are too many gaps and no matter what I do I can't seem to find a way to fill them. Something happened here, Merryn, something that affected the brothers forever and ended up with my mother's death. It's all tied up with why Armand left me the island, but I just can't work out what. Oh!" In frustration she slammed her fist against the rock, grazing her knuckles and making her eyes smart. "I have to get to the bottom of it."

"I know," Merryn said. "I know."

Gently, he took her sore hand and raised it to his lips, brushing her skin with such tenderness that her breath caught in her throat.

"I'll do my best to help," he promised. "Even if I have to nag my granny for a month, I'll find out whatever I can. We'll figure it out."

His hand stroked her cheek and Ness knew it would be easy to pull him close and lose herself for an afternoon. She imagined that Merryn's kisses would be gentle, with none of the tight-leashed passion she'd sensed in Max Reynard and certainly none of the conflict that had followed. If Max was like the deep and mysterious depths of the pool, then the man with her right now was akin to its sparkling surface. She could have fun with Merryn and the idea was very tempting. Yet like all temptation it would come at a cost, and Ness wasn't sure that she wanted to pay that price. Merryn was a resident on the island and any involvement with him would complicate things. The balance between them all was already fragile.

She pulled away a fraction and the moment slipped out of her grasp.

"We should head back," she said.

Merryn nodded. "Maybe you're right. Annie sends out a search party if people are out of sight for too long. And if the tide's coming in I may find some passengers and earn a few pennies. What is it they say? Every little helps?"

Once she'd got dressed again – with the fabric of her shorts now sticking to her salty legs, and her vest clinging to her wet bikini top – Ness followed Merryn up the steep path from the beach and back to the castle. Already boats were setting off from the town, their white lines of wake lacing the sea. Any visitors stranded on the island would be milling about on the quay in hope of a ride back to the mainland. Ordinary life beckoned and already their charged moment on the beach was taking on an unreal quality. Ness was relieved that nothing between them had changed.

"I'll take the bottles back to the tea room," she told Merryn when they crested the hill and the path forked. "It's the least I can do. I had a lovely time."

"Me too, Ness."

Instinctively, she rose onto her tiptoes and kissed his cheek. The golden stubble rasped against her lips and fleetingly she wondered how it might have felt against her throat. She suspected that the answer was utterly delicious.

And she'd stepped away? Mel would think she'd flipped.

Actually, forget Mel. Ness was starting to think she'd flipped!

Laughing to herself, Ness pushed open the tea-room door, the smile freezing on her lips when she saw a man sitting at a table, sipping coffee and looking for all the world as though he had every right to be there.

Annie said huffily, "He insists you want to see him. He won't say why."

Ness couldn't speak. Just the sight of this visitor banished all thoughts of Merryn in an instant. Any fleeting attraction she'd felt towards Merryn was insignificant compared to the raw and dreadful fascination gripping her now. With shaking hands, she steadied herself against the counter and tried to slow her racing heart. Nothing could have prepared her for the shock of seeing this visitor.

"Hello, Ness," said Max Reynard.

Chapter 15

Max Reynard sat in a window seat, watching Ness and the blond fisherman as they made their way along the path. Interesting. So that was how the land lay, was it? It certainly hadn't taken the new owner of Pirran Island long to find herself a bit of local entertainment. His expression thoughtful, Max swirled his coffee. Just as well he hadn't been thinking that what they'd shared was something special.

His lips quirked upwards. With any luck Nessa Penwellyn's attachment to the island would prove just as fickle. In Max's experience women were generally easy enough to persuade when the price was right. Why should she be any different?

And here she was now, walking into the tea room with that glorious sunset hair in wild tangles, and a dusting of freckles across the bridge of her nose like cinnamon kisses from the Cornish sun. She was smiling to herself (probably something to do with the very wet vest top clinging to her curves, Max thought wryly) but her smile soon faded when that old boot, Annie Luckett, pointed him out.

"Hello, Ness," he said.

Her big green eyes widened. "What are you doing here?"

He gestured at the cup and saucer on his table. "Having coffee. Care to join me?"

There was a silence.

"The cake's good too," Max added. "It was worth a trip over for the Victoria sponge alone."

Ness snorted. "There are loads of coffee shops in St Pirran, and most of them sell cake too. Why come all the way here?"

"My boat needed a run?" he ventured, jerking his thumb in the direction of the pier where his speedboat was moored. This reason was true enough; for the huge amount it had cost him, the Sunseeker really did need to do something more than bob up and down in St Pirran's harbour. To be honest, Max winced whenever he looked at it. Foxy Lady was a stunning boat and a big floating advert for wealth and success, which was of course why he'd succumbed and purchased her. Slicing through the waves on that beauty, with champagne cooling in the chiller and bikini-clad girls sunning themselves on the deck, was supposed to say that a man had made it – although Max secretly suspected it actually said the man in question was a complete tosser. He didn't dare to think what his father would have made of such excess. Whenever Max was at Malcom's Place, the shelter set up in his father's memory, he felt queasy at the thought of what this one ridiculous boat would equate to in terms of beds and meals.

Nessa Penwellyn didn't seem impressed either. Hands on her hips, she glowered at him across the tea room. Oh dear, thought Max. He really was in the bad books.

"OK, you've caught me out. I'm actually here to see you," he confessed.

"Well, you've seen me, so you can go now."

"You might not be so keen to get rid of me once you've heard what I have to say," Max replied calmly.

"I doubt there's anything you've got to say that I'd want to hear. Besides, when it actually mattered you didn't seem nearly so eager to talk."

"Is this because I haven't called, honey?" he quipped. He was rewarded with a glare. "Sorry, that was a joke, and not a very funny one. But seriously, Ness, I think we've got off on the wrong foot. Can we start over?"

"Why on earth would I want to do that?"

This was going to be harder than Max had anticipated. Usually women didn't take long to be persuaded to his way of thinking. If speedboats didn't work, then self-deprecating humour normally did the trick – but unfortunately Ness was proving immune to that too. Her lips, which he knew to be extremely kissable, were now set in a tight line. Her chest, impossible to miss in the lime-green bikini top glowing through her wet white vest, was rising and falling in agitation. He was reminded of how soft and pliant she had felt in his arms, utterly feminine yet filled with fire too. Max felt himself stir at the memory.

And this was why you should never mix business with pleasure, he reminded himself sharply. In future he'd stick to pretty girls with brains like Swiss cheese. Life was simpler that way.

Simpler, but less interesting. Persuading Nessa Penwellyn to sell Pirran Island to him now was going to be quite a task, but if there was one thing Max Reynard loved it was a challenge. He'd never met one yet that he hadn't overcome, and there was no reason to think Ness would be any different. He just needed to take the right tack, that was all. The problem was that while she stood there in her skimpy cut-off shorts, with her wild red curls tumbling over her shoulders and the shape of those glorious breasts perfectly accentuated by the translucent fabric, Max didn't stand a hope of figuring out what that tack could possibly be. For once in his life, his razor-sharp mind couldn't function at all.

This was why he stayed away from women like Ness. Max's world of property development was cut-throat and fast moving; he needed his wits about him and every iota of concentration trained on the business. Distractions weren't an option at any time, even less so when the future of a flagship development depended on his being ahead of the game and finding a way to make the situation work for Reynards. Jamie might have proved to be of little use, but there was no way Max was giving up on this project now; he had way too much invested in it. Besides, defeat wasn't in his vocabulary. Already he could tell that his crew was getting antsy. The arrival of Ness and the lack of a sale had unsettled them, and even the ever-loyal Adam was starting to voice concerns. Max was more determined than ever to clinch the deal, which was why he'd decided to visit the castle in person and see Ness. She'd have her price. People always did. All he had to do was find out what it was...

Sensing his gaze, Ness crossed her arms over her wet torso and raised her chin.

"Are you going to tell me why you're here? Or are you just going to stare at my chest all day?"

Max gave her an unashamed grin. "Sounds like a great way to spend time, but I'm going to have to pass on that invitation."

"It wasn't an invitation!" Ness howled.

Interesting that she was so angry, Max thought. All he'd done was come and have a cup of coffee on the island; he was putting money into her coffers by giving her his custom. She should have been pleased about that. Instinct, and his knowledge of women, told him she was more upset about the episode on the beach than she liked to admit.

"I'm teasing," he said gently. "Look, we need to have a chat but," he nodded his head in the direction of the kitchen, where he strongly suspected Annie Luckett would be standing by the door with her ears out on elastic, "not here. Is there somewhere we can go?"

Ness looked as though she was going to protest, so he added, "There are some things that are probably better staying between us, don't you think?"

"Don't mind me," called Annie. "I can make myself scarce if it helps?"

Ness flushed. "We can talk outside, if you really must."

"Sounds good to me. Would you like a coffee?" Max asked. And maybe twenty sugar lumps in it to sweeten you up, he added under his breath.

But Ness had already stalked out of the tea shop, the door slamming behind her. She was clearly seething. Max was a little bemused by the strength of her reaction. Looking back on their evening together, maybe his behaviour hadn't been altogether gentlemanly. His rushing away from the beach hadn't been a reflection on her, or how he'd felt that evening, but rather a mixture of haste to take the call and shock when he'd realised who she was. He sighed. Why did women always take things so personally?

Outside the sun was bright. Automatically Max reached for his shades, before deciding against them in case Ness assumed that wearing sunglasses was some kind of ploy. Fortunately, she'd chosen to sit at a picnic table in the cool shade of a ruined wall, where he'd be able to speak to her without being forced to screw up his face like Gollum.

"You've got five minutes," she told him icily.

Max glanced at his Breitling wristwatch. "I'd better get on with it then, although I really should tell you that the bikini and wet tee shirt combination is going to make it very hard for me to concentrate."

Her cheeks flushed pink. "There's no point trying to distract me. We both know this isn't a social call."

"With all due respect, I'm not the one who's doing the distracting here," said Max. "Look, Ness, I want to apologise about the other evening. It was beyond rude of me to race away like that and I don't blame you for being upset. It was unforgivable and absolutely no way to treat a lady."

"You think I'm upset because you walked away? Unbelievable!" She shook her head, and even her riot of curls seemed to boing with indignation. "Absolutely unbelievable. I couldn't give a hoot about that! In fact, I think I had a lucky escape, all things considered. No, what's really pissed me off is that you didn't have the decency to tell me who you were. But that wouldn't have suited you, would it? Much better to worm your way in with me first and get what you wanted."

He stared at her. "What the hell are you talking about?"

She shrugged. "Oh come on, there's no need to pretend now. I can take it: I'm a big girl. Tell me, Max, exactly when were you going to make me an offer for the island? Just before we slept together? Or maybe during? Or were you planning to have as much fun as you could and ask me afterwards?"

Her words were harsh and, even though he sensed the hurt that lay beneath them, Max was taken aback. Taken aback and insulted. What the hell was she accusing him of here? A proud man, and with high standards, he'd never needed to trick a woman into his bed – and he never would, either.

"Are you accusing me of seeking you out on purpose in order to seduce you and steal the castle?" he asked incredulously.

Green eyes met his fearlessly. "I'm not accusing you of it. Isn't that exactly what happened? I bet you were gutted when we were interrupted."

The truth was that Max had actually been very sorry when Val Brown had appeared –not because he'd been attempting to manipulate Ness, but because he'd been enjoying her company. He genuinely hadn't had the faintest idea who she was. All that had mattered was that he'd been drawn to her, in a way he hadn't been to a woman for a very long time. As soon as he'd learned of her identity he'd stepped right away, ironically for the very reason she was so angry now. Talk about a lose-lose situation.

"I had no idea who you were," he said now. "If I had done I wouldn't have come near you, believe me. If you think I sought you out and concocted some elaborate plan to sleep with you in order to get my hands on the island, then you're painfully deluded because that's not how I do business. Please don't flatter yourself, Nessa, or waste any more time being so incensed. You've totally misjudged the situation."

There was a taut silence during which they glowered at one another. Max didn't break eye contact and finally Ness dropped her gaze.

"Everyone saw us together," she said in a quiet voice. "Val saw us on the beach. You can imagine what they all thought."

"Yes," Max replied curtly. It was nice to know he was so highly regarded in the local community. So much for creating employment and encouraging tourists to visit St Pirran. As far as the townsfolk were concerned he was still the big bad wolf, buying up the houses of straw and twigs as investments and gobbling up any little pigs who got in his way. It didn't matter that the little pigs had been only too happy to sell him their houses or that they earned their livings working for him; he was an incomer and as such he was hated and resented. It was profoundly depressing.

"They thought I was planning to develop the castle," Ness added. "Everyone thought I was making plans with you. You should have said what you did for a living. I thought you were an artist."

Max exhaled wearily. "I am an artist. That was me, Ness. I like to sketch."

"And you're also one of the biggest property developers in the country, which seemed to slip your mind!" She looked up and there was still anger in her expression. It didn't matter what he said; she wouldn't believe him.

"That too," he agreed with a note of resignation. "Look, I'm sorry if our meeting made things difficult for you." He could only imagine the reception Ness would have received from the likes of Annie and the other townspeople. They would have thought Armand Penwellyn's bequest was a reprieve, and they'd have been incandescent with rage to imagine the new owner was planning to sell.

Max had some sympathy with the likes of Annie Luckett, but he was also realistic enough to see that without a serious cash injection a great deal of Pirran Castle would be beyond repair in less than a decade. Adam, one of the most experienced stonemasons in his field, had already expressed grave concerns about the viability of the project, and unless something changed soon the place would be lost forever. It drove Max wild that people didn't seem to be able to grasp this. They clung on to the past, fought change every step of the way, and refused to see that without people like him who were prepared to pump millions into a project the very thing they loved would be gone. Yes, he stood to make a lot of money and yes, he'd wanted to own the island since he'd first clapped eyes on it as a kid, but there was far more to this project than profit. Max wanted to safeguard the island and this way was the only way he knew how.

He glanced across the motte to the ruined towers and crumbling walls. With the best will in the world, tea shops and boat trips weren't really doing the job.

"Difficult?" Ness was saying disbelievingly. "Try impossible! I thought Merryn was going to tip me overboard, and several times Fern looked as though she wanted to throttle me."

"So it wasn't worth it then?" Max asked softly. He could still feel the heat of her body, the press of her breasts against his chest, the way she had fitted against him. No doubt about it, he'd enjoyed every minute. Even now he was trying his best to keep his thoughts from racing away to a place where he'd be able to lay her down gently, peel away the damp vest and dust kisses over every inch of that soft skin...

Ness turned her head away and lowered her lashes so he couldn't see into her eyes – but Max wasn't fooled. He knew she felt it too. Whatever complications had followed, that moment on the beach had been worth every conflicted second. When she looked at him again she met his gaze boldly and there was no anger there, only mingled curiosity and defiance.

"What do you want?" she asked.

There was no point labouring it. Max was well known in his world for being good to deal with because he cut to the chase and always kept his word. Ness would come around to his way of thinking; he was sure of it. If he kept business and pleasure strictly separate then she would be able to see that his plan was the best one for the island, for the castle and for her. Then, once the business was all concluded, they would be able to concentrate on the pleasure side of things. He already looked forward to kissing that delicious mouth again.

"I want to buy the island," he said bluntly. "That's no surprise to you, so I won't insult your intelligence by pretending otherwise.

Regardless of what passed between us, I've been preparing to purchase Pirran Island for a while now and I've already got a fantastic team assembled to work on it. Until recently I'd been under the impression that Jamie owned the place but, to be frank, who owns it is immaterial. I'm ready to push the button as soon as you are."

"You're assuming I want to sell."

"I don't think you have much choice. The castle's falling into disrepair. You must see that?"

Her silence told him that she saw it very well indeed.

"Then there's the upkeep, the insurances, the repairs to the pier and the landing area," Max continued. "Unless your uncle left you a huge amount of money, which according to Jamie certainly isn't the case, then there's no way you'll be able to keep the place running, let alone from falling down."

Ness raised her chin. "I'll find a way."

Max admired her determination, however misplaced. Quite what Armand had been playing at was anyone's guess, but he'd certainly picked a worthier recipient for his legacy than the sneering Jamie.

"The only way to save the castle is to sell it," he said. He knew it sounded harsh, but it was the truth of the matter. "Without money it will fall down and you'll end up selling anyway. I'm prepared to offer you five million for the island and the castle. I'll make certain that all the work done is sympathetic – you'll have my word on that – and I'll even give you an apartment too as part of the deal."

"Five million?" Her voice was faint.

Max felt a flicker of disappointment. He'd expected a protest, even just as part of the dance, but it seemed that what he'd offered was enough to quell her conscience. So Nessa Penwellyn was no different from any other woman then. Money, jewellery, shoes... He should have learned by now that these things bought them easily enough. It was the reason why he was still single.

"Tempted?" he asked.

Ness pushed her hair behind her ears. She looked stunned. "I wouldn't be human if I wasn't."

"The plans are already drawn up and you can go through them with me," Max said. "I've also hired a master builder who'll take charge of the renovations – and I have a wildlife expert on side too, who'll be advising the project team every step of the way."

"And what about everyone else who lives here? Fred? Lucy? Merryn? Fern? And the visitors?"

"I can't keep them on, because the island will be a private residence," Max explained. "You have to understand that any clients wishing to purchase an apartment in the castle will be very wealthy people who value their privacy."

"You already have a list of people who want to live here?"

"As I said, this development has been in the planning for a long time."

Ness shot him a disgusted look. "Since way before my uncle even died, by the sound of it. I can imagine you and Jamie could hardly wait for him to die. No wonder he left the place to me. Well, bad luck, Max. Pirran Island isn't for sale."

This was more like it.

"Seven million," said Max calmly. He'd been set to offer Jamie ten, so this way was going to prove much more lucrative for Reynards. He'd push to nine if he had to. She'd bite. They always did when they sensed a fortune was within their grasp.

"You could offer me seven billion. I still won't sell. This was my father's home and my mother's too. It doesn't just belong to me. It belongs to everyone. Fern, Lucy, the town, the visitors; it's theirs just as much as it's mine." Ness's voice was low and charged with emotion. "You can take your money and get off my island because it isn't for sale. It never will be. I'm going to make it pay. You just watch."

"Everything's for sale, Ness," Max said mildly. "And if not now, then at some point it will be. You should save yourself all the heartache and work, and sell to me now. My next offer might not be as high."

"I don't care what your next offer is! The answer's no!" Her chest was rising and falling again, and Max forced himself to concentrate on her glittering green eyes. God, he'd love to paint her; sitting there opposite him and spitting with rage she was as elemental as the harsh granite cliffs and spiky cliff top grasses. The wildness in her made him feel alive.

"Fine," he said. "Now, how about having dinner with me?"

"What?"

"Dinner? We can go anywhere you like. Stein's? Fifteen? Or there's a great seafood shack in Falmouth I know that does the best mussels. You like seafood, right?"

"Yes, I love it, but what on earth are you going on about? I just told you: I'm not selling."

"I know, I heard that loud and clear," Max replied patiently. "This is dinner. Something very different."

"Why on earth would I want to have dinner with you?"

"Because you like me? Because we both know there's unfinished business between us? Because it might be fun to conclude that unfinished business?"

Ness started to laugh, a bubbling, joyous sound that made him want to laugh too. Those lips, now that they weren't pursed in disapproval, were simply crying out to be kissed. He found himself wanting to find more ways to make her smile rather than scowl.

Christ, he needed to get a grip. What was going on in his head? He wasn't here to make Nessa Penwellyn smile. He was here to buy her castle and with any luck enjoy a no-strings fling too. Wasn't that how these things went? Then he could get back to normal.

"No thanks," Ness answered, once she'd got her breath back. "And that's to both offers, by the way."

"You'll change your mind," Max said.

A smile was still playing on her lips. "About the castle?"

"About both."

They stared at one another for a moment, during which the world seemed to stop turning, the clouds hung still in the sky and even the gulls were quiet. Then Ness stood up.

"I don't think so," she said. "This discussion's over. I'll never sell to you. And as for dinner? I think I'd choke. Have a nice afternoon on your powerboat, Max."

And then she was striding away across the grass, every sinew of her slender body taut as she focused on ignoring him.

Max watched her go with a mixture of amusement and regret. She'd be back. Of course she would. She would take him up on his offer.

But which one? And more to the point, which of his two offers did he most want her to accept? He was no longer able to say.

Chapter 16

The little piano was dwarfed in the medieval hall where it now stood, but Lucy found she enjoyed having it there. It had only been gathering dust when it had been tucked out of sight in Armand's bedroom, whereas now it was coming back to life here in the centre of the castle. Everyone walked through the Small Hall at some point during the day and it was unusual not to hear a faltering tune being picked out by Ness or a flurry of notes when Josh came to visit. Lucy herself often took a minute or two to sit down and run her fingers over the familiar ivory keys. Once again music was at the heart of castle life.

At the moment Josh was the one playing the piano, and as she began to prepare supper in the kitchen Lucy smiled to hear the music drifting through the ancient rooms. He was such a talented boy and teaching him had quickly become one of her greatest joys. There was nothing better than sharing your love of a certain composer and seeing delight dawn in another, especially one whose ability far outshone that of his teacher. Already Josh was playing scores Lucy struggled with. His confidence was growing too, and in just the few weeks since he'd begun visiting the castle his face had lost the pinched and unhappy look it had had when they'd first met. Admittedly his father was still working flat out by all accounts, and Lucy imagined that the kids at school were still vile to Josh when they thought there were no adult eyes upon them, but he had another life now at the castle and had quickly become a part of the island family. Belonging somewhere and feeling safe could make all the difference, as Lucy knew well from personal experience.

As Josh played today's choice, Beethoven's Moonlight Sonata, Lucy lay down her knife and abandoned chopping vegetables to lean against the Aga, close her eyes and let the music sweep her away. This had been one of Armand's favourite pieces and on the rare occasions when her uncle had played the piano it had been one of his choices. She could picture him now, seated at the Steinway with his fingers moving across the keys. He'd be immersed in the music, his eagle-like profile trained on something far away that she couldn't see. Was it a place or a person he was searching for? Beethoven had famously dedicated the fourteenth sonata to his beloved. Had her uncle been thinking of someone he'd loved and lost? She'd never know now. A lump rose into her throat.

Every few bars the same key jammed, jolting the fluid beauty of the music, and Josh tutted loudly. When it happened for the fifth time the music stopped abruptly; instead there was an ugly crashing of notes as the little boy brought his hands down on the keys in frustration. Oh dear, thought Lucy as she opened her eyes and headed to the Small Hall, not again. Josh certainly had the artistic temperament that accompanied talent, and that troublesome key had been driving him crazy. She really must call a piano tuner out to look at it. This job was on her long list of things to do but she'd been putting it off, dreading to think what piano tuners must cost these days.

Money worries were starting to wake Lucy up in the small hours; she'd found herself rooting through her possessions at three o'clock this morning, wondering what on earth she could sell to free up some funds. She had her mother's engagement ring and pearls, but Lucy treasured these. It would break her heart to part with them. On the other hand, what choice did she have? Armand had left all of his shares to Jamie, and whatever royalties she might receive from his music weren't due in until the autumn. In the meantime, her own bank account was dipping a toe into the red and poised to dive in properly. The thought of being in debt made her feel quite giddy with terror because there was no way she could ever pay it back. Lucy didn't dare ask Ness to help. Her cousin was already starting to look a little wild-eyed when it came to any discussion of finances, and Lucy was loath to put Ness under any more pressure – especially for something that was a luxury, like the piano. Having already used her savings to buy food and pay the last electricity bill, Lucy knew the pearls would have to go. She'd take them into Truro next week and get them valued. Her mother would have understood.

"That stupid key's stuck," Josh complained when she joined him. "It's happening all the time."

"I know it's annoying but please don't take it out on the piano, sweetheart," Lucy said gently. "It's very old and tired."

A bit like me, she wanted to add – except that the piano could be tuned or restrung, whereas there wasn't much hope for weary, penniless spinsters without careers. If Ness couldn't hold onto the castle and Max Reynard had his way, Lucy dreaded to think what her future held. Did workhouses still exist?

Josh's bottom lip stuck out mutinously. "I want the old piano back."

Lucy sighed. "We all do but it's not coming back, Josh, and we have to accept that. It's Jamie's piano now and he's taken it to his house."

The little boy shot her a pitying look. "No he hasn't. He's sold it. He said so yesterday when he came to get more of his stuff, remember? He said this one was good enough for oiks to play so we could keep it."

Not for the first time lately, Lucy could have throttled Jamie. He'd turned up the day before (luckily missing Ness, who'd gone off somewhere with Merryn) and helped himself to anything he felt entitled to. Lucy had trailed after him – partly to make sure he didn't take anything he shouldn't and partly because she was trying to find out if he and Max Reynard were still in cahoots – but, apart from gloating over the piano, Jamie had barely had a word to say to her. In the end she'd beaten a retreat to the tea room. She'd hoped that Josh hadn't heard any of her brother's unkind comments but, like most children, he didn't miss a trick.

"He's a bit upset," she began, but Josh shook his blond head and pulled a face.

"No he isn't! He's mean and nasty. No wonder your uncle gave the island to Ness! Anyway, you didn't get the island either and you're not horrible like him."

Oh dear, thought Lucy. Even a child could see she was making excuses for her brother. Perhaps it was time she stopped. Even as Jamie had sped across the causeway, cutting it fine as always and with his tyres sending spray flying, she'd tried to tell herself that he was hurting deep down. Very, very deep down. Behaving like an arse was just an act to cover his pain; there was still a decent man in there somewhere.

The trouble was, even she no longer believed this. Annie had told her that Max Reynard had come looking for Ness – and the fact that Max had been skulking around at the same time as Jamie was a coincidence too far. They were in league together to get their greedy hands on the island, and it made Lucy wild. If Max Reynard dared to cross her path he'd wish he hadn't, she promised. Who did he think he was, rolling up here and playing Mephistopheles? Fury took her breath away.

"Are you all right, Lucy?" Josh asked. "You've gone a really funny colour."

Lucy put her hand on her heart and felt it leaping beneath her ribs. She'd need anger management at this rate, or beta blockers. She needed to calm down. Getting incensed like this wasn't going to help. To outwit the likes of Max Reynard and her brother, Lucy would need to use her brains rather than her temper. Planning revenge ought to be like writing poetry or composing a melody: "emotion recollected in tranquillity" and all that.

So as always when she was upset, Lucy turned to music.

"Let's play a duet," she suggested, sitting beside Josh and nudging him to budge up. "How about the opening cadenza of the Island Suite?"

Thinking about it, playing Armand's most famous piece on an out-of-tune and very tired piano probably wasn't the most tactful way to deal with Josh's indignation, but before long their four hands were flying over the keys and Armand's notes were filling the room. Lucy was soothed to realise that although Jamie had taken the Steinway away, he couldn't rob her of the music or the pleasure it gave her. That was something she'd shared with her uncle and could now pass on to Josh; it was a gift from Armand far more valuable than shares and expensive pianos. The memories this piece brought back were indelible. Exhaling, Lucy lost herself in the music. For the next ten minutes nothing else mattered.

It was only when they reached the end of the piece and the final notes had trembled into the air that Lucy noticed she and Josh were not alone. A stranger had stepped out from the shadows and was clapping his hands.

"Well done!" he cried. "That was absolutely wonderful!"

Oh! With a jolt of recognition, Lucy realised this wasn't a stranger at all but the stonemason she'd met in town, the same one who'd told her she ought to buy the polka-dot dress. His thick blond hair was dusty and his combat trousers and Metallica tee shirt had seen better days, but the brown eyes were just as twinkly and his smile every bit as warm as she recalled. But what on earth was he doing in the Small Hall?

Josh answered this question for her by leaping off the piano stool and hurtling into the visitor's arms.

"Dad! Cool! Did you like it?"

The stonemason was Josh's father; of course he was. Now that she saw them together Lucy realised that the similarities were obvious. They shared the same mop of butter-coloured hair, big melting Malteaser eyes and crinkly smiles, as well as freckles and tanned skin. Josh's father had lines fanning out from his eyes – and judging by his lean frame he didn't eat quite as many biscuits as his son – but otherwise there was no mistaking the resemblance.

"I'm so sorry to turn up unannounced, but this monkey's turned off his phone and I couldn't get hold of him," the man was saying, ruffling Josh's hair.

"The battery ran out, Dad!" Josh protested.

"Not good enough, mate. It has to be kept charged otherwise I'm going to worry. Embarrassing but true," he added as his son rolled his eyes and groaned. "You know the rules."

Lucy pushed the stool underneath the piano and closed the instrument's lid before turning to face Josh's father.

"I'm so sorry you were concerned, Mr…" Her voice petered away as she realised she had absolutely no idea what Josh's surname was. Goodness. That was awful. Here she was with the little boy practically a member of the family and she didn't even know his full name. That was definitely a St Pirran thing, of course. She couldn't remember what Fern's surname was either, and most of the other people she could think of here were known by their trade. It was usually "Fred the Gardener" or "Bryan the Chippy", or something of the sort. All the same, not knowing someone's name must look odd to an incomer.

But Josh's dad didn't look perturbed. Instead he was holding his hand out and still smiling that sunbeam smile. Lucy took it and they shook hands politely. His was strong and rough from physical work, which made her feel a lot better about her own tatty nails and the calluses from gardening.

"Lucy Penwellyn, I presume?" he asked. "I'm Adam Miller and I'm really pleased to meet you properly at last. Josh talks about you all the time and he's spot on: you are very pretty and nice, and you're definitely a wonderful music teacher too. I could hardly believe my ears just then."

Lucy blushed. She didn't think she'd ever received so many compliments at once. In fact, when was the last time she'd received even one? Probably when she'd first met Adam outside the dress shop.

"I haven't done anything," she insisted. "Josh has an amazing talent."

Adam nodded. "Yes, yes he does, but you've nurtured it. I can't begin to say how grateful I am. Coming here has changed so much for him. He's started to get his sparkle back."

"Dad! Yuk! Stop it!" Josh groaned, raising his eyes to the beamed roof.

"Am I embarrassing you again?" Adam asked. His brown eyes met Lucy's and he gave her a rueful smile. "And there I was thinking I was a cool dad. I even brought the boat over in case you wanted to sail back, mate. But if that isn't cool then I'll just go home."

"It's cool, Dad! I'll get my bag!" His son punched the air in delight and tore out of the Small Hall and into the kitchen, where Lucy knew he'd also be helping himself to a couple of her cookies before he returned. Once his son was out of earshot, Adam turned back to Lucy – and now his expression was serious.

"I mean it, Miss Penwellyn, you've done a wonderful thing for Josh and I can't begin to tell you how much I appreciate it. Coming over here and finding the heart for music again has really made a massive difference to him. Did you know that after his mum died he stopped playing the piano?"

Lucy didn't but this made sense. Josh played the piano like a swimmer gasped for air after a deep dive. "He told me his mum played the piano but I had no idea he'd stopped."

"Elly was a wonderful pianist," Adam said, keeping his voice low in case Josh reappeared. "She taught Josh and always said his talent would outstrip hers, which from what I've just heard today seems to be coming true already. I think when we lost her he couldn't bear to play the piano without his mum – but he must have missed it dreadfully. Here, with you and in this beautiful place, he's found his way back to it. It'll never be the same as it was, but do you know what? Sometimes different isn't all bad, is it? We just have to look for the parts that are good."

Lucy thought about Armand's death, the loss of the grand piano and the times in the night when she woke up panicking about money and her uncertain future. These things were undeniably difficult, but without losing Armand she would never have found her cousin Ness, of whom she was growing very fond. Adam was right – and if someone like him who had suffered dreadfully could still face the world with a smile and find the good in things, then she certainly could.

"Absolutely," she agreed. "And please, call me Lucy. Miss Penwellyn sounds like a character from a Dickens' novel. I feel I should be wearing a tatty wedding dress and presiding over a rotting feast!"

"Hardly," said Adam. "By the way, did you ever buy that spotty dress?"

She pushed her hair behind her ears and looked down at her shabby trainers, about as far from strappy sandals as it was possible to get, and laughed awkwardly. "No, of course not."

"Of course not? What do you mean by that?"

"I live here," Lucy said simply. "If I'm not baking then I'm gardening or cleaning. I don't go anywhere that needs a dress like that."

"Well, that's got to change. We need to take you somewhere to wear it," Adam told her firmly. He had a way of saying things that suggested an air of command, and his chin was now raised at the same determined angle that Josh always tilted his when his mind was made up about something. "I've been very remiss here. I should have been over to visit before rather than relying on Merryn to do all the collecting and picking up, and I apologise for my total lack of manners. My only excuse is that I've been working flat out, but that's coming to an end now and I've got some free time before the next job begins."

"Wonderful," Lucy replied politely, while her brain whirled round like a hamster on a wheel. So the slave-driving Max had another job lined up for Adam, did he? And what was that? Developing a castle?

"So in some of that spare time I'd very much like to take you out for dinner," Adam said, adding quickly when he saw the look of terror flicker across her face, "as a thank you for all the help you've given Josh. Not for any seedy reasons, I promise. I'm not cracking onto you or anything. Not that a man wouldn't want to crack onto you... I, err..." Now it was her visitor's turn to blush and Lucy started to laugh because the more he floundered the worse it was becoming.

"Oh dear," Adam groaned, clapping his palm to his face and peeking out through his fingers. "I've just made a total idiot of myself, haven't I?"

"Of course not," Lucy said, feeling sorry for him. He was only being kind. Of course he wasn't cracking onto her; she knew that. Adam Miller would have no trouble choosing from his pick of women in the town, so she knew she was safe from his attentions. "It's a very kind offer, but really there's no need. I've enjoyed having Josh here and he's reminded me just how much I love to play too. My uncle was really very ill towards the end: he had cancer and it was quick but pretty savage. I suppose I just slipped out of the habit of playing the piano myself because there was so much else to do."

"You nursed him? Here?"

She nodded and Adam looked grave.

"That couldn't have been easy. Not many people would be able to do it."

Lucy looked into his eyes and saw an understanding she rarely encountered. Had Josh's mum had cancer too? It was somehow too intimate a question to ask, but she felt the tug of mutual sympathy and suspected that he knew just how hard her task had been.

"It wasn't, but it was the least I could do for him. My uncle gave me a home when I needed one and he might have been a strange old soul – cantankerous probably describes him best – but he was family. Yes, it was hard, but in a way it was a privilege too."

"And on top of all that you've been lumbered with my son," said Adam, breaking the sombre mood as Josh returned, his cheeks bulging suspiciously and with crumbs dotting his mouth. "I dread to think what piano lessons would cost, so I think one dinner is the least I can do. No arguments. If Josh is going to carry on coming to the castle I won't hear of you saying no."

"Please can I keep coming?" Josh asked, through a mouthful of pilfered cookie. "Please, Dad? I'm teaching Lucy to use her iPhone too, so I am useful."

"He certainly is," Lucy agreed. "I'm hopeless with it but thanks to Josh here I'm able to text now."

"I'm going to show her iMovie and Facebook," Josh said, "so I have to keep coming, don't I?"

"It's up to Lucy," his father replied, those brown eyes crinkling. "She knows what the deal is if she wants to escape from the digital wilderness!"

Now two pairs of beseeching brown eyes were trained on her. Lucy would have needed a heart of stone to say no. Luckily for Josh her heart was more like melting butter and all she could do was throw her hands in the air and agree that yes, she would have dinner with Adam.

"Make sure you go to a restaurant: he's a terrible cook," Josh warned as the three of them walked out into the warm evening.

"You ungrateful child! I make wonderful beans on toast!"

Outraged, Adam pretended to cuff him and Josh retaliated by trying to trip his father up. They scuffled and play-fought all the way down the path that led across the lawn, past the tea room and to the pier, where a pretty sailing boat was waiting. There was no mistaking the closeness between father and son, and Lucy found herself wondering how Jamie would have turned out if he and Maudsley had enjoyed a similar relationship. Their father had been distant and troubled, given to bouts of black depression and introversion, and had rarely had time for his children. Lucy couldn't begin to imagine what Adam had been through, but she could see that Josh was his world. It was a shame Max Reynard worked him so hard; it was another black mark against Max, to add to all the others in Lucy's book.

The wind was freshening in the east and the sky now had an ominous purple hue, as though the clouds were bruises flowering against pale flesh. The sunshine was still bright but had taken on a sickly yellow intensity, ripping through the clouds and stippling the sea with patches of light and shade. A sense of unease ran down Lucy's spine. A storm was threatening, and judging by the white horses now cantering across the bay it would break soon. Having lived in St Pirran all her life Lucy knew the signs. If Adam and Josh were to make it across the water before the weather turned they would need to leave now. Merryn's boat was already moored, the extra bowline telling Lucy that her instincts were spot on.

"The weather's closing in," she told Adam.

He nodded, his expression growing serious. "The forecasters were saying there'd be a storm, but they reckoned it would be later."

"Never mind the forecasters. See those rocks to the east?" Lucy asked, pointing to the farthest headland.

Adam shaded his eyes against the bright light and then shook his head. "No."

"That's because the rain is already falling there so you can't see them for the squall. Usually that happens about ten minutes or so before it reaches us," she explained. "Don't bother with the sails; just use your outboard motor and get across as fast as you can. This looks bad."

Adam didn't question her judgement or sneer as Jamie would have done. Instead he nodded again and immediately began loosening the moorings in preparation for casting away.

"Hop in, Josh, and start her up," he called to his son, who was on deck in an instant, donning a life vest. Soon the engine was running and the boat was poised to race for the mainland.

"I'll throw the bowline down to you," Lucy called to Adam as he untied the stern. "You guys get going."

Adam leapt onto the deck and, landing with ease and with his legs braced against the motion of the waves, grinned up at her. "Aye aye, captain!"

Fat spots of rain were falling now, spattering lazily on Lucy's jeans. The sun had disappeared behind orange-edged clouds, and the sky seemed to swell and press closer to the earth. Lucy's fingers, deft from years of sailing, eased the reef knot loose – and then the boat was free, its rope flying towards the deck. Adam, tugging on his life jacket, gave her a thumbs up before taking the wheel and turning for St Pirran.

"Bye, Lucy!" Josh called. "Thanks for having me!"

She waved. "It's a pleasure. See you soon! Now get going!"

"We will, just don't forget that dinner!" Adam called. "And buy that dress!"

Lucy had no time to reply; the little engine roared into life and the boat was zipping across the bay, leaving behind a white slash of wake in water that was now the same dark colour as the castle's walls. She stood on the pier waving until her arm ached and their boat was no more than a smudge dashing towards the town.

Only when she could no longer see them did Lucy stop and turn for home – and even then, the heavy raindrops and driving wind couldn't steal her smile. She was experiencing an unusual emotion, and it was only as she ducked through the gate and hurried across the grass that Lucy identified the feeling.

She stopped dead in her tracks, halted by surprise and oblivious to the slicing rain and her soaking clothes. The unfamiliar sensation driving out the cold and warming her deep inside was happiness. Wet and bedraggled she might well be, but Lucy Penwellyn was feeling happy.

Goodness. What on earth was that all about?

Chapter 17

After Max Reynard's visit and his mind-boggling offer of seven million pounds, Ness's composure had vanished along with the sunny afternoon. Still seething from his utter nerve - how dare he just turn up on the island and try to buy her off with obscene amounts of money - Ness had decided that the only way forward now was to try to figure out how to make St Pirran pay for itself. She'd stomped back through the gardens, underneath the Pilgrim's Gate and back into the castle with his words ringing in her ears and her skin prickling with irritation because, no matter how much she wanted to deny it, some of what he'd said was spot on.

"The castle's falling into disrepair. You must see that?" he'd said, and Ness hadn't been able to think of a suitably stinging reply. Of course she could see it. Lucy and the others might be able to kid themselves that everything was wonderful, but as a newcomer to the island Ness's gaze was fresh. It was obvious to her just how much work was needed.

Max's comments about the huge expenses involved in maintaining, let alone restoring, the castle had also hit home. His observation that she lacked the funds to cover these costs couldn't be denied, and in spite of her brave words Ness was worried. There was no missing the crumbling walls, broken windows and cracked masonry. Just as it was impossible to ignore the crack in the pier, or the fact that the flowerbeds were overgrown with nodding valerian, or that dog roses and ivy now stitched the castle's stonework. Everything was looking shabby and tired.

Actually, forget tired. The place looked ready to collapse from sheer exhaustion.

In spite of this, Max's utter confidence infuriated Ness beyond belief. Did he really think that once he waved a big enough sum of money under her nose she'd smile sweetly and then take the cash? He'd regarded her with that penetrating grey gaze and, even when she'd refused, had remarked evenly that everything was for sale.

Well, not her! He could offer a billion trillion gazillion pounds and she wouldn't take it. Max Reynard would soon discover that Nessa Penwellyn couldn't be bought. And as for the bare-faced cheek of him asking her out for dinner? As if that would ever happen! No wonder she'd laughed at him. What did it matter that he was handsome enough to take her breath away or that, as hard as she tried, she couldn't quite put aside the memories of that moonlit evening on the beach? Rich and arrogant and selfish, Max was everything she despised; Ness would rather starve than have dinner with a man like him.

And anyway, what had he been playing at by even asking her in the first place? Was it just a warped power game, or did he really think he'd be able to seduce her into selling the island? He might have already denied this but Ness wouldn't put anything past Max Reynard. He was so devious he'd make Machiavelli look like Mary Poppins. She'd met men like him before – her ex, Stephen, had been the same type of spoilt rich boy – and there was no way Ness would ever let herself be taken in by somebody like that again. When she thought how close she'd come to making a fool of herself on that first evening, she went cold inside. Talk about a lucky escape.

Incensed, she'd stormed into the castle. What if Max was right? What if it was only a matter of time before she had no choice but to admit defeat and sell the island?

I'll never sell to him, Ness thought savagely. Never.

With Biscuit now bounding at her heels and barking excitedly at what looked like a lovely game of chase, Ness raced up to the library. Once there, she dragged the castle's accounts book from the shelf and hurled herself onto the window seat. She stared at Lucy's neat royal-blue writing and carefully presented figures until she was cross-eyed and her head hurt. Try as she might, Ness couldn't see any way that Lucy might have made an error with her sums or conveniently missed out a few hundred thousand or so. Finally she gave up, slamming the ledger shut with a howl of despair.

Bloody, bloody Max Reynard. He was absolutely right: there wasn't enough money to run the place. No doubt Jamie had already given him the lowdown on the castle's finances and he was well aware just how dire things were looking.

"It's all right, boy," she told Biscuit, who'd been snoozing at her feet but was now staring up at her with big worried eyes. Ruffling the fur on his silky head, she sighed. "I'll find a way, somehow. Maybe I should blow what's left in the bank account on some lottery tickets?"

Biscuit cocked his head to one side and looked apprehensive.

"Okay," Ness conceded. "Maybe gambling isn't the best option. So if I can't gamble our way out of the financial mire, there has to be another solution. I just have to work out what it is."

At this the spaniel thumped his tail on the rug, in what Ness took to be approval.

Resting the ledger on the worn tapestry cushion of the window seat, Ness leaned her hot forehead against the glass and stared across the sea, her eyes widening when she saw that the weather had changed dramatically while she'd been absorbed in scrutinising the accounts. A summer storm was gathering on the horizon and growing closer with every passing moment.

Ness had believed that life on a Caribbean island had taught her all there was to know about storms. Every spring through to late December, St Antonians guarded their supplies of tinned food, bottled water and candles, and prayed hard that the weather would spare them this hurricane season. Past storms were talked about in hushed tones, as though so much as mentioning a hurricane was to wish one onto the island. The graveyards were crammed with marble headstones and pots of bright plastic blooms that were a testimony to the number that had perished. Living in a dive hotel right next to the ocean, Ness had watched electrical storms split the sky with jagged lightning slashes and heard thunder so loud it had triggered car alarms and made the hotel shake – but never had she witnessed anything as savage as the storm that was now starting to pummel the Cornish coast.

Before long the rain was falling, dimpling the grey sea and hurling itself against the window; as the clouds advanced with surly determination, the downpour intensified and the droplets became needle-sharp. The sky was no longer the baby blue of earlier but had darkened to a bruised plum colour. White-tipped waves galloped towards the beach. The wind was a low growl, growing louder by the second, and far below Ness's tower window the Cornish palm trees fringing the grass were tossing their leaves like horse tails plagued by flies. On Lucy's tea lawn, a bench flipped over as easily as though it were crafted from driftwood rather than oak, while Fern's slim figure dashed to the shelter of the castle as lightning ripped across the sky. Moments later Lucy was scuttling across the open grass, bent almost double against the force of the wind and with her hair plastered against her head.

As though sensing Ness's thoughts, Biscuit whimpered and fled out of the room, his claws clicking faster and faster as he hurtled down the tower's steps. Ness didn't blame him. It felt like being under siege as the wind battered the walls and the sea hurled fistfuls of salt spray up at the mullioned windows. She was returning the accounts ledger to its shelf and was about to follow Biscuit when there was a loud crack, swiftly followed by a crash. Tearing to the window, Ness saw that a section of the tea shop's roof had lifted and was twisting with every savage gust, flapping and floundering like a landed fish until another, stronger gust ripped it clean away. Slates were tossed across the lawn like confetti and the storm seemed to turn into a living, breathing entity as another section of the roof was raised, then fell back down and rose again like a ribcage housing a monstrous pair of lungs.

The castle would be safe, Ness reasoned. After all, it had stood on the island for centuries and withstood lifetimes of violent weather. The latches rattled against the glass, and draughts howled down the chimneys and gusted along the passageways, but the core of the old building would barely tremble. It was the newer sections and the ruined parts that were under attack now from the salvo of the wind and rain. The tea room and the small visitor centre were fairly recent additions, and although they were partly joined to what had once been the stables they were mainly constructed from glass and timber. They'd been designed to look pretty and make the most of the views, but they'd been built as cheaply as possible and the roofing was already rotten in places. It wouldn't last against a gale of this ferocity.

Ness raced down to the Small Hall. For once she didn't stop to look up at the portraits, but ran straight to the kitchen. It was hard to think clearly with the roar of the storm and the crashing waves adding to the pounding of her heart, but she was terrified of what might be about to unfold. The Pilgrim's Gate was weak, the ruined walls of the old chapel were precarious enough, and both the pier and the causeway already needed work. Max's words, spoken with a deadly honesty that even she had no choice but to acknowledge, echoed in her memory. The only way to save the castle is to sell it, he'd said. Without money it will fall down and you'll end up selling anyway.

Was Max Reynard some kind of evil prophet? Ness wouldn't have put it past him to have even the weather on his payroll. Men like him stopped at nothing to get their own way.

She burst into the kitchen where Lucy and Fern were huddled by the Aga, their clothes steaming while they attempted to dry their hair with tea towels. Fred was slumped at the table with his head in his hands and his cloth cap dripping steadily onto the battered surface.

"My plants! What about all my plants?"

"They'll be sheltered in the garden, Fred," Fern said gently. "When this blows over I'll help you sort them out. It'll be fine."

Fred didn't answer, although whether that was because he couldn't hear or because he was too lost in despair it was hard to say. The garden was his pride and joy.

Lucy's gaze met Ness's over the gardener's soggy cap. "Oh, Ness, it's just awful. We've lost half the tea-shop roof and the visitor centre too. I just don't know what we're going to do…"

Her words ended with a sob and Ness knew that Lucy didn't need to say any more. They'd lost more than the roof: if the tea shop was badly damaged they'd also lose the one small income stream that had been keeping them going. A deluge of rain and sea spray wouldn't do the building any favours, and repairing it was an expense they couldn't afford.

"We'll fix it," Fern said staunchly. "Won't we, Ness?"

"Of course we will," Ness agreed, although she had no idea how. Max and his seven million pounds flickered through her mind and she banished him swiftly. That was not the way. Maybe she could find an overlooked antique or something.

Lucy laughed bleakly. "Oh, girls! Fix it with what? Magic?"

"There's magic on this island, so why not?" Fern crossed her arms and raised her chin, looking very young all of a sudden.

"How did the roof come away?" Ness asked.

Her cousin sighed. "It's needed repairing for a while and Merryn's managed to keep it together as best he can. I was going to talk to you about getting a new one put on because I didn't think it would last a winter storm. I should have known better than to wait. Storms here can be just as vicious in the summer."

"But how could so much damage happen so fast?"

"The rotten part of the roof was only tacked down, so it started to lift when the wind first picked up." Fern filled the kettle and returned to the Aga; her small hands were shaking so much that the kettle landed on the hotplate with a clatter. "I was cleaning up when the storm came in. I should have thought of something to save it but I didn't know what to do. Before I had time the first section was already off."

"It's not your fault. The main thing is that we're all safe," Ness said. Then an awful thought occurred to her. Never mind stones and buildings. What about Merryn? Was he safe in his camper van over at Grace Note Bay? If the wind took that, he could be seriously hurt – even killed. "Where's Merryn?"

"I think he went to check the boat," answered Lucy. "I thought he'd be back by now."

Ness frowned. "You don't think he's still out there do you?"

"He's not come back," said Fern, looking worried.

"He'll be sheltering, that's why," Lucy reassured her. "Merryn's St Pirran born and bred, love. He can ride out a summer storm. He won't be outside in this weather. I would have thought he'd have headed here though. The castle's the best place to be when a storm comes in."

"What if he isn't sheltering at all but trying to save the tea room?" asked Ness slowly. Instinct told her this was just the kind of thing Merryn would do. He'd do anything not to let Lucy down and to help protect the island. "Could he have gone there?"

Lucy blanched. "Well, yes... I suppose so."

"It's exactly what he'd do," Fern agreed.

The three women looked at one another as horror dawned. Ness dashed to the window but could hardly see beyond the glass for the heavy rain. Before she had time to think about what she was doing, she was flinging open the kitchen door and stepping out into the gale. Instantly the breath was ripped from her lungs and rain needled her face as she lurched across the courtyard and hurried under the precarious archway, before staggering down the grassy banks to the tea room.

"Merryn!" she yelled, but the storm only snatched her words. With rain running down her cheeks like tears, Ness ran all the way to the tea room, hardly able to believe the sight that greeted her.

The blond wood façade had been ripped away, leaving the building wide open like a doll's house; the shop's display area was exposed as though ready for a giant hand to place a toy inside it. A good section of the roof had peeled away too, revealing bare beams and dangling wiring. Flakes of plaster were falling like snow and one of the outside walls listed drunkenly. Ness found herself stumbling as the gale blew harder.

"Careful!" shouted Fern, her voice harsh against the wind as she tugged Ness back. "This lot could come down at any minute."

Holding onto one another, the two women managed to make their way along to the tea room's back door, while the wind whipped around the courtyard.

"Merryn!" Ness shouted. "Merryn!"

Fern's fingers clutched Ness's arm, the silver rings biting in painfully. "Did you hear that?"

Ness strained her ears. Against the howl of the wind and the pounding of the waves it was hard to hear much at all.

"He's in there," Fern insisted. "Listen!"

Ness heard a faint calling from inside the building and, without a thought for what they might find inside or the danger it could place them in, she and Fern were clambering over the fallen plasterboard and rafters.

Merryn was in the wreckage of what had been, only half an hour before, the tea room's kitchen. He was sprawled on the floor, clutching his wrist – which was bent at an angle that made Ness feel queasy. There was a jagged cut above his left temple and his blond hair was matted with blood.

"Something fell," he gasped, his eyes dark with pain. "Jesus, Ness. I'm so dizzy. I can't move."

"Hold on," she called. "I'm coming."

Fern lay a warning hand on her arm. "What if he's got concussion or damaged his spine? We shouldn't move him, should we?"

Ness was well aware of first aid; usually she would have been in total agreement. This occasion, though, was going to have to be the exception to everything she knew. The building was swaying and creaking like a galleon tossed on the ocean. They had to make a decision and soon.

"He can't stay inside. It isn't safe. We need to get him out as fast as we can."

Ness ducked between the splintered beams and dodged broken plasterboard that stirred with every gust as though the building was in its death throes. Rain, tears and dust blinded her and the exposed sky was navy blue, throwing the wreckage into bleak relief. She glanced upwards and her heartbeat quickened as she realised the whole structure was reeling and rocking around her. Another roar from the wind made the place shudder and Ness knew there might only be moments before more of the roof caved in.

She crouched beside Merryn and, grabbing his good arm, tugged him to his feet. His face turned almost green.

"Shit! That hurts!"

"I'm sorry," Ness said, "but I need to get you out. It's not safe in here."

Her heart was playing the xylophone against her ribs. Fern was on his other side now and somehow they managed to drag him through the debris and out of the building. Moments later the visitor centre rocked for a moment, as though undecided, before collapsing like a house of cards, taking with it what little remained of the tea room's roof.

"That was close," breathed Fern.

"Too close," Ness agreed grimly. "Come on, we need to get Merryn indoors."

Together they half pulled, half dragged Merryn up the path to the castle and negotiated the steps up to the kitchen. By now all three were soaked to the skin and shivering. And this was June? thought Ness in disbelief. England certainly had crazy weather. No wonder her father had loved the heat of California.

"You're not even this much of a dead weight when you're pissed," Fern was saying to Merryn as they heaved him up the steps and all but fell into the kitchen, where Lucy was ready with towels and hot tea.

"I don't ever feel this crap when I'm drunk," Merryn groaned, collapsing onto the sofa next to the Aga. "I'm so sorry, Lucy. I couldn't save the roof."

Lucy was close to tears. "I don't care about the roof. I just care about you being safe." She glanced at his wrist and her hand flew to her mouth. "Oh my. That looks nasty."

"It feels nasty," said Merryn. His eyelids drooped. "God, I'm exhausted."

"Keep him talking. Don't let him sleep," Ness instructed Lucy. "He's concussed and I think his wrist's broken too. He really needs a doctor. I don't suppose we can get him off the island?"

Lucy shook her head. "Not until the storm blows itself out or the causeway's clear. That won't be for at least five hours though."

"Could we ask the coastguard to send a lifeboat?" Fern wondered.

"We can't risk a lifeboat crew for a broken wrist," Ness said firmly. On St Antonia she'd been miles from any hospital and had often been forced to make tricky decisions when there were accidents. She was sure they'd be able to look after Merryn until the tide turned in their favour. He seemed more alert now and she wasn't as worried as she had been earlier. Having him checked over properly was going to be a priority the minute it was possible, but until this could be done without risking anyone else they'd need to work together here.

Turning to Lucy, she said, "I need a first-aid kit and the biggest wooden spoon you've got, as well as a couple of old bed sheets and some masking tape."

"What are you planning on doing to me? A bit of S and M?" Merryn asked, with a ghost of his old smile when Fern brandished Lucy's wooden spoon at him.

That was more like it. If he could think about sex at a time like this then he'd survive, Ness thought!

"You truly have had a bump on the head if you think I'd sleep with someone who looks like an extra from Casualty," Fern shot back.

Merryn started to laugh and then winced. "Christ, pain's overrated. Christian Grey needs his head read."

"Talking of heads, can you let me know if your vision blurs or you feel sleepy?" Ness asked. "It's really important you do that, OK?"

"I can see two of you." Merryn said slowly. "Or am I just having an amazing fantasy?"

"You," said Ness, "are a dreadful patient."

At this point Lucy returned armed with bed sheets and tape, and Merryn's banter stopped abruptly. Lucy's face was taut with worry.

"I don't know what we'd have done if anything had happened to you, Merryn Hellier," she said, sitting down beside him while Ness gently did her best to splint his broken wrist with the wooden spoon.

Merryn's teeth were gritted through the pain. "You'd be fine. Probably get an odd-job man who could actually fix your roof."

"He wouldn't be you," Fern replied softly, taking his hand. She didn't wince when he squeezed her hand so tightly that it turned blue.

Ness was focused on ripping up the sheet and strapping up Merryn's arm, but she couldn't miss the expression on Fern's face. Did Fern have hidden feelings for Merryn? Thank goodness Ness had trusted her instincts and not kissed him earlier on. That could have made life very awkward.

Eventually Merryn's wrist was strapped up and his head wound had been cleaned. Fern was firing random questions at him from an ancient set of Trivial Pursuit, to ensure that he remained alert. The gale had quietened down somewhat: there were no more ominous crashes outside, and although the rain was still lashing the castle it wasn't nearly as heavy as it had been earlier. The violent summer storm was passing and before long they would be able to get Merryn to the mainland.

But for Ness the worrying wasn't over. She was still haunted by Max's prediction, as well as the terrifying numbers in the ledger. She had a feeling that for Pirran Island the biggest tempests were yet to come. Only time would tell if she would be able to weather them.

Chapter 18

The storm had blown itself out by dawn. As soon as the tide had retreated, Lucy had driven Merryn across the causeway to the mainland. There was a small cottage hospital in the town where he'd be able to see a doctor and get his wrist X-rayed. Of course, Merryn had claimed that he didn't need any of this, but Ness had insisted upon it.

"I'm pretty sure your wrist's broken," she'd said, while Lucy had started up her ancient car and Fern had bundled Merryn into the passenger seat. "Unless you want to spend the rest of your life attached to a wooden spoon, you need to get it sorted. And as for the bump on the head? You definitely need that looking at if you think you're fine."

Merryn had pulled a face but given in, and before long the tail lights of the car had retreated across the wormy sand and been swallowed by the grey murk of a lacklustre dawn. Ness and Fern had stood waving until they could no longer see the car; then they'd turned back to the castle to make yet more tea. Neither of them had slept and Ness's eyes now felt gritty with exhaustion as the sky grew pink and the light crept across the island. It would be many hours yet before she would get any sleep.

She placed her mug on the draining board and turned to Fern. "Are you ready to inspect the damage?"

Fern grimaced. "Not really. I think Fred has the right idea."

They glanced at the old gardener, fast asleep on the sofa with his cap over his face. His rumbling snores rendered him blissfully unaware of the damage outside. Fern had covered him with the knitted patchwork blanket that was usually folded over the back of the sofa, and Biscuit was snoozing by his feet. At this moment Ness felt very envious of them both.

"The sooner we know what's been affected by the storm, the sooner we can work out what we have to do in order to fix it," she said, injecting a degree of confidence into her voice that she was far from feeling.

"Maybe it isn't as bad as we think?" Fern said optimistically.

"Maybe," Ness agreed, but she didn't hold out much hope.

There was stillness outside and the sea had calmed; the waves were now breaking on the rocks with a sigh rather than the roar of earlier. Gulls called to one another from the sand, where their greedy beaks were rooting through piles of fresh seaweed. Ness and Fern made their way past the ruined tea room and visitor centre, unable to face looking inside, and crossed the lawn where picnic tables and benches were scattered like matchsticks. The palm trees had survived the assault, which didn't surprise Ness in the slightest, but the grass was littered with sharp fronds that the wind had ripped away.

The vegetable garden was set within the walls of what had once been the keep, and this had protected most of Fred's plants from the worst of the weather. They looked a little soggy but the watery sun would soon dry them out.

Fern crouched down by the strawberries and declared that they would probably be fine. She was remarking that Lucy could use them in the tea room – but then her face fell when she remembered that the tea room was in pieces.

"We'll set up an emergency tea room," said Ness quickly. Talk about trying to think on her feet. She didn't even know if this was possible. Wouldn't the castle kitchen need all kinds of health and hygiene checks first? It was usually filled with cats and sleeping gardeners, and the Aga was caked in the grime of decades. They'd be hard-pushed to pass an inspection. Still, they'd have to cross that bridge when they came to it. Perhaps they could have a cleaning party.

Digging her hands deep into the pockets of her hoody, Ness strode down the quay steps and onto the sand, to check the pier wall and the causeway. Her heart plummeted when she saw them: the pounding sea had been merciless.

"The crack in the wall is bigger, isn't it?" she observed.

"Yeah, it wasn't that bad before. It looks to me like some of the stonework is looser too," Fern replied.

They backed away, craning their necks as they peered up at the wall. There was no mistaking the extent of the damage. Was the pier still safe? Ness felt her stomach swoop. How could she tell? Who would she ask?

Closer inspection of the causeway revealed more bad news: a further chunk had been torn from it at the end nearest the island. Thank goodness Lucy was a cautious motorist, Ness thought as she and Fern assessed the damage. Anyone who drove fast along the causeway would be in danger of sliding off. Great. She'd just dig out a few of the million that Armand had left her so that she could pay for all the damage. Oh wait. Her uncle hadn't left her a penny, and Ness knew that the buildings weren't insured either. Lucy had already confessed that the insurance had lapsed some months before.

The castle itself had escaped relatively unscathed, which was hardly surprising given that it had been built to withstand far worse. The ruins looked pretty much as they always did to Ness, but the Pilgrim's Gate appeared a little precarious and several blocks of stonework had tumbled to the ground. They'd have to redirect their visitors, Ness decided as she gazed up at it critically – if they still had any visitors coming to the island, of course. She was no expert but there must be public liability issues here?

Did they even have public liability insurance?

"Thank goodness Armand isn't here to see all this," Fern remarked when they turned back to the castle.

Ness couldn't reply. As far as she was concerned, Armand Penwellyn had a great deal to answer for. Not only had he allowed the place to get out of hand, but he'd left it to her without the means to safeguard it. Whatever had been going on in his mind?

Max Reynard's offer was suddenly very tempting indeed.

By the time Ness and Fern returned to the kitchen, having checked all of the island – including Merryn's caravan, which miraculously had made it through the storm – Lucy had returned from the hospital with the patient. Merryn was all plastered up like something out of The Mummy. Annie Luckett was there too, busy giving him a lecture.

"You're going to move into the castle," she was telling him. "I've spoken to your grandmother too and she agrees. There's no way we're letting you live in a caravan with a broken wrist. So that's your choice: you either move in here or I'll frogmarch you back over the causeway and Rose can take charge."

"You didn't tell my gran?" groaned Merryn, looking at Lucy in alarm.

"I certainly did," Lucy replied staunchly. "I called her while you were being X-rayed. Better she heard it all from me than from one of the staff at the hospital and had a fright. You know how news travels here and how it gets exaggerated. You'd have been at death's door by the time Penny from the village shop saw your granny."

Merryn laughed. He knew she was right.

"Rose says she'll be over to see you as soon as she's finished cottage cleaning," Annie continued, plumping cushions and fussing around the patient. "She was going to call you anyway; she said her second sight told her there was a problem."

"Rose is amazing," Fern explained to Ness. "She's a psychic."

Merryn rolled his eyes. "She saw the weather forecast."

"She is psychic," Fern insisted. "She can read tea leaves and she knows everything."

"I wonder if she knows where my phone is then? I think it must be in the tea room, so she'll be going spare by now. Great. Gran on the case: just what I need," Merryn grumbled.

"Well, you'd better move in here then, or else you'll end up with Rose on your case twenty-four seven," Lucy pointed out. "No arguments, Merryn. You can't live alone in a caravan with a broken wrist."

"Of course I can," he laughed. "I'm a big boy. I can take care of myself."

"Bollocks," said Fern. "You won't even be able to put your own pants on. And before you ask, no I'm not helping you with that. Gross. No way. You'll have to ask one of your slappers from the town. There'll be a queue."

Leaving the two of them to bicker, Ness joined Lucy, who was heating soup on the Aga. With her hair scraped back from her face and violet smudges under her eyes, she looked shattered.

"What a mess," Lucy said.

"There's no insurance, is there?" Ness asked softly.

Lucy swallowed miserably. "No. It lapsed before Uncle died and I never got around to renewing it. There never seemed to be enough money and I really thought we would be able to hold out until the will was read. When Jamie was left the money I didn't know what to do."

The soup swirled in the pan and Ness's stomach swirled with it. Having no insurance meant they couldn't make a claim to fix anything: not the tea room, nor the causeway, nor the unstable-looking pier. It was an absolute disaster. There were no antiques left to sell, and the bare patches on the walls were a reminder that any paintings worth money had been sold long ago. Unless Ness could emulate the Famous Five and find treasure somehow, there would be no means to repair the damage. Without the income from visitors their future looked bleak.

The only way to save the castle is to sell it, Max Reynard had said. Without money it will fall down and you'll end up selling it anyway.

Oh God, thought Ness as despair wrapped icy fingers around her heart. What if he was right?

Unable to face the thought of food, she left the kitchen and headed back outside. The sun had given up shining and instead the world consisted of infinite shades of grey, from the granite rocks to the castle walls to the pewter-coloured sea. Deep in thought, Ness barely noticed the big black Range Rover hurtling along the causeway, until it bounced over the cobbles and almost flattened her.

Great. Jamie Penwellyn had popped across for a gloat. Could this day get any worse?

The window hissed down and, sure enough, her cousin's face – with its features set in their habitual sneer – leered out of the cigarette-scented interior. It took all of Ness's self-control not to recoil.

"Hello, Ness," he brayed. "I just thought I'd pop over for a visit, pick up a few more bits. I heard on the grapevine that there was a bit of an accident here last night? Nobody's badly hurt, I hope? All still alive here?"

Ness had a sudden image of Jamie perched on top of the Pilgrim's Gate trying to dislodge a chunk of masonry to squash her, Wile E Coyote style.

"We're all fine," she said shortly. "If you want to see Lucy, she's in the kitchen."

"I'm surprised she's got time to waste cooking. This place looks an utter state, or maybe I should say even more of a state than it usually does. You do know there's a massive chunk out of the causeway, by the way? More than one, actually. Have you been along and taken a look at it yet? And I'm loving what you've done with the tea room. Is it a Caribbean beach-shack look?"

Ness had never thought of herself as a violent person until now, but right at this moment she was filled with a white-hot desire to drag her gloating cousin out of the car and hold him down face first in a rock pool until the bubbles stopped. Restful as a few years at Her Majesty's pleasure would be in comparison to life on the island, she somehow managed to resist the urge. As she walked away, his mocking laughter rang in her ears.

Fuming, Ness stomped along the causeway and into town. Just as Jamie had said, there were several sections that had been swept away – and if the winter storms were anything like last night's summer one, repairs would need to be made fairly soon. Quite how she'd pay for them was anyone's guess. Did she really need two kidneys?

The beach was thick with seaweed, its pale roots exposed after the angry sea had wrenched up the underwater carpet. All the boats in the harbour were balanced on wooden legs and still lashed to the quayside with extra ropes. A few cottage roofs had bald patches where slates had slipped during the worst of the storm. Litter had blown from the bins; chip wrappers and polystyrene burger boxes were now scattered across the seafront. Ness climbed the steps up to the quay and splashed through puddles as she wandered into town. Where she was headed she had no idea. All she knew was that she needed some time out.

St Pirran was quiet. The bad weather had kept the tourists away from the seaside and sent them scuttling for cover in the Eden Project. Ness wandered through the narrow streets, looking in the windows but barely registering what was displayed in them. Rain began to spit and, as it grew heavier, she ducked into a coffee shop to shelter. She ordered herself an Earl Grey and squeezed into an empty seat. She was so tired that the warmth of the place made her eyes close. When a hand touched her arm, she jumped.

"Sorry, my dear. I didn't mean to frighten you."

An elderly woman stood opposite Ness, appraising her with lively blue eyes set in a lined brown face. It was a bit like being stared at by Mrs Tiggy-Winkle; there was an energy about her that was at odds with her stooped frame and age.

"I'm sorry, do I know you?" Ness asked.

"I'm Rose Hellier," the older woman said, lowering herself into the seat across the table and causing tea to slop into Ness's saucer. "We haven't met but you know my grandson."

"You're Merryn's grandmother?" Ness was jolted wide awake. So this was the same Rose Hellier who'd worked at the castle and who Annie thought might know something about what had really happened to Ness's parents?

"For my sins," Rose said, pulling a face, but the pride in her expression belied the words. "I believe my grandson owes you big time for rescuing him yesterday. From what Lucy's told me, you were incredibly brave."

Ness shook her head. "Not at all; anyone would have done the same."

Merryn's grandmother tilted her head to one side and regarded Ness thoughtfully. "I don't believe they would. Lots of people would have been afraid or would have waited for someone else to take the lead. I saw the weather come in yesterday and it was one of the worst storms I've seen for a long time. Going into the tea room when the roof could have caved in at any moment was very brave. You probably saved his life."

Ness coloured. "Merryn's a friend. He'd have done the same for me."

"Just a friend? Or is he more? You can tell me if I'm being nosy – it's all part of being an interfering grandmother."

It was just as well things hadn't gone any further between herself and Merryn, thought Ness. Rose Hellier had a way about her that made you feel she already knew the answers to the questions she was asking. Suddenly Fern's comments about Rose's psychic powers didn't seem quite so far-fetched.

"We're just friends," Ness said firmly.

Rose smiled. "I believe you, although there's a part of me that is a little disappointed." She took Ness's hand in her own. The old lady's skin was as thin as tissue paper, but there was strength in the fingers that turned Ness's hand over to trace the lines on her palm.

"May I read for you?"

Ness was a bit taken aback, but she didn't want to look rude. "OK."

Rose stared down at their entwined hands and sighed. "It's as I thought. Merryn isn't the twin flame you seek. That man is further away and closer than you can imagine. He has two sides and walks a dangerous path. That danger draws you closer and consumes you."

Ness stared at Rose. What on earth was she talking about?

"You have many questions too," Rose continued, her voice low and intense. "So many questions and no answers are forthcoming. The music is the key. Listen to the music: it will lead you to the answers you are seeking."

"What do you mean?" Ness asked. None of Rose's words made sense. Wasn't she supposed to tell her that a tall dark stranger was coming her way? "Rose? What's that supposed to mean, listen to the music? What music? What man?"

Rose blinked and slowly let Ness's fingers slip from her own. "I'm sorry, love, I have no idea. The messages just come through me. My guides don't tell me what they mean. Usually the people I'm reading for are able to make sense of them."

"I must be the one exception then, because I don't have a clue what any of that means," Ness said with an awkward laugh. "I suppose your guides are right about one thing: I certainly have a lot of questions, but they're not about romance or music."

But Rose was unperturbed. "That's what you may think now, but on a deeper level that's exactly what they're about. My guides are never wrong."

Right. What did you say to that? Ness really wasn't sure.

"Oh dear, I've made you feel awkward," said Rose. "That wasn't my intention at all. I only sought you out to thank you for what you did for Merryn. Feel free to ignore my ramblings. I'm sure he'll tell you I'm an utter menace. I bet even at this moment he's trying to think of a way to tell me tactfully that he doesn't want to convalesce at home. Ah! I can see by your face I'm right!"

"Now I'm starting to believe you might be on to something," Ness said, but Rose Hellier just laughed.

"That's nothing to do with being psychic, love. That's about being a grandmother! If Merryn were to live at home with me he wouldn't be able to get much past me. Of course he doesn't want to put up with that! Now, let me get you another tea – I promise not to read the leaves – and then you can ask me about your parents. And that's nothing to do with being psychic either. Annie Luckett told me you wanted to have a chat."

Rose fetched more drinks, waving away Ness's offer of payment, and then settled herself back at the table. She tipped several sachets of sugar into her tea and stirred it thoughtfully.

"I was working at the castle when your mother arrived," she said at last. "I used to go over a couple of times a week to give the housekeeper a bit of a hand. It was a different place then, you see, and there were quite a few staff employed. Your Uncle Armand was very sociable in those days and he often entertained."

Ness nodded. Lucy had said something similar. "Did you know my father?"

"I knew all three brothers. They grew up here and my son played with them as a boy," said Rose. "They were nice lads, although your father was a real monkey. I remember several occasions when I had to tell him off for something or other. He was always up to mischief."

"He wasn't much different as an adult," Ness sighed.

"They were wild as young men too," Rose recalled, sipping her tea and gazing over Ness's shoulder and out the window to the castle. "They weren't short of money, that was for sure. There were some wonderful parties. Armand was becoming quite famous. The Island Suite was making his name in musical circles. He was supposed to be writing a symphony and everyone was very excited about it."

"That's the symphony he never wrote," said Ness.

Rose shot her a sharp look. "How do you know he never wrote it?"

"It's what everyone says. He was meant to be writing this masterpiece but it never got written." Ness put her teacup down with a clatter. "He must have got the musical equivalent of writer's block."

Merryn's grandmother said nothing for a moment. Then she exhaled slowly. "Your mother was around at this time, Nessa. She was very much a part of their crowd."

Ness stared at her, heart pounding. "You remember my mother?"

"I couldn't forget Beth Lacey; nobody could. She was like a breath of fresh air sweeping through the place when she arrived. She came to play the violin and help Armand with his composing. She was very musical." Rose leaned forward. "Are you musical?"

"Sadly not," Ness sighed. She couldn't paint either. Addy had despaired.

"Beth was very gifted," Rose said. "She was beautiful and talented and she loved it here. I'd often see her walking on the beach, barefoot and with her hair blowing in the wind, and she loved the water."

"Did she?" Ness was thrilled to learn this. Was it from her mother that she'd inherited her need to live near the ocean and her love of diving?

"Oh yes. She spent hours out sailing or swimming in the Grace Note rock pool. It drove Armand mad trying to track her down when he wanted to explore a composition." Her eyes narrowed. "You look just like her, you know."

"Do I? I never knew her."

Rose slumped back in her seat and a shadow flitted across her face. "No, I know you didn't."

"So what happened?" Now that she was this close Ness had to find out more. "How did she meet my father? What went wrong?"

"She met your father at the castle," said Rose. She looked very old all of a sudden, the lines in her face tightening and her gaze somewhere far, far away.

"And?" Ness urged. "Was it love at first sight?"

"I was just a member of staff, love. I wouldn't have been party to any of their private business. It must have been a very swift thing though. They were inseparable and they certainly married very fast. I suspect you may have been something to do with that."

"I don't know. He hardly ever mentioned her to me. I thought he hated her," Ness said bleakly.

"Love and hate aren't as far apart as people think," Rose replied. "It was probably too painful for him to talk about her."

"Because she drowned?"

Rose didn't answer but instead looked out across the sea. The water was calm now, a different animal to the raging, spitting monster of earlier. That same water had closed over Beth Penwellyn's head and taken her away forever.

"Rose, if you know anything about what happened, please tell me," Ness pleaded.

"There were rumours of an argument between the three brothers but I don't know much more. I wasn't there that evening and everyone who worked at the castle would have been inside and out of the weather," Rose recalled. "I heard that Beth slipped into the water and it was dreadfully rough, like last night I should imagine, and Armand tried to save her. He dived into the water over and over again until he nearly drowned himself."

"My uncle tried to rescue her?" Ness was taken aback. "But what about my father? Where was he?"

Rose looked distressed. "Nessa, I don't know. I only know what I was told by the staff who were there that night. The brothers had had a big row. I think Adric tried to save her too."

"But what did the brothers argue about?" Ness cried, beyond frustrated. It must have been something pretty serious if they'd all run outside in the middle of a storm. The wild Cornish weather wasn't to be toyed with. And why was Beth there too? What had happened?

Rose set her cup down in the saucer with a rattle. "Look, all I can tell you is that the answer is in the music. Listen to the music and it will tell you everything."

"That's it? That's all you can tell me?"

"That's all I know." The older woman stood up slowly. Her face looked grey, as though their conversation had taken an enormous amount of energy. "I'd best get going if I'm going to make it across the causeway and see that grandson of mine before the tide turns."

Ness forced herself to smile and nod. After all, it wasn't Rose's fault that Addy had been so secretive. If anyone had kept the truth hidden it had been her father. She just had such a nagging sense that she was missing something huge.

The answer is in the music.

Great. That was a really good piece of advice for a girl who was tone deaf.

Once Rose had left, Ness stared out across the beach and watched the stooped figure make her slow progress across the causeway. The disappointment at being given only a riddle, rather than the answers she needed, was overwhelming. She'd pinned so much hope on Rose knowing something important; that she knew no more than anyone else was a real blow. How many more dead ends would there be?

As she sat in the café and thought about her lost parents, the damage to the island and the rapidly spiralling costs, Ness didn't think she'd ever felt quite so alone. What if there were no answers at all? And what if Armand's trust in her had been misplaced and she couldn't carry this new burden? What if she had no choice but to sell the island?

The answer is in the music.

Ness frowned. Maybe if she figured out what this meant everything else would fall into place. That was a hope she had to cling to.

One thing was for certain, anyway: nothing could possibly get worse than it already was.

Chapter 19

"The tea room's ruined, the causeway needs some urgent repairs and another good storm will finish the pier off. You can bet your entire fortune that Lucy won't have been able to afford to keep the insurance up to date either. So basically, they're screwed."

As he described the damage that last week's summer storm had wreaked on Pirran Island, Jamie Penwellyn could hardly keep the expression of glee from his face – and he was lounging in the office chair as though he owned Reynards. Although Jamie was the bearer of what might be considered good news, Max found he was itching to wipe that smug smile off his visitor's gloating face. What sort of man revelled in seeing his family's fortunes brought so low and enjoyed the thought of his sister struggling? Or saw a situation where she could have been injured as a cause for celebration?

The answer was one like Jamie: a spineless individual who'd always look for the path of least resistance. Of course, without his type companies such as Reynards wouldn't have made nearly as much money. There were always Jamies to be found, happy to cash in an inheritance for a quick buck or sell a legacy as it slipped out of an elderly relative's grasp. Of course there were. How else would a big developer acquire so many plum properties? Such greed and desperation had played straight into Max's hands on many occasions.

Unable to bear looking at his unexpected guest any longer, Max swivelled his leather chair around and gazed out of his office window. The floor-to-ceiling glass afforded him a dizzying view of London. Planes circled in a cloudless sky and countless windows glittered in the sunshine while the traffic moved by below, soundless and smooth from this vantage point. But Max wasn't seeing this living picture. He was seeing Nessa Penwellyn – with her angry sea-green eyes, determined chin and cloud of red hair – as she told him she'd never sell to him. Try as he might to banish the image, he was also seeing those lush curves in that clinging wet vest top. He recalled that although her words had told him to keep away, Ness's body language had been saying something completely different.

This mental picture was proving very hard to erase – a fact that left Max feeling caught off balance. He was used to being able to take or leave women. It was unsettling to find himself thinking about Ness and hoping that she was safe and not too distressed.

By all accounts the unexpected summer storm had been severe; Adam had alerted Max to the extent of the damage in the town and to their potential development. It sounded bad and, even before he'd received Jamie's gleeful update, Max had guessed that the island had been hit hard. Apparently Adam's son, who usually played the piano up at the castle, had stopped visiting for the time being, while Lucy concentrated on the tea room and the local ferryman recovered from an injury. When Max had asked just how serious the damage was, his best friend had seemed reluctant to tell him.

"What's all this?" Max had demanded, rather put out. "Are you going native on me? You'll be up there rebuilding the place for them next. Shall we rename you Dances with Islanders?"

He'd been joking but Adam hadn't seen the funny side. Instead Adam had replied rather stiffly that he would certainly be giving Lucy Penwellyn a helping hand if she asked, because she'd been good to Josh.

"Traitor," Max had teased. "I thought you were on my side?"

"I didn't realise we were taking sides here, Max," Adam had said before ringing off.

Max frowned. Adam had always been his wingman, the Goose to his Maverick, and to find that his friend's loyalties might have shifted a little made Max uneasy. Adam was employed to head up the team that would renovate and develop the castle; it was no good him getting sentimental at this stage. Likewise, Max couldn't allow his thoughts to drift to Nessa Penwellyn. This was business. There would always be plenty of women. Ness might be sexy as hell but she was also an obstacle he could do without. Dinner, some fun and a sale. Then she'd be out of his system. That was how it usually worked.

Still, Max hoped she was all right. The storm must have been savage if the damage was anywhere near as bad as Jamie was telling him.

Christ. What was the matter with him? He wanted the bloody castle, not the woman who lived in it. What did it matter what happened to her? The main thing was getting Nessa Penwellyn to sell. How he achieved this didn't matter. All that counted was the final result.

Infuriated with himself for dithering for as much as a nanosecond, Max spun the chair around again to face Jamie, who was staring at him expectantly.

"So could you advance me some more funds? Maybe another twenty grand or so? Just until the sale is sorted?"

Max wasn't often surprised in business, but Jamie Penwellyn came close to making his mouth fall open with disbelief. Jamie had seriously come here to ask for more money? Things must be bad. Adam had described how Jamie had taken the grand piano away and presumably sold it for a good price. He must be motoring through the cash. In Max's experience, that made him a loose and rather dangerous cannon.

"You owe me a lot of money, Jamie," Max said slowly and with an edge of menace in his voice. "You promised me all sorts of things that you haven't delivered, and I'm not feeling inclined to be patient. What are we going to do about it?"

"The place is in a state, old boy. They've lost the tea room and it's going to cost a fortune to fix the causeway. There's no money left anywhere and I know for a fact that none of the organisations that have helped in the past would be willing to dish out grants while the place is in such a hazardous state. There's no more in the pot. That's a fact. Nessa will have to sell up because it's game over."

Max steepled his fingers beneath his chin.

"That wasn't the answer to the question I asked. What are you going to do to get things moving? I seem to recall that you promised me you would make sure everything was sorted. Or was that all hot air?"

"I will sort it!" Jamie retorted. An angry flush spread across his cheeks.

Max raised a cynical eyebrow. "I look forward to seeing how. Maybe we should just settle up now? You sold a Steinway recently, I believe? That should just about cover anything I loaned you."

"How the hell do you know that?" Jamie looked genuinely shocked.

"I have my sources. So, shall we cut our losses?"

Not even a flicker of his eyelashes gave away the fact that Max was toying with his visitor. Judging by his waxy pallor, Jamie believed he was only seconds away from having to admit he was broke. Max didn't even want to imagine where Jamie's money went, but unless he was suffering from hay fever in this air-conditioned office, his perpetual sniff was a bit of a giveaway.

"Let's not be hasty," Jamie was saying now, leaning forward across the desk in his desperation to impress. "I think the storm will do all the work for us anyway."

"You could be right, which renders you redundant," Max agreed. "I need you why, exactly?"

"I'll visit again. I'll persuade Lucy to get Ness to see reason," Jamie promised. "Lucy will agree once I've finished. I swear it."

It wasn't Lucy who needed to agree, Max thought with growing irritation. He was tired of Jamie and, amusing as it was to goad him, this wasn't getting them anywhere. Max needed to chat with the organ grinder rather than the monkey – and when the organ grinder (so to speak) was a sexy redhead he couldn't stop thinking about, talking to her rather than an intermediary made even more sense.

"Let's hope so," was all he said to Jamie, who nodded and then left as hastily as he could, no doubt en route to whatever loan shark or dodgy broker he could find. Poor Lucy would be getting an ear bashing too – which of course would be totally pointless, since it was obvious that Nessa Penwellyn was a woman who made up her own mind and stuck to it. She wouldn't be bullied or railroaded; she was as bloody stubborn as they came. In spite of his frustration with the project Max smiled, because people probably said just the same about him.

It was time they had another chat. Maybe this time she'd be a little more inclined to listen to reason?

Max picked up his desk phone to instruct his PA to hold all calls. Then he plucked his mobile out of his jacket pocket. Scrolling through the contacts, he found the number he was looking for and pressed the green call button. As he spun his chair around to watch the city street beneath him, Max listened to the ringing and imagined the phone shrilling for attention in the cool depths of Pirran Castle.

"Hello?" The answering voice was breathless, as though its owner had run through passageways and climbed stairs to reach the phone. Maybe she had, who knew? Max hadn't been inside the castle for a while but he did remember how vast the place had felt to him as a boy.

"Ness." He leaned back in the chair, the leather creaking as he cradled the handset against his ear. What a stroke of luck that she'd answered rather than Annie Luckett or that surly Merryn. "It's Max Reynard."

There was a gasp at the end of the line. "How did you get this number? Did you bribe somebody? Or did you have one of your minions torture a local until they talked?"

He laughed. "A beer would be far more effective than torture in St Pirran. No, as much as I'd like to say that I bribed several people and then killed the one who gave the information away, I'm afraid the actual answer is far more banal. I found the number for Pirran Castle ages ago in the telephone directory."

"Oh. Right." Ness sounded wrong-footed and there was a pause before she added sharply, "I'm guessing this isn't a social call?"

"It could be if you'll have dinner with me?" In the tinted glass, Max's reflection was smiling. He was enjoying this game of social chess very much.

She snorted. "I'd rather starve."

"From what I hear about the damage to the castle and the causeway, that might happen," Max said evenly. "Look, Ness, I couldn't live with myself if I allowed you to fade away. One dinner?"

There was a brief hesitation. "So you can pump me for information, I suppose?"

His lips curved at this. He could imagine her blushing, aware of the double entendre. "How uncharitable," he replied.

"How accurate." Ness sounded bitter. "You've heard about the storm and you've come sniffing around again to buy at a knockdown price, haven't you?"

"Not at all. I'd offer you the same as before. Seven million." Beyond the window the city sparkled and glittered, a man-made shrine to mammon where seven million was to so many what seven quid was to others. For a fleeting moment Max imagined his father's look of disgust. Malcom Reynard wouldn't have had any time for city boys who made their money from gambling with possibilities. Good honest work was what Malcom had respected. Making a cheeky offer to a woman who was in a desperate situation was not something his father would have done either. Feeling a prickle of shame, Max said quickly, "Look, I'll even go to eight if we can move fast."

Now it was Ness's turn to laugh. "Eight million? You're talking fantasy numbers here."

"These figures are real, believe me. My legal team move fast, Nessa. That money could be yours by next month. Eight million pounds."

Max wished he could see her at this moment. What would the expression on her face be? Greed? Excitement? Disgust? There was no way of reading somebody over a telephone.

"It might as well be eight million magic beans. I'm not selling to you. You can offer me whatever you want. Pirran Island is not for sale."

A challenge. Max sat up. "Are you trying to push me higher?"

"No. I said I'm not selling to you. The island isn't for sale."

"Nessa, come on. You have to be realistic. There's more damage to the castle than you can handle. You've got no money and no hope of any income or grants in the foreseeable future. How on earth will you make it pay?"

"That's my business," she snapped, and Max knew he'd hit a nerve. Nessa Penwellyn didn't have a clue how to solve the mess she was in. She was probably scouring the castle in the hope of finding any antiques Armand and Jamie might have overlooked.

"But it doesn't have to be just your business," he said softly. "Ness, this must be a huge burden to carry. Let me help. I've already said we can work on the project together and I'll give you an apartment. Imagine how it would feel to see the castle come back to life and know that it was thanks to you. If you don't sell now the whole place will be in disrepair and probably beyond salvaging. You're not doing Pirran Island any favours by clinging on."

"And I won't be doing it any favours by selling out to you. Don't give me all that crap about saving the place. You just want to make money out of it. That's all people like you care about." Her voice was shaking with fury and Max was stung by her accusation.

"I certainly care about the castle but it needs money to be protected. If you can't see that then you're naïve at best and stupid at worst."

"Naïve and stupid," Ness repeated slowly. "Well, we'll see about that. Take your millions, Max. I hope they make you really happy. This island is not for sale. Not now, not ever, and certainly not to you."

Then all Max heard was the dial tone. Ending the call, he placed his iPhone on the desk and stared sightlessly across the city. There had been a steely edge to Ness's parting words and Max knew he'd played his hand badly. Ness wasn't the kind of woman to be cajoled or intimidated or persuaded. She was independent and strong and utterly determined to succeed. Now she would do everything in her power to prove him wrong. Of course she would. It was exactly how he would react if it had been him. For the first time in his life, Max Reynard had met somebody as purposeful and bloody-minded as himself.

And he didn't have a clue what to do next.

Chapter 20

Ness wasn't usually inclined to call meetings but desperate times called for desperate measures. Besides, this wasn't so much a meeting as a council of war.

Almost a week had passed since the storm had hit St Pirran, a week in which Ness very quickly realised that the damage would run into tens of thousands to put right. Thanks to the efforts of Josh's stonemason dad, Adam, and some of Merryn's friends, the tea shop's roof had been patched up and made watertight. Meanwhile, Annie and her team of volunteers had cleared up the mess inside. These were only temporary measures though, and if another gale struck it was doubtful whether the repairs would hold. The Pilgrim's Gate seemed stable enough to Ness but Adam had strongly suggested that they shouldn't allow any visitors near it. And as for the causeway and the pier? His worried expression had said it all.

"I'm not a structural engineer but this looks serious to me," he'd told Ness and Lucy when the tide had been far enough out to allow for close inspection of the pier. "I'd say it's a job for a specialist team. That crack could stay the same way for another decade or one big storm could split the top section clean away. My advice would be to fix it as soon as possible in case things deteriorate further. I certainly wouldn't recommend leaving it beyond the autumn."

Lucy had looked close to tears. "But won't that be very expensive?"

"I expect so," Adam had said gently. "But there are grants for these kinds of thing. I'll look into that for you, if you like."

Ness had felt close to tears herself when they'd moved on to examine the causeway. The mile-long path looked like a Curly Wurly bar that a hungry giant had taken big bites out of. Unlike the pier, the repairs to this wouldn't require experts. Adam was sure that a team of local builders would be able to handle the task, but Ness knew they wouldn't come cheap either.

"Isn't the council supposed to look after roads?" she'd asked hopefully, but Lucy had soon put paid to any such idea.

"The causeway's a private road so we have to maintain it," she'd explained. "In any case, they'd probably say that we can still use boats to reach the island. There's no way the council will help. It's hardly a matter of priority."

So, short of investing in some amphibious vehicles or resigning herself to not being able to get anything that wasn't a four-by-four across to the island, Ness was going to have to find a way of stumping up for repairs. She'd been on what had to be her fifth sweep of the castle in search of any stray Ming vases that might save the day, when the phone had rung in the Small Hall with bloody Max Reynard on the line offering her the answer to all her problems.

Eight million. It was an amount that Ness couldn't even imagine and one that would certainly solve all her difficulties. Eight million pounds. It was a vast sum of money, the kind that lottery winners had printed on giant cheques or that celebrities spent on Hollywood mansions. Nevertheless, it was an offer she wouldn't contemplate for even a second. There was no way she'd dream of selling to Max Reynard. She wasn't going to watch him turn the castle into luxury apartments while ripping the heart out of the place. He might try to sway her with all his talk of rescuing the building but Ness wasn't fooled; a man like Max only cared about money.

She wouldn't sell to him. She'd be buried in the rubble first – which was looking more and more likely by the day if she couldn't come up with some rescue plan soon. Still simmering with anger after the telephone conversation, Ness had decided that it was time to lay her cards on the table with the island's other residents. She might technically own the place but, as the newcomer to St Pirran, Ness knew she had a great deal of catching up to do as well as needing all the help she could get. It was time to pool the knowledge of everyone here.

The Small Hall was an obvious gathering place. The refectory table seated everyone and as the evening sun streamed through the high windows, Ness glanced up at her uncle's portrait reproachfully. What on earth had Armand been thinking to leave her, a total stranger, his estate but no money to maintain it? Lucy could keep saying that he would have had his reasons until she was blue in the face, but Ness wasn't convinced. What possible reason could he have had for placing everything in jeopardy? He must have lost his mind.

"Shall we make a start?" Annie asked Ness. She glanced at the longcase clock with a frown. "There are only a couple of hours until the tide turns and I've walked over."

"I could take you back," Fern offered from her place opposite. "If I drive the boat, Merryn can tell me what to do. It can't be that hard."

Merryn, whose wrist was still strapped up, rolled his eyes. "There's no way I'm letting you loose with Guardian Angel, squirt. I'd still like to have a boat to work once I'm out of plaster."

While they squabbled and Lucy tried to distract them by dishing up slices of apple cake, Ness took a mental roll call. Yep, all present and correct. Annie was sitting at the far end with a spiral-bound notepad and brandishing a red biro, Fred was dozing beside her and even Biscuit had shown up. She took a deep breath. This was it. It was time to let them know just how bad things really were.

"Max Reynard's offered me eight million pounds for the island," she began. Talk about the shock factor! Leaping in with this had certainly got their attention. Even Fred looked up in amazement.

"Bloody hell," said Fern. "He's not messing about, is he?"

"Max Reynard never messes about," Annie remarked. "When he wants something he generally goes after it until it's his."

"Eight million though," whispered Lucy, looking stunned. "Oh Ness, none of us would blame you if you sold for that price. We all know how hard it is here."

"I told Max he can offer me whatever he wants, I'm not selling," Ness said firmly. She was rewarded with a collective sigh of relief. "But," she added, holding up a hand before they could all start asking questions, "he did make one really good point, which is that the island does need a lot of money spent on it. There were huge amounts of work to do even before the storm."

"And we don't have any money." Merryn shook his blond head. "I can see that in your eyes, Ness."

Ness looked away, embarrassed. "Admittedly there's very little left in the pot now to support the day-to-day running of the estate, let alone cover any repairs after the storm," she replied.

"So basically we're skint," said Fern.

"That's one way of putting it," Annie agreed. "Ness, maybe you should seriously consider selling while there's a good offer rather than be forced to sell further down the road and possibly for less."

"I'm not selling," Ness said. "Not while we still have options, anyway." There was silence as she glanced around the table at their serious faces. "Oh dear. This is the point where I was really hoping somebody would come up with a genius idea and save the day? Or tell me that there's a priceless antique somewhere we've overlooked?"

Fern perked up. "There are lots of paintings here, aren't there, Lucy? And lots of lovely furniture. Those must be worth something, surely?"

But Lucy shook her head. "Sorry, Fern, but I really don't think so. This is a family home. It was bought by my grandfather;

it was never a Downton Abbey style estate. All the furniture was bought at auctions and the paintings are mostly by Ness's father. Talented as Addy obviously was, they're not worth a great deal. Anything that was valuable was sold long ago."

"It doesn't make sense," said Annie. "Armand was such a clever man. To leave the estate but no income to support it seems pointless. I simply cannot believe he'd do such a thing. What did he expect would happen?"

"He always told me the solution to everything was at my fingertips, whatever that meant. He did love his riddles. I was always playing musical ones with him," sighed Lucy.

Annie nodded. "Yes, that sounds like the kind of cryptic remark he liked to make. Armand might have enjoyed guessing games but it's not very helpful now. Oh! If the old bugger wasn't dead already I would throttle him right now!"

What was it with these old people and their riddles? wondered Ness. It was all very annoying. When Ness was old she'd make a point of telling everyone exactly what was what.

"So the bottom line is that we need a lot of money," Merryn said. "I'd offer to sell my body but I don't think it's up to much right now."

His comment lightened the atmosphere briefly and there was a ripple of laughter.

"Sell veg," hollered Fred from the far end of the table, making them all jump.

"It's a good idea," Annie said kindly, reaching across and patting his hand, "but we'd need to sell quite a lot."

"I could try approaching banks for loans," Ness suggested to Annie, who grimaced.

"Yes, that's a possibility I suppose. I guess I'm old-fashioned, though. Borrowing money makes me nervous."

"Wouldn't it be a no-brainer for a bank? In return for a loan they'd have an interest in an eight-million-pound investment," Merryn pointed out.

"Will they lend to me?" asked Ness. "I've not been living here long enough, surely?"

They all stared at her glumly.

"What about a venture capitalist of some sort? Or some other kind of lender?" wondered Fern.

"Isn't that a bit risky?" said Annie. "The buying and selling of debts is how these companies make money. You don't know who you could end up in hock to. I'd say anything like that should only be a very, very last resort."

Ness didn't comment, but it occurred to her that this might be worth looking into. Her ex's father had been a venture capitalist. It was one of those jobs that people on St Antonia had talked about and that she didn't really understand. Perhaps it was time she found out?

"I'll willingly donate all my royalties from Uncle's estate," Lucy offered. "They don't come in for a while and I'm not sure how much there's going to be, but it's going to help, isn't it?"

Ness smiled at her. Lucy had to be one of the most generous people she'd ever met. Not once had she complained about things being unfair – yet out of all of them it was she, who'd nursed her uncle through his illness and clearly still mourned him, who'd been the most overlooked. If Armand Penwellyn had appeared at this moment, Ness would have been inclined to have a sharp word with him.

"Of course it will," she said warmly.

"So we've established that there are no antiques to sell – and of course there's no immediate income either, with the tea room in a state of disrepair." Merryn's usually cheerful face was serious. "Max Reynard's offer is a no go and the royalties from the music won't be in for a few months."

"There's enough money to continue like this until the early autumn, but after that..." Lucy's voice tailed off and she looked around helplessly. She didn't need to say any more.

Ness's fists clenched beneath the table. There had to be a way to carry on. Giving up was not an option. Maybe it would have been if Pirran Island was still unknown to her and just an idea, as relevant to the sweltering beachy world of St Antonia as inheriting a chunk of Mars, but now the place had wound its way into her heart. There were secrets too that she knew were waiting to be uncovered. How could she leave while Beth Penwellyn's death was still unsolved and her father's exile remained a mystery?

The answer was that she couldn't. While the others discussed various ideas, Ness vowed to do everything she could to prevent the island falling into Max Reynard's sweaty hands. The fact that his hands were actually tanned and strong and had made her tremble was one she chose to ignore.

"But Jesus came to this island!" protested Fern, and Merryn laughed bleakly.

"By the sounds of things, even He can't save us now."

"Whatever happens, I'm not selling to Reynards. I'd rather let the whole place fall down." Ness glanced around the table at the worried faces. "I mean it. This place isn't for sale. We just need to think of other ways we can raise money. Enough country houses have managed it, so why not us?"

Annie nodded. "Ness is right. We already open parts of the castle up for two days a week in the summer. If we could think of some other good ideas it would be a start."

Merryn looked doubtful. "We're talking a lot of money. Just maintaining a property this size takes thousands."

Annie fixed him with the same steely stare that had reduced several generations of St Pirran's schoolchildren to jelly. "I know that. I'm not completely gaga, but we have to try something. Surely between all of us we can come up with a plan?"

There was a collective grinding of mental cogs as everyone did their best to think of a solution. This was followed by a flurry of ideas, some of which made more sense than others. Fred's shouts of "vegetables" could have meant anything from developing a range of premium organic foodstuffs to manning a market stall, and Ness wasn't convinced that Annie's murder mystery weekends set in the grounds would work in the depths of winter. On the other hand, she did agree that a festival of some kind could be good.

"What about a rock concert?" Merryn said. "We've got local bands, and lots of celebs live nearby. We could even provide camping areas."

"Or we could have a fairy festival!" Fern's eyes lit up. "With yurts and music and fire-eating."

"We could rent the castle out for filming too," added Annie. "Look how successful Poldark was."

"Or how about glamping?" Lucy chipped in. "Everyone loves to holiday in Cornwall, don't they? We have the most amazing water and beaches here, even if it is cold."

Ness nodded. Tourism was something she did know about and it had crossed her mind that this could be a solution of sorts. The gin-clear waters off the island were beautiful, and the marine life was breath-taking. With a good wetsuit, the diving would be fantastic – and with the amount of wildlife that surrounded them, ecotourism could be another direction for them to take.

"Nude calendar?" Fern was saying, grinning across at Merryn. "I bet lots of local girls would pay to see you with your kit off! Or maybe not actually? Most of them have already seen that!"

"Lucky for you I'm injured," Merryn said good-naturedly. Turning to Ness, he added, "I think we've got some really good ideas here. Why don't each of us take one and then do some research? We can meet again in a week and see what we've got."

At this point the meeting drew to a close as everyone decided what their pet project would be. Although they were still in a precarious position there was now an air of optimism in the room and a buzz of energy too. If gathering together had only succeeded in raising spirits then it had been worth every minute.

Lucy gathered her paperwork up and smiled at Ness. It was a weary and sad smile which said she knew exactly what they were up against. Once they were alone Ness was able to voice her deepest fear.

"You think it's too late, don't you?"

"I'll be honest with you, Ness. Short of a miracle, I can't see what could possibly be done."

Ness bit her lip. She knew in her heart that, as much fun as all their ideas were, it was all far too late in the day. What had their uncle been thinking?

"I'm going to need to borrow money, aren't I?" she said quietly. "I need to go to the bank."

Her cousin sighed. "Much as it pains me to say it, maybe we'll have to consider doing some kind of a deal with Max Reynard. He could be our only hope of saving this place."

Ness said nothing. Just the thought of the satisfaction in those grey eyes if she admitted defeat was enough to harden her resolve. She'd make a point of asking anyone but him.

There was really only one choice left now: Ness was going to have to swallow her pride and go begging for money. Surely somebody would want to take a chance and invest?

If not, she'd live in the ruins rather than go cap in hand to Max. Whatever happened, there was one thing she was very sure of: Pirran Island would never, ever be his.

Chapter 21

Lucy was running late. The meeting had gone on far longer than she'd expected, and without Merryn to ferry her across to the mainland she had to beat the tide and use the causeway. She was finally meeting Adam for their promised dinner. She hoped he wasn't intending to eat anywhere smart where her outfit of trainers, combats and a long-sleeved tee shirt would let him down. She'd been intending to wash her hair and hunt out some make-up, but time had simply run away from her and now she was striding it out to town with a bare face and her hair in a ponytail. Not really how she'd imagined looking on a date.

Not that this was a date, Lucy scolded herself sharply. Where had that ridiculous thought come from? This was just a chance to have some food with the father of her star pupil – a father who also happened to be a nice man. Adam Miller was friendly and there was no denying that he was attractive in a twinkly-eyed and easy-going kind of way, but there was nothing more to her association with him than that he was Josh's father. Adam was being kind and thanking her for the time she'd spent with his son; that was it. To read anything more into this invitation would be absurd.

The tide had reached the side of the causeway and bubbles edged the cobbles. Ten minutes more and she would have missed her chance to get to the mainland. Even though she'd seen the damage every day since the storm, Lucy was still shocked by its extent. Getting supplies over to the island was going to be more difficult now and she suspected they'd have to rely more heavily on boats – which was fine at this time of year, but tended to be tricky in the winter when the seas were heavy. She could only hope that Armand's royalties were unusually good this year and that some of the ideas raised in the earlier meeting proved useful.

Lucy sighed. It seemed unlikely and, although she'd never admit it to anyone, she felt dreadfully let down by her uncle. If he'd wanted the island sold then he should have just left it to Jamie rather than involving Ness and raising all their hopes. It was beyond cruel to leave them to struggle without even the minimum income needed to run the island. For all Armand's cryptic comments about the answers being at her fingertips, Lucy was no closer to finding a solution to their problems. It made her heart heavy to even think it for a second, but she was afraid that it was already way too late. If Max Reynard made Ness another offer then maybe her cousin should admit defeat and just accept it? Where Lucy would go and what she would do, she didn't know. Caring for her ailing parents and then her uncle hadn't left her with time to forge a career of her own. She guessed that with some cottage cleaning, baking and piano tuition she'd get by. In any case, this wasn't Nessa's concern, and Lucy would never dream of burdening her cousin with her own worries.

"Hey, that's a glum face. Is the thought of eating with me really so bad?"

Adam was halfway down the quayside steps, smiling his crinkly smile – and in spite of her gloomy musings, Lucy discovered she was smiling in answer.

"I haven't dressed for dinner, I'm afraid," she apologised, as they met at the foot of the steps. "We had a lot on and I've only just managed to get away."

Adam leaned forward and kissed her cheek. He smelt of fresh linen and oranges, Lucy thought. Oh dear. What did she smell of? Jeyes Fluid and despair probably.

"You've had enough on this week without having to worry about anything like that," Adam told her. "How are things?"

As they climbed the steps and headed into town, Lucy filled him in on the latest developments and Adam listened sympathetically. Once the storm had blown itself out he'd been one of the first to offer his help – and in a practical way too, as well as in his professional capacity. What he'd had to say about the state of the quay and the Pilgrim's Gate hadn't been easy to hear, but she'd appreciated his honesty just as much as she'd appreciated his help in shoring up the tea room. It was a shame he worked for Max but Lucy wasn't going to hold that against Adam; it was hard enough to find work these days, and with Josh to think about he'd have to take whatever was offered. Still, she held back from telling him quite how bad things really were. Adam worked for Max, after all, and the less insider information that man had the better.

"So that's where we are," she finished. "We're looking for ideas to raise some money to help with repairs. So if you have any, feel free to tell me."

Adam looked thoughtful. "Hmm, I'll get my thinking cap on. I like the festival idea very much though, and what a setting! I've got a friend who's been crew for a couple of festivals. I think he did Glasto too. I could put you in touch if that helps?"

"That would be great," said Lucy.

"Least I can do, after all you do for Josh. He's desperate to come back and play the piano, by the way."

"Tell him to come over tomorrow. I'll be inside baking. We're opening part of the tea room again because it's one of our days for visitors. I could do with an iPhone lesson too, if he's up for it?"

"Josh is always up for any excuse to be on the island!"

"What's Josh up to this evening?" Lucy asked.

"He's with a school friend. I know, isn't that something?" Adam said, when her eyes widened. "Honestly, Lucy, the change in him since he's been coming over to Pirran Island is incredible. He's got so much more confidence and I can't thank you enough."

"It's nothing to do with me," Lucy protested, but Adam shook his head.

"I won't have you saying that because it's got everything to do with you. You've been there for him, encouraged his music again – which is something a tone-deaf numpty like me could never do – and you've made him feel that he belongs." He stopped in his tracks, placing his hands on her shoulders and turning her to face him. "Lucy, I really mean it: I can't ever thank you enough for what you've done."

Lucy felt her face grow warm. "I love having him there and, honestly, it's a privilege to be able to teach such a talented boy. He truly is exceptional."

"He's not the only one. You are too," Adam replied, but so quietly that Lucy wasn't sure if he'd really said anything at all. Before she could speak his hands fell away, and only the warmth left on her skin told her that she hadn't imagined the charged moment.

"Right, food." Adam rubbed his hands together. "You're not wearing that lovely dress and I'm still covered in masonry dust, so I don't think the Italian will be very pleased to see us. I know it's slumming it a bit, but what do you say to fish and chips on the harbour?"

Lucy smiled. "I can't think of anything I'd like better!"

The St Pirran chippy had undergone something of a transformation from the tired and dated shop of Lucy's childhood. Now that Cornwall was well and truly on the foodie map, the establishment was all chrome fittings, blond wood furniture and organic produce.

"I never knew cod and chips could be so complicated!" Adam grinned once they were sitting on the harbour wall and unpacking hot parcels. Handing Lucy a chip fork, he added, "Bon appétit!"

There was something about eating fish and chips outside and overlooking the sea that made the food taste all the more wonderful. Whether it was the fresh air, the gilded rays of the slowly sinking sun or the cries of the beady-eyed gulls circling overhead, Lucy wasn't sure, but she couldn't remember ever having enjoyed a meal so much. The chips were golden and fluffy, the batter just the right degree of crunchiness and the fish inside so flaky and delicious that she relished every mouthful. While they ate, Adam and Lucy chatted as easily as the water flowed across the causeway and over the glistening sand.

"Thanks so much for dinner," she said, mopping her mouth with a paper napkin and placing her hands on her full stomach.

"That wasn't dinner. What kind of cheapskate do you take me for?" Adam waggled his sandy eyebrows in mock offence. "I said dinner and I meant it. We're still going to that Italian. No arguments either, Lucy. I'm a man of my word."

"But this was perfect. I can't think of anything better than eating here," Lucy protested. She meant it too. There couldn't be a better restaurant view in the entire world than this deep blue bay and the sky streaked with pinks and oranges.

Adam nodded. "It's amazing, isn't it? I feel so lucky to live here. It really is such a special place. This probably sounds a bit nuts but I think there's something healing about it too." He paused and Lucy waited for him to continue; something about the expression in his eyes said that he was miles and several years away. "Elly – my wife – has been gone for a couple of years now, and when Josh and I first got here we were pretty raw. Everyone says that time heals, don't they? But they never tell you quite what that timescale is."

Lucy thought about her own quiet, private grief for her uncle. Grumpy and difficult Armand had certainly been, but she missed him every day. He'd been her sounding board, her musical companion and her reason to get up and do things; when he'd died the void had been vast. But Armand had been old and his death, however unwelcome, was a part of the natural cycle of life. How much worse must it be having to face every day when your soul mate had been snatched too soon? And what was more, to have to put your own grief aside in order to carry that of your child? Her throat grew tight.

"It wasn't until we moved to St Pirran that I started to feel there was hope for a new kind of life," Adam continued, staring out across the bay. "I'm not saying that we miss Elly any the less, but being here feels right and it's where Josh and I belong now. I don't expect to see Els here. She isn't in the garden, or the kitchen or in the street, and there aren't the same memories in our new place. We're making different ones, I suppose, and this is our life now. Maybe that's how grief works?" He turned back to her and smiled. "Don't the counsellors say acceptance is the final stage of the process?"

The Penwellyn family were of the get on with it school of thought, but Lucy recalled how the sharp edges of misery from losing her parents had been smoothed by the passing of the years, until she could think back on the happier times without her eyes prickling.

"I think so," she said softly. "It must be hard though, Adam."

"It's been bloody hard, especially for Josh. That's why knowing that he's happy visiting the castle and that he's actually playing the piano again means so much to me, and why I need you to know that." His brown eyes were bright with emotion. "He's so talented and to see him playing again means that he's healing too. That means everything to me."

Lucy didn't think about what she did next; it was as instinctive to her as breathing. Reaching out, she held and squeezed Adam's hand.

"He's a wonderful boy, Adam, and you're a wonderful father," she said softly. "I'm so glad that coming here's been good for you both."

Adam didn't remove his hand but returned the pressure of her fingers. Lucy said nothing but let him recover his composure before gently sliding hers away and busying herself collecting up the fish-and-chip wrappings.

"I might regret moving here if I eat like this too often though," Adam said eventually, and Lucy laughed.

"You are kidding? All the walking around in this town will keep the pounds off."

Not that Adam had any extra pounds. When he stood up and stretched, his tee shirt rode up to expose a slice of tanned torso.

Lucy looked away hastily, feeling as coy as a heroine in a Georgette Heyer novel.

"Yeah, the novelty of parking miles away from the cottage soon wore off. Heaven help me in the winter!" he was saying, oblivious to her pink cheeks. "And the job's really physical, not that I'm complaining. I'm lucky to have it, especially since it allows me to spend more time with Josh."

Lucy could imagine exactly how hard Adam worked. Max Reynard pushed his staff to the limit. You only had to pop into The Castle Inn on a Friday evening to hear the local builders moaning about what a slave driver he was.

"Which is why you can't keep coming over in your spare time to work on the castle," she said firmly. "We really appreciate all you've done to help, but you need time to relax and be with Josh."

"Is this the same Josh who'd rather be on the island?" Adam asked. He gathered up the rubbish and they walked together along the seafront to find a bin. Seagulls eyed them hopefully, screaming their irritation when he managed to stuff all the papers in without dropping any leftovers.

"You have quite enough on," Lucy insisted. "Building must be such a physical job."

"It is," Adam agreed. "But the thing is, Lucy, I'm not just working here as a builder."

He wasn't? Lucy was confused. "But aren't you working on the church?"

"I'm the Project Manager and a master stonemason," he told her. "I know I look like a disorganised mess most of the time but somehow I've ended up being a bit of an expert in my field. Pirran Castle and its restoration is the kind of project people in my game dream about. Any help I can give you is an absolute pleasure. Never mind what you've done for Josh, you'd be indulging me too. I'd love to lend a hand when I can."

"Goodness," said Lucy, taken aback. They had an expert who wanted to help them for free? For the first time since Ness's meeting she felt a little flicker of hope. "Wow, thanks."

"It's my pleasure. Making a difference and preserving the past is something I'm passionate about."

"You're the opposite of Max Reynard then," Lucy observed.

But Adam shook his blond head. "I think you'd be surprised. Max isn't what you think he is."

Lucy wasn't convinced. The changes in the town, the rapid development of the church, the flash boat and now the attempt to buy the castle suggested to her that Max Reynard was exactly what she thought he was: a ruthless man who'd stop at nothing to make money. Nonetheless, Lucy was aware that Max was also Adam's employer, so she chose to say nothing. As far as Lucy was concerned the jury was still out when it came to Reynards.

Having finished their meal, Adam and Lucy strolled back towards the harbour steps, where several boats were collecting holidaymakers keen for a sunset trip out across the bay. Lucy waved to one of the skippers, who gave her a thumbs up.

"There's my ride home sorted," she said.

"It certainly beats the London Underground," Adam remarked.

Lucy laughed at this. "There's no Oyster card and I'll have to pay him in cake, but it seems to work."

They'd paused at the top of the steps. Suddenly Lucy felt shy. It hadn't been a date but something had shifted between them.

"Thanks for dinner," she said, and Adam gave her a stern look.

"That wasn't dinner, remember? The Italian meal is still waiting, but let's not leave it too long. I love seafood pasta." He leaned forward and brushed her cheek with his lips. "Thanks for a lovely evening, Lucy. I'll see you in the next few days, I'm sure. I've got some ideas about how we can salvage the Pilgrim's Gate."

The gate. Of course. It was the castle he was excited about, Lucy reminded herself as she descended the steps and hopped on board the small tripping boat. She must bear that in mind and not allow herself to get swept away with silly daydreams and fantasies. He was a master stonemason and she lived on an island that offered a once-in-a-lifetime project, that was all.

Still, as the boat slipped its moorings and Adam waved to her with the evening sunshine turning his hair to fire, it was very easy to dream. It was only when the skipper drew alongside the island's pier that Lucy realised that for the whole journey home she'd had her fingertips pressed against the exact spot where Adam's mouth had touched her cheek.

How was it possible that her skin still felt warm?

Chapter 22

"There's absolutely no way she'll sell to you, mate. I should just give up trying to tempt her with huge amounts of cash. From what I can see, she's not impressed with that kind of crap."

Adam handed Max a Coke and leaned back against the Sunseeker's cabin. Although Adam was wearing Ray-Bans, Max knew exactly what the expression in his best friend's eyes would be: a mixture of exasperation and sympathy. He took the can and, glancing around his expensive boat and at the stunning blonde sunning herself in a tiny bikini on the foredeck, raised it in an ironic toast.

"Looks like I'm screwed then, doesn't it?"

It was a beautiful summer's day, the kind when England looks its best and all the grey rainy days are instantly forgotten and forgiven. Tired with the heat of London and the grind of the office, Max had driven down to Cornwall the night before, keen to kick back for a couple of days and enjoy the water. With her clean lines and ice-white hull, Foxy Lady was perfect for slicing through silky blue water. Now that she was moored in the bay the beautiful boat was attracting a lot of attention. At least, Max thought it was his super yacht that everyone was admiring, but then again Aimee's bikini was very skimpy and her long honey-coloured limbs wouldn't have been out of place at Aintree. Bringing her with him had seemed like a good idea yesterday, but after twenty-four hours in her company he was starting to wonder. Coming to Cornwall and flaunting his boat, wealth and gorgeous girlfriend was supposed to make Ness Penwellyn look out from her crumbling castle and feel impressed and (hopefully) jealous, but he had his doubts now.

Yes. That had been the plan – and in London, where supercars cruised the streets and the West End teemed with the designer-clad wealthy, it had seemed like a good one. The only problem was that down in Cornwall, where people wore cut-off jeans and zipped about in boats that probably cost less than his deck shoes, Max was starting to feel a bit of an idiot.

All right then, scratch bit. He was feeling like a complete tosser. If Adam was right – and, given that his best friend was now well and truly going native, Max had no reason to doubt him – Ness was far more likely to be looking across the water and laughing. Just imagining the scorn in those green eyes made Max take a big swig of his Coke. At times like this he wished he drank alcohol.

"Yep, totally screwed," said Adam cheerfully.

"Thanks for the support, mate," grumbled Max. "I thought you'd be a bit more sympathetic, seeing as you're the one heading up this project."

Adam shrugged his brown shoulders. He was very tanned, Max noticed with a small jolt of envy. Christ, it must be nice to work outside rather than being cooped up in an office pushing paperwork about and pandering to planners and government officials. He wasn't often tempted to throw in the towel and retreat to Cornwall for a life of pottering about on the water, but sometimes it appealed. If he could only persuade Ness that developing the castle was the right thing to do then he could be justified in finishing with this project – maybe even take some time out to actually enjoy what he'd achieved, rather than hurtling onwards to the next big thing like a hamster on a bloody big wheel.

The island was slumbering just ahead, the waves so calm that they barely seemed to break on the rocky necklace ringing it. Shimmering in the haze and bold against the bright sky, it looked like something out of a novel. Max's gut tightened with longing.

If he could only get his hands on it. What an amazing place it could be and what a project! It would be the pinnacle of his career. Perhaps then he could turn his attention to the shelter and his charities and to actually having a life.

If only that stubborn, infuriating, gorgeous woman across the water would see some sense...

"I offered her eight bloody million," he said, scowling at the horizon. "What more can I do? Should I go to nine?"

Adam spluttered into his can. "Nine million? Jesus, Max, have you gone mad?"

Max said nothing. He wasn't going to tell Adam what his actual budget for the purchase could be, because for the first time in their long friendship he wasn't entirely sure where the other man's loyalties lay. Instead, he pressed the windlass switch and raised the anchor before knocking the engines into gear and steering the boat towards the island. On the bow, Aimee didn't stir so much as a golden hair, while Adam simply raised his face to the sunshine. Max resisted the urge to let the powerful boat fly and instead crept slowly across the water, picking his way through the tripping boats and elegant white-sailed yachts, before turning towards the back of the island and opening up the throttles. This was Grace Note Bay, a private and sheltered spot that was perfect for swimming and snorkelling. When he owned the island, Max was tempted to sink an artificial reef a little farther out to attract even more marine life. Diving was a passion of his and to have his own dive haven would be a dream come true.

"There might be seals over here," he called to Aimee, who didn't reply. To be honest, Max wasn't even sure why he thought she might. Unless it was a seal from Louis Vuitton or Chanel, Aimee wouldn't be impressed. A city creature through and through and something big in PR, she was good as a companion at corporate functions or dinner parties, but otherwise the conversation was limited. Then again, Max didn't usually spend time with women for their conversational skills.

"Cool!" said Josh, who was sitting in the bow. Clad only in his swimming trunks, he looked as brown and as healthy as his father. "Can we swim?"

"If your dad says it's OK," answered Max. The idea of diving into the water very much appealed to him right now; in fact, he could hardly wait. He was still a young boy too, deep down inside – although his board members might be amazed to know this.

"Fine by me," said Adam. "It'll be cold though. Maybe put your wetsuit on?"

Josh crinkled his nose. "Don't be such a sissy! Ness and Merryn swim there all the time and they wear swimming costumes."

Max tried not to think about Nessa Penwellyn in a swimming costume, firstly because it felt inappropriate when Aimee was on board and secondly because he needed to concentrate on navigating around the hidden rocks that guarded the entrance to Grace Note Bay. It soon became evident that he wasn't focused on this task at all: if it hadn't been for his echo sounder he'd probably have sunk the boat. Christ. He really needed to buy this island and get Nessa out from under his skin.

Once they were safely through the razor-sharp maze of barely visible rocks, Max dropped anchor again, cut the engines and admired this side of the island. You couldn't see the town from here and it felt as though miles and miles of ocean separated the boat from the shore. Seabirds called, wild grasses blew in the wind and fat seals lounged on the rocks, growling and grumbling to one another. There was an enormous splash as Josh launched himself into the water, and a shriek from Aimee as the icy spray covered her taut tummy.

"He loves it here," Adam said to Max. "It's done him so much good. I owe you, mate."

The two men watched Josh swimming. Adam threw him a snorkel and soon Josh was busy exploring the watery world below.

"I'm glad it's worked out," Max replied. "You've both had a shit time."

Adam nodded. "It's not been great but I do feel like we've turned a corner now. This place suits us both. But, mate, I have to ask: what's going to happen if this sale doesn't come off? There's not going to be the work I'd hoped for, is there?"

Max's eyes were storm-cloud grey. "Of course the sale will come off. You're not having doubts as to whether I can do this, are you?"

"I never doubt you," said Adam, "but I've met Nessa Penwellyn and I promise you she's not going to sell. You could offer her twenty million pounds and she'd still turn you down. It's not about money."

"Rubbish. Everything's about money," scoffed Max. He glanced at Aimee, prone and plugged into her iPod. From her designer bikini to her French-polished toenails to her expensively dyed hair, she reeked of money. In his experience women loved the stuff.

But Adam looked doubtful. "Not for Ness. She really loves this place and she'll do everything to keep it in the family. The last thing she wants to see is some greedy developer carving it up."

"I'm not carving it up. I'm bloody rescuing it!" Max cried, exasperated. He loved this island and stretch of Cornish coast; for years he'd dreamed of being able to make his mark, nurture it and claim his own small piece of heaven. Jesus, he'd known as a schoolboy that this was what he was meant to do. Everything he'd achieved so far was just the precursor to this.

"You and I know that, but Ness doesn't," Adam pointed out in his usual reasonable way. "If I was you, mate, I'd focus less on floating phallic symbols and big amounts of money and more on all the really good stuff Reynards does. Why don't you tell her about the affordable housing? Or the university sponsorships? Or the homeless shelter? If she knew about those things then she'd see the real man rather than the corporate monster."

"Corporate monster?" Max was amused. "Is that how you see me? Some kind of boardroom Godzilla?"

"I know you hate violent movies, would rather have a pizza than a gourmet meal and play a mean round of burp tennis, so no!" Adam laughed. He reached into the ice bucket and helped himself to another beer. "But she's a woman with integrity, Max, and I don't think fast boats and fat wallets will impress her. Just tell her the truth."

"Firstly, I haven't played burp tennis since primary school and, secondly, all that charity stuff is private." Max was adamant about this. His private life was something he guarded closely. He did the charity work because it actually meant something to him; it wasn't supposed to be a PR exercise for the likes of Aimee to spin. Max cherished the honesty and anonymity of volunteering at Malcom's Place. There he was just another helper who dished up food on Christmas Day or mopped the floors. Nobody cared what watch he wore or what car he drove: at the shelter he was simply Max. The idea of that changing made Max sick to the stomach. He'd never use his charities to impress a woman or to seal a deal. Malcom Reynard would never have dreamed of it and neither would his son.

"I understand, mate. I just think that those things are more you than all this shit." Adam swept a hand in the direction of the deck. "But it's totally your call and I swear I won't say a word."

He peered over the gunnels. "What's the water like, bud?" he called to Josh, who'd surfaced and was blowing water out of his snorkel.

"Cold!" his son called back. "Are you coming in, Dad? Are you, Max?"

Adam threw a challenging look at Max. "Fancy a swim?"

Max thought about it for a moment. The clear blue water might look inviting but he knew it would be freezing. Maybe next time he wanted to show off with a boat he'd stick to the Med. On the other hand, it was better than sitting here brooding over an island he couldn't buy and trying to make conversation with Aimee.

"Yeah, why not?" he answered.

Max tugged his tee shirt over his head and kicked off his Sebagos. His wetsuit was in the bow locker but he couldn't be bothered to disturb Aimee mid tanning, so his board shorts would have to do. Adam had already dived overboard; Max followed, gasping when the cold water snatched his breath away. For a moment or two he trod water, watching as his godson and best friend splashed one another, before turning to look at the beach. It couldn't be more than a quarter of a mile away – a good distance that he would easily make. Exercise always cleared Max's mind and right now a clear head was something he could do with. Surging into his powerful crawl, Max Reynard headed for Pirran Island.

Ness had been in town very early to catch the tide and had caught a ride back over with one of the tripping boats. As she'd lugged her bags down the beach steps and clambered aboard, she'd reflected that losing the causeway was going to make life doubly hard. It was a sharp reminder of just how much she had to do before the winter set in. A few days had passed since her meeting with the other residents of Pirran Island, and everyone now seemed busy pursuing their respective ideas. Already there was a buzz of excitement building in town regarding Fern's baby, the newly named Island Fest. Quite how this was going to work, Ness wasn't sure – but Fern seemed confident and Adam's roadie friend, Zak, was happy to help too. So far Ness hadn't had time to get involved: she'd been too busy putting her own plans into action.

The next stage of those plans would have to wait until next week though, when she would be making a trip into London. This weekend Ness was determined to actually enjoy life on the island and to make the most of the glorious weather. As the small boat had carried her home, she'd watched a Sunseeker zipping across the water, towing rings and skiers – and she'd immediately recognised the lithe form at the helm. Even hundreds of metres away it was impossible to mistake the determination in the tilt of that dark head or the ease with which he held the powerful boat in check. It was Max Reynard, showing off in a flash boat and with some blonde Playmate type draped across the deck. Ness's top lip had curled with scorn. What an absolute cliché. He did know this was Cornwall and not Miami?

Shaking her head, Ness had carried the groceries up to the castle kitchen and unpacked them. There was nobody at home: Lucy was presumably doing her best to man the tea room together with one-armed Merryn, and Fern was helping Fred in the gardens. The place was still and cool, and for once Ness found herself feeling uneasy. Usually somebody was about, even if it was just Biscuit to chat to. All alone in the echoey kitchen, she became very aware just how ancient the castle was. The stillness was thick and heavy. How many people had passed through here over the years? How many previous occupants had unpacked shopping or leaned on the sill and stared out of the arched window? And how many of them had lain awake at night with panic pressing down upon their chests as they desperately tried to think of ways to keep the place afloat?

She needed a break from all this, Ness decided. The weeks since her arrival here had been intense and strange, and there'd barely been a moment to stop and reflect. To think she'd once considered her life in St Antonia hectic! At least there she'd been able to dive most days or just float lazily in the Caribbean Sea. Diving and swimming had soothed her soul after Addy's death, and she'd taken these activities for granted. Whenever she was stressed or sad Ness always yearned to be near water; she'd found it difficult to be so far away from it when her father, who'd never been a fan of the sea, had decided to move them inland. Perhaps the ocean was in her blood.

In her blood and literally on her doorstep, so whatever was she waiting for?

Having unpacked her shopping, Ness had grabbed a bottle of water, snatched a towel and then run up to her room to change into her bikini and shorts. Armed with some sun cream, her Kindle and a rare free hour, she'd swapped the cool quiet of the castle for the bright sunshine and Grace Note Bay. There she'd swum in the clear water and afterwards basked in the sunshine with her book. It wasn't the Caribbean but the sand was almost as white and the water every bit as blue. And just as in St Antonia, there were idiot millionaires with speedboats who thought they could behave as though they owned the place.

Ness had been dozing by the rocks, her limbs salty from the sea and gritty with sand, and enjoying the rhythmic sighs of breaking waves and the barks of seals. The warmth of the sun and the swim had made her drowsy – so it was annoying to have the peace interrupted by the roar of a speedboat. She sat up, shading her eyes against the glare of the light on the water, and groaned when she realised who'd arrived.

Just typical. Was nowhere sacred?

There was the clanking of an anchor chain over rollers before the engines were cut and a small figure dived into the water. Then a woman shrieked and there was the sound of male laughter, followed by conversation. Irked at being interrupted, Ness reached for her sunglasses and did her best to ignore the goings-on in the bay. Two more splashes signalled that the men had both dived into the sea as well. Ness watched as one lone swimmer struck out for shore while the other two drifted about with snorkels. The woman didn't move but continued to soak up the sun on the bow. If it hadn't been for the goose bumps that dusted her skin when the breeze blew, Ness could have been right back in St Antonia.

The swimmer was slicing through the waves with a strong front crawl, each stroke making easy work of the distance. Ness sat up a little straighter and squinted. He was headed for the shore, and the closer he came the more certain Ness was of his identity. Only one man around here would power through the sea with the same determination and certainty as he powered through business deals or swept a girl off her feet. It was Max Reynard; of course it was.

Mesmerised, she drew her knees up against her chest and wrapped her arms around them as his glistening torso emerged from the sea. In spite of her annoyance she couldn't help but notice how toned his upper body was and how sculpted his arms were. He strode out of the surf and onto the beach, shaking seawater from his face and hair. As he did so, rivulets of salty water trickled over his pecs and ran down from his narrow waist and muscular brown legs. Ness knew she was staring but she couldn't help herself. It was a pure Mr Darcy moment and she simply couldn't look away.

"Hello, Ness," Max said, those grey eyes amused to have caught her gawping at him. "You look a little surprised. Didn't you think I could swim?"

Ness could have ripped her eyes out. Thank goodness she was wearing sunglasses. She wished she was wearing more than her green bikini though; as his eyes raked her body she was acutely aware of how revealing her choice of swimwear was. Alas, if she made a dive for her shorts and tee shirt he'd know she was feeling awkward, and Ness didn't want to give Max that satisfaction. Oh well. Judging by the blonde draped all over his ridiculous penis extension of a boat, Ness's bikini revealed nothing much that Max Reynard hadn't already seen before. Telling herself this, she stood up and pushed her shades onto the top of her damp head.

"What are you doing here?" she demanded.

"It's nice to see you too, Nessa."

Max Reynard didn't miss a beat; if he was at all bothered about being on someone else's private beach clad only in his shorts and looking like he'd stepped from a Calvin Klein advert, then not so much as a flicker of that handsome face gave it away. Instead he stood on the sand, legs proudly apart and with his hands on his hips, as if he owned the place, inhaling deeply to recover his breath after the exertion of the swim.

"This is a private beach," Ness snapped. "You're trespassing."

Max inclined his dark head. "Yes, you're right. Sorry about that. I just thought I'd have a quick swim to the shore while the others snorkelled."

"Your girlfriend isn't snorkelling," Ness pointed out.

She was rewarded by another amused look from her uninvited visitor. "Ah, so you saw Aimee? Don't be jealous, Ness.

She's nothing serious and not nearly as sexy as you are in that tiny bikini."

"I'm not jealous!" Ness shrieked. Her hands flew to her chest and she felt herself grow hot. "And I can wear what I like on my own beach."

"You certainly can," he agreed.

Oh! He was infuriating. Trying her best to ignore his grey eyes as they roamed over her body, Ness decided to take a different tack.

"Anyway, this is my beach. You don't own it yet," she said coldly.

A smile played on his lips. "So you think I will one day, then?"

"No! Of course not! I didn't mean that."

Max mightn't be wrong-footed but Ness was totally thrown. While he was standing there in all his well-honed masculine glory, she was horrified to discover that she could hardly think straight. It was as if the sunshine had gone straight to her hormones. To her dismay she found herself wondering what his chest would feel like beneath her fingertips. She could imagine flicking her tongue over the smooth flesh and tasting the salt water...

What on earth was the matter with her?

"My offer still stands," Max was saying. "Eight million and an apartment. In fact I'll even throw one in for your cousin too. How does that sound?"

Even clad in shorts and on the beach Max had an air of arrogance and command that took her breath away. He was talking business to her here? Seriously, did the man never give up?

"How does it sound? Like you're getting desperate," she answered.

He shrugged his broad shoulders. "Not at all, Ness. I can afford to wait but that offer of an apartment for Lucy might expire. I'd think about it seriously if I were you."

"You can't bribe me," said Ness scornfully.

"Bribe? That's unkind." He stepped forward and now there was a dark gleam in his eyes which made her pulse quicken.

"Persuade is the word I'd have used. Maybe you could persuade me to change my mind? From what I remember, Nessa Penwellyn, you could persuade a man to do anything. I'm willing to take that risk if you are. Beaches are our place as I recall?"

His voice was low but the meaning was clear: he was referring to that first intense kiss they'd shared on the night she'd arrived in St Pirran. It had been perfect and Ness could have kissed him forever that evening. She'd thought about it since far more often than she liked to admit, the way he'd almost been drinking her in and the way her bones had melted. Sometimes she'd dreamed about it and woken up in the pitch darkness of her tower bedroom with her heart racing and longing for more...

But that was before she'd known who Max Reynard was and before she'd discovered that he would stop at nothing to possess the island. Her feelings didn't matter; she would put those aside. But as for his? Ness almost laughed out loud at her own stupidity for wavering for so much as a millisecond. He was just a good actor and he'd do anything he could to get his way.

She had to tell him that there was nothing he could do or say, that she wanted him to go away, that she wished she'd never set eyes on him – but the words simply wouldn't come. When those grey eyes held hers she lost all thought and reason. All she could think about was how his mouth had felt against hers and how she'd wanted nothing more than to pull him closer and deeper.

"Ness?" He was only inches away from her now, so close that she could feel the coolness of the seawater on his limbs against the heat of her own skin. Her name was a whisper of longing and, before she knew it, Max had cupped her face with his hands and lowered his mouth against hers, his lips hard yet gentle, hot and yet cool, pressing kisses onto her bottom lip and the corners of her cupid's bow. Then, as her lips parted, his tongue met her own with such hunger that her body turned limper than the seaweed strewn along the shoreline.

Ness felt herself falling. For a moment she was kissing him back, matching his hunger with her own and lost in the million and one sensations from just the skimming of his thumb over her cheek or the warmth of his palm against the small of her back. She was melting like Cornish ice cream in the sun, and if Max carried on kissing her she knew there would be no holding back. Somewhere in the back of her mind a voice was shouting at her to stop and think about what she was doing. This was no stolen, unknowing kiss under the big-eyed moon. This time she knew exactly who this man was and what he was about. Lips could lie in more ways than one.

She broke the kiss first and they stared at one another, their breathing ragged and eyes dark with desire.

"Do you want me to stop?" Max asked softly.

Ness couldn't speak. What on earth was she doing, kissing this man? She knew exactly what he was: an opportunist who would stop at nothing to get his hands on the island. But did she want him to stop?

Oh Lord, no. Of course she didn't.

"This isn't a good idea," was all she could say, taking a wobbly step back and giving his bare chest a shove. If she could maintain some distance between them for a moment, then maybe she would just about find the strength to say stop. But if he so much as touched her again, Ness knew she would be lost.

He gave her a penetrating look. "Because you don't want to or because of the island? That's just business, Ness, not pleasure."

"Are you sure the two aren't intertwined?"

His lips curved as his eyes dipped to her breasts. "I'm not saying pleasure isn't involved in some capacity, but maybe that can work for both of us? We can surely come to an agreement that works in every way?"

It was all about the business with him. How could he separate the two so coolly? His touch, his mouth on hers, had almost made Ness lose control – but Max Reynard would never be so weak. Had she just been played?

"Ness?" Max was frowning. "What do you think? Can we work together?"

His question was enough to jolt her out of her haze of desire and back to reality. This ability of his to switch so swiftly from passion to business was exactly what she needed to bear in mind. None of what had just happened had meant anything to him. It was all just another game and, like a fool, she'd very nearly fallen for it.

"Nice try, Max," she said, "but the answer's no."

His eyes narrowed. "No to which question?"

Her head was still spinning from his kiss, and no matter how hard she tried Ness couldn't order her thoughts. Max Reynard turned her world to quicksand; everything she'd thought she knew was suddenly uncertain.

"All of them," she cried. "All of them, OK?"

And then, before he had any chance to try changing her mind – or, even worse, to touch her again and weaken her resolve – Ness spun on her heel and tore away, leaving her bag, her towel and Max Reynard behind.

She'd never sell Pirran Island to him. Never. No matter what he offered or how hard he tried to convince her.

And, more importantly, she certainly wouldn't be kissing him again. She wouldn't be able to trust herself if she let that happen.

Chapter 23

The following Monday found Ness in London, doing her best to negotiate Piccadilly in a thunderstorm. Although she was used to tropical showers, she'd never seen a downpour where the rain was both vertical and horizontal at the same time. Londoners might have the whole thing down to a fine art as they swarmed out of the tube stations under the cover of their umbrellas, seemingly oblivious to red buses swishing by only inches from their elbows, but Ness was struggling. She was absolutely drenched. She probably looked more like a half-drowned urchin rather than a groomed and confident businesswoman.

By the time she stood dripping in the foyer of Ambrose Investments, Ness was cold, fed up and longing for St Antonia. Things here were just so complicated and the weather made it all twenty times harder. All she wanted to do was see Stephen's father and discuss an investment opportunity. Looking as though she'd swum here from Cornwall hadn't been part of the plan.

The offices of Ambrose Investments were on the fifth floor of a smart tower block situated just one street back from Green Park (and conveniently close to the Ritz, should any investors wish to pop over for afternoon tea). As she took the lift, Ness did her best to dry her face and hair with a tissue, although the handkerchief was soon disintegrating faster than her earlier belief that coming here might be a good idea. A glance in the mirrored interior made her wail. She looked even more of a mess than she'd imagined. Her mascara had run and her carefully styled hair was now a riot of tight, springy curls. The cream linen shift dress she'd purchased in St Pirran and which had looked so chic hanging on its padded hanger was limp and creased from her long journey. She looked distinctly out of place in this building, with its smart-suited, briefcase-carrying occupants. Small wonder the reception staff had looked a little surprised when Jonathan Ambrose had confirmed he was meeting her.

Ness's mind wandered back to her kiss with Max. It had unnerved Ness because it was the closest she'd ever come to losing control. When it came to him she was weak. Max knew that now, which made the situation doubly dangerous. He'd do his best to persuade her to his way of thinking and would stop at nothing to own the island. With her finances vulnerable and the future of the place more uncertain than even Max could guess, Ness had realised that she had to take action. And fast. Fern's concert was gathering momentum, Lucy had done a sterling job of resurrecting the tea room, and Adam had been a godsend too. He'd shored up the worst of the damage, but he needed a team and serious amounts of money just to keep the buildings as they were, never mind restore them. The only real solution was to borrow from someone.

As she'd lain awake in her tower room, trying her best not to relive Max's kiss, Ness had made a desperate attempt to come up with a solution. The only answer she could find was approaching a venture capitalist who might be willing to invest in something a standard bank might find too risky. Ness had seen TV programmes like Dragons' Den and Shark Tank, in which people put forward their business proposals to potential investors, but she didn't have time to audition for shows; nor did she have the inclination to give away fifty percent of her inheritance in exchange for a few pounds and some ideas. She needed big money and good terms, and there was only one person who might be able to help: Jonathan Ambrose, the father of her ex-boyfriend Stephen.

As Ness took a seat in the plush reception area of Jonathan's headquarters, she reflected that this was probably the longest long shot ever in the entire history of long shots. Things hadn't ended particularly well between her and Stephen – which had been more to do with his inability to stay faithful than anything else – and there was no reason why his father should harbour any kind thoughts towards her. In fact Ness had only met Jonathan Ambrose a handful of times when he'd visited St Antonia to meet with his attorneys. Ness's acquaintance with him hadn't strayed beyond a few brunch trips out on the obligatory flash boat. He'd been polite and chatted to her about the diving, but that had been about the extent of it. On several occasions Ness had caught him watching Stephen, who was usually necking champagne or showing off in his own boat, with something approaching exasperation. When their gazes had met, she'd known that Jonathan wouldn't be surprised when she called it off. Which she had done, of course. All the same, blood was thicker than water and there was no knowing what kind of reception she'd receive today. Ness exhaled slowly to steady her nerves. That she'd got this far had to be a good sign, surely?

"Mr Ambrose will see you now," announced the immaculate receptionist.

Still feeling like she'd been dragged through a hedge backwards, Ness stood up and walked towards the office. She hoped she didn't look as terrified as she felt.

"Nessa! What a wonderful surprise!"

If Jonathan Ambrose was taken aback by her dishevelled appearance he was far too polite to say so. Instead, he strode across the deep-piled carpet and kissed Ness soundly on each cheek, before stepping back and regarding her with sharp eyes. He was tall like his son, but his once blond hair was now a thick grey pelt and – unlike Stephen, who worked out obsessively – Jonathan's generous waistline suggested that long lunches and fine wines were his thing rather than hitting the gym.

"You look as ravishing as ever," he was saying now. "My son was an idiot to ever let you go."

"He didn't let me go. I left him," Ness said, before she could stop herself. Immediately, her hand flew to her mouth. Nice work, Nessa. Just remind him you dumped the son and heir. Why not tell him he's put on weight too? Really insult him?

But luckily Jonathan seemed to find this comment amusing.

"So you did, and good for you. Did Stephen good to have someone stand up to him for once," he said approvingly. "Boy's spoilt rotten and it's probably all my fault, but I imagine a smart young woman like you figured that out a long time ago."

It wasn't a question, so Ness was spared the awkwardness of having to think of a tactful reply. Instead, he motioned for her to take one of the big leather seats that was positioned opposite his enormous desk. Ness sat down. It felt a bit like being summoned into the headmaster's office; she realised her hands were shaking.

Jonathan Ambrose lowered himself into the even bigger chair opposite and steepled his fingers beneath his chin. A signet ring cut into the flesh of the little finger on his left hand.

"So, pleasant as it is to see you again, I gather this isn't a social call?"

Ness shook her head. "I've got a business proposition for you."

The grey head was inclined in affirmation. "I thought that might be the case. Well, we've all seen Dragons' Den, so you know what happens next." He gave her an encouraging smile. "This is the part where you give me your pitch."

Ness reached into her bag and pulled out a sheaf of paperwork that she'd prepared. Lucy's ancient printer had managed to choke out some faint type and the pictures she'd taken of the castle were printed too, albeit in lurid colours that made the place look rather like a migraine – but hopefully it would give him an idea of what her primary asset was. While he flicked through all this, his face devoid of any reaction, Ness explained her situation and what she was proposing. Then, once she'd talked herself to a standstill, Jonathan Ambrose gathered the paperwork into a neat stack and set it down on the desk.

"Nessa, this is a very simple one from my point of view. You have real estate of significant value but in a huge state of disrepair and haemorrhaging money at an alarming rate. You say you urgently need a quarter of a million pounds to get the place fixed and to a point where it can begin to earn some kind of an income. Correct?"

"Yes," Ness said. Her mouth felt dry. She could hardly believe she was asking to borrow a quarter of a million pounds when she'd never even had a credit card and didn't like to go into overdraft either. Unlike Addy, who'd been constantly on the run from bailiffs, Ness had a horror of debt.

"You're a smart woman," Stephen's father said. "You know that the risk for us is very small. That's not a large amount of capital for us to lend and, unlike you, we have no emotional attachment to the property. You've shown me a business plan, of sorts, and I have no doubt that all those ideas could be successful, given time. The eco hotel and diving school, for instance, are particularly attractive possibilities. I daresay we'd even be willing to stretch to half a million, although obviously the terms would be different in that case. That's something we'd need to discuss, of course."

Ness stared at him. "You're saying yes?"

"I'm saying that this is certainly something I can sanction in principle," he agreed. "However, you need to be fully aware of what it would mean for you. If you fail to meet the terms of your loan with Ambrose Investments then I'm afraid you'll have an uncomfortable choice to make. You'll either have to sell the property in order to pay us back, or throw us the keys, walk away and let us deal with it."

"But if I can generate enough income to repay the loan in full with interest then we're quits," Ness shot back.

"Yes," Jonathan said smoothly, "that would be the preferable option for you, of course. We'd give you a three-month window before you'd have to start paying interest on the loan, and we'll talk terms that suit both parties."

Ness's brain was whirling. Three months. It was June now, so the loan repayments wouldn't begin until the end of September. She could get the repairs done before the winter storms, raise some money and buy them some time. It was doable. If she didn't take this risk she'd lose the castle anyway.

"It sounds good to me," she said.

"Are you sure?" Jonathan leaned back in his seat and regarded her sternly. "Be certain this is what you really want and that you can take the risk. If you can't service the loan you'll only end up having to sell anyway, and probably for less money. It might be wisest to sell the property now. You've written in your supporting statement that you've already had an offer of eight million. Perhaps you ought to accept?"

"No way!" Ness was incensed and her red curls bounced in indignation. "I'm not selling to Max Reynard. Never!"

Jonathan Ambrose was instantly on alert, like a gun dog scenting game. "Max Reynard made that offer? The CEO of Reynard Developments?"

"Yes," said Ness.

He whistled. "You do know they call him 'Midas' in the City?"

Ness didn't. Personally she preferred to call him an underhand, cunning, Machiavellian git, but that was her choice. Still, mentioning Max had certainly made Jonathan Ambrose sit up.

"Max never misses a trick," he told Ness. "If he sees that property as being worth eight million you can triple the value by the time he's finished with it. In fact you can probably quadruple it."

Ness had suspected as much. All his talk about restoring the place and saving it was a pack of lies. The only thing Max cared about was profit. She shouldn't be surprised but she was oddly disappointed.

"So, as you say, the risk to Ambrose Investments is very low – especially if we keep it to a quarter of a million rather than half

– and the opportunity to make money is high," she said. "Do we have a deal, Mr Ambrose?"

She held out her hand. It was still trembling, but from a surge of adrenalin rather than fear now. She could do this! She knew she could. With the funding agreed they could afford to hire Adam and a specialist team to fix the castle, as well as refurbishing the tea room and perhaps doing bed and breakfast. The possibilities were endless.

And best of all? It would be a massive V-sign to Max Reynard.

Jonathan Ambrose took Ness's hand and shook it. His grip was like iron.

"Congratulations, Miss Penwellyn," he said. "It looks as though we're in business."

Chapter 24

Lucy couldn't believe it. There was money in the account, Adam had been hired to put a specialist team together and begin the restoration of the Pilgrim's Gate, and a local firm of builders was already fixing the causeway. Ness had assured her the tea room was next on the list and then they would be refurbishing the castle in order to start a boutique bed-and-breakfast business.

"How on earth have you managed it?" she'd asked Ness on several occasions, but her cousin had just winked and said something about calling in a favour from an old acquaintance.

"Some favour," Annie Luckett remarked on a blustery Tuesday morning in early July as she and Lucy waited in the Small Hall to show the first group of visitors around the castle. "I dread to think what she's had to do to find the money to start all this work." Her lined face was creased with concern. "I hope she's not done something daft like borrow money from somebody disreputable."

Lucy hoped so too. "Nessa's not stupid. She wouldn't do that."

"Hmm," said Annie, which was short for I have my doubts.

Lucy didn't blame her; she couldn't think of any other explanation apart from a loan. If Ness's lottery numbers had come up, surely she would have said something. It wasn't as if there was any hope of finding an unexpected inheritance, either – and nobody knew this better than Lucy. What choice had Ness really been given? They'd been only weeks away from bankruptcy.

Only a handful of tourists had arrived this morning. The weather was unusually chilly for the time of year and, rather than exploring the island, most of them had headed to the tea room where Fern was making drinks and Merryn was doing some one-handed waiting of tables. Meanwhile Ness was in the library, which she'd turned into an office – and very busy she was too, Lucy thought, with coordinating builders, sorting out insurance for the music festival and generally balancing the books. There had been a bustling and purposeful atmosphere about the castle in recent days, which it probably hadn't experienced since Armand had hosted his legendary parties at the height of his fame. The energy was contagious and, buoyed with optimism, Lucy had finally taken the plunge and treated herself to the spotty dress. Tonight she and Adam were going to visit the Italian restaurant – just as friends, of course – to give the frock an outing and to celebrate Josh passing his Grade Six violin exam with distinction.

Lucy was lost in daydreams about the possibilities of entering Josh for the equivalent piano exam when Adam strolled into the Small Hall. The work on the church conversion was all but complete, so he was doing a couple of days a week at the castle now. Already he and his team had made considerable progress.

"Morning all," Adam said, with that grin which made Lucy's heart turn somersaults. "I'm looking for Ness. Is she about?"

"Library," said Annie. She peered at him over her half-moon spectacles. "Not so fast, young man! You're covered in dust and we've spent an hour sweeping the floor this morning before our visitors arrive. If you're going inside you can take your boots off. And your overalls."

Adam grinned. "My boots are fine to come off, Miss L. The overalls though you might object to. It's hot work lifting granite and I've only got my boxers on underneath."

That was an image Lucy knew she wouldn't get out of her mind. Now every time she looked at Adam in his blue overalls she'd be imagining him stepping out of them like something from Magic Mike. Oh dear. That wasn't the way she was supposed to think about a man who was just a good friend.

But Annie didn't turn a hair. "You may freeze because it's always cold in here," she warned him. "Perhaps it would be prudent to have clothes on in the future?"

"Yes, Miss," teased Adam.

"What's this about putting clothes on?" asked Ness, who'd just joined them. Her eyes widened as she caught sight of Adam in his overalls – which were now unzipped to the waist to prove his point, revealing a bare chest dusted with golden hair. "Did I green-light a male stripper business without realising?"

"Adam was getting dust everywhere," Annie began to explain, but Ness held her hands up.

"I don't need to know where Adam's getting dust," she laughed. "I was actually looking for Fern? There's been a man on the phone for her and I think it must be about the concert. He's very persistent."

Ness held the castle's phone in one hand and a spiral-bound notepad in the other, and her wild red curls were skewered to the crown of her head with a biro. She looked like this a lot recently, Lucy thought, probably because she was so busy. The light in the library burned deep into the small hours, the telephone was constantly shrilling and there always seemed to be a stream of tradespeople traipsing in and out of the place.

"Fern's in the tea room," Lucy told her. "I can take a message if you like? What did he say his name was?"

Ness frowned. "He didn't. He just said Fern would know him and that he'd be in touch. Do you think there's a problem?"

"I don't know. I hope not." Lucy felt uneasy. Nobody knew where Fern had come from or why she was all alone at such a tender age. Lucy remembered the bruises on the girl's thin arms and the haunted look she'd had for months, and a sixth sense told her this caller was not good news.

"Now that you're here and I don't need to strip off," Adam was saying to Ness, "unless Miss Luckett wants me to, that is, I just need you to clarify that we can go ahead with the next stage of the gate? We'll be needing three more masons, if that's still okay?"

Ness nodded. "That's all fine. Just try and keep it within budget if you can? Under would be better, obviously."

Adam looked doubtful. "I'll do my best, Ness, but it won't be easy."

"No," shouted another voice, "it won't be easy, because you're supposed to be bloody working for me!"

This angry interruption, called across the Small Hall from the open entrance to the kitchen, made Lucy jump and Ness spin around. Max Reynard was framed in the doorway. The expression on his face was as black as his hair.

"You could have knocked," Ness said, and was rewarded with a glower from those slate-grey eyes.

"The door was open. Perhaps my project manager left it that way so that the rest of my employees could wander in too?" His words dripped with sarcasm and Adam winced.

"Mate, where I choose to work is up to me," Adam said evenly. "The same goes for my team too, since they're freelance."

"You've all been hired by Reynards!" Max blasted, striding across the flagstones until he and Adam were practically eyeball to eyeball. "I go away on business for a fortnight and when I come back I find that my project manager's walked off the job and is moonlighting somewhere else. What the hell are you playing at?"

Everyone in the room was struck dumb. Max's icy grey gaze swept contemptuously around the Small Hall before returning to Adam.

"Well?"

Adam sighed.

"Come on, Max, you know as well as I do that the work on the church is all but finished. My part in it certainly is. There's nothing more for me to do there and I'm not going to sit on my backside, twiddling my thumbs and taking your money for nothing. I'm off the payroll since last week when my team finished. I had thought that was just until our next project, but now..." He paused and let the silence speak for him. "Now I'm not too sure."

"I'm sorry you feel like that," Max said curtly. "But the work isn't completed. There's more to do."

"Mate, there really isn't," Adam replied patiently. "It's all finished and that other project you mentioned isn't quite coming off as planned, is it?"

"It will," Max said crisply. "And your working here for free won't make it happen any quicker."

"He's not working for free." Ness stepped forward. "I'm paying Adam in his professional capacity."

"What?" Max turned to face her, his feet slightly apart and every sinew of his lithe frame tensed. "Don't be ridiculous. You can't do that. You couldn't possibly afford it."

"Says who?" answered Ness.

"Don't play games with me, Nessa. We both know how things stand here." His handsome face wore a sardonic expression. "There's no money to fund it."

"Interesting that you seem to know the ins and outs of my finances," Ness remarked. "And even more interesting that you seem to be totally wrong. There's plenty of money to get us started on some repairs now that I've asked Jonathan Ambrose to help."

Max stared at her incredulously. "You've borrowed money from Ambrose Investments? Are you absolutely insane?"

He looked ready to explode, and Lucy's heartbeat accelerated.

Ness merely shrugged her slender shoulders. "There've been a couple of occasions lately where I've wondered that myself," she agreed.

A dark look passed between them. Intriguing, thought Lucy. Had Ness seen more of Max Reynard than she'd been letting on? Surely not? After the sneaky way he'd tricked her when she'd first arrived, Ness had made it clear she couldn't stand the man.

"Why didn't you come to me?" Max was clearly shocked. "Why on earth borrow from a shark like Ambrose? I'd made you an offer for the castle. We could have done this together."

"You've borrowed money?" Annie looked horrified.

"It was the only way to get things started," Ness said. "Don't look so worried, Annie! I haven't been to the local loan shark. I've an arrangement with one of the biggest venture capitalists in the City. There's nothing to worry about."

"Until Jonny Ambrose calls the loan in!" Max was shaking his head. "You should have come to me, Ness. This is madness."

"That's your forte, waiting for people to get desperate and then pouncing, isn't it?" Ness's voice was filled with scorn. "Excuse me if I'd rather not just hand the island to you."

"So you'd rather let Jonathan Ambrose screw you over?" Max was unable to hide his disbelief. "Have you any idea just how tough these guys can be? They exist to make money. They're not the good guys here."

Her top lip curled. "And you are, I suppose?"

"I'd like to be. Come on, Ness. Why don't you give me a chance and let me help?"

"Because I don't trust you," Ness said bluntly.

They stared at each other and Lucy felt the atmosphere crackle. She looked at Adam, who raised a blond eyebrow – a gesture that confirmed he felt it too.

"Fine," Max said coldly. "It's up to you. I'll just wait until Ambrose calls in the debt – which you'll never service, by the way – and buy the island then. It makes no difference to me, Ness, but it would have done to you. I'll probably buy it for less than I offered you now."

With that, he turned on his heel and strode out of the Small Hall. Lucy knew it was a ridiculous thought, but he seemed genuinely upset by what Ness had done. She wasn't sure how she felt about the loan herself, but what other choice had there been? Without the causeway they'd be in huge trouble; not only that, but no tea room meant no income, and the repairs to the Pilgrim's Gate would never have got under way if her cousin hadn't found some cash from somewhere. Desperate times did call for desperate measures.

But just how desperate they were yet to get was what really worried Lucy. From the look on Max Reynard's face this was far from the end of the matter.

"He calmed down eventually," Adam assured Lucy later on that evening. They were seated in the window at Sorrentina, St Pirran's pretty Italian restaurant, tucking into piles of delicious seafood pasta. He leaned forward and topped up her glass.

"I'm glad to hear it," Lucy answered. "Whoa, that's enough! I'll never make the walk back otherwise!" She placed her hand across the top of the glass. Her cheeks were already glowing and the red shoes which matched her dress were hard enough to walk in when she was stone-cold sober, never mind when tipsy and navigating cobbles. "He was really angry though. I hope we haven't got you into trouble with your boss?"

Adam laughed. "The day Max is my boss is the day I know I'm doomed! We're old school friends, Lucy. My dad worked for his, back in the day when Reynards was just a building firm. Max is my best mate and probably the closest thing I have to a brother." He paused and a faraway expression filled his brown eyes. "To be honest, if it hadn't been for him, I don't know how I'd have managed after Elly died. Max picked me up and dusted me down, and he was there for Josh too. I know he gets a bad press here, but trust me on this: he's one of the good guys. Josh adores him and he's a brilliant godfather."

Lucy was taken aback to have her view of Max Reynard turned upside down. It was a bit like discovering that Cruella de Vil worked for the RSPCA and had actually been saving little puppies.

"The thing you have to understand about Max is that he feels things very deeply," Adam continued. "He loves this town and he loves the island too. His ideas might not be the same as Nessa's but they both have the same goal in mind."

"If Max buys the island then it'll get developed and it'll be for private use only. The place will be gone forever and the magic will be lost."

"I totally agree," said Adam, "and I think Max will too in the end, but he needs to figure that out for himself. I think he and your cousin could be a really good team if they actually worked together rather than fought one another."

"Work together? They hate each other!"

Adam took her hand in his, brushing her palm with his thumb. "Are you so sure about that? Sometimes people's feelings creep up on them. Enemies discover they don't dislike one another as much as they thought, or good friends come to realise there could be more between them..."

His words faded away but the thumb continued its delicate caress. Lucy's pulse skittered. Sitting here with Adam, wearing the dress he'd admired all those weeks ago, and with her hair and make-up just right for once, she felt a million miles away from her usual self. She'd glimpsed something in his eyes that had made the breath catch in her throat and given her hope that maybe, just maybe, there was a new version of Lucy Penwellyn waiting to be discovered.

"Do you believe friends can sometimes become more?" Adam asked softly.

Lucy's eyes widened. "Are you saying—"

But she never managed to finish her sentence. The door of the restaurant flew open and her brother Jamie burst in, scanning the place until he spotted her. Lucy shrank into her seat and slid her hand away guiltily.

"They told me in the pub that you were here," her brother shouted, oblivious to the annoyed glances thrown his way by the other diners as he glanced off their tables, sending glasses rattling and wine sloshing on his uneven route to reach her. "So much for being there for me. So much for all your I love my brother shit. Why weren't you at the castle? You knew I was coming down this evening to visit and you should have been there to meet me. That bitch told me to get off her property. How bloody humiliating do you think that was for me? And it's your fault she was able to say it. If you'd been there she wouldn't have dared."

Lucy had a horrible sensation in the pit of her stomach, as though she were descending fast in a lift. She'd known Jamie was due to collect yet more things that he'd been insisting were his, but with all the excitement of the past couple of weeks his visit had completely slipped her mind.

"Jamie, I'm really sorry," Lucy said, but her younger brother was in no mood to listen to apologies. His face was scarlet with rage. Lucy's heart sank; although it was Ness he was furious with, Lucy knew that Jamie would take out his anger on her instead.

"You let me take that crap from her while you're out having dinner with your bit of rough," he spat. "Nice to know you have your priorities right, sis. A little loyalty wouldn't have gone amiss."

"I'd say that some manners wouldn't go amiss from you, mate." Adam rose to his feet. He was much taller than her brother, Lucy realised, and all the lifting of masonry and physical work he did for a living had rendered him muscular and powerful. "Your sister's out for dinner, and so are all these other people around us. I suggest you go away and come back in when you've sobered up."

Jamie's face, set in its perpetual sneer, grew redder still. Lucy knew he wouldn't calm down now. If she didn't defuse the situation somehow, he'd be making an even worse scene.

"Are you going to let your oik talk to me like that?" Jamie demanded.

Lucy smelt the sour taint of whiskey on his breath and groaned inwardly. Her brother was always foul when he drank spirits. He must have been trawling the drinking establishments of St Pirran looking for her – and if he was staying at the hotel he'd have had a few there too. Jamie was a horrible drunk, belligerent and unpredictable. She had to get him out of here, and fast.

"I'm so sorry," she said to Adam, mortified by her brother's words.

But Adam was looking amused. "That I'm your oik? Hey, I'm cool with that if you are?"

Lucy couldn't think of anything nicer. Not that Adam was an oik, but that he was happy to be her anything. She was just about to say this when Jamie, incensed at being ignored, made a lunge across the table at her companion. As Adam neatly sidestepped the assault, the inebriated Jamie overbalanced and landed face first in Lucy's spaghetti marinara.

"If we'd known you were that hungry mate, we'd have got you a plate," Adam remarked as Lucy's brother lurched back to his feet.

Jamie's hair was laced with spaghetti and a mussel sat jauntily on top of his head. He glowered at Adam, tomato sauce dripping from his face. "I won't forget this!"

"Neither will I!" Adam said. His lips were twitching. "I know I'm an oik but I'd always assumed people generally dive for seafood before it's plated rather than after? Or is this a public school tradition I'm unaware of?"

Jamie's only answer was to shoot Adam a truly evil look, before stomping out of the restaurant with as much dignity as a man covered in tomato sauce and flakes of lobster could.

Pausing at the door, he barked at Lucy, "Well, come on then. Don't just sit there like an idiot!"

Pavlov's dogs had nothing on Lucy: she was on her feet and reaching for her bag in seconds, the dinner and her pretty frock forgotten now.

Adam caught her wrist. "Lucy, what are you doing? You're not seriously going to follow him, are you?"

"He's my brother."

"He might be your brother but nobody should treat you like that. Christ, he's a liability." He shook his head. "Lucy, please, let him go."

But Lucy couldn't. Jamie, for all his faults, was still her little brother. Right now he was drunk and angry – a bad combination anywhere, but especially bad in Cornwall where there were cliffs and riptides and high quay walls. Anything could happen if he stormed off alone. She had to go after him.

The door slammed in her brother's wake and the waiters exchanged weary looks. The people of St Pirran were used to Jamie

Penwellyn, but this didn't make Lucy feel much better. If anything, it made her feel even worse.

"He's really drunk. I promise he's not usually this bad," she told Adam. Even to her own ears this sounded a pitiful excuse.

"I think we both know that's not true," Adam said quietly.

"I can't just leave him."

Adam looked her right in the eye. "You can. He needs to grow up sometime; pandering to him isn't going to help."

"I'm not pandering to him!" Stung, Lucy pulled her wrist away from his grasp. "He's family and I can't just stand back and watch him self-destruct."

"Even if he's going to do his best to destroy you in the process? Lucy, I mean it. He's not on your side. Stand up to him. For your sake, please, don't go. Stay here, Lucy. Stay with me."

But Lucy couldn't do this any more than she could change her blood type or her love of music. Caring for Jamie was what she did. If she didn't go after her brother then guilt would certainly destroy her from the inside out. She couldn't win.

With a strangled cry of misery, she fled the restaurant with her little red shoes scuffing against the pavement and her carefully applied make-up running as the tears fell. She'd left Adam alone with the overturned pasta and an empty seat. He must feel insulted and abandoned.

Lucy feared that things between them would never be quite the same after this.

Chapter 25

Fern felt sick. She sat on the floor in the Small Hall with the telephone held limply in her hand and waited for the room to stop whirling. She didn't notice the unyielding stone floor against her bare legs or feel the ache of cold spread over her flesh. None of this mattered to Fern, because the world had lurched and pitched and tipped her upside down. What had once been safe was now fraught with danger and where there'd been sunshine there was nothing but shadow.

Logan had found her.

This time he wouldn't let go, not until he'd managed to destroy everything – and this time there was nowhere to hide. The shock of hearing his voice whispering her name in that low possessive way of his was almost too much to bear. She'd hoped never to have to hear it again. All she wanted to do was curl up somewhere, close her eyes and give up. She was tired of running, tired of looking over her shoulder and, most of all, tired of being afraid. In a strange way it would be a relief when Logan arrived. The worst would have happened and there would be no more fearing it.

The day had started off so well. Most of the arrangements for the island's festival were in place. Several big local bands had confirmed and the hotel had agreed to loan its wedding marquee. Adam's friend had wangled stage and sound equipment for them and persuaded some of his colleagues to help set it all up in return for a free weekend in Cornwall. The insurance had come through too, and although the cost was high Ness had been willing to pay it. The only things left to worry about were organising marshals and sorting out refreshments. With tickets at twenty pounds a head and the county fired up about the festival, Fern had already been hopeful that they'd make a decent profit. Then a local fireworks company had called and said it was willing to put a display on for free if it could use the event for advertising.

On a roll and feeling inspired, Fern had set to work; several phone calls later she'd managed to get Cornish Beach FM on board – which was quite a coup, as the local celebrity DJ was going to broadcast his flagship drive time show from the festival and had promised lots of mentions about how great a venue Pirran Island was. In need of a break, Fern had strolled into the garden, meandering through the herb beds and brushing her hand through lavender and thyme to release the soothing scents, until a shout from Lucy had told her she was wanted on the phone. Thinking it would be the final band confirming their slot, Fern had sprinted back to the Small Hall to take the call. Smiling, she'd cradled the receiver between her chin and shoulder and had given a cheery hello.

"And hello to you as well, Fern," a soft voice had said.

Her body had frozen with horror; her inability to move had been the only thing that had stopped the phone clattering onto the flagstones.

"Nothing to say to me? That's so disappointing, Fern, when we have so much catching up to do."

"What do you want, Logan?" Her voice had been little more than a whisper.

He'd laughed. "You, of course, Fern. I never left, did I?"

How had he traced her? Who'd given him her number? Was he nearby? As the questions tore through her mind Fern knew that the answers didn't really matter. All that mattered was that Logan knew where she was.

And he wouldn't give up until he reached her.

She'd tried to quell the rising panic. When she was filled with terror like this Fern couldn't think straight – and she couldn't afford to give Logan that advantage. If he detected that she was afraid it would only give him strength; her fear would feed him like some dreadful, monstrous entity until he grew even more powerful. If she kept reminding herself that he was just pathetic and weak, every bit as dependent upon the drugs he peddled as the unfortunate creatures he drew into his web, then it helped her feel stronger. She'd untangled herself from him.

She was strong. She was a fighter. She could handle him now.

"I know you're missing me, Fern," Logan had said softly. "Me and the life we had. We had the best of times, didn't we? And we'll have them again. You'll see. It'll be me and you together again, just like before."

"No," she'd answered. "It's over, Logan."

"Don't say that, Fern. It's never over with us. We're good together. We belong together. You'll see."

"I won't." Her hands were clenched into fists.

"Yes you will," Logan had said firmly. There was malice beneath the quiet words, like a flick knife hidden inside a woollen sleeve. "You owe me, remember? Don't think I've forgotten that, Fern. I don't like thieves and I always call in debts. Your payment is long overdue, and with interest."

He'd ended the call then and although all she could hear was the dialling tone, Fern had slumped to the floor. For all her firm words and resolutions, she was afraid. Afraid of Logan and of what he could do. She knew him so well. She knew how he thought. He'd think that she was still the timid and sheltered girl he'd picked out, the one who'd felt special being the centre of an older man's attention. He'd assume that she'd be easy to manipulate because she'd be too scared and ashamed to tell anyone the truth.

Was she still ashamed? As she rose to her feet, her legs as weak as a foal's, Fern searched her heart for the truth. Secrets gave people like Logan Barrie power; she could see that now. They were a great device for making someone vulnerable feel special. It's just you and me or Don't tell your parents: this is just for us were his specialities, and before she'd been aware of it those serpentine words had slithered between Fern and her family, hissing venom into what had once been a close relationship. Fern's eyes filled with tears now as she recalled the bitter arguments with her mother and the ugly words she'd hurled at her father. When you were sixteen and thought you were in love it was exciting to rebel. A smoke here, some weed there... It had felt rebellious, and with Logan to encourage her she'd tumbled headlong into the abyss.

And what an abyss it had been. What was exciting when you were rebelling wasn't quite so thrilling when you were cold and aching from withdrawal or when your face was smarting from the back of your boyfriend's hand. Much of that time was a blur and Fern didn't like to think about the dank bedsits or what Logan had forced her to do when they'd both been desperate. He'd been clever, never giving her enough to let her become dependent, but tempting her with just sufficient to keep her to heel. Fern choked back a sob because it was so intensely painful to think about the person she'd been then. Ashamed and addicted, she hadn't dared to contact her parents for help. Besides, as Logan had often pointed out, they wouldn't want anything to do with her now. She belonged with him. It was too late.

Fern dashed the tears away with the back of her hand. She wasn't that person anymore. She'd fought too hard not to be that miserable shadow of a girl: she wasn't going to let him ruin everything now. She'd beaten the addictions and although her past wasn't something she was proud of there was no way she'd let it define her. She'd go and find Merryn and ask him for help. Merry was her friend. He wouldn't judge her and she always felt safe with him. Merryn was the person she felt closest to in the world and so many times she had almost told him the truth, both about her past and about how she had come to feel about him. How seeing his face was the highlight of her day and how when he'd been trapped during the storm she has thought her heart would stop with terror. Only fear that she might ruin everything between them and destroy a friendship that had come to mean the world to her had kept Fern silent. Now she knew that the time had come to tell the truth. Merryn understood that people made mistakes. Armand Penwellyn had understood that too.

Fern and Logan had been living in Plymouth, dossing in a squalid flat after skipping the rent on a place in Bristol. For once Logan had had some paid work lined up. It had only been for a few weeks but he'd managed to gather some cash together. The notes had been rolled tight and hidden inside a balled-up pair of socks – a place he didn't think Fern had noticed.

He'd been wrong.

For several days Fern had bided her time. Then one morning, once Logan had headed out, she'd grabbed the cash and made a break for freedom. She'd made one call to her parents from the bus station, leaving an answerphone message to say she was well, before hopping on a bus heading over the Tamar and deep into Cornwall. With her temples throbbing from lack of nicotine and weed, and terrified that at any moment Logan would find out what she'd done and drag her back for a beating or worse, Fern had found herself alighting in St Pirran.

Cornwall. It was a magical place and as soon as the salty air had filled her lungs Fern had known that she was somewhere she could heal. It was a feeling deep in her heart, a peace that enveloped her when she stood on the harbour wall and gazed out over the sea. Fern's childhood holidays had been spent in Rock or Watergate Bay; she had so many happy memories of eating sandwiches on the beach or water-skiing behind her father's boat. As she'd wandered along the causeway to the island that day, Fern had been convinced that she could discover herself again here. If she could find a way to stay she knew that her toxic association with Logan and drugs would be in the past.

The castle had been full of visitors, so it had been easy for Fern to slip away and explore. The place was wild and tumbledown in places, and it hadn't taken long to find somewhere she could hide. The coach house had a hayloft above, accessible via a rickety ladder, and there was a tap in the courtyard too. If she could swipe some food from the tea room at night then Fern had reckoned she'd be on to a good thing. The blonde woman running the tea shop looked fraught and if the odd pasty or two seemed to vanish or an entire cake dissolved into thin air, then she'd probably put it down to being exhausted and making mistakes. That and mischievous Cornish piskies.

This plan had worked, for a couple of days at least, until the old gardener – whose eyesight was unfortunately better than his hearing – had spotted her and told Armand Penwellyn they had a squatter.

Fern glanced up at the old man's portrait. Those blue eyes held hers as powerfully now as they had the first time she'd met him – if met was quite the right word for a landowner confronting a runaway hiding in his empty coach house.

"Old Fred's right: you're a state," was all he'd said. "For Christ's sake, girl! Come up to the castle and have a bath and something to eat. You make me feel like a factory owner from a bloody Dickens novel."

Fern, her stomach clenching with hunger (she'd found very little in the bins outside the tea room that day), had been stunned into acquiescence. She'd followed him into the castle, where Lucy – doing her best not to look shocked at the state of their unexpected guest – had heaped a plate with stew and dumplings and then run her a bath. The rest had been history. The next day Armand had offered Fern a place to stay in return for some chores. When she'd tried to explain her story, he'd said that he could guess.

"I'm old, not stupid," he'd snapped in the curt fashion she'd soon learned was just his way. "Stay for as long as you want, girl. This is a safe place."

And it had been a safe place – until today's phone call.

Merryn would be working on the boat, Fern thought. His wrist was slowly healing and he was learning to do lots of his marine chores one-handed, although he'd said he could always do with help hand-tightening nuts or selecting spanners. She'd go down to the pier and tell him the truth about her past and her feelings for him. It was long overdue.

The sun was playing hide-and-seek with the clouds and as she crossed the courtyard Fern shivered. She was passing under the Pilgrim's Gate when a hand came down onto her shoulder, yanking her around. The seconds it took Fern to realise this wasn't Merryn messing around cost her the opportunity to escape: before she knew what was happening, the person's other hand had been clapped over her mouth.

It was Logan.

As Fern's eyes bulged, he shook her so hard that her teeth rattled. "Surprised to see me? Aren't mobile phones great?"

Fern writhed to free herself but Logan, although skinny, was strong. He pulled her round and held her tightly against his chest while she continued to struggle and fight. His face, once boy-band handsome, had become sallow and his cheeks were sunken. He still kept his hair long but it was lank now and there was a crop of angry red spots near his mouth. In his appearance Fern saw the road her life would have taken if she hadn't found the strength to run away or had the gruff kindness of Armand to support her. Her friends here, her garden and her new island life had saved Fern from becoming someone she despised.

"You're probably wondering how I found you," Logan continued, his sharp fingernails biting into her skin. "It wasn't easy. You did a great job of going to ground and I'd never have thought for a minute you'd be here. Call it luck or call it fate, but I was listening to the radio and I heard the DJ mention that somebody called Fern Morris was organising a festival here."

Fern hadn't dreamed the DJ might mention her name on air. She could have kicked herself for the oversight – and kicked herself twice as hard for not adopting a new name when she'd first arrived on the island.

"So now we're reacquainted," Logan said softly, dragging her away from the gate and towards the ruined part of the castle, where people seldom ventured, "it's time I reminded you why taking anything of mine is a very bad idea."

Fern tried to kick him but it was no use: Logan was stronger than she was. She had no doubt that he could hurt her if he really wanted to. It wouldn't be the first time – but in the past he'd been drunk or high, and for a long time she'd been able to tell herself that he didn't really mean it.

Today he most definitely did.

"Three hundred quid you stole from me, you bitch," he hissed, his clammy hand still clamped over her mouth. "That was my hard-earned money."

Fern disagreed. The way she'd seen it, the cash was the least he'd owed her. Managing to twist her torso, this time Fern kicked him sharply in the shin. For a moment Logan released her, but the victory was short-lived; the hand swung back and dealt her a stinging blow to the face.

The castle walls dipped and rolled and Fern lurched backwards, her vision blurring. She raised her hands to shield her face, knowing from experience that the worst was still to come.

Except it didn't.

Unseen by her ex, Merryn had appeared behind him. Before Logan had a chance to strike again he was rugby-tackled to the ground, landing with a thud and a yelp of pain. Then Merryn's left hand dealt him a punch to the jaw, followed by another and another. Even though Merryn was fighting with only one hand, Logan didn't stand a chance: Merryn was six foot of pure muscle and rage. Within seconds Fern's ex was curled up with his arms across his face, trying to protect himself as the other man rained blow after blow down upon him.

"What the hell do you think you're doing?" Merryn was shouting. "Well? Want to tell me, you worthless piece of shit? Or shall I hit you with my plaster cast?"

Logan couldn't have told Merryn even if he'd wanted to. Blood and saliva bubbled from his split lip and he was gasping for air. Although her head was still pounding, Fern knew that she had to pull Merryn off. Her friend was white with fury and he was pummelling his felled opponent like a rag doll. It was so strange; she'd known Merryn for a year or so now, but she'd never seen him like this before. For the first time Fern realised just how strong and powerful he was.

"Not so much fun picking on women now, is it?" Merryn said scathingly. "Not such a big man now, are you?"

Logan's head walloped against the dry earth with every shake Merryn gave him. He looked terrified – and Fern didn't blame him. Merryn was like a man possessed. His blue eyes were navy with fury and his usually smiling mouth had curled into a snarl. Her ex looked pitiful, and as she stared down at him Fern realised he didn't scare her anymore. Logan looked exactly like what he was: a pathetic and cowardly bully.

He was nothing.

"Merry! Merry! That's enough!" she cried, grabbing his left arm and tugging him back from the cowering Logan. "You'll hurt your good wrist."

"It'll be worth it," Merryn said. "I take it this is the piece of crap who gave you those bruises you arrived with?"

And there was she thinking she'd done a good job of hiding everything. Wearily, Fern nodded.

"I'd like to kill him for that alone, never mind what he's just done. Nobody would miss a lowlife like him, would they? The castle well's pretty deep. I'll just throw him in," Merryn deadpanned, winking at Fern.

Logan, who didn't see this exchange, whimpered.

"Believe me, he's not worth polluting the well," she said, taking Merryn's sore hand in hers and gently pulling her friend away.

"It is if he's hurt you," Merryn answered fiercely.

"But he can't hurt me anymore," Fern said slowly. "I don't need him now. There's nothing he can do."

"He can't get away with it," Merryn insisted.

Fern glanced at Logan, who was nursing his bloody nose. "He won't. The life he leads is punishment enough and if he ever, ever comes near me again then I'm calling the police. And they might be very interested in what I have to tell them. Some of Logan's associates wouldn't like to think that he'd turned grass. They don't take well to that kind of thing."

Her ex paled. "You wouldn't dare."

"Try me," said Fern. "You'll soon find out, won't you?"

She eyeballed him and Logan looked away first.

"All right, all right. I'm going, all right?"

"You've got five minutes to get off this island before I call the police," Merryn said coldly. "Now get out of my sight before I change my mind and throw you in the well."

Logan didn't need asking twice. With a groan he hauled himself up, shooting them an ugly look before scurrying through the scaffolded gate. He didn't glance back.

Fern's heart rattled against her ribs with relief.

"Thanks, Merryn," she said.

"You don't have to thank me."

"I do. You could have been hurt and I couldn't bear that."

"So you know exactly how I feel then, don't you?"

Fern stared at him. "What's that supposed to mean?"

"Let me show you," Merryn said.

Then he stepped forward and folded her in his arms and the world turned inside out all over again, only this time it had nothing to do with Logan's fists. This should have felt strange – Merryn was her friend and her sparring partner – but it didn't feel strange at all.

It felt absolutely right.

"There's so much I need to tell you," Fern whispered as Merryn pulled her against his chest. His sling scratched her cheek but she didn't care; it just felt so good to be safe and close to him. "I don't know where to start."

"All that can wait. There's something far more important to do first." He smiled at her, a smile filled with such tenderness that it took Fern's breath away. "There'll be time for talking after."

Fern tilted her head back and looked up at him. Oh! The expression in Merryn's eyes was one she hardly dared name.

"After what?" she whispered.

"This," said Merryn. Then, to Fern's delighted surprise, he kissed her. It was a kiss that she knew was the start of something so wonderful that Logan's threats, the bruises and her painful past melted right away.

Chapter 26

Max Reynard sat in the spotless kitchen of his beautiful holiday home with a blank sketchpad beside him and a pencil dangling between his fingers. Things must be bad if he couldn't even draw. After all, this was a glorious spot looking out across the bay, with spectacular views of the island and castle. When he'd first bought the house he'd loved it; its white minimalist decor and windows filled with blue seascape were reminiscent of being at sea on a stately ocean liner. He'd imagined holidays here with friends and family, enjoying long sunny evenings barbecuing or days boating out in the bay, but the reality was that he worked too hard to spend much time here – and when he was here the view of the castle was only a constant reminder of his greatest project's failure to materialise.

Had he jumped the gun with this development and allowed his emotions to overrule his business sense? Max wondered. Several months ago he'd been so sure that the project was a done deal and that the island would be his. He'd wanted to devote all his professional experience to it, sparing no expense and seeking out the most knowledgeable experts and the most skilled craftspeople in order to save the ancient building and return it to the state of splendour it deserved. From the second he'd laid eyes on the place this had been Max's ultimate goal; everything he'd worked towards had been leading to this. It had never really been about making money. Nice as it was to be wealthy, cash wasn't Max's god and he was quite content to pour most of his income into his charity work. Developing Pirran Island was about far more than boosting Reynards' already healthy profits. It was about fulfilling a childhood dream and doing something important for posterity. When Jamie Penwellyn had visited his office in London that first time, Max had truly believed that this was fate and that the island he loved was meant to be his.

Now he wasn't so certain.

Ness Penwellyn loved the place too, that was apparent, and she was working flat out and against all the odds to save it. It was her inheritance, so it was hardly surprising – but her task was impossible, and now that she'd involved Jonathan Ambrose it was only a matter of time before the island was on the market and Max could snap it up. Oddly this didn't make him feel nearly as happy as he'd expected. In fact, he felt very uncomfortable with the way events were panning out.

Since he'd first seen Ness in the hotel bar, something within Max Reynard had changed. It was as though she'd ignited a spark in him – and her determination not to give in or be impressed by money had only fanned the flames. When those scornful green eyes had held his that last time at Grace Note Bay, emotions that Max hadn't previously believed in had stirred deep in his heart. In spite of all his cynicism about women and his experience of girls like Aimee, he'd found himself unable to stop thinking about Ness.

Max was exasperated with himself. Nessa Penwellyn was the reason he was not yet in possession of Pirran Island. It was because of her stubborn refusal to see sense and accept his offer that this project, his flagship development, was in danger of falling months behind schedule or, even worse, not happening at all. She constantly thwarted him and scoffed at his suggestions, defying all logic and common sense with her ideas of running the place alone and on a shoestring budget. Jonathan Ambrose had loaned her a tiny amount – Max's contacts had swiftly found this out for him – and it wouldn't go far at all. She'd be needing more very soon. It wouldn't be long before Ambrose Investments had a sizeable stake in the island. That was how these companies operated. Posh loan sharks was how his father would have scathingly described them. Why hadn't she come to Max for help? He'd offered her an apartment and a say in the development and all she'd done was laugh at him.

Well, there was nothing he could do to help Nessa now. If she got in any deeper then he would be buying from Ambrose. Either way he'd win and Pirran Island would be his. It was only a matter of time.

I ought to be pleased, Max thought. But he wasn't. The truth was that he was feeling torn about the whole deal and the thought of seeing Ness fail. Watching the fire in her burn to nothingness would give him no joy.

Christ. What the hell was wrong with him?

Max had hardly been able to sleep last night; instead he'd sat staring out over the dark water towards the sole lit window, which he knew must be hers. He'd imagined Ness there, that flame-red hair loose over her shoulders as she sat in the tower – perhaps staring straight back at his window. God, he was mooning about like a teenager. It was ridiculous. If he hadn't already been tetchy from lack of sleep, a hammering on the door now and the arrival of Jamie Penwellyn definitely put him in a bad mood.

Max didn't often miss drinking, but right now he could have done with a whiskey. These days Jamie was proving very hard to shake off.

As he showed him into the kitchen, Max observed that his old school acquaintance was looking even less together than he had in London. His hair needed a comb, his skin was sallow and although he wore an expensive shirt there was a ring of grime around the collar.

"If this is about more money," Max said, "you're wasting your time. Our arrangement's at an end."

Jamie raised his sandy eyebrows. "You're not giving up, are you? We're nearly there, I swear to God. It's only a matter of time before Ness sells. You'll see."

Max narrowed his grey eyes. "Lucy might be terrified of your temper tantrums but I don't think you have any influence over your cousin. Nessa's made of sterner stuff."

"I'm disappointed by your lack of faith, Max old man. I promise you, she's only days away from giving up and when she does it'll be me you have to thank. I think that's worth another ten thousand surely?"

Something about the way he said this set Max's mental alarm bells ringing. There was no legitimate way Jamie could persuade Ness to sell. A sudden recollection came to Max, of how Jamie had blackmailed a classmate who'd been caught in a compromising situation with a copy of Playboy. Max tensed. He'd have to be careful not to spook Jamie if he wanted to find out what he was up to.

"You have my attention," he said evenly. "Tell me more."

But Jamie merely tapped his nose with a forefinger. "That's my business, old sport, but it's going to work a dream. It's surprising just how much bad luck Nessa is having. Visitors tripping, unhygienic tea rooms, freezers defrosting themselves. It's such a shame and it must be costing thousands in compensation payments."

"What?"

"You heard. There's more than one way to skin a cat. You should know that. It's amazing what people will do to earn a few quid, isn't it? Then again I guess you already know that."

"What are you talking about?" Max demanded.

Jamie looked at him as though he was stupid. "Find a way to get Lucy to persuade Ness to sell: wasn't that what you wanted? Well, I'm certain I've found a way. By the time I'm finished Nessa will be begging you to take the place off her hands. To be honest, old man, I'm surprised you haven't already thought of doing it yourself."

Max was on his feet and consumed with murderous rage.

"I want to buy the island, not play underhand games!" He couldn't believe what he was hearing. "Under no circumstances would I ever condone such things!"

"Oh chill out, Max. All's fair in love and business," Jamie said airily. "As long as the bitch sells up, what does it matter how we achieved it? You should be thanking me. By the time I'm through, Nessa will be desperate to give the island away!"

Max thought he was going to explode with fury. Red spots danced before his vision and for a dreadful moment he thought he was going to strangle Jamie.

"Are you insane?" he asked, his voice filled with menace. "You've seriously been paying people to sabotage cafés and put in false claims for compensation? That's criminal behaviour! What the hell else are you up to?"

But Jamie, realising too late that Max wasn't reacting with the enthusiasm he'd expected, wasn't going to say another word on the matter.

"I didn't say I'd done anything," he said. "I don't much like your accusations. Anyway, you can't prove a bloody thing."

"Don't play games with me!" Max snarled. "Whatever you're up to, you can put an end to it right now."

Jamie laughed nastily. "You can't order me about, old man. I don't work for you, remember? Besides, this isn't about you."

"It is when you owe me thousands," Max said. He took a deep breath and did his best to fight his anger. "Look, whatever you're up to just forget it. I'll give you longer to settle up. I'll even write the whole lot off. Just stay away from Nessa and the island."

"Jesus. You must want to get into her knickers really badly," Jamie observed.

And that was it: Max saw red. Grabbing his visitor by the scruff of his grubby neck, he towed Jamie through the kitchen and shoved him through the front door.

"Get out," he said.

Max was shaking with rage. How had he managed to get embroiled with someone as low and cunning as this? He'd known back in his schooldays just what kind of a sorry excuse for a human being Jamie Penwellyn was, but his desire for the island had blinded him to the truth in more ways than one.

"I don't like your tone," Jamie said slowly. "Be careful, Max. This is personal now and, like you, I don't give up easily. Not when things are about to liven up a bit. Maybe I'll see you at the festival? It should be great fun. Not for Nessa, but certainly for me! Do pop down, old boy. I guarantee it'll be interesting."

With this cryptic parting shot, he'd sauntered down the cliff path. Max stared after him with a sense of dread. That Jamie Penwellyn was petty and unbalanced was beyond doubt. He was a loose cannon and, as such, this made him dangerous. What was he up to and how could Max stop him? How could he keep Nessa safe?

Hold on. Didn't he mean, how could he keep the island safe and ensure its future with Reynards?

Max thumped his fist on the kitchen worktop in pure frustration. He barely registered the crack of bone against marble or the flare of pain in his knuckles. This was nothing compared to the anguish of a realisation that was slowly dawning: it wasn't the thought of owning the island that consumed him anymore. If he was honest, it hadn't been for some time now.

It was Nessa Penwellyn.

Adam Miller had known Max Reynard for a very long time and had always believed his old friend to be honest and straight in his dealings. Yes, Max could be ruthless and he was certainly determined – yet he was never underhand and he always played fair. He knew his own mind and was driven in business, but he'd reached the top by being the best rather than manipulating the system or looking for shortcuts. If there was one word Adam could have chosen to describe his best friend then it was honourable. That might sound old-fashioned but there was something a little old-fashioned about Max. He was a gentleman in the truest sense of the word and proper in everything he did.

So why, then, was Jamie Penwellyn coming down the path from Max's holiday home? What business did he have being there?

It was a hot Friday afternoon and Adam was sitting outside, relaxing for once as he made the most of a rare day off from working on the castle. Josh was out with the sailing school, in one of the little toppers that was zipping across the bay. Adam had been enjoying listening to the strains of music drifting across from the island, where the sound stage had been set up for the following day's festival. According to the forecasts, the weather was going to be fair for the weekend; better still, every hotel and bed and breakfast in the town was booked and all the tickets had been sold days ago. Adam was already looking forward to a day of chilling out in the sunshine with a picnic and listening to some music. Josh was excited too. His band from school was going to play a set, and a local folk group had asked him to accompany them on the violin. His son's confidence was growing by the day. Besides that, Adam had work coming to him from the castle, the sun was out and everything was looking good.

So why then did a shiver ripple over him when Jamie Penwellyn passed by with a face like thunder?

Adam knew he was biased – it was hard not to be when the younger man was so objectionable and treated Lucy appallingly – but he also prided himself on being a good judge of character. Just as he knew that Lucy was generous and honest, he also knew that her brother was rotten to the core. Lucy could plead Jamie's case all day long (and she'd certainly done her best to try to explain away the scene in the restaurant as a drunken one-off), but Adam wasn't fooled. Jamie Penwellyn was a thoroughly nasty piece of work. He'd turned up this weekend for one reason only: to cause trouble.

Adam sighed. He didn't hold Lucy responsible for her brother's behaviour but he couldn't help feeling that by making excuses she was condoning it. He was no psychiatrist but Adam wasn't convinced that being let down by your uncle and feeling neglected by your father were valid reasons for behaving like an utter cock. In Adam's opinion, Jamie needed somebody to stand up to him once and for all – and that person had to be Lucy. The problem was, she was so afraid of upsetting her brother that she'd probably spend the rest of her life scurrying around in a fruitless attempt to placate him. When Lucy had left the restaurant and followed Jamie, Adam had been disappointed but not surprised. He'd stepped away from her a little in the weeks since. Lucy was a lovely person – he enjoyed her company and certainly found her attractive – but it was clear where her priorities lay. She wouldn't hear a word against her brother, even though it was abundantly clear that he revelled in any disaster that beset Lucy and those living on the island. Jamie was her blind spot, and until Lucy saw for herself exactly what her brother was like, Adam knew there could be no future for them.

Jolted by this thought, Adam took a hasty slug of his beer. He'd been thinking he and Lucy might have a future, he realised now. Had his feelings for her crept up on him stealthily? This had happened to Merryn and Fern, hadn't it?

Like everyone else in St Pirran, Adam was delighted to see these two together. It was obvious they were made for each other. Their banter and teasing friendship had been a slow burn to something even deeper. For two people who usually shied away from opening up, their feelings had swiftly blossomed into a closeness that would bring a tear to the most cynical eye. Adam certainly had a lump in his throat when he saw them together. The tenderness with which Fern strapped up Merryn's wrist and the protective way he drew her close as they walked through the grounds reminded him of how he and Elly had been. At least he could think about Elly now without that clawing sense of loss. Acceptance was the final stage of grief, and Adam did now accept that she was gone and would never return to him. Acknowledging this fact didn't stop the dull ache of missing her; that would never go away. Nevertheless, for a while spending time with Lucy had lulled him into believing – hoping – that the future might not be as bleak and as lonely as he'd feared.

But Lucy had chosen her brother over him, and although Adam knew that she'd felt unable to do otherwise, he'd been hurt by her decision all the same.

So now, as Jamie Penwellyn strode towards the town, Adam decided to follow him. It was maybe a sixth sense or perhaps just a distrust of Jamie after everything that had happened, but he couldn't help noticing that whenever Lucy's brother chose to spend a few days in St Pirran problems soon arose on the island.

Adam had been working on the Pilgrim's Gate for several weeks and during this time there had been a number of incidents. None of them had been significant enough to arouse suspicion at the time, but to Adam's mind they seemed almost too much of a coincidence to be unrelated. A tourist claimed to have fallen on an uneven part of the castle and had threatened them with a claim unless he was compensated. Another visitor had found a cockroach in her slice of Victoria sponge, which had prompted a public health inspection. And yesterday the tea shop's freezer had somehow become unplugged, ruining all the contents and costing hundreds of pounds to replace the spoiled food. Ness, despite looking worried, had dealt with all these problems in the calm manner that was her hallmark – but she was already in hock to Ambrose Investments, and doubtless wouldn't want to incur further borrowing unless she had to.

Adam frowned. It was a little odd that Jamie's arrival in town always coincided with these unfortunate incidents. It wouldn't hurt at all to see what Jamie was up to. Like all the visitors in town, Jamie was probably here for the festival and Adam was being paranoid – but he'd walk into town anyway, grab a quick pint and collect Josh from sailing club. Maybe they could pick up fish and chips on the way home.

Adam's heart constricted as he recalled the night he and Lucy had enjoyed their al fresco takeaway and watched the sunset. The conversation had flowed so easily and he'd felt the warmth of simply being happy with someone. If only things could have stayed that way...

Jamie Penwellyn had reached the far end of the path and was heading into town. Still holding his empty bottle, Adam followed Jamie into St Pirran. The streets were thronging with visitors eating ice creams and milling around outside gift shops. Bunting fluttered in the breeze and there was already a carnival atmosphere as a busker strummed his guitar outside the pub and a troupe of Morris dancers assembled on the quay. It all boded well for Island Fest, Adam thought, as he drank in the scene with pleasure.

Unfortunately, all this distraction was enough for Adam to lose Jamie in the crowd. He'd probably ducked into The Castle Inn for a pint or had returned to his hotel. Adam felt a little foolish now. Honestly, what was he thinking following Jamie? He was a stonemason, not Jason Bourne! And his quarry was just an upper-class nitwit, not some international gangster. He must have been sitting in the sun too long; either that, or that beer had been stronger than he'd thought!

Shaking his head at his own behaviour, Adam turned into one of the town's narrow side streets so that he could get to the pub without having to elbow his way through the holidaymakers. He'd only walked a few hundred yards when he spotted none other than Jamie Penwellyn standing in a shadowy doorway, deep in conversation. Adam stopped abruptly. Had Jamie seen him? And if he had, would he even recognise the "oik" who'd been in Sorrentina with his sister?

Who was Jamie talking to? In the gloom of the side street it was hard to see, but whoever it was, he was a skinny, unhealthy-looking individual. He had the pallid skin of someone who rarely saw fresh air and lank dark hair that kept flopping across a sunken-cheeked face. He seemed to irritate Jamie, whose voice had risen loud enough for Adam to overhear.

"We agreed a price! We had a deal!" Jamie cried.

"Keep your bloody voice down or the whole thing's off," the other man shot back. He wasn't shouting, but there was menace in his tone and instantly Jamie was contrite.

"Don't be hasty, Logan. Look, how about another forty?" Jamie reached into his jacket and pulled out a wallet. Peeling off some notes, he held them out hopefully.

The other man laughed. "Double it and we might be getting somewhere."

Jamie glanced over his shoulder. Instinctively, Adam crouched down and made himself look busy tying a shoelace. When he glanced up, Jamie was still talking, but softly now, and the other man was counting money. As far as he could see, absolutely nothing else had changed hands. Not wanting to be spotted, Adam straightened up and left them to it – but he couldn't help feeling uneasy. Whatever their exchange was about, Adam's gut instinct told him it wasn't good news.

Something was very wrong here.

Very wrong indeed.

Chapter 27

"Aren't you going to come and listen to the next band? They're supposed to be amazing. I've called you over the radio a couple of times and I'm starting to think you're ignoring me."

Ness looked up from her clipboard to see Merryn, clad in his high-vis steward's tabard and brandishing a walkie-talkie.

"Sorry, I didn't mean to make you jump," he said. "It's just you're working so hard and we all think you should come and enjoy the festival. Chill a bit. The hard work's done, Ness. Look around! This is a massive success!"

Merryn was right: the festival was a hit. Visitors had been streaming onto the island since eight o'clock that morning. The English weather had been on side for once, and all the grassy areas had been claimed by people enjoying picnics as they sunbathed and listened to the music. The stage was surrounded by people dancing; even the security guards hired for the event were tapping their toes in time to the beat. Meanwhile the hog-roast stand was doing a roaring trade and the inner courtyard was crammed with an eclectic mix of stalls selling everything from hair wraps to local artwork. Down at the tea room customers were queuing out of the door – Lucy and her team of helpers hadn't stopped all day – and the seagulls were gleefully feasting on any leftovers and scavenging through the bins.

"It's not over yet," Ness reminded him, and then laughed. "Lord! I sound such a killjoy, don't I? You're right: it's been wonderful so far."

"Then come and enjoy it," Merryn insisted. He started to steer Ness away from her post by the Pilgrim's Gate. "Seriously, Ness. At least have ten minutes off. There's enough people helping out for you to take a break."

Ness allowed herself to be gently guided towards the lawn. Although she was touched by the way her friends kept trying to persuade her to enjoy the music or grab a burger, she knew she wouldn't be able to relax until the fireworks had lit up the night, the last visitor had left the island and the event was over. Her nerves were as taut as guitar strings, and although it sounded crazy she just couldn't shake the feeling that something was going to go wrong. It was paranoia, of course, because everything was well planned and running beautifully – but even so, there was a niggling sense of unease that she couldn't ignore. It might have had something to do with the fact that Jamie Penwellyn was here. Ness was certain he took no pleasure from seeing her fundraising attempts going so well, so why was he wearing that smug expression? She didn't like the look of the pale and shifty character he'd been talking to either. Neither man had seemed in the festival mood, and they hadn't talked for long, but for some reason her insides had started to knot. Ness guessed it was because she trusted Jamie about as far as she could hurl his grand piano.

"I wasn't entirely joking: I really was beginning to think you were avoiding me," Merryn was saying as they wove their way through the press of people.

Ness looked at him, confused. "Why on earth would you think that?"

"Because of me and Fern getting together. After that time you and I went to the beach... Well, you know."

Merryn looked worried, but he didn't need to be. In truth, whenever Ness thought about being on the beach with a man, that man was always Max Reynard. Max, with his penetrating grey-eyed gaze and lithe panther's grace.

"I thought that when we went swimming that time you thought we were... I was... Oh shit! I'm making an idiot of myself, aren't I?" Poor Merryn was turning red, and his light-blond hair seemed even brighter against the scarlet hue of his skin.

Oh! He was thinking about the time they'd swum in the rock pool. That day felt like another lifetime to Ness; so much had happened since then. Yet there had been an attraction, albeit a pale imitation of the white-hot desire she'd felt when Max had kissed her, and Ness took pity on Merryn.

"You're never an idiot and of course I'm not upset," she said gently. "I'm thrilled about you and Fern. You're made for each other, you always were."

"I love her," Merryn said simply. "I didn't realise just how much until I saw that bastard hurting her. Honestly, I could have killed him. She's so special, Ness, and so brave."

It sounded as though Merryn had solved the mystery of Fern, thought Ness. She supposed this was one less secret the island was hiding. She was no nearer to finding out the truth about her mother's death, the family feud or her uncle's odd legacy. Rose Hellier's words hadn't helped at all. Maybe she'd never know.

"Fern's lucky to have you on her side and so am I," she told him. "I'm lucky to have found all of you."

"We're the lucky ones. Without you none of us would still be living here, that's for sure."

"I just hope it can stay that way," Ness said.

"If it doesn't, nobody could have tried harder," Merryn assured her. "You never met Armand, Ness, but he'd have been proud of you. You're a lot like him too – he would never take any crap or sell out either. Whatever the future holds and whatever his reasons were for leaving the island to you, you need to know that everyone around here thinks you were the right choice."

Ness's vision swam with tears; she blinked them away rapidly, before Merryn saw them. Luckily at this point their conversation was interrupted as a popular local band took to the stage and began to belt out a set, much to the delight of the crowd. Giving Ness a thumbs up, Merryn set off on a sweep of the area, leaving her to enjoy the performance.

As the group played, Ness glanced around and felt a warm glow to see so many people having fun. This was the perfect setting for a summer festival: the grassy slopes were just right for containing the audience, and the granite walls of the castle provided amazing acoustics. Maybe they could rent the island out for more events like this. Perhaps even big names might come to play here, like they did at Eden and Powderham. She felt a thrill of optimism. After all, there had always been music on this island. Some of the best-loved works of the past century had been composed here, and every day the castle rang with Josh and Lucy's playing. Ness hoped her uncle would have approved of today's events. In her heart she felt sure he would have done, because it was something very special to see so many people rapt by music. Armand would have known that joy too.

The sun was lower in the sky now, bathing Pirran Island in pinks and golds. Ness raised her face to the warmth and for the first time began to relax, letting the exhaustion and tension slip away as she lost herself in the melodies. Perhaps this was the turning point?

"Hello, Ness."

Max Reynard had made his way through the crowd, and was standing just inches away from her. Ness was instantly jolted from her thoughts.

"Max. I didn't think you'd be here."

"Why not?"

He looked at her quizzically and she was struck again by just how handsome he was, with those intense grey eyes and that inky dark hair. As his confident gaze flickered over her, Ness felt her stomach flip. Despite the effect he had on her, she tried to steel herself for the inevitable battle of wits between them. Any second now, he'd probably offer her ten million.

"Because I turned your offer down," she replied.

"Which one?" Max asked. The question was loaded and she found that she couldn't look at him.

"Selling this place, of course."

"Ness, that's business." Max raised his bottle of Evian water to her. "This festival is fantastic. You should be very proud."

"Are you being serious?"

"Absolutely," he said quietly, inclining his dark head until his face was close to hers.

In order to hear him against the loud music, Ness hadn't had any choice but to step closer to him, which she knew was dangerous. Max could be devilishly charming when he wanted to be. Careful! she warned herself. He's probably just trying to work out another way of persuading you to sell.

"I mean it, Ness. You've done an amazing job. Turning this place around would make most people head for the hills – but not you. You've met every challenge head-on. You're an incredible woman."

She stared at him. Was he being sarcastic?

"I mean it," Max repeated, probably able to tell by her incredulous expression that she thought he was playing with her. His voice was low but his eyes held hers with that penetrating grey stare. "I know we haven't always agreed on everything—"

"That's one way of putting it! All you ever do is keep telling me how I should sell to you and how I'm letting the place go to ruin! I bet that's what you're thinking right now, isn't it? That I should sell to you?"

He held up his hands. "You got me. Guilty as charged. Look, Nessa, I develop property and I love this island, so I'd be lying if I said I didn't still want it or think I could do a great job here, but that doesn't mean I can't see that you've worked your socks off to get this far or that I'm not quite impressed."

"Wow," said Ness drily. "Quite impressed. You really know how to make a girl feel good."

Max grinned, and she was surprised to see how much his face was transformed by the smile. It was like the sunshine appearing after a storm. She noticed the dimple in his cheek and how boyish it made him seem all of a sudden.

"You know I do," he said softly.

"Do I?" Ness knew this was a dangerous challenge but she couldn't help herself. Something about Max Reynard made her reckless. "Really?"

"Yes," Max replied – and, moving closer, he kissed her gently, brushing his mouth against hers. It was such a fleeting kiss, lighter than gossamer, that Ness was shocked by just how hard her heart was beating; she wouldn't have been surprised to hear it thudding above the bass of the music. She shivered with sudden longing and before she could stop herself she rose onto her tiptoes and kissed him back.

Max's hand cupped the back of her head, his fingers threading into her curls; Ness slid her hand under the cool linen of his shirt to trace the sinews of his back, the heat of his skin searing her fingertips. She could blame it on the sun, the intensity of the day or anything she chose, but all she knew at that point was that she longed for more. Enemy. Rival. Sparring partner. Nemesis. None of this mattered anymore, not when she was melting at his slightest touch.

A loud and rather awkward throat-clearing behind them broke the moment. As Ness and Max sprung apart like teenagers caught snogging behind the school bike sheds, she noticed Adam standing in front of them. He was accompanied by two policemen and a man in a suit.

Adam's usually cheerful face was serious. "Sorry to interrupt, guys, but these officers would like to have a word with Ness."

Ness's heart went into free fall. The last time policemen had come looking for her it was to break the news that Addy had wrapped his motorbike around a fence.

"No one's hurt, are they?" she whispered.

"Is there something wrong, officers?" This was Max, his voice firm. His hand reached out and took hers, and Ness found that she was clinging to it as though it was all that was keeping her steady.

"I need to speak to Miss Penwellyn?" said the suited man.

Ness swallowed her rising terror. "That's me. Can I help?"

"I'm Detective Chief Inspector Allen, Kernow CID. I'm afraid a serious allegation has been made."

Ness didn't understand. "What do you mean? What kind of allegation?"

"We received an anonymous phone call this afternoon. A member of the public claims that drugs are being sold on the island and that this festival is being used as a means of dealing them." DCI Allen's gaze was unfaltering. "The caller also claims that children are being exposed to drugs and that they're being sold from the stage area."

"That's utterly ridiculous," Max said firmly. "Who's made these allegations?"

"As I said, sir, it was an anonymous call, but CID have it on good authority that an individual known to us has indeed visited this island recently and been seen in the vicinity." DCI Allen turned back to Ness. "I'm sure you understand that we can't ignore such an allegation?"

Ness nodded. Her mouth felt dry with fear. "Absolutely, I do."

"We'd like to search the stage area, if we may."

This was her call and her call only, Ness realised. The creeping dread she'd been trying to shake off all day was intensifying now. There was no real choice: of course she'd let them search.

There was a pause as the band finished one song to rapturous applause before launching into another number.

She nodded again, and that was all the go-ahead that was needed. As the band played and the audience danced and sang and enjoyed the set, the police moved through the crowd. There was a dog with them and it strained at the leash in its haste to reach the far side of the stage. Following, Ness and Max watched as the dog made a beeline for a canvas holdall that was lying next to a pile of empty guitar cases. Within seconds this was unzipped to reveal hundreds of polythene bags, each containing what looked very much like an illicit substance.

"Who does that bag belong to?" DCI Allen asked Ness.

"I've absolutely no idea." Ness was feeling as though she might pass out. "I've never seen it before."

Her protest sounded feeble even to her own ears, especially as it was clear that this amount of drugs wasn't just for someone's personal use. An amount this large was intended for one thing only: to supply.

She looked at the DCI in shock. "This is nothing to do with any of us or the festival. Somebody must have planted it!"

"I can guess who," Max said. His mouth was set in a grim line.

"No prizes there," Adam agreed.

A look passed between the two men, and if she hadn't been so upset Ness would have asked them exactly what they meant. As it was she was too busy trying to fight the rising panic of knowing that she would have to stop the festival and deal with a possible drugs charge to worry about anything else.

"That bag's been planted," Ness said again, her voice wavering. "It's nothing to do with anyone here."

Max took her hands in his and held them tightly. "We know that and so do the officers, I'm sure, but you're going to have to let them do their job and search. It's all going to be fine."

But Ness was shaking too much to speak. How was it all going to be fine?

She felt completely on her own now – and she feared the same would be true for Pirran Island.

Chapter 28

Lucy sat at the kitchen table with yesterday's local papers and felt herself slide deeper into despair. She'd made a pot of coffee and poured a cup, but it was long cold and her plate of toast was untouched too. As she scanned the pages the print jumped about and blurred before her eyes, as though her exhausted brain couldn't bear to read another word or try to make sense of recent events. She wasn't sure what to do next or even if there was anything she could do next. It was a disaster.

She placed her head in her hands. What Lucy would really like to do was phone Adam and talk things through with him, but since their calamitous dinner at Sorrentina the closeness that had been growing between them appeared to have withered away. Previously they'd been in the habit of meeting up for coffee or spending lunchtimes together on the island, whereas now they could only manage to exchange a hello in passing. The easy chatter they'd once shared had been replaced by awkward silences. She missed their friendship terribly.

She missed Adam terribly.

The castle was eerily quiet. It happened to be one of the castle's open days, but Lucy couldn't imagine visitors feeling inclined to come to Pirran Island now, unless out of mawkish curiosity. The place was deserted. Ness had left at first light to catch the train to London. Meanwhile Fern was still utterly heartbroken and blaming herself for everything. She was refusing to talk to anyone except Merryn; Lucy supposed he was with her now, seeing as he hadn't shown up for breakfast. She glanced at her watch. It was almost ten o'clock. Annie Luckett would be over at some point, but Lucy had already decided she would send her home again. She couldn't face opening the tea room today. In fact, Lucy wasn't sure she would ever feel like opening it again. All she wanted to do was hide away and try to ignore the dreadful suspicions that were growing stronger and stronger.

If only Adam had been working here today. She would have swallowed her pride and told him she was so sorry about walking out of the restaurant that night; she'd have admitted that she'd made one of the biggest mistakes of her life and asked him if they could go back to the way things had been before. How was it possible that in such a short time a total stranger had become the centre of her world? She'd been happy before Adam had arrived on the scene, hadn't she? Life had been busy and she'd had more than enough to occupy her with looking after her uncle and running the tea room. How had Adam Miller managed to fill such a huge void when she'd never even noticed one existed?

It wasn't just Adam that Lucy missed. Usually Josh was here too, chatting about something or practising his scales. He'd eat her cakes, make her improve her iPhone skills or be tearing around the place with a barking Biscuit, like a gap-toothed scabby-kneed whirlwind. But today there was no Adam because work on the gate had skidded to a very abrupt halt, and Josh was yet to arrive.

Oh God, Adam didn't believe all the furore about the drugs, did he? She hadn't seen him since the festival had been interrupted in such a dreadful fashion, but surely he didn't think any of them here were dealing drugs? It was all totally absurd! On the other hand, the papers were full of half the story, predictably the shocking and sensationalist half, and she could only imagine that a responsible father like Adam would be concerned about what his child could have been exposed to. Her hand hovered over her phone as she toyed with the idea of calling him to explain. Then Lucy pushed the handset firmly out of reach. If Adam Miller was really her friend then he'd know it was all nonsense.

"I guess we'll just have to wait and see, won't we?" Lucy said to Biscuit, who simply looked up at her with sad brown eyes. The spaniel was probably missing Josh too, Lucy thought bleakly. It seemed that they'd both grown fond of the new additions to their island family and were going to find life without them rather empty.

She took a sip of cold coffee, grimacing at the bitter stewed flavour, and forced herself to return to the newspapers. Merryn had fetched them over the day before. Even though she knew it was all rubbish, Lucy wasn't finding the coverage of the festival easy to read. "Drug Fest" was what the papers had dubbed it. If it was true that mud stuck, then the inhabitants of Pirran Island were going to be trying to pressure-wash this lot off for a very long time to come.

Lucy cast her mind back to the moment it had all started to go so wrong. She'd been in the tea room, making what had felt like her millionth pot of tea, when the music that had been a background thud for over five hours stopped. Shortly after that, a river of people had flowed across the causeway.

"What's going on?" Annie had flipped her tea towel over her shoulder and was standing by the door, shading her eyes against the bright sunshine. "We're not due to finish yet, are we?"

Lucy had put the teapot down and joined her. "Absolutely not. The fireworks display doesn't start until half nine."

"Is there a problem? Are they evacuating the island?" Annie had fretted. Her family had come to the island today to watch the bands, and her immediate thoughts were for their safety. Lucy had done her best to reassure Annie that everything was bound to be fine, but it had been difficult to convince somebody else of this when Lucy herself was so worried. Apologising to the customers still queuing, she'd abandoned her duties; leaving Annie at the helm, she'd run across to the stage area to find out what was happening. Everyone had been headed in the opposite direction, and as she'd passed by she'd caught snatches of conversations that had left her horrified. Drugs? A police raid? Dealing? Lucy hadn't been able to believe her ears. What on earth was happening?

Lucy had never raced up the steep path so fast.

"What's happened?" she'd asked, grabbing hold of Merryn's unplastered arm and pulling him around to face her.

If Lucy had been worried before, she was doubly so when she saw how white Merryn was. In front of them Ness was deep in conversation with several policemen. Even more concerning was the fact that Max Reynard was there too.

"What's Max done?" Lucy demanded. Whatever calamity had taken place was bound to be down to that awful man. He'd stop at nothing to get his hands on the island.

Merryn shook his head. "For once this is nothing to do with him. Lucy, you're going to have to hear this from someone, so it may as well be me. The police are searching the island. They think there's drug dealing going on here."

Lucy had started to laugh because this was totally ludicrous. "That's ridiculous! Of course there isn't. Do they think Fred's growing marijuana in the vegetable garden? Or I'm baking hash cakes?"

But Merryn wasn't laughing. "They had a tip-off from a member of the public who said they'd seen suspicious goings-on backstage. Apparently they've found a bag full of drugs and now they want to search the whole place."

"You're not serious?"

"They've found a lot of drugs, Lucy. This is as serious as it gets."

Lucy shook her head as though trying her best to shake away the unpleasant memories. It hadn't seemed real. She, who rarely even took an aspirin, was now being accused of dealing drugs? It was mad! This was Cornwall, not Colombia!

Fern had been inconsolable.

"This is all my fault," she'd sobbed, tears running down her face and streaking her make-up into sooty rivulets. She'd looked so young and Lucy's kind heart had gone out to her.

"Of course it isn't," she'd said firmly. "There's no way you can blame yourself, love. When you suggested a festival you weren't to know this would happen."

Merryn had tried to pull Fern into his arms but she'd shaken him off impatiently.

"Don't, Merry. You know I'm right. Logan's done this because I wouldn't go back to him. He's done it to get his own back after what happened the other day."

She'd burst into another storm of weeping, gasping for breath and gabbling out a complicated story about punches and insults and drug-dealing ex-boyfriends, growing more hysterical by the second. It was only when Annie Luckett, veteran of many teenage emotional tempests, grabbed her by the shoulders and spoke very firmly that Fern calmed down enough to explain herself.

And what a tale it was. Tutting sadly at the memory, Lucy got up to refill the kettle. As she waited for it to boil she leaned against the Aga and marvelled again at how cruel life could be. That a young girl, barely sixteen and no way old enough to know her own mind, could be manipulated by an older boy and find herself spiralling into despair and desperation was hardly an original story – but that didn't make it any less shocking. Armand would have known, of course. That was why he'd let her stay. There'd been a heart of gold under that gruff exterior and today Lucy missed him more than ever.

"So when this Logan came back and started threatening Fern, I saw red," Merryn had finished, squeezing Fern's hand. Lucy couldn't help noticing how small Fern's hand seemed, and how bitten her nails were. "I saw him off all right. He won't be back."

"You mean you punched him." Annie raised her eyes to the tea-room ceiling. "It's good to know you learned something from being excluded from school, Merryn Hellier."

"He was really brave," said Fern defensively.

"No, Annie's right," Merryn sighed. "I've given Logan even more of a grudge – and not just against you either, Fern, but against me and the island too. If he's planted drugs then it's to get back at me."

"No one's to blame apart from whoever did this." Lucy had been adamant on this score. Besides, she wasn't entirely sure that all the drama had been caused by this unsavoury Logan character acting alone. Deep down inside, a small part of her was starting to have a suspicion that she was terrified to even acknowledge.

Surely not? Jamie couldn't hate them all this much, could he?

By the time Ness had finally joined them, grey-faced and shaken, Lucy had been vacillating between feeling hideously guilty for thinking this way and wondering if she might actually be right. When Ness told them that apart from the one bag of cannabis that had attracted the sniffer dog, the holdall was actually filled with packets containing nothing more sinister than Italian seasoning and icing sugar, Lucy's fears had been confirmed. Jamie had played this trick on a schoolmate and almost got him excluded. It was only when he'd been cornered that he'd admitted it, but he'd never once seemed sorry. Her brother was never sorry, was he?

The suspicion alone had sickened her, but Lucy always trusted her gut feelings. This one was telling her that it was Jamie's school prank again all right – only this time he'd involved somebody very nasty to help him. Over the years she'd tried her best to convince herself that Jamie's persistent sniff was hay fever or a winter cold, but who was she really kidding? His constant need for money and his foul moods all made sense when she stopped making excuses for her brother. There was every chance Jamie would come across a lowlife like this Logan character.

"I don't understand," Annie Luckett had said with a frown. "If not this man, then why would anyone do such a dreadful thing?"

"DCI Allen says we're the victims of a malicious hoax." Ness had buried her face in her hands. "Whoever tipped the police off wanted to ruin the concert and totally discredit us."

"Well, that won't work when they know it was just herbs that were found," Merryn had said, hugging Fern. "It's going to be fine."

But Annie wasn't so sure. "I think they may need a little convincing, Merryn. You know what it's like here once rumours begin."

"And rumours apart, I'm going to have to refund everyone," Ness had added.

"So we won't have made a penny." Fern's eyes had shimmered. "I'm so sorry, Ness."

"It's not your fault," Ness had said. "But I'm afraid there's something worse than not making a profit, and that's making a loss. This will have cost us money and I don't think I can claw it back from here. We were just about to break even if this had worked out, but now..." She'd shaken her head. "I don't see how with the winter coming we can pay the loan back and keep the castle running. We haven't even started to look at the pier yet, and the surveyors said it probably won't last through the winter. There simply isn't any money left."

Everyone had fallen silent. They all knew exactly what this meant.

"I'll go and see Jonathan Ambrose early next week and see if I can buy us some more time," Ness had said quietly. "If he'll extend the repayment schedule for six months and maybe lend us a little more, it may be enough."

"He'll do that, won't he? If it makes him money?" Fern had asked hopefully.

Ness had shrugged. "To be honest, I have no idea. It's also about whether we can even afford to do that. The terms were clear – if we default then the loan will be called in. I'm so sorry. I've made things even worse for us."

"Nonsense. Nobody could have tried harder than you," Lucy had said firmly.

"Absolutely," Annie had agreed. "I don't always claim to have a clue what Armand Penwellyn was thinking, but he certainly did the right thing putting you in charge – no disrespect, Lucy."

Lucy had waved her hand. "None taken. You're right, Annie. Ness has given it everything and more. She's a Penwellyn through and through."

"And at least you never sold to bloody Max Reynard," Fern had added.

At this Ness had dashed another flood of tears away with her sleeve. Goodness, thought Lucy, Max must be a monster if just the mention of his name makes her cry. Adam might insist that Max was one of the good guys, but Lucy wasn't convinced.

"I just keep feeling that there's something I missed. It's like there was always a solution to this but I just can't figure it out," Ness had sighed. "I know it makes no sense but surely our uncle left the island to me for a reason? We just haven't discovered it yet."

"Uncle Armand always used to tell me there was a fortune at my fingertips," Lucy recalled. "I think it must have been his idea of a joke."

Annie had frowned. "Armand was never one for joking. Quizzes and cryptic puzzles yes, but he didn't say things unless he meant them."

"Your granny told me the answer was in the music, whatever that meant," Ness had said to Merryn, who'd rolled his eyes.

"Yeah, that sounds like my gran. She loves to come out with a cryptic line. If she ever offers to read your tea leaves, don't be fooled. She uses teabags."

In spite of her heavy heart, Lucy had smiled. "Ignore him. Rose is the real thing, so let's just keep hopeful. Maybe something will come up after all?"

It wouldn't if these papers were anything to go by, Lucy decided now as she returned to the kitchen table with a fresh pot of coffee. Predictably the local press had chosen to focus on the drugs haul and the stories of possible dealing, rather than the far less exciting reality. Just because a sizeable amount of drugs hadn't yet been discovered didn't mean they weren't there, was the implication. Lucy threw the papers away in a fit of disgust. If only she could talk to Adam and share her deepest suspicions. She hadn't dared voice them to anyone else, partly because she felt so disloyal and partly because she was convinced she was right.

Lucy drained her cup and set it down with a thud as the caffeine hit her bloodstream. There was only one thing for it: she would have to confront Jamie. He wasn't her cute little brother anymore, and neither was she the cowed and nervous spinster without friends or purpose. Everything had changed – and most of all her, she realised.

Jamie was going to be surprised, that was for certain. This encounter was way overdue.

Chapter 29

"Nessa, my dear, I wish you'd told me you were coming to London. I would have spoken to you over the telephone and saved you a long journey."

Jonathan Ambrose was sitting at his huge desk as before, resplendent in a Savile Row suit and looking every inch the successful businessman. Ness, crumpled and wrung out after the events of the past few days, waited to be invited to take a seat – but the invitation never came.

She swallowed back her nerves. The five-hour journey to London had given her long enough to ponder her circumstances and she'd reluctantly reached the conclusion that she was powerless in this situation. Before, she'd been full of confidence and convinced she could turn the island's finances around. It had been a high-stakes gamble but Ness had thought the odds were stacked in her favour. Now, however, she was terrified that she'd been wrong. What if it turned out that she'd bet everything on red when black was the winning spin, so to speak?

Enough with the gambling metaphors, she told herself sharply. This was no time to be introspective. She had to hold her nerve; men like Jonathan Ambrose could smell fear and weakness from a mile away. It was how they made their millions.

"I left a message with your PA," she said politely.

"Ah yes, she did tell me." He exhaled and glanced at his Rolex. "OK, Ness, I can give you five minutes. Have a seat."

Five minutes to plead her case. Wow. That was harsh and nothing like their last meeting. On that occasion Jonathan Ambrose had been all smiles and flattery, whereas today she was about as welcome as the tax inspector. Ness supposed she was surplus to requirements now that he had what he wanted.

Or else this was revenge for dumping his son?

She settled herself into the chair and did her best to smile. She needed to act as though she was in control of all this, even if the exact opposite felt true. Aware that her fingers were gripping the armrests far too tightly, she forced herself to relax her hands and look like she was here to do business rather than to plead. She had to keep a level head or he'd sense she was really in trouble and then everything would unravel.

It had all felt dangerously close to unravelling on Saturday. While the police had searched the stage area, Ness had watched in shock. Only Max holding her hand had kept her from tumbling into despair. It was odd that in her moment of need it had been her worst enemy who'd stepped up to the plate, but she supposed he was keeping a close eye on the island, biding his time. It hadn't felt like that, however; if she'd had to describe it, then Ness would have said it felt as though Max actually cared – which was crazy because of course he didn't. Like Jonathan Ambrose, he was playing a very clever game.

She'd spoken to the crowd, telling them that the festival was over. It had been a nerve-racking experience. Ness knew that for the rest of her life she'd wake up dreaming of that moment, her heart pounding as she relived the disbelief on those faces staring up at her and heard again their cries of anger.

As Ness dredged up the last of her courage and prepared to pitch her case to Jonathan, she realised that Annie was right. It didn't matter that there hadn't been any drugs on the island, apart from the small amount used to lure the sniffer dog. People would still choose to believe the worst. The most precious thing Ness owned wasn't the castle or the land it stood on, but the island's reputation.

"You can probably guess why I'm here," she began, hoping Jonathan Ambrose couldn't hear the thudding of her heart.

He didn't say a word, so Ness ploughed on.

"I'd like to renegotiate the terms of our agreement. If we could put the repayments back until the spring, that would help in the short term, and I'd also like to take you up on the extra credit that you suggested before. I'd like to make it half a million instead of a quarter."

"Ah." His pudgy face folded into a concerned expression. "I thought this might be what you wanted to discuss. I'm afraid it really won't be possible though."

Ness was prepared for games. He'd play her – make her squirm and grovel before offering her something that wasn't anywhere near what she needed, to lure her even more into the mire. It made her sick to the stomach but what choice did she have? Without an extension to the loan, they were finished. She may as well throw the keys to Max.

"We've had some bad luck–" she began, and Jonathan raised his eyebrows.

"I'd hardly call a drugs bust bad luck, my dear!"

"It wasn't a drugs bust! It was all a huge mistake and the tiny amount that was found was planted there to create the worst possible disruption to our festival!" Ness wasn't having anyone, no matter how wealthy or powerful, accuse her of criminal activity. "The DCI said that himself! He thinks it's likely to be somebody with a grudge against us."

"How unfortunate if so – and doubly unfortunate that your venture is now associated with drugs." Jonathan Ambrose didn't miss a beat. Neither did he look concerned.

"Anyway, how do you already know all this?" Ness asked.

His lips twitched. "Let's just say that I have my sources. It's prudent for an investor to know what's going on."

"You mean there's a spy," Ness said bitterly. It didn't take the detective skills of Hercule Poirot to figure out who that might be. And to think that for a brief, stupid, wonderful moment she'd been naïve enough to imagine that Max Reynard was on her side. No wonder she'd not heard a word from him since Saturday. He'd been busy turning her bad luck to his advantage. How he must have been laughing.

It was funny though. At the time it had felt as though he really cared...

"Spy? That's a little harsh, my dear. I think you probably mean 'helpful contact'. And that person was right to think I'd want to know if one of my investments had been involved in a drugs scandal. I'm glad they were so keen to tell me, before the press made the connection. You can surely see how this puts Ambrose Investments in a very awkward position."

Ness wasn't interested in his pompous and self-righteous talk – not when she'd lived in the Caribbean and seen first-hand just how unscrupulous Jonathan Ambrose really was. After all, he operated in a tax haven where everyone looked the other way.

"The property's worth a large amount of money and you said yourself that the risk to you was low," she shot back, not sure where her sudden courage had come from but thrilled to find it. "You offered to extend me half a million pounds before, and I only took half of that amount. Today I'm here to ask to borrow the rest and I'm offering you the chance to have an even bigger stake. I'm prepared to take the risk. How about you? Are you brave enough?"

He whistled. "That's some speech. You certainly know how to roll the dice, young lady."

Ness didn't say a word. She couldn't: she was holding her breath.

Jonathan Ambrose stood up and walked to the office window.

"You don't give up easily, do you, Nessa?" he said slowly.

Ness supposed she didn't; in that respect she was the opposite of her father, who'd always run the second there'd been as much as a whiff of trouble. Perhaps she was like her mother. Maybe Beth Penwellyn had been the one who'd fought for what she wanted?

Jonathan Ambrose turned back to face her. His expression was serious and a little regretful. "Even if I do want to help you, which I have to admit would be my inclination, I'm afraid that it's not going to be possible. In short, I've sold my interest in Pirran Island."

Ness couldn't believe what she was hearing. "No! You can't have done. I signed a deal with you!"

"And in that deal it was made very clear that Ambrose was at liberty to sell its stake to another party. Taking recent events into account, I didn't feel that the investment was right for my company anymore. I no longer have any say over the future of Pirran Island, Nessa." His tone was mild but deadly and Ness knew that she was in way, way out of her depth. Jonathan Ambrose hadn't just been diving with the sharks in those blue Caribbean waters; he'd been taking master classes from them. "I'm afraid you'll need to speak with the new owner of those interests if you want to renegotiate your terms."

"So who's that?" Ness demanded. Her mind was racing as she tried furiously to think of a way she could save this situation. "Another company?"

"In effect, yes. Reynard Developments has bought the investment. In fact I was just about to have someone send out a letter to inform you of the change."

Ness couldn't believe her ears. "You're telling me Max Reynard owns your stake in Pirran Island? Since when?"

He glanced again at his expensive watch. "Since I spoke to him about an hour ago. You've just missed him actually."

Ness wasn't going to listen to this for a minute longer. Her temper was simmering. Any moment now she knew she'd explode in a way that would make Mount Etna look like a damp firework. She spun on her heel and tore straight down the stairs rather than waiting for the lift. As soon as she reached the ground floor, she flew across the concourse, shot out into the street and hailed a taxi.

"The main offices of Reynard Developments," she gasped, to the surprised cabbie.

"Bloody hell, love! When women fall panting into my cab they normally ask for the nearest maternity hospital," he grinned. Nevertheless, he spun the taxi around and headed into the City, while Ness sat in the back gnawing her nails. By the time the car stopped outside a chrome and glass monstrosity of a building, Ness was so wound up she was almost ready to chime.

How typical of Max to have his office in a giant phallic symbol, she fumed as she waited for the receptionist to dial up to Reynard Developments' headquarters. No doubt he was there now, laughing his head off because he'd pulled a fast one on the silly girl who'd been naïve enough to almost believe he cared and who'd definitely been foolish enough to lie awake in her turret bedroom, staring across the dark waves at the single light burning in his house. He'd probably known that she was reliving his kisses and dreaming of more. She'd bet anything that duping people like her was how he got his hands on most of his property.

Could she have been more stupid?

"Is Mr Reynard expecting you?" asked the pretty receptionist, her heavily mascaraed eyes flickering over Ness critically. Catching a glimpse of herself in the tinted glass behind the desk, Ness saw that she was wild-eyed and even wilder-haired, her long red curls having escaped the neat bun to snake crazily over her shoulders. She looked savage.

Good. Savage was exactly how she was feeling.

"He'd better be," Ness told her grimly. "Tell him Nessa Penwellyn's here."

To her credit, the receptionist did a good job of appearing unflustered. (Then again, maybe Max just had them all lobotomised? He clearly liked his women thick.) Within minutes, Ness was riding the private lift right up to the penthouse office.

What a cliché, she thought, as the doors swished open and she stepped out into a light room with a jaw-dropping view of London tumbling away beneath it. A penthouse, a blonde PA and now what? Greed is good? Lunch is for wimps? Or how about an explanation of why he'd chosen to stitch her up and not had the balls to tell her?

"Ness! This is a lovely surprise!" Max was wearing a white shirt, the sleeves rolled up above his tanned forearms, and as he crossed the room to meet her his muscular body dominated the large office. In spite of her fury, Ness felt the strong pull of attraction and her rage intensified.

"Is it?" she hissed. "I'd describe my experience today as being closer to a shock."

"Ah. You've spoken to Jonathan Ambrose."

"You bet I have." Hands on her hips and green eyes bright with rage, Ness rounded on him. "It didn't take you long to pounce did it, Max? Were you on the phone to him the minute you left the festival?"

One corner of his mouth quirked upwards. "You really don't have a great opinion of me, do you?"

"What do you expect? You've been playing me since the moment we first met. So did you tell him about the raid?"

He held her gaze steadily. "No, I most certainly didn't, although I did call him the minute I knew he was looking to offload the investment. Why so quick to believe the worst of me, Ness? What are you so afraid of?"

She shook her head, livid with herself for the currents of emotion that were pulling her in so many strange directions. "There's nothing about any of this that I'm afraid of, because I'm not the one who's been playing a double game, am I? Tell me, Max, did you pay someone to hide that bag behind the stage?"

"Are you accusing me of planting those drugs?"

"We all know how much you want Pirran Island! It's hardly a secret!"

His eyes narrowed. "Be careful, Nessa. That's a very dangerous accusation to throw around. I'd think twice before saying something like that. Besides, do you really think that's how I operate?"

"Yes! No! I don't know! Oh!" Frustrated with the entire situation, Ness dug her hands into her hair and tugged furiously at her curls as she glowered at him. "I don't know what you'd do, Max! One minute I think I've got you all worked out and the next I'm totally confused. What are you playing at?"

"Nessa, stop it." He moved forwards and a shiver of anticipation rippled over her skin when he placed his strong hands on her wrists, gently untangling her fingers. "Why are you always fighting me?"

"Because you're always fighting me!" Ness half shouted, half sobbed. "Since the second I arrived you've been waiting for me to trip up so that you could step in and buy the island. Go on, admit it! You know it's true."

Her hands were free but Max still had hold of her wrists, and with a tug he pulled her closer until she was only inches away from him. She held herself rigid, struggling not to inhale the scent of fresh linen and clean male skin, resisting the longing to sag against him and let the fight slip away.

Then Max sighed. "Fine, I admit that when Jamie didn't inherit I was annoyed, especially since he'd told me the place was as good as his and been advanced a fair sum too. Then it occurred to me that the situation could work to my advantage. You were new to the place and didn't know what it involved, and I'd already decided that I'd give you enough time to mess up and then make an offer. I wasn't lying in wait for you at the hotel though! Dammit, Ness. I didn't need to. It was bloody obvious you didn't stand a chance. You didn't need me to cause trouble: you already had quite enough of your own to contend with and far closer to home."

They stared at each other for a moment.

"It was Jamie, wasn't it?" Ness said slowly. "Of course it was. It's been him all along."

Now things were starting to fall into place – all the mishaps and bad luck, things that had happened all at the wrong time and could only have been orchestrated by someone who knew the castle and the way the island ran. Jamie had access to Lucy too and, as sweet as her cousin was, Ness knew that she was weak when it came to him. There were things she could easily have let slip without meaning to, and whenever Jamie had visited her he'd have been able to see what was happening at the castle. It wouldn't have been difficult for him to find out that Ness had borrowed money from Ambrose Investments, either. A five-minute snoop around the library would have been more than enough to tell him all he needed to know.

"I'm afraid I think you could well be right," Max agreed, "and I'm sorry to say that I might be responsible for that. He thinks that if I buy the place the agreement still stands – I mean the one that he and I had when he was expecting to inherit the island."

"You were going to pay off his debts and give him an apartment," Ness said. Of course he was. It was exactly the deal that Max had offered her; no doubt he'd once offered the same to Jamie.

"Yes." Max was still holding her wrists but his grip loosened. "I'm so sorry, Ness. With his deviousness and the costs involved in running the place you never stood a chance."

"You're wrong, Max! It was working. I had plans and I could have seen them through if I'd just had more time."

"With Jonathan Ambrose pulling the strings?" Max gave a harsh laugh. "I hardly think so. If anyone was going to pounce then it was him. He was just waiting for you to use the noose he'd given you."

"I could have done it!" Ness insisted. She wasn't going to cry. Not in front of him. No way. "If you hadn't ruined things I could have renegotiated and made it work. I know I could."

Max let her wrists slide from his grasp and he shook his head wearily. "No you couldn't, Ness. The odds were stacked against you from the start. I don't doubt you've got fire and I know you've got passion, but it was always impossible. You should take heart though; your vision for the island's certainly changed mine."

"What do you mean?"

"I mean that when I first thought of buying it I wanted Pirran Island as the flagship development for Reynards. I wanted Pirran Castle to be a byword for luxury and privacy – somewhere so exclusive that the world's wealthiest aspired to be there and to boast about it. It was going to showcase the very best of Reynards. It was to be the jewel in our crown."

Ness shuddered as a vision of oligarchs and sheikhs, speedboats and keep out signs flashed before her eyes. "It sounds hideous."

"I agree," he said.

"You agree?" Ness was taken aback. Those two words, quietly spoken, rang with sincerity and punctured her wrath. "How can you agree? You want to develop the place. You said so."

His hand rose to brush a curl back from her flushed cheeks.

"Can't a man change, Ness? Isn't he allowed to see things differently when someone he cares about opens his eyes? I see the beauty of the place, the same wild untamed spirit that I see in you, and I can't feel the same way about owning it and controlling it as I used to. All the things that make the island special were there before, and of course I saw them – but I never felt them." His hand fell to trace the curve of her cheek and Ness was mesmerised by his intensity. "I still want to develop the castle and I truly think it's the only hope of saving the place from ruin, but there's a better way to do it. A way that I think could preserve it for everyone. It's a magical place and it needs to stay that way. So you see, Ness, that's the vision I have now. Your vision."

For a second Ness almost believed him. Heaven only knew she wanted to believe him. Those compelling grey eyes brimmed with emotion, and as all their past encounters spooled through her memory it took a supreme effort not to tumble head first into trusting him. The first moonlit meeting, their kiss at Grace Note Bay and finally his calm presence beside her as the festival had unravelled. He'd been the anchor that had held her firm amid a sea of panic. But then she remembered how he'd been in league with Jamie from the start and probably still was. How could she ever trust Max Reynard? Even now he was probably pursuing his own ruthless agenda.

What did she mean, probably? Of course he was. He was the ultimate chess master.

"Well, you'll be able to make your dream come true," Ness said quietly. As quickly as it had consumed her, the fight had slipped away and now she just felt utterly exhausted. "You own the debt; you know I can't pay it back and I know you won't extend it, so I guess that's it. You've won, Max. You don't have to play these games anymore."

His dark brows met. "You think I'm playing games?"

"Isn't that how you operate? Come on, Max, give me some credit here. We both know how much you wanted the island. You played me from the minute we first met. And well done: you've got me where you want me. I owe you money that you know I haven't a hope of repaying. You've achieved what you set out to do."

Max threw his hands in the air. "Jesus, Nessa! What the hell does a man have to do to make you trust him?"

"Stop playing games with people? Tell the truth?"

"Are you calling me a liar?"

"If the cap fits," Ness said bitterly.

Once again, his eyes narrowed. "Nobody questions my integrity, Nessa. Not even you."

He looked furious and Ness realised she'd gone too far. Then again, what did it matter that he was upset? Sometimes the truth hurt, didn't it? Max Reynard was a player and a ruthless businessman. She'd been a fool to believe even for a heartbeat that he was anything else.

"Then maybe they should," she said. "You wouldn't even know the meaning of the word."

"Is that what you really think of me?" Max stared at her. The expression in those grey eyes was suddenly impossible to read.

Was it what she really thought of him? Ness wasn't sure. He'd played games, toyed with her and made no secret of the fact that he wanted the island – but he'd also been there when she'd needed him, and he'd kissed her in a way that had melted her bones. He was infuriating and frustrating and magnetic all at the same time and she hated him.

But did she think he was a liar? Deep down Ness knew the answer to that, but she wasn't prepared to admit it; at this moment she was angry and cornered and wanted to hit back. Hard.

"Absolutely," Ness spat. "I hope the island makes you happy, Max. My solicitor will be in touch, I'm sure, but don't contact me again. Ever."

She turned and stepped into the private lift, jabbing her finger on the button. Max didn't reply but she felt him staring after her, as brooding and as dangerous as the waves on a stormy night. As the doors closed Ness shivered. She had the strangest feeling that this wasn't the last she'd see of Max Reynard.

It was frightening just how much her heart leapt at this thought.

Chapter 30

The library was one of Lucy's favourite rooms. It was always light during the daytime, and it was high enough up to command a breath-taking view. On days like this when the sunshine poured in there was nothing nicer than curling up in the window seat to read, or even to watch the beach fill with holidaymakers. From this vantage point up in her tower, Lucy could see the causeway stretching out over the golden sand below, and she could watch for anyone who might choose to make the crossing from St Pirran. Unlike previous inhabitants of the castle she wasn't lying in wait to tip boiling oil over them – however tempting that might be – but she did feel a little under siege knowing that the enemy was on his way.

The other point in the library's favour, apart from the glorious view, was that it had a full mobile phone signal, which meant that Lucy was able to make calls and send emails from here. The first of these activities she'd already done and the second she intended to do very soon, provided everything went according to plan and she kept her resolve.

Lucy swallowed nervously. She really hoped she'd be able to stick to her guns and not weaken. It was going to be hard to break the habits of a lifetime, but the time had come to make changes and to stand up for what she believed in. She'd spent far too long in the shadows with her head down. If she was ever going to make any kind of a life for herself, she was going to have to be brave and take control of her own life.

Maybe this was what Uncle Armand had wanted her to do all along. Perhaps he'd known that leaving the island to Ness, cutting off their income and forcing his family to work together would bring everything to a head. In spite of her nerves, Lucy smiled. This was exactly the sort of thing her uncle would have loved plotting. Just as his musical scores were filled with technical tripwires and tricky arpeggios, in daily life he'd loved riddles and keeping everyone on their toes.

Was leaving Ness the island his biggest puzzle yet? His way of making them all figure things out and get on with life without him?

"Well, if it was, then you certainly succeeded, Uncle Armand," Lucy said aloud to a faded photograph of her uncle, resplendent in white tie and tails as he shook hands with the Queen after some long-ago Royal Gala performance of his work. This picture took pride of place on the mantelpiece; it was a startling reminder of just how famous and influential he'd been in the musical world. Looking at it, Lucy was struck anew with sadness that his great symphony, his life's work, had never materialised.

What was her life's work? If she were to die this afternoon, which was highly likely if she provoked the response she was hoping for, what would her legacy be? Some nice cakes? Being remembered as a good piano teacher? A sister who'd indulged and spoiled her little brother? A woman who'd chosen to walk away from the truest, kindest man she'd ever met?

It wasn't a list that made her feel proud. Lucy's resolve hardened; it was time to change things and put them right.

A black car was making its way along the causeway now, racing across the cobbles with a reckless speed that even from this distance made Lucy catch her breath. Jamie, of course, and driving way too fast as always. So he'd got her message and taken the bait. Of course he had: he thought there was money in it for him, and money was Jamie's god. It was the only reason he was still hanging around St Pirran – he'd known more about the island's finances than he'd let on.

Lucy bit her lip, because if Jamie knew all about their financial affairs that was surely her fault too. She'd let him visit her on several occasions, to take items that he'd claimed were personal. While she'd been working in the tea room her brother had probably been having a good old snoop through any paperwork he could find. Oh! There she went again, making excuses for him! There was no probably about it; the word she was looking for was definitely. Jamie was a born sneak. As a child Lucy had lost count of the times she'd caught him rifling through her father's desk or reading her diary. He'd been in trouble for it at school too, she seemed to remember, although nobody had actually been able to pin anything to him. Somehow Jamie had always avoided the blame in the end.

Today, that was going to change.

She glanced down at her iPhone. The battery was fully charged and there was still a strong signal. By the time her attention returned to the causeway there was no longer any sign of the black Range Rover. When Armand had been alive he'd always complained about Jamie speeding like that. Lucy's uncle had been a cautious driver; on the rare occasions when he'd ventured out in his elderly Morris Minor, he'd proceeded so slowly that tortoises had probably overtaken him.

"He'll come a cropper one day, you mark my words," had been Armand's constant refrain, usually followed by a fervent, "and I hope I'm here to see it."

There'd been no love lost between Jamie and her uncle. Armand had tolerated him for Lucy's sake, while Jamie had scarcely bothered to hide his impatience with his elderly relative's idiosyncrasies – an attitude that made her uncle's legacy even more baffling.

"There you are. Why the hell do you insist on hiding away all the way up here? You're hardly bloody Rapunzel," Jamie grumbled as, red-faced and perspiring, he stomped into the library.

No, she'd sent her prince away, Lucy thought sadly – and she was the only person who could rescue herself now. It was like a bleak feminist version of the fairy tale.

Her brother glanced around the room, his hard blue eyes flickering over the remaining items of art and furnishings before settling back on Lucy as he mopped his face with a handkerchief. "It's like a sauna in here, sis. Bloody place needs air con."

"I like this room," Lucy said mildly.

"Well, make the most of it while you can, sis, because you won't be spending much more time up here, not once Max has the paperwork sorted," he replied. "I'm sure dear cousin Ness will bung you some cash, enough to maybe buy one of those affordable houses at the top of town. You know? The ones made of papier mâché and Sellotape. If you're really lucky you'll be able to crane your neck and look across at this dump."

What on earth was Jamie talking about now? Lucy had always suspected her brother indulged in too much drink and the odd line or two of cocaine, but now she was convinced. His speech was rambling and his expression maniacal.

"Ness won't sell to Max," she said firmly, but Jamie merely laughed.

"She won't have any choice. Ambrose Investments somehow got wind of the drugs raid here and they were suddenly very keen to dump the place. Wasn't it lucky that a little bird told Max so that he was able to snap up the debt?"

"Reynard Developments has bought the island's debts?" Lucy wouldn't have believed it if it hadn't been for the gloating look on her brother's face. Her heart sank. Max Reynard really was utterly ruthless.

"Yep." Jamie sauntered across the room, perched one meaty buttock on the corner of the desk and folded his arms. "Nessa's debts are his now. Lock, stock and barrel. He couldn't have done it without me either, so Max Reynard owes me big time. I'll be getting an apartment here, I expect, as a thank you. Maybe you can visit me? Won't that be a turn up for the books? I would put in a good word about the tea room, but I expect he'll bulldoze it. Just as well. I hear there are cockroaches."

Lucy felt sick. "Whatever did I do to make you hate me so much?"

"Whatever did I do to make you hate me so much?" mimicked Jamie, the whine in his voice making her flinch. "Oh, grow up, Lucy. I don't hate you. You're far too pathetic to hate. I'm over being jealous of you too, because let's face it, there isn't much to be jealous of now, is there?"

"Jealous?" Lucy couldn't be hearing that right. How on earth could golden boy Jamie have been jealous of her? "You can't have been jealous of me."

He rounded on her like a striking cobra.

"Don't you dare tell me how I felt! You were the favourite, Lucy, weren't you? Who got to stay at home and who got packed off to bloody boarding school like an unwanted parcel? Who was Pa's golden girl? And who did our miserable old bastard of an uncle like best? You, of course. It's always been you. Lucy. Lucy. Lucy. That was all I ever heard. It's still all I ever bloody hear. Lucy runs a wonderful tea room, Lucy is so good to her uncle, Lucy is an amazing music teacher. Jesus. I'm sick to death of hearing just how much everyone loves you. I've heard it my whole bloody life. I'm more than aware I'll never be as good as Saint sodding Lucy."

The unexpected invective stung like a lash and Lucy was stunned. None of this fitted with reality as she knew it. Jamie had been the longed-for son, the child who'd been gifted an incredible education, the one who'd been free to live a city life while she'd had to nurse a succession of elderly relatives. Jamie felt that he didn't compare to her? But that was crazy.

Was this just another of Jamie's mind games? Did he suspect that she'd worked out his last trick? Perhaps he did. Maybe he was trying yet again to make her feel bad enough that she'd cover for him. Lucy had always caved in before, so he'd be expecting more of the same. It would have been so easy for Lucy to have fallen into that trap – and for a dangerous moment she wavered. But then in her mind's eye she saw Ness's stricken face and Fern sobbing, and she recalled Adam's bleak expression when she'd left Sorrentina that night. The memories of the hurt Jamie had caused them all were enough to pull her up short.

"That's nonsense," she replied firmly. "I don't believe a word. Besides, how can you say Uncle Armand didn't care about you? He left you a Steinway and his entire share portfolio!"

"A portfolio of shares which tanked when the bloody bottom fell out of the market," Jamie shrieked. Spittle flecked his lips. "Most of them are worthless! Worthless! And probably will be for years. I bet the old bastard knew it too."

"Oh dear," said Lucy weakly.

He raked a hand through his lank hair. "Oh dear? Are you kidding? Christ! Don't you even watch the news?"

Actually, Lucy was a big fan of Radio 4 but she'd been far too busy trying to figure out whether they could afford milk and pay the electricity bill to keep an eye on the FTSE 100. On reflection though, she wasn't surprised to learn that his portfolio had plummeted in value lately.

"So that brings me neatly to why I'm here. You said you'd found something here that was meant for me? Something valuable?" He pinned her with a desperate stare. "Whatever it is you'd better hand it over. I'm not leaving it for that bitch."

Lucy took a deep breath. "Actually it would have been more accurate to say that the police found something valuable that was yours – a bag full of drugs, at the festival? I take it you know exactly what I'm talking about?" She picked up her phone. "I've got you to come here because I want to know the truth. Shall I call the police right now and let them hear what I think, or shall we keep this between us? I'm not messing, Jamie. I mean it: I want the truth."

He threw her a scathing look. "As if you'd grass me up. I'm your brother."

But Lucy was still holding the phone. "I mean it," she repeated. "I'll call them right now and get you fingerprinted."

His top lip curled. "Do what you like. They won't find my prints on that bag."

"No," said Lucy, setting the phone down carefully beside her on the window seat, "but they might be able to find Logan Barrie, and I bet he'll be willing to tell them all they need to know."

She was familiar with the expression "as white as a sheet", but Lucy had always thought it was just a clichéd simile, trotted out by lazy writers. Now she realised she was wrong. Although Jamie's cheeks had been flushed from his sprint up the tower steps, they were now drained of colour. From his expression, Lucy knew that her hunch was correct: her brother had come into contact with Fern's unpleasant ex.

"How the hell do you know about him?"

"This is a small town. Word gets around. Maybe I should ask how you've come across the charming Mr Barrie? He's not from here, is he?"

"I've no idea where he's from," said her brother, "and I couldn't care less. He's pretty small time, although he fancies himself as a big shot. My usual guy put me onto him."

"Your usual guy?" Like Alice in Wonderland, Lucy felt as though she was tumbling down a rabbit hole. Jamie had a usual dealer? "You've bought drugs before? Here? In St Pirran?"

"Christ, Lucy, don't be so bourgeois. Of course I have. How do you think I keep awake on the trading floor? Colombia's best keeps half the City marching. It wasn't hard to find someone like Logan who was happy to earn a little extra and hide that bag for me. I was lucky because he seemed as keen on this place as I am. He'd had a run-in with that no-mark friend of yours, so he didn't take much persuading."

"So you deliberately set out to ruin the festival by planting drugs?" Lucy felt sick. She'd suspected the worst but having it confirmed was hideous. "I take it you were the member of the public who tipped off the police?"

He laughed and gave her a mock bow. "Of course. Did you like the way I made sure they found it too? Didn't the mixed herbs and icing sugar look convincing? It's a good trick I learned at school. That public school education wasn't wasted. Once the teachers think you're just a wag they never look too closely again – it's the same for the police. Besides, I'd have hated to waste my real stash; I can make far more selling that in London than I could to a bunch of hicks here."

"You've been dealing?"

"Everyone does a bit," he said. "It's nothing to get your knickers in a knot about. If you want to be pissed off about it then blame bloody Uncle Armand. He's the one who gave my inheritance to some tatty hippy. A chap's got to make cash somehow."

"Not by selling drugs," whispered Lucy.

"I didn't sell any drugs at your precious festival, so chillax. I just managed to make sure it was an utter disaster and that the investment became very unpalatable to Ambrose. That way I could make sure Max was able to pick the loan up." Jamie flopped into the chair opposite and crossed one plump leg over the other.

"So Max Reynard put you up to all this?"

"Hardly." Jamie could scarcely keep the scorn from his voice. "Max doesn't have the balls to take action. He's as much a goody-goody now as he was at school. If it was left to him we'd all be sitting around playing by the rules and waiting for it to happen the slow way like frightfully good chaps. He's no idea how hard I've been working – and even if he did, he'd not appreciate it. Or any of the other stuff. He's pathetic."

Lucy realised she was shaking. Her brother had deliberately planted drugs at the festival and watched as the police had swooped. What else had he done?

"Other stuff?"

"God, you're like a parrot," Jamie said. "Come on, Lucy. Are you thick? The tourist who slipped and wanted to claim? Who do you think paid him? Cockroaches in the food? Blocked toilets? Unplugged freezers? Honestly, the things school kids will do for a tenner these days."

"You were responsible for all that?" Even at the time it had seemed like a dreadful and improbable spate of bad luck. When Lucy thought how hard they'd worked and how every setback had cost money and shattered dreams, she felt absolutely savage. She was filled with fury. "How could you?"

"Because the island should have been mine!" He leapt up from the chair and began to pace the room. "Who the hell is Nessa Penwellyn anyway? Why should she have what's rightfully my inheritance? I'll do anything I can to make sure she doesn't keep it. Anything. Believe me, I've hardly even started."

"Jamie, what you've done is criminal," Lucy said. "I'm going to tell the police."

"Tell them what? The mad ramblings of a sad old spinster? They'll laugh at you."

She picked up her phone, fiddling frantically with the keypad while her brother sneered.

"You can't even work a mobile. Call away; they can have a laugh at your menopausal ramblings. It's proof they want, not a pathetic fantasy."

"Good job I was videoing this entire conversation then. Hopefully that will be all the evidence anyone will need."

Jamie's mouth swung open. "What?"

"You heard me. I recorded our entire conversation using the video camera app. You see, Jamie, one thing we sad spinsters have on our hands is time. Time to figure out how drugs appear in holdalls and how to use apps." She couldn't believe how calm she sounded when inside she was quaking. "Isn't that something?"

"You're bullshitting," Jamie said scathingly. "You don't know how to do all that."

"Really?" Lucy looked him right in the eye. "I know, why don't you check your mobile and see? I've compressed the file and emailed it over for you. Isn't technology amazing?"

But her brother was too busy fishing through his jacket pocket to reply. Yanking out his phone, he peered at the screen in disbelief, howling in rage when he realised that she wasn't bluffing. Lucy sent out a silent thank you to Josh. His patience while teaching her the rudiments of iPhone wizardry hadn't been wasted. Maybe she'd take him up on Pokémon Go too? Who knew where that could lead?

"You sly bitch!" Slamming his phone onto the table, Jamie made a lunge for her handset, ripping it from her grasp and hurling it at the stone fireplace. There was a sharp crack but Lucy knew the gesture was pointless. The file was saved in her email folder but, more importantly, she'd copied Adam and Ness in too. There was no way his confession was going to be lost.

Jamie glowered at her. "You're supposed to be my sister!"

"And you're supposed to be my brother!" Lucy shot back. She was close to tears. Having him confess her darkest suspicions had been horrible, almost as horrible as the cold sense of betrayal creeping over her. "Look, let's go to the police together. Maybe with Ness too? There wasn't enough cannabis in that bag for the police to press charges. They'll probably let you off with a caution. I'm sure Ness won't want to press charges either if you put things right and apologise."

"Put things right? I was putting things right! I was getting my inheritance back!" he screeched. "But you couldn't bear that, could you? You had to spoil everything! Well, I hope you're happy now with your precious Ness. Good luck when she loses everything! And as for you, you old bastard," he added, sweeping his hand across the mantelpiece and sending Armand's picture tumbling to the floor with a crash, "if you weren't already dead, I'd kill you."

With this parting shot he stormed out of the library. Moments later Lucy heard the kitchen door slam, followed by the roar of the Range Rover's engine. Where was he going? Craning her neck to look down from the high tower, she saw that the tell-tale bubbles were already edging the cobbles of the causeway. Surely he wouldn't make it to the other side, even driving at his usual pace. It was madness to even try.

But Jamie wasn't thinking clearly. He'd always thought he could succeed where Canute had failed – and Lucy could only watch as the black car accelerated into St Pirran's Bay.

Chapter 31

Summer days didn't come any better than this, Adam Miller decided as he found a seat on the hotel terrace and set his cold beer down on the table. He had a drink, his work was done for the time being and the sun was shining. As always in high summer, the beautiful people had flocked to Cornwall and were lounging on rattan sofas with wine glasses held loosely in their hands. The men were wearing open-necked shirts in nautical tones, the women were clad in floaty dresses and the children were playing on the beach in their shortie wetsuits. The tide was racing back in over the golden sand and soon they'd be jumping from the outer pier with shrieks and big splashes. Maybe this afternoon he and Josh could sail to the next bay and grab some supper too.

All things considered, life in Cornwall was very good. Not better than it had been before with Elly, but good nevertheless and in a different way. Perhaps some things hadn't panned out as he'd hoped – and his friendship with Max had certainly been tested – but St Pirran was most definitely home. Moving here had been the right choice. Adam only had to look at Josh, tanned and freckled now and with his hair bleached from sunshine and salt, to know this.

"Can I have another?" his son asked, slurping up the dregs of his cola through a straw.

"Mate, I've only just bought you that. What did you do, inhale it?" Adam asked, rather alarmed by the speed-drinking. It didn't bode well for when his son discovered pints.

"I'm thirsty," Josh said. "It's really hot. Can I have another one? Please?"

Adam ruffled his son's hair. "That stuff will rot your teeth. Besides, it's bad for you. Did you know they use it to clean blood off roads after accidents?"

"Cool!" Wide-eyed, Josh looked impressed – which wasn't the effect his father had hoped for. "Mum used it to clean the stains down the loo."

She did? That was news to Adam. No wonder there'd never been any left whenever he'd gone on the hunt for a sugary hangover hit. He was just about to make a comment to this effect when he was struck by a realisation that momentarily robbed him of speech.

Josh had just spoken about his mum. He'd not been prompted by Adam or cajoled by a counsellor but had mentioned Elly as casually as he was now chatting away about being allowed a second fizzy drink and some crisps. There were no tears or worried expressions. In fact, he was smiling.

There was a lump in Adam's throat. This was the moment he'd been praying for and it had arrived without any fanfare.

"Well, who am I to say no on such a hot day?" he said. "Another bottle of Mum's loo cleaner coming up."

Josh giggled at this, and Adam found he was smiling too. He was just pushing his chair back to head to the bar when his phone beeped to herald the arrival of an email. Automatically, Adam checked it. He'd been tentatively putting out some feelers for work ever since it had become obvious that the castle project was grinding to a halt from both directions, so hopefully this was good news. Opening the folder, he was taken aback to see a message from Lucy waiting in his inbox.

Since when did Lucy email?

"Josh, did you give Lucy my email address?"

The little boy nodded. "Yep. I've been teaching her how to use her phone. She was rubbish before. It's a bit like a swap, Dad. She teaches me to play the piano and I teach her how to play with the iPhone. Cool, huh?"

Adam frowned. There was a video file attached to a blank message. His finger hovered over the keypad. He hoped it wasn't a virus.

"You shouldn't give out my personal details to people, son," he said.

Josh looked at him as though he was mad. "Dad, Lucy isn't people. She's Lucy! Anyway, everyone knows you want her to be your girlfriend."

They did? Adam was so stunned by this that he pressed the phone's screen quite by accident, and now a film was starting to play. Great. A clogged-up mobile was the last thing he needed if he was going to be job-hunting.

"I think she'd be a nice girlfriend for you," Josh was saying matter-of-factly. "You always smile when you're with Lucy. The only bad thing is you might get fat because she makes very nice cakes. Also I think we'd have more cushions in our house if Lucy lived there too. But Biscuit could come and that would be well cool."

"Mate, I don't think—" Adam began, his face hot, but he stopped mid-sentence when he realised what the film was. In spite of the sun's warmth, unease trickled between his shoulder blades; he was watching a puce-faced Jamie screaming at Lucy. Turning away from his son, Adam raised the volume of his handset so that he could hear the entire conversation. By the time it was finished he was filled with dread. The film had been shot scarcely ten minutes previously, and although it had confirmed his own suspicions, it worried him that Lucy was alone with her deranged brother.

Adam had to get to her. Jamie was unbalanced and there was no telling what he might do.

"Josh, show this film to Val at reception and tell her to call the police, at once. They need to get to the island," he told his son, crouching down and handing him the phone. "Then wait with Val, OK? Understand? Can you do that for me?"

"Yes, Dad," Josh said. He sprinted across the terrace and into the hotel, all thoughts of cola and crisps forgotten.

The tide was racing in across the sand, bubbling at the edges of the path. The locals always took this to be a sign that the cut-off was imminent. Adam knew there was hardly any time to waste if he was to make it across to the island. He tore down the hotel steps onto the beach and ran over the sand towards the causeway. If he was fast enough he could make it to the castle on foot. But if not? Then he was going to bloody well swim. Adam wasn't leaving Lucy alone for a second longer than he had to. She'd finally been brave enough to stand up to her brother and he was going to be there for her.

And if she wanted, he'd be there for a lot longer too...

Adam was halfway between the hotel and the causeway, seawater swirling around his ankles, when a black Range Rover hurtled across the castle's sloping lawn and hit the causeway at speed. Spray flew from its tyres in the driver's haste to beat the incoming tide. Already the water was lapping across the cobbles. The big vehicle might be designed for all terrains but it wasn't amphibious – and travelling at that rate across a surface that was still damaged was destined to end in disaster.

Jamie.

He was flooring it. The automatic gearbox and traction control were doing their very best to keep the low-profile tyres close to the slippery cobbles, but the clever engineering could only do so much: it could hardly be expected to compensate for Jamie's reckless driving. As the car grew closer, Adam saw to his huge relief that Jamie was the sole passenger. Lucy was safe on the island.

He hoped.

The waves were breaking over the causeway now. As Adam watched in disbelief, the speeding car struck the water like a skater on ice, aquaplaning across the surface with balletic grace before spinning one hundred and eighty degrees and lurching over the edge of the path. The sudden drop, combined with the force of a couple of tonnes of Land Rover's finest crashing into the sea, created an enormous wave that swamped the bonnet. The motor gulped saltwater for a moment, before a second wave took hold of the car and returned it to the edge of the causeway. Adam started to laugh. He suspected there was no car in the world that could have managed to get Jamie Penwellyn out of this one. The vehicle had already been almost entirely submerged, and now the water was creeping steadily up its metal flanks again.

Jamie opened the door and clambered out, the expression on his face as black as the paintwork. By the look of things, he had no choice but to wade to shore and hope one of the local mechanics took pity on him. Somehow, Adam didn't think help would be forthcoming. The "oiks" in St Pirran had long memories.

The tide was sweeping over the sand. In an attempt to beat it, Adam made his way to what remained of the beach, where he could cut to the halfway point of the causeway. Jamie was headed straight for him but Adam couldn't have cared less about that; he just wanted to reach Lucy. He hopped up onto the cobbles and tried to run, but they were greasy and he slithered dangerously.

"Sir! Wait here! Don't go across, please."

Turning around, Adam saw that a police Discovery was parked up on the harbourside. Two policemen and a familiar grey-haired man in a suit had joined him and were watching Jamie with faint amusement.

Adam felt a glow of pride. So Josh had done his bit.

"Shall we apprehend him, DCI Allen?" asked one policeman.

"I don't think he's going very far," the suited man observed wryly. Then, as Jamie tried activating the locks on his stranded car, the man added, "And I don't think he's in any danger of having his vehicle stolen either. Interesting he wants the boot secured. I wonder why?"

"Shall we wade over, sir?" the younger of the two policemen asked eagerly.

The Detective Chief Inspector smiled. "I think we should let him come to us. After all, where else is he going? Back to the castle? Or maybe France?"

"My friend's in the castle," Adam interrupted. "Lucy Penwellyn? I need to make sure she's safe."

"She's fine, sir. We've already spoken to her," the DCI said. "She's understandably very upset but she's unhurt. As soon as Mr Penwellyn is taken care of you're free to go across – although you may have to swim over at this rate."

Adam nodded but he was filled with impatience. Could bloody Jamie move any more slowly? It seemed to take forever before he reached them, and even when he did he showed no sign of stopping.

"Jamie Penwellyn?" The DCI stepped forward. "Detective Chief Inspector Allen, Kernow CID. We'd like you to accompany us to the station and help with some enquiries."

"And I'd like a gold Ferrari but I'm not about to get one, am I?" retorted Jamie rudely. "Can you get out of my way? As even you can see, I've got a car to sort out."

"Ah yes, that's going to be a danger to shipping soon. I'll have to inform the coastguard," deadpanned DCI Allen. "Leave that with me, sir. We'll take care of it while you come with us to help answer some questions."

"About what?" Jamie demanded. "Something my hysterical halfwit of a sister's said? You're wasting your time. Anything I may have said to her was just a joke."

"With all due respect it isn't a funny one, sir." DCI Allen certainly wasn't looking amused. "Anyway, by strange coincidence we were already on our way here to have a little chat with you before we were made aware of any other issues. You might be interested to know that we have an acquaintance of yours in our custody. A Mr Logan Barrie?"

"Never heard of him," snapped Jamie, but Adam noticed that a muscle near Jamie's eye had started to twitch.

"How strange. He seems to know you very well," said DCI Allen, a note of faux surprise in his voice. "He's told us all sorts of interesting information that I'm sure you'll be very keen to set us straight on."

"If he's a lanky guy with dark hair and pale skin, I saw Mr Penwellyn handing him some cash in Bay Street last week," Adam said slowly. "I'd be happy to make a statement to that effect if it helps."

The look Jamie shot Adam should have laid him out flat on the seabed.

"I might have known you'd be behind this," Jamie hissed.

Adam shrugged. "Just doing my civic duty. Besides, if you don't know Mr Barrie then it doesn't matter what I think I've seen, does it?"

A crowd was gathering on the quayside, and even from here the onlookers' murmuring and excited chatter could be heard. Aware that he was becoming a spectacle, Jamie attempted to barge past – only to find his way blocked by the two uniformed officers. He had a choice between leaping into the sea or assaulting a policeman; in other words, no choice at all.

"Are you arresting me?" he asked.

"Only if you won't come with us voluntarily, sir." The DCI seemed nonchalant, which was understandable given that Jamie was neatly trapped. "The choice is yours. Personally, I'd come willingly as it'll look far better for you if you cooperate. But if you want to give the good townspeople the excitement of watching an arrest, that's entirely your call."

"Fine, I'll come with you," Jamie spat and, shoving his way past, splashed across the causeway.

Detective Chief Inspector Allen turned to Adam. "I think that went pretty well, all things considered. Feel free to go across now, if you still want to and if you still can. We'll be in touch about that statement."

Adam didn't need asking twice. Nothing was going to stop him from reaching Lucy. Barely noticing the icy temperature of the water or the fact that it was almost to his shins, he surged through the rising tide towards the island. He needed to be quick, otherwise the water would soon race in and sweep him off his feet completely. Adam was determined that if anyone was going to be swept off their feet today, it would be Lucy. She'd been her brother's prisoner in that castle for far too long and it was time she was set free.

Somehow he managed to increase his pace, and by the time the water was swirling around his knees Adam was staggering up the slight incline where the causeway met the island slipway. He didn't think he'd ever feel his feet again, and his deck shoes had long since been taken by the sea, but none of this mattered a jot now that he could see Lucy running down the path towards him. Her face was blotchy with weeping and her hair was falling loose from its ponytail, but to Adam she'd never looked lovelier.

"I'm sorry, I'm sorry, I'm sorry," she gasped. "I should have listened to you. I should never have believed Jamie. I'm so sorry!"

"None of that matters," Adam said simply. "I promise nothing matters but you, Lucy, absolutely nothing."

"Really?"

He held out his arms. "None of the rest of it matters at all. Just that you're safe. Don't you see? I love you, Lucy. I love you."

She paused momentarily before her lip wobbled. Then, with tears spilling over her cheeks, she stepped forward into his embrace. Adam held Lucy Penwellyn against his heart, his arms wrapped tightly around her trembling body as he pressed kisses onto her soft hair, her wet eyelids and her poor red nose. Life was brief, and sometimes cruel, but love was a precious gift; it was something to be cherished. As Lucy nestled against him she felt so right, so familiar, and so very Lucy that Adam vowed he'd never let her go again. He wanted nothing more than to fold her into himself and love her, keep her safe and find a million and one ways of making her happy.

So when he raised her chin with his forefinger and brushed her soft mouth with his own, Adam Miller looked deep into Lucy's eyes and knew with all his heart that he wanted to love and protect her for the rest of his life.

And the rest of his life began right now.

Chapter 32

July's promise of long sunny days and balmy barbecue evenings slipped into a sullen August. Just like the tides, visitors ebbed and flowed from the island. They drifted through the castle and ate cake in the tea room, but there were too few of them to sustain the island financially. With a heavy heart Ness admitted to herself that the summer's end would herald not only the autumn of this year, but also the autumn of her time on Pirran Island.

There had been no recovering from the reputational damage associated with the festival. People were still talking about the drugs raid and were well aware of Jamie's subsequent court appearance. Moreover, Ness had felt honour-bound to refund every ticket and compensate any traders who'd paid for pitches. Once the costs of insurance and publicity were taken into account as well, she'd been horrified to discover that the festival had actually made a loss. With winter approaching and a lack of immediate income (other than Lucy's royalties and whatever Merryn's fishing might bring in), Ness could find no way of balancing the books. The causeway had been patched up as best as her budget would allow, but maintenance work on the castle had ground to a halt. She feared that any future gales would cause severe damage to it in its current state. Max was right: if something wasn't done soon, the problems would become so extensive that repairs would no longer be viable.

She sighed. Since that charged visit to his office she'd heard nothing from Max. Foxy Lady hadn't moved from her berth and the blinds in the big windows of his holiday home hadn't been raised for weeks. The loan arrangements between them had remained the same, but it wasn't the interest and repayments that were keeping Ness awake in the small hours so much as Max's silence. What was he plotting? When would he pounce? He'd said that he wasn't playing games, so what was happening? She'd seen Lucy's footage of Jamie saying that Max had known nothing about his underhand tricks, and her heart had lifted. Maybe, just maybe...

Oh! Ness shook her head, furious with herself. Maybe what? Maybe Max had feelings for her? Maybe he was thinking about her as much as she was thinking about him? Reliving their kisses on an hourly basis? Who was she kidding here? He was a player. Men like Max Reynard took their amusement wherever they wished and used whatever means they could find in order to succeed. Just because he'd made a pretty speech about how she'd changed his vision didn't mean a thing. Of course it didn't. He was just spinning her the lines that all women wanted to hear. Jane Eyre had changed Rochester. Lizzy had changed Darcy. Ness had changed Max. It was nonsense. After all, Cathy had never changed Heathcliff – and dark, brooding Max had far more in common with him.

"You keep sighing. Is something wrong?" Merryn asked.

He was sitting opposite Ness at the kitchen table, with his socked feet up as always and munching his way through one of Annie's doorstep bacon sandwiches. Newly freed from his cast, Merryn was itching to get back to work and was busy writing a business plan on Annie's ancient laptop. Annie had been helping him by dictating bits of it and correcting his punctuation. While Merryn had been in plaster he'd been teaching Fern how to drive Guardian Angel; he and Fern were now putting together a plan to go netting once the mackerel arrived. The two of them envisaged making a fortune with their new venture, Pirran Island Fishing Holidays. They were so excited that Ness didn't have the heart to tell them this would never happen – not unless Max allowed it, anyway.

It was time for Ness to face the harsh truth: she couldn't pay Max back and she'd be lucky if she even managed to cover the island's running costs until next month. Her uncle's faith in her had been misplaced. She'd failed. The numerous invoices spread in front of her couldn't have announced that fact more clearly if they'd jumped up and danced around the table.

"What a daft question, Merryn Hellier!" Annie rolled her eyes. "You have been present the last couple of months, haven't you?"

He frowned. "But everything's all right now, isn't it? Jamie's confessed about the drugs and had a massive kick up the bum, and the causeway's been patched up. We'll have a brilliant autumn. You'll see. Everyone will come to Cornwall and we'll have lots of visitors."

"I think it might be a bit too late for visitors to save the day," Ness said gently.

"You mean you'll have to sell?" Fern asked, glancing up from the Aga where she was waiting for the kettle to boil. She looked shocked.

"I don't think I'll have much choice," Ness replied. "Not unless something amazing happens."

"Like a lottery win?" Merryn reached into his pocket and pulled out a pink ticket. "Already on it, Ness. See! I'm Camelot's bitch!"

In spite of everything Ness laughed. "Gambling! Now why didn't I think of that?"

"Mock all you like," Merryn told her as he folded the ticket up and placed it under the table mat, "but I know that jackpot's ours."

"We don't need a jackpot; we need a miracle," Ness said.

Annie reached across and patted her hand. "Don't give up, love. Miracles do happen."

They fell silent for a moment and then the rain began. Before long the dark skies were flinging handfuls of heavy drops against the glass.

"I'd better head to the tea room and give the girls a hand. They're going to get busy now," Annie said, hauling herself to her feet. "Ness, could you let Lucy know I'll do the next shift for her? She's busy with Josh and I don't want to interrupt. Besides, the state she's in these days she's as good as useless. Her head's so in the clouds she's likely to ice a sausage roll or put soup in a teapot!"

Ness laughed again. This was so true. Since her cousin and Adam had got together, Lucy had been on cloud nine. She looked ten years younger, sang constantly and couldn't stop smiling. It was wonderful to see, and Ness thought nobody deserved happiness more. At least if things fell apart here, as she feared they would, Lucy would be ready to move on. Merryn and Fern had their whole lives ahead of them and even Fred was talking about going to live near his daughter in Looe. Where that left her, Ness wasn't sure. She'd be losing the funny little island family who'd come to mean everything to her, as well as the place she'd fallen in love with, and no amount of money would ever make up for that.

While Annie hunted for an umbrella and Fern replaced her as Merryn's spellchecker, Ness wandered along the corridor towards the Small Hall. The bad weather made the space even darker than usual and she shivered, feeling as though invisible eyes were watching her from the shadows. Was it her Uncle Armand? Or maybe even her parents? Were they disappointed with her for not solving the puzzles they'd left behind? Were they angry that she'd failed?

"Oh! There has to be an answer!" she said aloud. "Just show me what it is!"

Listen to the music, Rose Hellier had said. It will lead you to the answers you are seeking. That was all very well, Ness thought, but it hadn't meant anything to her. Pirran Castle was always full of music, whether it was Fred's whistling or Merryn's radio or Lucy playing the piano. Sometimes they listened to the Island Suite on the ancient CD player in the solar, but to see and hear Josh Miller perform the piece was something else. He was such a talented boy and Ness felt privileged to witness it.

Lucy smiled and patted the seat beside her. Ness slipped into the Small Hall as quietly as she could, her socked feet silent on the cold floor as she took her place on the tired sofa by the fireplace. As always her uncle's portrait surveyed them from the wall where he was flanked by his brothers. Beth's portrait caught her eye. Ness studied it for the hundredth time, wishing she knew what thoughts were hidden behind those slanting, mysterious eyes.

Josh sat at the tatty upright piano, his fingers flying over the keys as he coaxed melodies from an elderly instrument that even Ness could tell was way past its best. Every now and then a note stuck and his face screwed up with irritation. When it happened for the fifth time in quick succession Lucy jumped to her feet and joined him, placing a calming hand on his shoulder.

"I know that's annoying, love. I'll get it tuned as soon as I can."

Josh's bottom lip jutted out. "It's getting worse." He slammed his finger down on the key and yet again there was no corresponding note. "It feels like there's something stuck in it."

Lucy grimaced. "Lord, don't say that. It's probably a rotting mouse or something ghastly."

"Or a dead body! Cool!" The little boy's face lit up. "Can we look? Maybe there's a skeleton of a dead smuggler inside the piano?"

"Or a pirate?" Ness suggested, leaping up to join them.

"Yes! Like Jack Sparrow!" Josh agreed.

"He'd have to be very small! It's more likely to be his parrot!" Laughing, Lucy gently nudged Josh off the stool. "Ness, would you give me a hand?"

Kneeling on the stool, Lucy popped a couple of catches and lifted the front of the piano off to reveal its strings and hammers. Passing this to Ness to put onto the sofa, she then unhooked the lid too and placed it carefully beside the instrument.

"Oh!" Lucy leaned forward. "That's odd!"

"What?" said Ness.

"Is it a dead pirate?" Josh asked.

"Not quite. Have a look at this." Lucy stood aside and pointed to the piano's intestines. "There's paper wrapped all around that string and blocking the hammer. No wonder the note wouldn't work."

"Maybe it's a message from the pirate? Or a treasure map?" Josh suggested, hopping about excitedly.

"More likely it's another bill," Ness said.

Lucy was unwrapping the yellowing paper. It was tightly coiled and even when she'd freed it the paper insisted on springing back. As she smoothed it out, she looked perplexed. "How strange."

"What is it?" Ness stepped forward and peered over her cousin's shoulder. "Oh! It's a piece of music." It might as well have been a message written in Chinese. "Is it one of our uncle's compositions?"

"If it is, it's a very strange one," Lucy said, flattening the paper down once more so that she could examine it. "Josh, would you do the honours?"

"OK!"

Josh resumed his seat at the piano. He leaned forward and squinted at the music, which kept rolling up again until Lucy trapped the edges of the paper beneath two music books. Then he played the notes, frowning at the jumble of sound.

"Is it a modern piece? Like a musical Picasso or something?" Ness asked.

"You mean some kind of weird tone poem?" Lucy shook her head. "I don't think so. It sounds like nonsense."

Josh played the piece again and Lucy looked even more confused. "There's nothing of any musical merit there at all as far as I can see."

"So why would it be there inside the piano? Had it slipped?" Ness was doubly bewildered.

Her cousin laughed and pointed at Armand's portrait. "It's there because he put it there. Firstly it's his writing and secondly I can't see how anything could slip into a closed lid and then coil itself around a piano string, can you?"

"No," Ness admitted. Goodness, but her uncle had been a strange man. And she'd thought Addy was difficult. It must have run in the family!

"I wish it was a pirate map to take us to the treasure," Josh said wistfully.

Lucy stared at him. Her blue eyes were wide. "Oh my God!" she breathed. "That's it! Josh Miller, you are a genius."

"I know that," said Josh. "Can I have a Coke please?"

"Not right now, but you can go and get me a pen and some paper from the kitchen table," Lucy said. "If you fancy a treasure hunt, that is?"

Josh didn't need asking twice and flew to the kitchen.

"Treasure hunt?" Ness echoed. "Do you think you know what this is all about?" Listen to the music: it will lead you to the answers you are seeking. Was this what Rose Hellier had meant?

"Our uncle liked to play games," Lucy said excitedly. "When he became poorly he was often bedbound, which drove him mad. One of his favourite distractions was to devise musical cryptograms and make me figure them out. Josh and I have played with these a bit too, just for fun. It's a nerdy muso thing. Great! Thanks, Josh," Lucy added as, panting, the little boy returned with some paper and felt pens. Spreading the blank paper out on the old trestle table, she began to draw a grid and fill the boxes with alphabetical letters.

"What's a musical cryptogram?" Ness was feeling lost. Addy had clearly neglected her education in more ways than one.

"It's a puzzle," Josh explained kindly. "It's a bit like when spies do stuff, like hide a message and use a code. What was the word you said it was called, Lucy?"

"Steganography. It's when there's a message hidden within some other kind of information that's not secret. So for example it could be concealed in an ordinary-looking piece of text or a picture – or music, of course. Uncle Armand showed me ages ago. It involves writing the letters of the alphabet in a grid like this one." Lucy finished drawing and stood back. "OK, Ness, I reckon this bizarre tune is actually a cryptogrammic sequence of musical notes. In other words, there's a message hidden in that music which can only be cracked if we have the right method. Now, if Josh doesn't mind me leaning over his shoulder, I'll see if I can decipher the code while he plays the music again. We may as well hear the notes while we're trying to figure out whatever message Uncle Armand hid in them, I suppose. The wily old rascal told me the answer would be at my fingertips!"

So Josh played the harsh and jumbled sounds very slowly while Lucy, her face filled with concentration, matched the musical notes to the letters on the grid. Note by note and letter by letter, Ness watched transfixed as the words appeared in felt pen. It was only when the last musical note shimmered into nothingness that she realised she'd been holding her breath.

Finished and never heard, a symphony of regrets, a lifetime of loss.

Her legacy is yours.

She watches from the wall.

Love is the key.

Ness's heart was hammering so hard that she thought she was going to faint.

"My mother's portrait," she whispered.

Lucy's eyes were huge. "You think he hid something there?"

Ness nodded. She did, and what was more she knew exactly what it was.

Between the three of them they managed to drag the heavy table across the Small Hall to the wall dominated by Addy's paintings. Being the tallest, Ness clambered up until she could reach Beth's portrait.

"Is there anything there?" Josh asked impatiently.

Ness clawed her fingers underneath the elaborate frame. The stone wall rasped against her knuckles, but the frame felt smooth beneath her fingertips. Reaching the farthest corner, she crept her hand up a little until she felt the cool kiss of metal tucked into the frame. Carefully and hardly daring to breathe, she drew out a small golden key.

"No wonder we couldn't find it," she said to Lucy. "Not the most obvious place to look."

It didn't take them long to run up to Ness's tower bedroom, where the locked chest was waiting. Scooping off her piled clothes, Ness fitted the key in the lock and turned it. There was a click as the clasp released, followed by a large creak as Ness lifted the heavy lid.

No! It was impossible! She couldn't believe her eyes. Nestled in the case, as though put there just for her, was the same violin Beth Penwellyn was holding in her portrait.

Ness reached into the chest, her fingertips brushing the glowing wood. Her hands were trembling. Her mother had touched this instrument and holding it now was the closest Ness had been to Beth since she was a baby.

"A violin!" Josh was hopping from foot to foot. "Cool!"

"What's underneath it?" Lucy asked as Ness picked the violin up and cradled it in her arms. Ducking under Ness's arm she pulled out a foolscap folder and a brown envelope.

"It's got your name on it!" said Josh. "Look! It says, To Lucy!"

Lucy didn't reply. She sank onto the rug with the folder clutched against her chest. She shook her head incredulously before she began to sob.

"Lucy! Are you all right?" Josh cried.

Ness was alarmed too. Lucy was usually the calmest of them all. "What is it? What's wrong?"

"Nothing's wrong." Lucy looked up and smiled through her tears, a smile of utter joy that took Ness's breath away. "Oh, Ness, nothing's wrong at all. Uncle Armand didn't forget me any more than he ever lost his greatest work." She held the folder up and fresh tears spilled over her cheeks. "The symphony wasn't missing at all. It's here! And he's left it to me!"

Chapter 33

Lucy didn't know what to do first. Laugh? Cry? Call the London agency that had represented Armand and give them the good news? Open the score? It lay in her hands and the responsibility was terrifying. Within the yellowed pages were sequences of music unheard for over a quarter of a century; every note had been inspired by the life her uncle had lived and the emotions he'd felt so deeply. There must have been a reason why he'd hidden the manuscript away until he was gone, and to open it up and play his composition felt like an intrusion.

"He's left me the symphony," she whispered, looking up at Ness. "It was the most precious possession he had. I can't believe it."

Ness's green eyes shone with tears. "Who else would have deserved or known its value? He knew all along that Jamie would choose material value above anything else, which was why he let him pick his bequests!"

Lucy thought this was exactly the kind of trick her uncle would have loved to play. "How it would have amused him to know that the real legacy was hidden in something that seemed worthless."

Ness grinned. "I think our uncle would also have known all I could ever buy you was time to figure it all out. He sounds like a wily old boy and my guess is that Armand knew he had to wait for Jamie to reveal his true colours so that you'd stand up to him and keep the castle from his clutches. Only then could everything else fall into place."

Lucy nodded. "That's more than likely. He'd have seen it as the ultimate riddle."

"Or a quest? Only the truly worthy deserving the prize?" Ness suggested. "A bit like finding the Holy Grail?"

"So it was a treasure hunt?" asked Josh. He looked puzzled. "But where's the treasure?"

"It's here. It's this music." Lucy hugged the score to her chest. "Josh, remember how I told you that my uncle was a famous composer and everyone was sad that his greatest work was lost? This is it. It wasn't lost at all. He'd hidden it away for all those years!"

"I'd want everyone to hear it. Why would he do that?" Josh said.

It was a good question and Lucy had no idea what the answer might be. Jamie hadn't even been born all that time ago, so why would Armand have hidden the symphony? Especially when the music world had been waiting for it so eagerly. Why had he chosen to sabotage his career?

"I don't know," she replied. "All I do know is that this is something very special and that maybe the answers to lots of questions are in here."

"I hope so," said Ness, still cradling the violin against her heart. "Why was it hidden with my mother's violin? Why did he put the key behind her portrait? Why leave me the castle?" She glanced around her bedroom, at the faded yet still pretty curtains and threadbare rug. "Was this her room? Did she live here? You said that it was never used before I came, yet he'd locked everything in the chest..."

Lucy shook her head. Why were there still so many mysteries? "I really don't know. All I can tell you is that what I'm holding is something so valuable that it terrifies me. It's the musical equivalent of finding a new Shakespeare play."

Ness looked stunned. "Seriously?"

"Seriously," said Lucy. "This is going to be massive in the musical world. Once they know about it then it'll change everything."

The responsibility of having Armand Penwellyn's finest work in her possession was overwhelming, and Lucy longed to call Adam and share this with him. He was the beginning and end of her every thought these days; it amazed her how in a short space of time their friendship had melted into love. It was a love that gave her a warm, contented glow whenever she thought of it. There was passion too – something she'd never dared hope for or even dreamed of – but above all Lucy felt that with Adam she'd finally reached the quiet harbour of utter happiness. Now that this unexpected legacy had sent ripples across the smooth surface of that harbour, it was only right he should be there so that they could talk it through together.

Ness rose to her feet. "You need a little time alone with all this before you make any decisions. I can see from your face how huge it all is." She held out her hand to Josh. "How about we go and see if we can find that Coke you wanted? And maybe one of Annie's cakes?"

Lucy appreciated her sensitivity. Ness was right: there was far more to all of this than there appeared to be – and there was something else, which Lucy hadn't shared with her cousin. Accompanying the score had been a sheaf of notes covered in her uncle's distinctive writing, and on those notes the name Beth appeared over and over again, sometimes almost scratched into the surface with the pressure and passion of his pen. Lucy wasn't sure what all this meant, but she had her suspicions.

Clutching the manuscript tightly, she made her way to the music room. The empty space once occupied by the grand piano still looked strange, and since she'd shut the room up dust had fallen onto every surface. There was a sense of stillness, as though the room was holding its breath, and as she placed the score on a music stand Lucy had the oddest sensation that she was about to perform in front of an unseen audience. There was no piano, so she liberated a violin from its dusty case, nestling it under her chin and allowing the instrument to become a part of her as she tuned it. Although she wasn't a particularly talented violinist (she was nowhere near Josh's standard), Lucy was suddenly sure that this piece would have been composed with a violin in mind. She didn't even need to flip the score open to know for certain; her heart told her it would be so.

With a shaking hand Lucy turned open the cover of the manuscript, which hadn't seen the light of day for so many years. Sure enough, there it was written boldly in that slanting hand:

Island Siren
A symphony
for Elizabeth Penwellyn

Over one hundred bound pages of a score for piano, first violin and a full orchestra. There were scribbles, crossings outs, slurring marks and scrapped cadenzas. It was untidy, heavily annotated and completely raw, but as she began to play Lucy knew that none of this mattered. The melancholic notes sobbed from the instrument in her hands, sounding so heart-breaking that as she played Lucy wept too. There was love and loss and pain and joy here, like life itself. Even with her clumsy playing, it was the most beautiful music she had ever heard. There was no doubt about it: the lost symphony was a masterpiece.

While she played Lucy became the music, losing all track of time and space. Outside, the tide turned and the rain eased and then intensified again. It was only when the last note trembled away that she became aware of the crick in her neck and the soreness in her fingers. She'd been utterly transported, just as the entire musical world would be when they heard the symphony. Imagining this score being played by a full orchestra made the hairs rise at the back of Lucy's neck. She had to call Armand's agents in London, because this piece was priceless and needed to be shared. It couldn't be hidden away for a moment longer.

Lucy placed the violin back in the case. Her head was still full of the music and the passion that was in every note – the sharps, the flats, the minor keys. She thought she understood it. Did she even need to read the notes that accompanied the piece when Armand's music had told her more eloquently than any words ever could why he had given up composing? For a moment she hesitated, feeling again that sense of snooping into something so painful and so private that it had remained a secret for a lifetime. Then she remembered the bleakness in Nessa's face as she'd cradled the violin. There were answers to her cousin's questions here and Ness deserved to hear them.

With the notes in her hand, Lucy sat down in the window seat and prepared to read. Oh! But these weren't notes at all. They were the pages torn from her uncle's diary. Her mouth parched at the significance of what was held within them. Armand had left Lucy his diary and instructed her to read it. There was something here that he wanted to share. In death this most secretive of men was ready to tell his story – and Lucy owed him the respect of reading it carefully, however hard she knew she would find this.

When she'd finished, Lucy stared out at the sea for a long time. Beth Penwellyn had met her end in that water, and what a tragic tale it was. No wonder this symphony was so powerful.

And no wonder her uncle had hidden it.

Lucy took a deep and steadying breath. Until Ness knew the truth, this symphony had to remain a closely guarded secret. Letting it out into the world, no matter how valuable or how much of a work of genius it might be, was no longer her choice. Only Ness could make that call.

She rose to her feet, gathering up the diary pages and tucking them into the score, before setting off for the Small Hall. She needed to speak to Ness – and Lucy knew that this was going to be one of the hardest things she'd ever have to do.

Ness loved Lucy and she loved Grace Note Bay too, but walking up the hill on a stormy afternoon and being buffeted by the wind was putting that love to the test. The day had already been weird enough, Ness thought as she followed Lucy and the bounding Biscuit up the narrow path to the summit, and now it was getting weirder. Finding the key to the chest, holding her mother's violin and realising that she'd been sleeping in Beth's room all along had made Ness feel as though she was in some kind of dream; it was as if the flagstones beneath her feet had turned to sponge. The lost symphony turning up was something else entirely though, and Ness was thrilled for her cousin. She was no expert on music but she could imagine the excitement there would be in the press about this. Her uncle's masterpiece was probably worth a fortune. Lucy would be set up for life and nobody deserved it more.

So why then did her cousin look so worried? And what on earth was this route march about?

Several paces ahead, Lucy ducked to the left. Following her, Ness saw that another path veered off here, dropping away to a hidden spot cut into the granite where the grass grew even longer and swathes of pink and white valerian bloomed. Even as the wind and drizzle blew past, this half-cave in the cliff was dry and sheltered.

"My goodness, I had no idea this was here." Ness was taken aback. She thought she'd explored every inch of the island, but she'd missed this secret place.

"That makes two of us," Lucy said.

"I don't understand."

"It's well hidden and unless you were looking how would you know it existed?" Her cousin sat down, her back pressed against the mossy granite of the cliff.

Ness joined her. She hugged her knees close to her chest and clasped her arms around them tightly, then looked out across the endless expanse of the sea and shivered. It didn't look very friendly.

"What's going on, Lucy?" she asked.

"There wasn't just music in the folder. There were notes too. Or more accurately, pages from Armand's diary," replied Lucy, in a voice that was soft yet edged with concern and worry. The nuances in her speech told Ness there was far more to this than finding a symphony.

She looked at her cousin and suddenly Ness realised she knew the story. Of course she did. It all made perfect sense.

"The notes were about my mother, weren't they?"

"Ness, this was where Armand and your mother used to meet."

Ness's voice was a whisper. "They were lovers?"

Lucy sighed. "It seems so. Armand wrote the symphony for your mother, Ness, and he wrote it for you too. When it was finished he hid it away because he couldn't bear to ever hear it again."

And suddenly Ness understood everything. It was as though she'd been looking at a tapestry from the back: the stitching was there under the mass of coloured threads, and the patterns and images were partially visible, but it was only when you turned it around that you could see the whole piece clearly and that the design made sense.

"Armand was in love with my mother, wasn't he?"

Lucy nodded. "The symphony charts everything. From their first meeting, to their love affair, to the affair being discovered and then your mother's dreadful death. I can't do anything with it until you know the truth, Ness. It may have been left to me but it's your legacy too. This music is your story."

Ness pinched the bridge of her nose hard. She would not cry. "I think you'd better tell me everything."

There was a rustling as Lucy pulled the pages from her jacket pocket. "It's all here, Ness. It's Uncle Armand's diary, his journey through composing the symphony, right the way through to nearly destroying it. It explains everything. Here. It's all yours."

But Ness shook her head. "I don't think I could read anything right now. Can you explain it, Lucy? Tell me what it says?"

So Lucy told her, and as Ness listened so many things that had never quite made sense before suddenly became clear. Finally she understood how three brothers, all talented and close, had ended their lives as bitter enemies. Armand, the eldest, had lived for his music and been at the peak of his success. Armand had been particularly driven and aloof, though. It had only been when he'd met the beautiful and gifted Beth that he'd finally fallen in love and composed the music that had marked him out for greatness: the famous Island Suite. Unused to feelings of passion and longing, Armand had written violin parts for Beth and poured his heart and soul into composing for her and her alone. He'd known that this woman was the love of his life. Before her arrival, music had been Armand's only mistress – but now his passion for Beth consumed him.

The trouble was, Beth had then fallen in love with and married his younger brother, Addy. She might live on the island, and he would see her every day, but she would always be out of Armand's reach. The diary told how this tore him apart.

"It was a long, hot summer," Lucy said. "Your father was painting non-stop and you were a small baby. Addy locked himself away and concentrated on his art. According to the diary entries he'd do that a lot."

That was about right, thought Ness. Addy had frequently done this throughout her childhood, locking himself away for days on end and cocooning himself in his work with brandy and goodness only knew what else for company. As Ness had got older he'd even taken off for weeks on end, leaving her with whatever friends were kind enough to pick up his slack. He was a genius, everyone said so, but he'd also been very hard to live with. If it had been difficult for his daughter, what must it have been like for a young woman with a baby?

"She turned to Armand because my dad neglected her," Ness said. No wonder Addy had never talked much about Beth. Taking responsibility for his behaviour had never been one of his distinguishing traits and he'd remained bitter for the rest of his life.

Lucy sighed. "It seems that way. I should imagine that it was hugely flattering for her to be pursued by a famous composer and hailed as a muse. To be the object of such an intense passion must be intoxicating when you've felt lonely and unloved. Uncle Armand would have been the opposite of your father, I guess?"

"If he was more interested in my mother than in himself, then I imagine so," Ness said sadly. She'd loved her father desperately but he'd been a selfish genius. If Beth and Armand had a shared love of music, that would have drawn them closer too. As an adult she understood this – but as Beth and Addy's child she wanted to cry.

"It must have been overwhelming for Uncle Armand," Lucy commented, "to have never fallen in love at all and then to have this grand passion that swept everything aside and fired him up to write his greatest work."

Ness saw in her mind's eye a climbing sun, boating in coves, tanned limbs, searing heat and the lassitude of long summer days, swimming naked in the sea, making love under the blue sky...

"I wonder what my mother did with me?" she said aloud. "If Dad was on one of his painting binges and she was with Armand, where was I?"

"With the village woman paid to look after you," Lucy said quietly. "You can probably guess who that was."

"Rose Hellier." Now things were making sense. "She kept their secret all this time? Even when I asked her outright?"

"She was keeping Armand's secret. I guess she felt she couldn't tell you, even now when he's gone. People here are loyal like that." Lucy looked sad. "It seems our uncle had a lot of secrets."

"What a lonely life that must have been," Ness observed, and her cousin nodded.

"He told me towards the end that he had a lot of regrets. I think that was why he tried so hard to put things right where he could. Fern staying here, for instance, and his letting Merryn live here too. Giving Rose's grandson a home was the least our uncle could do in return for her silence."

"So what happened next? How did your father fall out with Armand and Dad?" Ness asked. She was trying to take it all in but it was like hearing the plot of a movie, one filled with picnics, music, boats and paintings as well as people whose names she knew but whom she'd never met. Only Addy felt real – and knowing him, Ness could understand how her mother might have felt. Handsome, fun Addy would sweep you off your feet and then drop you just as quickly. Ness had lost count of how many times she'd cried her eyes out because he'd let her down or been dismissive. With Addy you were constantly on the back foot, always trying to be good enough and earn the golden sunshine of his smile. Once granted it was impossible to live without.

"My father found out and Armand persuaded him to keep quiet," Lucy continued. "Dad did, but he must have been really torn. I think the guilt ruined his life and he blamed himself for everything that happened next. I never really knew him when he wasn't depressed." She gave Ness a sad smile. "Uncle Armand destroyed my father. That's why he gave me a home and left me the music. It's a legacy of guilt."

"No," Ness said. "That's wrong. He left you the music because he loved you, Lucy. You and Jamie were both Maudsley's children, after all, and he didn't leave it for Jamie."

Lucy dabbed her eyes with her sleeve. "Thanks, Ness. I loved him too. You never knew him, but I promise he really wasn't a bad man. He fell in love with the wrong person with dreadful consequences and he spent the rest of his life trying to atone for what happened. He even destroyed his brilliant career as a punishment."

Ness realised she was going to have to know the rest of the story, however uncomfortable it might be.

"Lucy, I already know that my mother drowned. But it was a wild storm by all accounts and I've seen for myself what it can be like here when bad weather comes in. She must have known it'd be dangerous. Why would she have ventured outside? Something happened, didn't it?"

"In the final movement of the symphony, a storm tears across the sea and drives away the heat," Lucy murmured. She held out her left hand and Ness was shocked to see that the tips of her fingers were raw. "I played the whole thing through earlier on and I have never, ever had to pull so much pain from a violin. It's brutal. In the diary Armand writes that your father found out about the affair, Ness, and he was furious. Addy confronted Armand and Beth and there was an enormous row."

For an awful moment Ness thought she was going to pass out with horror.

"My father didn't— He didn't—"

"No! Oh, Ness, no! Nothing like that, I promise." Lucy put her arms around Ness and hugged her. "As far as I can gather your mum realised she loved Addy. He stormed out of the castle and she followed him, begging him to forgive her. She shouted that she loved him and always had, that she didn't love Armand at all. She said it was madness and it didn't mean anything. Uncle heard all this, of course, and it broke his heart. But it was savage outside and your dad couldn't hear her above the storm. He was heading to his boat and Beth followed him, shouting at him to wait, but the wind whipped the words away. Your uncle wasn't far behind, trying to stop her, but she ran ahead onto the pier yelling at Addy to come back. She was wearing heels and she slipped. You know how it is out on the pier in the rain."

Ness did. The pier was greasy in good weather; in the rain walking on it was like trying to balance on ice. Beth wouldn't have stood a chance.

"So my mother fell into the sea," she whispered, seeing in her mind the cold, swirling water that Addy had spent the rest of his life trying to escape from in the deserts of California or on the back of a motorbike.

"It was a terrible accident. Armand dived in after her. So did your father. They dived and dived but they never found her." Lucy's face was wet with tears. "Armand writes in the diary that he dived for her every night in his dreams and for the rest of his life. He believed that his love killed Beth and he never, ever forgave himself. Every day was another day of punishment."

The sad tale drew to a close here because Ness knew the rest better than anyone. Addy had left with her, never to return. Armand had become a recluse and given up composing after writing his final symphony. Maudsley slid into depression and despair. Their family had been torn apart by love. Although she'd lost her mother a lifetime ago, Ness's heart broke again to know the truth. She cried onto Lucy's shoulder for a while as the grief consumed her all over again. All those lives wasted.

"Our uncle left me the island because he thought he took away my mother," she said finally, wiping her eyes on her sleeve.

"That would make sense," Lucy agreed. "He lived with the guilt for the rest of his life."

"My dad never spoke about any of it. Not properly, anyway," Ness remarked quietly. She wished so much that he had done, because she understood Addy a whole lot better now.

"None of them did. I suppose it was too painful – but the whole story's there in the symphony Armand wrote, and it's the most powerful thing I've ever heard. Sad and haunting and beautiful."

"Would you say it was even more powerful than his other work?" Ness asked.

Lucy considered this for a moment. "I think so. I'd also like to think that if something good could ever come of such tragedy then maybe this is it? But it's up to you. This is your story as much as theirs and mine, and if you'd rather it stayed in the past then I won't argue. We can lock the symphony away and forget about it."

Ness stared at Lucy. Was her cousin crazy? "That's insane. It must be worth a fortune."

"There's more to life than money," answered Lucy.

Ness looked out to sea. She loved this place. It was tragic and beautiful and challenging and part of her. She loved Lucy too, and she loved Merryn and Fern and Josh. Her past, present and future were bound up in Pirran Island. Hiding from what had gone before wouldn't make these things go away or change them. But maybe letting go could heal the past?

"People make mistakes," she said slowly. "I think it's what we do to put them right that matters. Armand punished himself for long enough – and so did my dad and yours too, by the sound of it. My mother certainly paid a high price. As you say, maybe it's time something good came out of it all. Besides, the music doesn't really belong to me or to you, does it? It belongs to the island and it belongs to everyone else. We can't keep that hidden. It would be wrong. You must publish it, Lucy."

"That's exactly what I think," Lucy said softly. "Thank you, Ness."

"So what now?" Ness asked.

"I'll call Armand's agents later and share the good news. I think they'll be very excited. This is huge, Ness. I can't even begin to tell you just how huge."

"My mother was a muse," Ness said thoughtfully. "That symphony's her legacy too and it really shouldn't be lost. Maybe this is the start of everything being put right? Do you know, I have a feeling that was what Uncle Armand had hoped for."

They smiled at each other.

"Your mother inspired great loves and passions, didn't she? Yes, she made mistakes, and she paid dreadfully for them, but if there's one thing I do know about love then it's that it's complicated. Things don't always work out as we expect them to or hope they will. Sometimes we don't even fall in love with the right person," Lucy said.

Ness pictured grey eyes and a familiar, handsome face and her heart constricted. Was she in love with Max Reynard? Her enemy?

This was a question she didn't dare answer.

"Beth must have been a very special woman," Lucy continued, "and now I know you, I can understand why she inspired such strong feelings. If you have a fraction of her grace and determination and passion then it's no wonder poor Max Reynard is crazy about you."

Ness laughed. "Hardly! He just wants to get his hands on the castle. Believe me, that man isn't to be trusted an inch. Poor Max? As if! All he cares about is money."

But Lucy didn't look convinced. "No, I can't agree with that at all. Perhaps at first that's what he wanted but I think that changed when he met you. Adam says he's never seen Max so subdued. He's not heard from him for ages."

Adam and Lucy had been discussing her and Max? Ness was nipping this in the bud.

"He's busy plotting how to screw us over, that's why."

"I really don't think so, Ness. That doesn't sound like the man Adam says he is. There's more to Max Reynard than you think. Why don't you give him the chance to prove that?"

Oh dear, thought Ness. Being in love must have done something to her cousin's brain. Lucy was sounding like a bad romantic novel.

"People don't change," Ness insisted.

"I didn't say he's changed. I said that his objectives had changed," Lucy shot back, rising to her feet and brushing dried grass from her jeans. "Max has always been a good person. We just couldn't see it before because we were too busy letting the trappings get in the way – and maybe our own prejudices clouded what we saw too. He's Adam's best friend, which means there must be more to him than greed and cash. So he owns our debts. He hasn't called them in yet, has he? Maybe you should talk to him? Let him explain?"

"There's nothing to explain. He's played us," Ness said bleakly.

As she followed Lucy down the track back towards the castle, Ness's head was already aching from all she'd learned. With Max Reynard thrown into the mix as well she thought it might just explode. She liked Adam very much but friendship, like love, could be blind.

"I shouldn't tell you this either, because Adam will kill me and apparently Max refuses to talk about it, but he spends most of his spare time doing voluntary work and ploughs a huge amount of money into charities," Lucy added, over her shoulder. "He's the funding behind Malcom's Place. You know, the homeless charity? And he's built lots of affordable housing in cities too. He's not the playboy you think – I thought – he is."

Ness was stunned. All those accusations she'd hurled at Max and he'd never once mentioned any of this? Why ever not? When she thought about the words she'd flung at him that day at Grace Note Bay, she felt a prickle of remorse. He could have shot all her criticisms down in flames in about two seconds.

"Why are you telling me this?"

Lucy shrugged. "Maybe today's made me see that keeping secrets, no matter how good the intentions, really isn't a good idea? And that living with regrets is a huge waste? All I know is that I'm not going to live my life like our uncle did, Ness, and I don't think you should either. It doesn't really matter what happens to the castle. It will always be here in one form or another. I think Uncle Armand's left you the chance of finding something far more important."

As her cousin strode ahead, Ness was left wondering whether Lucy was right. If she was, whatever could Ness do about it? She couldn't stop thinking about Max Reynard and she wondered whether she ever would.

Or, worse again, if she even wanted to stop thinking about him.

Chapter 34

It was the first week in September. The days were still warm and golden but in the mornings the air was sharp and by the evenings it was rich with the tang of blackberries and wood smoke from bonfires. High holiday season was over and St Pirran was settling into a new rhythm. The streets were less busy and the beach was no longer sprinkled with windbreaks and stripy towels. The tripping boats still headed out to sea each day, but the harbour steps weren't as crowded with queuing visitors. Meanwhile, on the island, the tea room was empty. Soon the nights would draw in and the seagulls would head to the cliffs for the winter.

The seasons were turning and it was the right time for change; the autumnal scenes all around Ness matched the autumnal feelings in her heart.

"Are you sure about this?" David Brown placed his hand on hers to stop the pen from moving across the document. "Once you've signed this it changes everything. There's no going back."

Ness and the solicitor were sitting in the library. The paperwork Ness was about to put her signature to was the product of weeks of discussion, negotiation and feeling humbled by the generosity of others. She'd had to learn to accept help, just as she'd also had to learn that stepping away from something you'd come to love was sometimes the only way of proving that love.

"I've changed my mind. Let's sell the island to a developer after all and make millions," she joked, but David wasn't laughing. Instead he looked deadly serious.

"That's still an option, Ness, and one I'd urge you to consider." He gestured to a folder that was resting on the chair beside him. "Three firms have made offers. The details are all there in writing, if you want to take another look at them. If you were to accept one of their offers, you'd be a very rich young woman – but if you sign that document in front of you, you'll be left with very little financially."

"It's not about the money, David," Ness said gently. "We've talked about this and spent weeks working it all through. All of us agree it's the right thing to do."

The solicitor nodded. "For what it's worth, I think so too – but giving up an inheritance like this is a huge sacrifice."

Ness supposed he was right but it didn't feel like a sacrifice to her. Ever since she'd learned the truth about why her uncle had left her the island, she'd felt a deep sense of unease. It was a legacy bound up with guilt and despair, and although she didn't blame any of the players in that unhappy story for what had happened, she wasn't comfortable about profiting from a tragedy. Armand had done all he could to protect the place and keep it safe, and he'd shielded her from the truth in his way, but Ness knew the time had come to move on from what had gone before. It saddened her to think that her uncle had died blaming himself for a terrible accident, just as it broke her heart to have witnessed how Addy had spent the rest of his life running away from it. She loved the island and the castle, and had come to love the people living there too, but Ness just couldn't shake the feeling that her legacy was tainted.

She'd had to find a way to put the past to rights, a way to keep the island safe forever so that none of it would have been in vain.

The answer had come soon and in an unexpected way. Just as Lucy had predicted, there had been considerable excitement about the lost symphony and several of the biggest names in the music world had made offers to buy it. When it had finally gone to a sealed-bid auction, the price raised had been staggering – and that was before the royalties from the rest of Armand's body of work came in. The story hit the national and international news and prompted a resurgence of interest in Armand's music. The late summer had seen a flood of visitors to the island, and a special BBC prom had taken place in his honour. Meanwhile, downloads of Armand's earlier compositions had soared, sending him to the top of the classical music chart. Ness couldn't have been more pleased for Lucy. Part of her was also thrilled to know that Jamie, who was currently sulking in London, was bound to see all this and be eaten up with envy. His sister was set up for life – make that several lifetimes – and he only had his own greed to blame. After all, nobody had forced him to choose the shares and the grand piano instead of the rights to his uncle's compositions and the old upright that had contained Armand's secret message.

Ness glanced down at the document. Hers would be the last signature and the one that completed the paperwork. Lucy's was above and, seeing it now, she was moved almost to tears.

"No way," Ness had said when, shortly after their heart-to-heart at Grace Note Bay, her cousin had come to find her in the library with a proposal. "I can't let you do that."

Lucy had fixed her with a determined look. "With all due respect, Ness, it isn't your decision. I've already spoken to David and I'm not changing my mind. All the money from Island Siren is going to the castle and Pirran Island. I don't want a penny of it."

"It's a fortune." Ness was stunned. How many noughts?

Her cousin had agreed that it was a lot, and then named the exact figure that the rights had been sold for. It was the kind of money even Max Reynard would have thought twice about spending.

"The symphony's a legacy for the nation, not just for us," Lucy had said firmly.

Ness had nodded, an idea starting to form in the back of her mind. "The same is true of the island where it was written," she'd mused. "Lucy, how about I do the same? Why don't we form some kind of trust for the music and the island? We're the custodians of something bigger than us now."

"A charitable trust, you mean?" Lucy's blue eyes had lit up. "That's a brilliant idea, Ness. With the castle as a museum and tribute to Armand's work? And a memorial to our parents too?"

"And safe from developers," Ness had added with feeling.

"Ah. Like Max?" Lucy had asked carefully. "Has he been in touch?"

Ness had shaken her head because she'd not heard a word from Max. She'd emailed his office, tried to call and even been up there using the trip to the prom as her excuse, but there'd been no sign of him and nobody had breathed a word concerning his whereabouts. Max, it appeared, had severed all links with her and with the castle. His holiday home remained shut and Foxy Lady's hull was growing green and slimy.

Ness supposed there was nothing here he wanted now.

She gripped David's heavy Montblanc pen, poised to sign on the dotted line. This was it. All the paperwork had been done, so that Pirran Island could be held in a charitable trust. As soon as she signed it, the place would no longer be hers; instead it would be kept for the nation and managed by a board of carefully appointed trustees. The island family would be able to remain there as lifetime tenants if they wanted to, but Ness already knew that Lucy would move in with Adam, Fred would leave, and Merryn and Fern would soon be off enjoying new adventures. As for her? Ness simply had no idea. Pirran Island was in her heart and soul, but maybe like Addy she would need to move on too. What else could she do? Everywhere she looked she thought she saw that familiar lithe frame and those grey eyes – and each time, her heart raced until she realised she was mistaken. Was it also her fate to be haunted by the loss of what could have been?

"Once I sign this, it's done." She tightened her hold on the pen. "We pay Reynards off for good and then the island and the castle are safe."

The solicitor smiled. "Ah, there's a piece of good news I was saving for you, Nessa. There is no loan to repay."

"What?" Taken aback, she put the pen down again. "No, that's not right. I owe Reynards the capital I borrowed plus the interest the loan accrued. It's all in the paperwork I passed you."

"I know that. The point is that there is no loan to repay. Max Reynard's legal team contacted me this morning. They've donated the sum you owed to the new charitable trust. They've faxed me the paperwork and it's all above board, I assure you." He plucked some documents from his folder and pushed them across the table. "Have a look."

Ness read the facsimile through. Sure enough, the debt had been written off and transformed into the trust's first donation. It didn't make sense.

"The documents say this is a donation from Reynards towards the restoration project, with the proviso that Adam Miller is to be placed in charge," she said hesitantly.

"That's right," David replied. "I told Max Reynard's legal team that I didn't think that would be an issue. I'm sure Lucy will be thrilled." He looked perplexed. "I thought you'd be delighted, Ness."

"We're talking over a quarter of a million pounds here! Why on earth would Max do all this and have nothing in return? Is it a tax thing, do you think? Or is he just thinking of Adam? Or is there something we've missed?"

"Is that a slur on my professional capabilities?" David asked with a smile. "I'm afraid I'm not even going to dignify those questions with answers. Sometimes people do things because they're the right thing to do, Ness. Not everyone has an ulterior motive. And maybe Max Reynard wants to show you that he cares about more than just money, hmm?"

"Have you been talking to Lucy?" enquired Ness despairingly.

He tapped his nose. "Now that would be telling! Suffice to say that it hasn't gone unnoticed in the town that a certain developer has changed somewhat. There's been quite a lot of speculation as to why that might be, too. My Aunt Val has a theory about that – and it's one Lucy Penwellyn and I share!"

Ness felt her cheeks grow warm. Had Max written off the loan because he had feelings for her? Had she misjudged him all along? She felt confused and wrong-footed.

"The point is that this is all above board and legal, and actually a marvellous start for the St Pirran Trust," David said, taking pity on Ness and returning to his usual business like manner. "I'd be inclined to accept it graciously and in the spirit it's been offered."

Ness nodded. She would do so and then she would hunt down Max Reynard and discover what this was really about.

She glanced down at the paperwork. She was the last to sign it; all the other names and signatures were there already. Annie, Fred, Merryn, Fern, David and Lucy – all witnessed and legal. No decisions would be made without a unanimous vote and never again would the island's future hang in the balance. It could never become the private haunt of the wealthy or an upmarket hotel but instead would ring with music and the chatter of visitors. There were plans for concerts and workshops, and there was even talk about a film of Armand's life – something Ness was considering very carefully. Lucy was also hoping to set up a music school for underprivileged youngsters. There was a wealth of good things waiting to happen.

One signature from her would set all this in motion.

Ness took a deep breath and signed with a flourish. There. It was done. She really hoped that somewhere her uncle could see what she'd chosen to do with his legacy, just as she hoped with all her heart that wherever they were now all the major players in his tragic story were at peace too. The truth about her family history hadn't been easy to hear but it was better than the silence of not knowing.

David placed the document in his briefcase, snapping the lock shut.

"Wonderful. We're all set," he said with a warm smile. "By the way, I spoke to Fern's father earlier on and he'd like to make a donation towards the first Armand Penwellyn musical scholarship. He says it's his way of thanking Armand for keeping Fern safe."

At least one good thing had come out of the festival mess and Jamie's involvement with Logan Barrie – Fern's reconciliation with her parents. Feeling protected from harm now that Merryn was beside her and her ex was in custody, Fern had got in touch with her family and started to build bridges. Her parents had been looking for her ever since she'd left home but the trail had grown cold when she'd come to the island. They were overjoyed to have been reunited with their daughter at last.

"That's fantastic news, and kind of him too. Will you write and let him know we accept and are very grateful?" Ness asked.

"Of course," said David. He picked up his briefcase. "It's been quite a journey, hasn't it? But I wouldn't have missed it for the world, Ness, and I think your uncle would have been very proud at all you've achieved."

"I hope so," Ness replied, and the solicitor smiled.

"I know so," he told her, before shutting the door quietly, leaving Ness alone with her thoughts and the ticking of the clock.

There. It was done. The castle was hers no longer but belonged to everyone – which was exactly as it should be. Ness had nothing that Max Reynard wanted. If it was only the island he'd cared about then she would never see him again. Nor would she be able to tell him how sorry she was that she'd misjudged him.

It was terrifying just how bleak these thoughts were.

Ness moved to the window and gazed out. She wasn't sure how long she stood there, lost in memories and daydreams. Her mother would have known this view, and her father too. Both of them had been flawed people who'd burned so brightly for a season, but at least now that Ness had made her difficult choice they would never be forgotten. They'd always be remembered through their music.

The sun slipped lower, casting long shadows across the bay and stretching golden fingers through the room. The tide was on the turn, and as Ness looked out at the glistening sand she caught sight of a lone figure walking along the beach. Her breath caught.

No. It couldn't be. She was imagining it.

Ness closed her eyes and opened them again slowly, hardly daring to hope.

He was still there.

Heart hammering, she flew out of the library and down the spiral stairs, her feet tripping on the worn flagstones in her haste to reach the bottom. Tearing across the Small Hall and through the kitchen, where Biscuit looked up from his basket in surprise, Ness burst through the back door and sprinted through the courtyard and beneath the Pilgrim's Gate. The path down across the lawn passed in a green blur and then she was on the causeway and racing over the cobbles. Although her breath was coming in gasps, Ness couldn't have slowed down even if she'd tried. Her heart had taken over and the sheer force of her emotion was going to take her across the beach no matter what.

Was it him or not? In the brilliance of the setting sun it was hard to tell. Maybe this was her mind playing tricks on her. Perhaps she was longing for something so badly that her imagination was placing it there for her, just as travellers lost in the desert saw water and shady palm trees.

But this mirage was solid. The late sun gilded his features, highlighting the strong cheekbones as he raised his hand to shield his eyes from the glare. Ness slowed to a walk. Her lungs were burning and her face was flushed from the exertion. With her curls tumbling from her ponytail she probably looked a state, but she'd never cared less about her appearance. Nothing else mattered apart from reaching Max. And it really was Max; Ness knew this now that she was closer. Even though the sun was dazzling her vision, every cell in her body was telling her she was home.

"You're here," she said, and her heart was thudding – although whether that was from the run or because of seeing him again it was hard to know. She was standing right in front of him now. He was deeply tanned and his dark hair was slightly longer than the last time she'd seen him. His face was thinner too, the eyes shadowed with tiredness. "Where have you been? I tried to get hold of you. Didn't they say?"

Max said nothing for a moment. Then he exhaled wearily as though he'd been holding onto something for a very long time.

"Yes, they told me but I knew nothing I said was ever going to change your mind. I've been away. I took a holiday."

"No you haven't. You've been working with your charity, haven't you? Building another shelter? That's where you went and why I couldn't find you. Don't deny it. I know about the charities."

He grimaced. "I see Adam's been telling tales out of school."

"Maybe," Ness admitted, "but don't be cross with him and Lucy. I can be very persuasive when I need to be."

"I can imagine. The last time I was alone on a beach with you I felt I could be persuaded to do anything," Max said, and the look in his eyes made her shiver.

"I'm sorry," she whispered. "I got everything wrong."

He shook his head and took her face in his hands. His pupils were so dark, so intense, that she saw herself reflected in them. He was just a kiss away.

"Not everything," he said. "There were some things you got exactly right."

Ness nodded. When she listened to her heart she heard the truth, but so much else had got in the way.

"That loan was worth a fortune. Why write it off?"

"I meant what I said, Nessa," Max told her quietly. "My vision for the island changed and this was the best way to prove it. You can start again now and without anyone else. Move forward. It's your inheritance and it's St Pirran's legacy too. Nothing should be allowed to threaten that."

"But you've chosen to walk away from the one thing you wanted above anything else. Why would you do that?" Ness asked, still staring up at him.

His low voice was like a caress. "Ness, you already know the answer to that."

Ness's heart was telling her that she knew, had always known, and she longed for nothing more than to acknowledge the truth. She was falling in love with Max, had been since that first moonlit night, but everything in Ness told her it couldn't happen this way. They had to be equals or nothing.

Gently placing her hand on his chest, the racing of his heart beneath her fingertips telling her Max felt the same way too, Ness took a step back.

"Max, that's a really generous offer but I can't accept it as it stands."

The sweeping brows rose into his dark hair. "Why ever not?"

"Because it doesn't feel right. It changes the balance of everything between us. It feels like charity."

"It is charity, Ness, but in the truest sense of the word. Jesus, have you got any idea how much money Reynards is worth? Let me write it off as a donation to the trust. Or how about we call it a fine for trespassing on a private beach?"

Ness shook her head. "It still feels like charity – or, even worse, being bought. Can you understand that? If I'm going to make Pirran Island work then I need to do it properly. Not with favours or donations. It feels wrong."

His grey eyes held hers like magnets. "Christ, you're so stubborn, Ness. Is it a Penwellyn thing?"

"Maybe," she admitted. Lucy was stubborn, refusing for so long to accept any criticism of Jamie, and her uncles had been too proud to mend their feud. Even Addy had never listened to anyone. Oh dear. It seemed the castle wasn't all she'd inherited.

"I need to do this properly, Max. It's what my uncle expected and it's the right thing. He didn't leave me any money or pull any favours or even let us keep the piano. I think this was about more than just inheriting the castle. It was about building a legacy. I can't do that if I feel I owe people favours or that I've been bought off. This all has to be done properly. It all has to be on the level."

"My father would have loved you, Ness," Max said, and there was a catch in his voice. "That's exactly the kind of thing he would have said."

"He sounds like a very wise man. I'm afraid I drove mine nuts," Ness remarked. "In fact if he can see me now he's probably banging his head on the pearly gates and yelling at me to just take the bloody money!"

"But you're not your father any more than I'm mine."

"No," Ness agreed, "I'm not. I'll accept the donation but there's one condition: I want you to be a trustee of the island. I want to do this with your help and your vision."

He sighed. "Ness, that's great, but I don't think I can. Please, accept the donation as my contribution to building something out of a childhood dream – but I won't be here to be a part of it."

"What do you mean?"

"I'm leaving St Pirran."

She stared at him in confusion. "But you can't! You love it here. You told me that as a child you dreamed of living in St Pirran. That was why you came back." Then a thought occurred to her. And she felt sick with disappointment. Had it only ever been about the island after all? "Is this because you can't buy the island?"

"No," Max said firmly. "That isn't it. The trust is a wonderful idea and the best way forward for the island. I know I'm a successful businessman and all of that nonsense, but even I won't be around for five hundred years. Hopefully the castle will be though – and if I can contribute towards safeguarding its future then that feels right to me. It's what I wanted to do, Ness. I would have tried to do that if I'd bought it and I want to play my part in doing that now. Yes, it was a boyhood dream to own the island, but there's so much more to it than that now. Besides, who owns it in reality? A place like this is only on loan to us, isn't it? Maybe it's closer to the truth to say that Pirran Island owns us?"

"And that's really why you wrote off the loan?"

"What can I say? The place has got to me."

"Just the place?"

Max chuckled ruefully. "Of course just the place."

Ness stepped forward and met that grey gaze head-on. "Fibber."

"Calling me a liar again?"

"I am," she said. "And this time you aren't telling the truth – are you, Max?"

"OK, not just the place," he admitted. "Maybe the people in it too?"

Ness laughed. "Wow. I never knew you liked old Fred so much! He will be touched!"

Max's brow crinkled. "Hmm, on second thoughts maybe I should more accurately say that there's one person I found I couldn't stop thinking about? When I should have been pushing to buy the place and moving forward with the development it was a shock to find that it wasn't really the castle I was thinking about after all. I can't stay here anymore. Not if that person doesn't feel the same way as I do."

Ness's heart was playing hopscotch. "So who were you thinking about?"

"You," Max said simply, and in an instant she was in his arms. Pressed against the heat of his body she could feel the rhythm of his heart beating as wildly as her own.

"I haven't been able to think about much else since that first night," he continued hoarsely, his lips against the top of her head. "The moon was so bright, do you remember? It was like daylight."

Ness nodded. She'd never forgotten it – would never be able to forget it, and goodness only knew how hard she'd tried. That perfect moment would stay with her for the rest of her life.

"Do you remember what else happened that night, apart from the full moon?" Max asked softly. His hands came up and he cupped her face between them again, staring down at her as though he wanted to sear her face in his memory.

"Val Brown interrupted us?" Ness teased.

"Ah yes, good old Mrs Brown." Max raised his eyes to the sky. "But no, fond of Val as I am, her appearance wasn't top of my list of great memories. Shall I show you what I was remembering?"

Ness closed her eyes, anticipating his kiss – and when Max's mouth brushed hers she almost wept with happiness, because she'd never experienced a kiss like it before. She'd waited so long for this, and now at last she felt the sweet relief of coming home. It wasn't the first time Max had kissed her, of course, but there had always been doubt lurking in the back of her mind before, whereas now there was none. His mouth tasted of sea salt and wood smoke, and she knew she would never be able to get enough of it.

She pulled away and looked into his eyes, softer than she'd ever seen them; they were no longer hard and challenging but instead were filled with an emotion she hardly dared name.

"I remember," she whispered.

Max took her hands in his and he drew her close.

"I think I should have told you a long time ago what I was feeling. The problem was that I couldn't work it out myself. The irony! I was managing my businesses, working between three time zones, coordinating teams of craftsmen – but I couldn't figure out what was going on in here." He tapped his chest and gazed down into her eyes with an intensity that was enough to make her own heart fly into her throat.

"And what is going on?" she asked.

"Love," he said simply. "I'm in love with you, Nessa Penwellyn."

But Ness already knew this because his feelings shone from those grey eyes of his, so honest and true that her own eyes filled with tears. How could it be that only a few months ago she hadn't even known Max Reynard and yet somehow, against all the odds, he'd already become the centre of her world? He was her enemy. Her rival. Her nemesis.

This change didn't make any sense to her and yet she utterly trusted it.

"Could you feel the same way?" he asked, and the uncertainty in his face as he laid his soul bare almost broke her.

"I already do," Ness answered quietly. "I think I've loved you since that first evening too."

And then Max kissed her again, a kiss so tender and so full of promise that there was no need for either of them to say any more. As they stared at each other afterwards, smiling in delighted wonder, Ness wished she'd admitted her feelings sooner. One thing she'd learned from her time on the island was that life was short and regrets were futile.

"So will you stay? Be part of this?" she asked. Her breath caught in her throat because she knew now that there was nothing she wanted more.

Max's answer was a gossamer-soft kiss. As she kissed him back, his touch told Ness that the future lay ahead of them, shining just as brightly as the sun's final rays.

When at last they drew apart, Ness found herself staring across at the castle. She knew it had to be a trick of the light, but for a few seconds she thought she saw a young man, sketchpad in hand; he was drawing a girl with long curly hair and eyes as green as the seaweed on the causeway, who laughed and twirled as she played her violin. Then Ness blinked and the vision was gone – but she could have sworn that the dying notes of a solo violin trembled in the air before they were washed away by the pounding surf.

Her imagination again.

Probably.

She threaded her fingers with Max's. The past, present and future seemed to blur together, but now this gave her hope and filled her with happiness. Any sadness and regret had vanished in the setting sun. There was so much ahead to look forward to. The rest of her life began right now.

"Let's go home," she said.

And, hand in hand, Ness and Max walked across the beach and back to Pirran Island as the waves sighed behind them and the shadows of the past gently faded away.

The End

The End

Author's Note

Dear Reader,

In 2010 my first novel, *Katy Carter Wants a Hero*, was published and my life changed forever. It had always been a cherished dream of mine to be an author and I'd written ever since I was a child – mostly stories about ponies – and as I grew older the passion for telling stories only grew stronger. In between teaching English at a big comprehensive school and moving to Cornwall, I wrote several novels – all of which were rejected by agents and publishers. Many times I felt close to giving up but when I met E V Thompson, the well-known Cornish author who advised me to "write about what you know and never give up", I picked myself up and penned *Katy Carter Wants a Hero*, the story of an English teacher who moves to Cornwall to follow her dream of being a writer.

The rest is history. This novel attracted the attention of TV's Richard and Judy as well as being splashed across the national press – feel free to Google that! The book was even shortlisted for the UK Romantic Novelists' Association's Romantic Comedy of The Year award in 2011.

Living in Cornwall is something I never take for granted and last summer I spent a lot of time boating just off Looe Island. The rhythm of the tides is also an important part of life here and has certainly wound its way into *The Island*

Legacy, as have my visits to some old and very beautiful Cornish properties. Mysteries and myths are threaded through this special place just as they are woven through the narrative of this book. I loved writing this story and I really hope you'll enjoy reading it. If you do, I would really appreciate a review on Amazon or GoodReads. These make all the difference to the success of a book and are like gold dust for writers.

I love to hear from my readers. Contact me at ruth@ruthsaberton.com and please visit my website, www.ruthsaberton.com to sign up for news of upcoming books.

Brightest wishes,

x Ruth x

About The Author

Ruth Saberton is the bestselling author of *Katy Carter Wants a Hero* and *Escape for the Summer*. She also writes upmarket commercial fiction under the pen names Jessica Fox, Georgie Carter and Holly Cavendish.

Born in London, Ruth now lives in beautiful Cornwall. She has travelled to many places and recently returned from living in the Caribbean but nothing compares to the rugged beauty of the Cornish coast. Ruth loves to chat with readers so please do add her as a Facebook friend and follow her on Twitter.

Twitter: @ruthsaberton

Facebook: Ruth Saberton

www.ruthsaberton.com